"YOU CAN NAME ROBERT LITTELL IN THE SAME BREATH WITH GEOFFREY HOUSEHOLD, HELEN McINNES, LEN DEIGHTON, AND THEN FORGET THOSE WORTHY VETERANS—THE YOUNG MR. LITTELL TOWERS ABOVE THEM."
—*Philadelphia Inquirer*

THE COMPELLING NOVELS BY THE MASTER OF INTRIGUE

THE DEFECTION OF A.J. LEWINTER

THE OCTOBER CIRCLE

MOTHER RUSSIA

SWEET REASON

N 0-553-25831-1>>395

THE SISTERS

CENTRAL INTELLIGENCE AGENCY
UNITED STATES OF AMERICA

"ENGROSSING... RIGHT UP THERE WITH THE NOVELS OF LE CARRÉ, DEIGHTON AND THE REST OF THE BEST."
—PEOPLE

ROBERT LITTELL

ACCLAIM FOR ROBERT LITTELL'S *THE SISTERS*

"SO CLEVER, SO OUTRAGEOUS AND CYNICAL THAT . . . YOUR BREATH IS TAKEN AWAY . . . WE'RE SEDUCED BY THE GAME OF WHO'S CONTROLLING WHOM . . . BY HIS AMUSINGLY QUIRKY CHARACTERS . . . ULTIMATELY, WE ARE HOOKED BY THE STORY, WHICH IT IS NOT MUCH OF AN EXAGGERATION TO CALL THE PLOT OF PLOTS."

—Christopher Lehmann-Haupt, *The New York Times*

"MORE THAN PLAUSIBLE. COMPELLINGLY BELIEVABLE—AND A THUNDERING GOOD READ!"

—Robert Elegant, author of *Manchu*

"DEFT . . . DIFFERENT . . . ENTERTAINING . . . ENGAGING."

—*Newsweek*

"EVERY STEP OF THE WAY, THERE IS A CHILLING REALIZATION THAT NOTHING SUGGESTED BY THE AUTHOR IS OUT OF PLACE OR BEYOND RATIONAL LIMITS. ESPECIALLY EFFECTIVE ARE THE SEGMENTS THAT OCCUR IN THE SOVIET UNION . . . SUCH MASTERY OF PLOT AND DETAIL PUT ROBERT LITTELL'S *THE SISTERS* AT THE TOP OF THE READING LIST FOR ANY SERIOUS STUDENT OF THE ESPIONAGE THRILLER."

—UPI

"THERE IS AN AIR OF JOHN LE CARRÉ IN ROBERT LITTELL'S *THE SISTERS*. IT IS ARTFULLY CONSTRUCTED, WELL WRITTEN AND HAS MORE SWITCHBACKS THAN THE ROAD UP PIKE'S PEAK."

—*The Detroit News*

"A MASTERFUL ESPIONAGE NOVEL . . . A TALE FULL OF INTRIGUE, DOUBLE-AGENTS AND BETRAYAL."

—*The San Diego Tribune*

"A THRILL-A-MINUTE RIDE THAT LEADS TO AN ASTONISHING CONCLUSION."

—*The Pittsburgh Press*

"WITTY, GRITTY, INGENIOUSLY PLOTTED . . . FULL OF TWISTS AND SURPRISES. *THE SISTERS* IS AN ENGAGING, INTELLIGENT THRILLER."

—*Fort Worth Star-Telegram*

Bantam Books by Robert Littell
Ask your bookseller for the books you have missed

THE DEFECTION OF A.J. LEWINTER
THE OCTOBER CIRCLE
MOTHER RUSSIA
THE SISTERS
SWEET REASON

THE SISTERS

Robert Littell

Bantam Books
Toronto • New York • London • Sydney • Auckland

THE SISTERS

A Bantam Book
Bantam hardcover edition / February 1986
A selection of the Literary Guild
Bantam paperback edition / January 1987

Library of Congress Cataloging-in-Publication Data

Littell, Robert, 1935–
The sisters.

I. Title.
PS3562.1782785 1986 813'.54 85-47797
ISBN 0-553-25831-1

Published simultaneously in the United States and Canada

PRINTED IN THE UNITED STATES OF AMERICA

KR 0 9 8 7 6 5 4 3 2 1

For my father,
Leon Littell

BOOK I

❦

Night

Outside it was night; inside too . . .

1

"I'm just thinking out loud," Francis was saying. An angelic smile manned the usual fortifications of his face. "What if . . ." His voice trailed off uncertainly.

"What if *what*?" Carroll prompted. A muscle twitched impatiently in his cheek.

"What if—"

They were, by any standards, the Company's odd couple. Office scuttlebutt held that when one itched the other scratched, but that wasn't it; that wasn't it at all. It was more a matter of symbiosis; of constituting two sides of the same coin. Looking at any given skyline, Francis would see forest, Carroll trees; Francis wrote music, Carroll lyrics; Francis would leap with almost feminine intuition in the general direction of unlikely ends while Carroll, a pedestrian at heart, would trail after him lingering over means.

"What if," Francis was saying, "we were to put our man Friday onto someone with Mafia connections?"

"Mafia connections?"

Francis pulled thoughtfully at an earlobe that looked as if it had been pulled at before. "Exactly."

Francis wore an outrageous silk bow tie that he had picked up for a song at a rummage sale. His sixth-floor neighbors thought it was out of character, which only showed that they didn't really understand his character. It was the unexpected splash of color, the tiny touch of defiance, the unconventional link in an otherwise perfectly conformist chain that set him apart from everyone else.

Carroll, on the other hand, liked to look as if he *belonged.* He favored conventional three-piece suits and starched collars that left crimson welts clinging like leeches to his thin, pale neck. Laughing behind his back, the neighbors spoke about his penchant for hair shirts worn, so they assumed, to atone for unspecified sins.

They were half right. There *were* sins, though Carroll never felt the slightest urge to atone for them.

"The Mafia is out of the question," Carroll announced flatly, a crooked forefinger patrolling between his collar and his neck. He looked past Francis the way he stared over the shoulder of anyone he deigned to talk to. "They will want to be paid in the end. And not necessarily in money. Besides, there's no compartmentalization. If this thing is going to succeed, it has to be tightly compartmentalized. Like a submarine."

"Quite right," Francis remarked, blushing apologetically. "I can't imagine what I could have been thinking of." His face screwed up, his eyes narrowed into slits, a sure sign that his mind was leaping toward another unlikely end.

Francis and Carroll were minor legends in the Company. Somewhere along the line one of the CIA's army of PhD's who majored in African dialects and minored in Whitman had dubbed them "The sisters Death and Night." The name stuck. If you mentioned the Sisters in an intraoffice memo, and capitalized the S, almost everyone tucked away in the Company's cradle-to-grave complex knew whom you were talking about. But only the handful with "eyes-only" authorizations in their dossiers had an inkling of what they actually did for a living.

What they did was plot.

And what they were plotting on that perfect August day was a perfect crime.

"What we will need," Francis thought out loud,

defining the problem, "is someone who can carry out an assignment without knowing it came from us."

"Someone who thinks he is being employed by others," Carroll ventured, lingering over means.

"Exactly," Francis agreed enthusiastically.

In an organization where people knew secrets, or made it their business to look as if they did, Francis stood out with his aura of absolute innocence. He invariably wore an expression that fell midway between curious and reluctant, and a Cheshire cat's pained smile that hinted at nothing more morally compromising than the death of an occasional rodent. It was common knowledge around the shop that he regularly lied about his name during the annual lie-detector tests—and always managed to fool the black box.

Compared to Francis, Carroll was an open book. When he felt frustrated, it appeared on his face like a flag. He had started out in the business with "Wild Bill" Donovan's Office of Strategic Services during the "Wrong War" (as he liked to call it; he felt that America had defeated the *wrong* enemy), and quickly made a name for himself by scribbling in the margin of one report: "The matter is of the highest possible importance and should accordingly be handled on the lowest possible level." What he meant, of course, was that *he* should handle it; at the tender age of twenty-nine, he had already been convinced of everyone's incompetence but his own. (Perhaps stunned by his audacity, his superiors gave him the brief. In due course Carroll engineered the defection of a German diplomat carrying a valise full of secret documents, and the betrayal to the Gestapo of the Soviet agent who had acted as their go-between. By 1945 Carroll was already focusing on the *right* enemy.)

Nowadays some of their Company colleagues whispered that the Sisters were past their prime, washed up, over the hill; old farts who amused the technocrats calling the tune; has-beens who gave the men in the Athenaeum (as the Sisters, classicists to the core, called the front office) something to talk about at in-house pours. ("The Sisters proposed that we . . ." "They weren't *serious*?" "I'm afraid they were." "What did you tell them?" "I told them they were *mad*!") There were even a few with regular access to the Sisters' product who recommended giving them medical discharges—and there was no suggestion that the problem was physical. They'd been around too long, it was said, they'd seen too much—as if being around too long and seeing too much inevitably led to deeper disorders. Still, several people in high places took them seriously enough to justify giving them space (which, with its Soviet magazines scattered around a shabby Formica coffee table, looked suspiciously like a dentist's office in Tashkent), a man Friday (whose real name, believe it or not, was Thursday) and a gorgeous secretary with an incredibly short skirt and incredibly long legs and a way of clutching files to her breasts that left the rare visitor noticeably short of breath. After all, it was said, the Sisters had had their share of triumphs. Not that long ago, with an almost Machiavellian leap of imagination, they had ferreted out a Russian sleeper in the CIA's ranks. While everyone else frantically searched the files for someone with a record of failed operations against the Russians, Francis thought the problem through from the Soviet point of view and decided that the merchants who ran the mole would have boosted his career with an occasional *success*. Working on that assumption, the Sisters combed the files looking for someone with one or two conspicuous successes and a string of failures. The suspect they uncovered was delivered to the tender mercies of the Company's most experienced interrogator, one G. Sprowls. After an intense interrogation that lasted seven months, G. Sprowls came up with the right questions and the suspect came up with the wrong answers. There was no trial. The suspect simply disappeared from the face of the earth, at which point the CIA awarded a medal and a pension to his widow rather than acknowledge that it had been infiltrated.

"Someone who thinks he is being employed by others," Carroll was saying thoughtfully—he appeared to be talking to the poster tacked to the back of the door that read "Fuck Communism!"—"can't very well point a finger at us if he is caught, can he?"

There was a single soft knock at the door. Without waiting for permission, the gorgeous secretary, who drew pay and broke hearts under her married name, Mrs. Cresswell, sailed into the dentist's office, wordlessly deposited a box of candies on the coffee table, and then, like a spider ducking soundlessly back into its hole, disappeared. Carroll tore off the lid and studied the contents. He detested nuts and cherries—one gave him hives, the other diarrhea—but could never for the life of him remember which ones didn't have them.

"Look at the code on the back of the lid," Francis said with an air of someone indulging his partner's idiosyncrasy.

"I don't understand codes," Carroll muttered. He snatched a candy at random, peeled off the tinfoil and, baring decaying yellowish teeth, gingerly bit into it. "Caramel," he announced with satisfaction, and he popped the rest of the candy into his mouth. He was working on his third caramel when he suddenly snapped his fingers. "I've got it!" he cried, though the caramel sticking to his teeth made his words difficult to understand. "What we need," he explained when he could finally articulate, "is someone who is highly skilled, intelligent, trained in fieldwork and willing to follow orders without inquiring into their source as long as they arrive in the correct form."

Francis said, "I don't quite follow—"

Carroll rocked back onto the rear legs of his chair. "What we need—" His lips twisted into an expression of grim satisfaction; another flag snapping on the halyard of his face.

"What we need," Francis repeated, his eyes watering in anticipation. Having come up with a perfect crime, he considered it in the nature of things that Carroll should come up with a perfect criminal.

"What we need—" Carroll whined, and because in his experience walls more often than not concealed *ears*, he plucked a pencil from a coffee table and finished the sentence on a sheet of scrap paper.

"—is a sleeper!"

"A sleeper, of course!" Francis wrote in turn.

Carroll retrieved the pencil. "But how on earth will we find one?" he wrote.

Francis grabbed the pencil out of Carroll's fingers. "We might get the Potter to give us the use of one," he wrote.

The Sisters melted back into their chairs, drained. Whistling softly through his teeth, Francis collected the scraps of paper they had written on; they had divided up office chores, and it was his job to shred all secret documents.

Carroll's cheek muscle twitched uncontrollably. "He might just do it," he said in a hollow voice, and in a gesture that had nothing, and everything, to do with ends and means, he waved vaguely, weakly toward the dirty window; toward the dirty city; toward the dirty world out there waiting to be *manipulated*.

They m
corrido
our ma
comme
how di
off-white even.

Carroll was too absorbed in his own schemes to worry about color schemes. "He's going to agree," he concluded, as if wishing could make it so. "I know him from the days when he ran errands for Dulles in Switzerland. He likes to keep several irons in several fires."

"Then we must make this seem like just another iron," Francis said under his breath, and flashing an ingratiating smile at one of the Pillars of Hercules, as the Deputy Director's two secretaries were known (one handled people, the other paper), he announced in a voice ideally suited to pulpits, "We are responding, like good dogs, to our master's whistle."

"Where *do* you get your ties?" the Pillar who handled people asked, waving them toward the appropriate door. She reached under her desk and dispatched a surge of electricity toward the appropriate lock. The door clicked open just as Francis reached it.

"What do you think of our halls?" demanded the Deputy Director, swiveling away from *his* man Friday to confront the Sisters.

"I would have made a case for pale green or off-e," Francis replied

ector, obviously disap-
ed the battleship atmo-
ay. Keep us all on our toes,

tor's man Friday nodded in brisk
immaculately dressed except for a
dandruff on his sloping Brooks Broth-

ll," the Deputy Director said enthusiasti-
pasted back a stray strand of battleship-gray
several fingertips. "If you don't mind, I'd like
e this a quickie," he announced. "I'm supposed
e up on the Hill in forty-five minutes. There will be
hotographers. I still have to have my hair trimmed." He swiveled back toward his Harry in panic. "You're absolutely sure I'm scheduled for Matthew? That new man who handled me last week butchered my sideburns."

"I checked on it myself this morning," Harry said impassively. "Matthew has cleared his book for you."

Relieved of another nightmare, the Deputy Director returned to the Sisters. "About this Op Proposal of yours"—he pulled a lemon-colored file card from a lemon-colored folder and tapped it with the back of a manicured fingernail—"you really think he may be ripe?"

Carroll arched his neck to relieve the pressure of his collar. "He's lost three sleepers in six months," he explained to a point on the wall over the Deputy Director's head. "His name is mud."

"He's been put out to pasture," Francis added hopefully. "He is bound to be nursing bruises. And then there is the matter of that wife of his . . ."

"*I* didn't know he'd been put out to pasture," the Deputy Director whined in irritation. "How did *you* know?"

"We learned about it from the Germans," Carroll said reluctantly; he had a journalist's instinct for sources.

"*Our* Germans or *their* Germans?" the Deputy Director wanted to know.

"Ours. It was buried in one of their Y summaries about a month ago," Francis added. "I suspect no one picked up on it because they identified him by his real name, Feliks Arkantevich Turov, as opposed to his working name, and not too many people put the two together."

"But you put the two together," the Deputy Director's man commented dryly. He was one of those who favored terminating the Sisters with medical discharges.

"That's correct," Carroll shot back without looking at him. "We have a head for names."

Francis added, "And faces. And places." And he beamed a smile of pained innocence in Harry's general direction.

The Deputy Director closed the lemon-colored folder with an irritated snap—he didn't mind dissension as long as it took place behind his back—and slipped it into a file drawer labeled "Current." "How do you propose to get at him?" he asked.

Carroll treated himself to a deep breath; they were almost home. "We'll use the Germans as cutouts," he said. "They'll farm the contract out to some free-lancers. If he's not buying, he's not buying from the free-lancers."

"If he buys," Francis chimed in, "we will plant our man Friday on the receiving line when he comes over. He will skim off the cream while it is still fresh and leave the milk for the farmers to market."

"You'll have to give the Germans something for their trouble," the Deputy Director commented unhappily.

"Maybe money," suggested Carroll. "Maybe access to the cream."

"Maybe only brownie points," offered Francis. "They wag their tails every time we toss them a bone."

The Deputy Director glanced quickly at his wristwatch. "Work linear," he advised. "Limit this to you two. Me. My man Friday. Your man Friday. We can circulate the product later to our clients without saying where it came from."

"We always compartmentalize," Carroll said matter-of-factly. "It is our trademark."

The Deputy Director cleared his throat nervously. "Just so long as you don't compartmentalize *me* out of the picture."

Everyone smiled at the utter absurdity of the idea.

Carroll had one hand on the doorknob when the Deputy Director called after them. "By the way, what is it you expect to get from him if he buys?"

The Sisters exchanged looks. "Odds and ends," Francis said, smiling innocently.

"Ends and odds," Carroll agreed, and he brought a palm up to his cheek to still his wildly twitching muscle.

3

❦

Under the angled beams of his attic workshop, in a cone of pale light cast by a naked bulb dangling overhead, the Potter, Feliks Arkantevich Turov, rinsed his small, powerful hands in a pan of lukewarm water, then kicked the wheel and leaned over the turntable. The fingers of his right hand curled around the outside of the damp clay. His left hand dipped delicately into the cylinder, the thumb hooked back over the lip so that it rested lightly on his right hand. The act of touching transformed the two hands into one perfectly coordinated pincerlike instrument. Wedging the clay cylinder between the tip of one finger and the joint of another, he brought up the wall.

The Potter had learned the art at the feet of a Japanese master who claimed that throwing a beautiful pot was as difficult as printing your shadow on the sidewalk. In the end, potting represented a classic case of mind over matter. Some days were better than others, but when the Potter was very good, he could overcome the natural tendency of the clay to become what *it* wanted to become; he could tame it, channel its power, control its pulse; he could force it to flower under his fingers into a form that already existed in his head.

If only he could control his life the way he controlled the clay! At fifty-six, the Potter already felt as if he were "tied up to the pier of old age" (Turgenev's phrase, first quoted to him by Piotr Borisovich, his last, his best sleeper). Turov's face resembled nothing so much as wax about to melt, giving him a distinctly blurred look; people who didn't know him well often had difficulty bringing him into focus. He was short to begin with—five feet, four inches. Since his obligatory retirement earlier in the year, his shoulders had gradually sagged, as if laboring under a great weight; his body had taken on a dwarfish appearance, underscoring its essential awkwardness. Only his forearms and his hands, conditioned by hundreds of hours of kneading clay, retained anything resembling youthfulness. To his own eye, he looked like one of those worn-out government functionaries visible in the streets at the start of any workday; they never seemed to hurry, eloquent evidence that they had precious little enthusiasm for getting where they were going. Like the bureaucrats, the Potter seemed to be living off emotional capital instead of income, the way a starving man lives off the protein already stored in his body.

The Potter fixed the lip of the cylinder, braked the wheel to a stop with a scuffed boot, then reached for the length of piano wire Piotr Borisovich had once fashioned for him and cut the vase off the wheel. He turned it upside down and tapped on the base, then set the vase on a shelf next to his electric kiln. When the spirit moved him, he would glaze it and fire it and offer it to some neighbors who always brought him a handful of mushrooms when they came back from their country *dacha*. Either that or he would smash it into a thousand pieces during another tantrum.

Outside, gusts of soot brushed past the grimy attic window. The Potter glanced at the sliver of Moscow River he could see off in the distance between two buildings. In the old days, when things were going well, when he had been the *novator*—the man in charge—of the sleeper school, he and Svetochka had occupied an apartment *overlooking* the river. There had been a bedroom, a living room, a study, a heated workroom for his potter's wheel, a kitchen, even a bathroom—an almost unheard-of eighty-eight square meters—and they had it all to themselves. Then, when Svetochka called him "my Jew," there had been affection in her voice. Nowadays they lived in a building with paper-thin walls and shared forty-five square meters with another family. And there was anger in her voice no matter what she called him. Or even worse, boredom. On more than one occasion he had caught her suppressing a yawn when they made love. If he didn't notice her suppressing yawns anymore, it was because he looked up less. With his head buried between her legs, he still managed to forget the unlaundered years (Piotr Borisovich's phrase; from the moment they met, the Potter had been struck by his way with words): the rats scurrying around the labyrinth in the late thirties, when he first joined what was then called the NKVD; the seventeen months spent behind German lines in the early forties; "sanitation" expeditions in the wake of the advancing Red Army in the middle forties; then the endless death watch of the late forties and early fifties as everyone wordlessly waited for the old buzzard in the Kremlin to give up the ghost.

The Potter could hear the telephone ringing under his feet. He could make out the sound of Svetochka's stiletto heels as she raced to answer it before the people who shared the flat could. In ten minutes the woman whom everyone invariably mistook for his daughter would slip into her imitation fur "soul warmer" and leave. Another rendezvous with another hairdresser, she would say. Another store selling imitation leather gloves that you can't tell from the real thing, she would say. Only when she came back later—much later—her hair wouldn't look any different, and there would be no imitation leather gloves in her pockets. They had run out just before her turn came, she would say.

It occurred to the Potter, not for the first time, that illusions don't die, they rot like fish in the sun. They torture you with *ifs:* what might have been if one of his sleepers hadn't refused to obey his "awakening" signal and disappeared; if a second, happier in America than in Russia, hadn't gone over to the other side; if a third, inside the CIA, hadn't been ferreted out by someone with an astonishing capacity to think the problem through from the Russian point of view. All within a six-month period. The Potter had trained the sleepers in question. He was accordingly rated on how well they performed. When the ax finally fell, there had been talk of exile in Central Asia, talk even of a prison sentence. But his record had been impeccable up to then. So they had put him out to what they thought of, all things considered, as generous pasture: a smaller apartment, a monthly stipend large enough to keep him in clay and vodka, even a self-winding Czechoslovak wristwatch delivered, without ceremony—with a certain amount of embarrassment—on his last day in harness. "For Feliks Arkantevich," the inscription read, "for twenty-seven years of service to the state." Service to the state! He might have been a street cleaner for all anyone could tell from the inscription.

Surprisingly, Svetochka had taken his fall in stride. Not to worry, she had said, Svetochka likes her Feliks even without access to the school's warehouse; Svetochka will always be Feliks' little girl. Eventually her last pair of American stockings had gone into the garbage, and her tone had begun to change. The Potter took to waiting on a side street near the warehouse; friends slipped him an occasional American lipstick or eyebrow pencil, and Svetochka would throw her arms around his thick neck and make love to him that night the way she had when he had been the *novator*. But neither the lipsticks nor her ardent moods lasted very long.

"Feliks!" Svetochka's high-pitched voice drifted up through the floorboards. "Can you hear me, Feliks? There's a phone call. Someone's asking for you. Feliks?"

"He's coming," Svetochka assured the caller, afraid that he was one of Feliks' friends from the warehouse and might get impatient and hang up. "Only a moment."

"So: I will wait," the voice said quietly.

"*Slouchouyou*," the Potter mumbled into the receiver. He had an instinctive distrust of telephones common to people who came to them relatively late in life. "What do you want?"

A voice with an accent the Potter couldn't quite place replied, "So: if you please, note the number I will give you, yes? If you need a private taxi, dial it and one will come to your corner."

The Potter's hand, suddenly damp with perspiration, gripped the phone. "I don't take taxis. They are too expensive. When I go somewhere, I use the metro or walk."

"Who is it?" Svetochka whispered.

"Please note the number," the voice on the other end of the line insisted. "You never know when you will need it. So: B, one-forty-one, twenty-one."

"What does he want?" Svetochka whispered.

"You have the number, yes?" the voice asked. "B, one-forty-one, twenty-one."

"I tell you that I do not use taxis," the Potter blurted out, suddenly frightened. "Go to hell with your number." And he slammed down the receiver.

"Who was that?"

"Nobody."

"How can you say it was nobody? Somebody phones you up and according to you it's nobody." Tears of frustration formed under Svetochka's heavily made-up lids. "Somebody is not nobody!" she cried in that tightly controlled voice that angry Muskovites use in communal apartments.

The Potter had a good idea of what the call was all about. He had made more than one like it during his four-year stint as KGB *rezident* in New York. It was a contact, an approach, an invitation to what the Merchants at Moscow Center called a *treff*—a secret meeting. Only it wasn't the Moscow Merchants who had initiated it; on that he would have wagered a great deal.

Svetochka began struggling into her soul warmer. "Where are you going now?" the Potter demanded.

"Nowhere," she sneered. "Nobody is who called. And nowhere is where I'm going."

The Potter sprang across the room and gripping the lapels of her coat in one fist, lifted her off the ground.

"You are hurting Svetochka, Feliks," she whispered. Seeing the look on his face, she pleaded, "Feliks is hurting his Svetochka."

The Potter set her down, slipped a hand inside her coat and clumsily tried to embrace her. "I only wanted to know where you were going," he remarked, as if it could account for the outburst, the months of tension that preceded it, the conversationless meals, the slow seeping away of intimacy.

"All you had to do was ask," Svetochka snapped, conveniently forgetting that he had. She fended him off deftly. "Svetochka is going to baby-sit for a girlfriend so she can go birthday shopping for her husband."

"Children are in school at this hour," the Potter said.

"Her child is too young for school."

"There are neighborhood nurseries for babies."

"This baby has a fever," Svetochka explained quickly. "He can't go out." With her teeth clenched, she spit out, "Svetochka doesn't ask you where you are going every time you put on your coat."

"You are lying," the Potter said simply, tiredly. "There was no hairdresser. There were no imitation leather gloves. There is no sick baby."

"You have a nerve . . ." Svetochka was screaming now. Down the corridor, the people who shared the apartment discreetly closed the door to their bedroom. "You didn't never use to . . ." Her phrases came in gasps; they no longer seemed to be glued together by grammar or sense. ". . . not going to only always take this . . ."

"Enough," the Potter muttered under his breath.

". . . think maybe you are doing to Svetochka favors . . ."

"Enough, if you please."

"Well, it don't even work like you maybe think . . ."

The Potter's arm swept out in anger, brushing a glazed bowl, one of the best he had ever made, off a table. It struck the floor, shattering at Svetochka's feet.

"Enough!" shouted the Potter.

Svetochka, who fancied herself something of an actress, could change moods in a flash. Now she screwed up her face to indicate that she had been mortally offended. "It is not Svetochka who will clean this up," she observed icily. Pivoting on a spiked heel, leaving the door to the corridor gaping open behind her, she stalked from the apartment.

The Potter poured himself a stiff vodka. When he had been *novator*, he had drunk nothing but eighty-proof Polish Bison vodka. Now he had to make do with cheap Russian vodka, to which he added the skin in the interior of walnuts to give it color and taste. Svetochka would come back later than usual to punish him for his outburst. He would mumble vague apologies. They would both act as if everything had been his fault. The Potter would shave for the first time in days, hoping she would notice and take it as a sign that he wanted to make love. He would watch her undress and make a clumsy effort to fondle her breasts. She would put on plastic hair curlers and turn away in bed, complaining about a headache. He would make an awkward declaration of love. Because the Russian language was devoid of articles, it would have the staccato quality of a telegram.

It was Piotr Borisovich who, during one of his English-polishing sessions with the Potter, had commented on the difference between English and Russian. Where English dallied, meandered, embellished, Russian took the shortest path between two points; Russian political thinking could trace its roots to the Russian language, Piotr Borisovich had said. In what sense? the Potter had asked. In the sense that Communism was essentially a shortcut. Are you against shortcuts? the Potter had asked; it had been early in their relationship and he was on the alert for ideological faults. I am all for them, Piotr Borisovich had replied, his head cocked, his eyes smiling, on the condition that they get you there sooner.

Curious he should think of Piotr Borisovich now. Or shortcuts.

The Potter shrugged. In his heart of hearts, he understood they were all connected: the phone call, Svetochka, Piotr Borisovich, shortcuts. For the next two days he tried to put it out of his mind. And thought he had succeeded. Then, without premeditation—he wasn't sure whom he was calling until he dialed—he picked up the phone and composed the number. He heard the phone ring once. Then the voice with the accent he couldn't quite place said, "B, one-forty-one, twenty-one?" as if it were a question.

Almost as if he were following a script, the Potter supplied the answer.

4

⚜

Carroll was spitting a cherry-flavored candy into the wastepaper basket when Mrs. Cresswell poked her head in the door. "Thursday said to tell you he's almost through with it."

Francis wrung his hands in anticipation. "Tell him to bring it straight in," he instructed her.

"As if he would do anything else with it," muttered Mrs. Cresswell.

"Secretarial help," noted Francis, staring directly at her knees, "is not what it used to be."

The message had arrived that morning on a direct scrambler channel from the BND, the West German Federal Intelligence Service, encoded in a one-time cipher that had been earmarked for the operation when the Sisters had sent the go-ahead. One-time pads represent the last word in compartmentalization. Their beauty, which is to say their security, lies in the fact that only two people on earth hold the key: the person who enciphers on the originating end, and—in this particular case—Thursday, sweating away in his windowless cubbyhole just down the hall from the Sisters' bailiwick.

"I take it as a bad sign that they're filing so quickly," Carroll mused. He scanned the box of candies for a promising shape.

"I don't know," Francis said. "If they had nothing

positive to report they would have let the string run out a bit more before filing a no-show."

Carroll bit into another piece of candy, made a face and spit it into the wastepaper basket. "The Germans—*our* Germans—are like schoolchildren, on that tiny point we can agree, I would think," he said. "They will set up their approach with meticulous care, make one pass at the target, then phone in with juicy details of their success or failure. It is part of their sense of insecurity that comes from having lost the wrong war."

Someone knocked at the door. Carroll sprang to open it, overturning his box of candies. Thursday stood on the threshold, vibrating with excitement. "He has bitten," he giggled. And he read the plain text from his yellow legal pad: " 'The fish is on the line.' "

Francis took possession of the page from Thursday's legal pad and the original coded message; at the close of the workday he would make sure they wound up in the office shredder. "The trick now," he remarked as if he were dealing with nothing more important than that evening's meal, "is to play him in very slowly."

5

For reasons of security, the Russians were keeping their distance. It was a Cuban cutout in New Orleans who contacted the Soviet agent known by his code name, Khanda. The cutout was a prostitute who worked a back street full of bars masquerading as nightclubs, so it was the most natural thing in the world for Khanda to saunter up to her and ask how much she charged. When she told him, he said he would be willing to pay twice what she asked if she, in turn, would be willing to accept American Express traveler's checks.

The cutout recognized this as the code identifying Khanda, and led him up to her room on the fourth floor.

Khanda had the instincts of a puritan; being with a whore made him uneasy. When the cutout invited him to take off his jacket and loosen his tie, he politely refused. He was in a hurry, he explained. What was it she had for him?

She rummaged through a sewing basket for her microdot reader, and handed it to him along with a picture postcard she had received from one of her regular clients in Mexico City. The message on it, and the address, had been typed on an old typewriter that had a new ribbon and no R. ". . . -eally g-eat time he-e . . ." it said. Khanda held the postcard under a lamp and examined it closely, but he couldn't see anything out of the ordinary. "It's the i in the word 'time,'" the cutout told him, and she handed him an eyebrow tweezers so he could pry the microdot from the dot over the i and insert it in the reader.

Khanda quickly copied the message onto the back of an envelope. When he had finished, the cutout casually asked him if he would like to make love. There would be no charge, she added, since they were, after all, colleagues. Khanda thanked her profusely but said he was expected somewhere.

Back in his own apartment, Khanda studied the message on the back of the envelope. His first reaction was to feel extremely flattered. They obviously had a great deal of esteem for him if they were assigning this mission to him. His second sensation was one of exhilaration. If he could pull it off, he would become what, in his wildest dreams, he had always wanted to be: important; a hero, even, in certain circles. He closed his eyes and imagined the blind man fumbling with the Order of Lenin, trying to pin it onto his lapel. He wondered if he would have to put up with a kiss on each cheek, or whether, in deference to his being a foreigner, they would agree to skip that part.

Khanda didn't like being kissed by men.

6

There were four people ahead of the Potter in the queue. Two empty taxis, their checkered doors splattered with dried mud, raced past in quick succession. Moscow was struggling under the heel of an unseasonal cold snap; temperatures had plunged during the night. The Potter pulled down the earflaps of his *oushanka* and stamped his feet, which were already beginning to feel numb inside his galoshes. A third taxi flashed by at breakneck speed.

"Bastards!" complained a heavyset man in front of the Potter. "They're warm as hell with their heaters going full blast. They don't give a damn for us stranded out here in the cold."

A fourth taxi wormed its way toward the corner along Zubovsky Boulevard, coming from the Krimsky Bridge. The skin on the back of the Potter's neck crawled; his *body* knew this one was it before he did. The cab pulled up before the queue. The driver, a squirrellike man with a worker's cap pulled low over his eyes and a scarf wrapped around his lower jaw, leaned across and rolled down the passenger window the width of a fist. The man in front of the Potter elbowed his way between the two women at the head of the queue and shouted out his destination. "The Exhibition of Economic Achievements, off Mistra Avenue, comrade." The exhibition was on the other side of the city, normally a profitable run for a taxi driver, because while the meter was running, he could pick up several passengers heading in the same direction and pocket their fares.

"*Nyet, nyet*," barked the driver, waving his hand in irritation.

The women who had been shoved aside smiled smugly. Each offered an address; each was refused in turn.

"And what about you, comrade fur cap?" the driver called when the Potter failed to come forward with an address. "Where are you heading on this arctic day?"

"Anywhere," the Potter replied, a sardonic grimace deforming his chapped lips.

The driver appeared startled. The Potter jumped to the conclusion that he had guessed wrong. And suddenly a sense of relief—of having gotten off a hook—flooded through his nervous system. He started to turn away; he would rethink this whole business.

Just then, to everyone's astonishment, the driver jerked his head toward the back seat. "Get in," he ordered.

The Potter hesitated. The heavyset man, the two women, stared at him, straining to place his face. If the driver agreed to take him "anywhere," he must be someone important. A member of the Central Committee perhaps. Or a manager of one of those new hard-currency stores that carried Western products.

Sensing the Potter's indecision, the driver reached back and pushed open the rear door. The Potter shrugged—it suddenly seemed easier to go with the current—and ducked into the back seat.

"Where are you taking me?" the Potter asked as the driver spun his taxi through a maze of side streets behind the Church of St. Nicholas of the Weavers. Ignoring the question, the driver turned into Pirogovskaya Street, then pulled up abruptly. He studied the rearview mirror; the Potter glanced over his shoulder. No one came out of the side street after them. Satisfied, the driver slipped the taxi into gear and headed toward the Novodevichy Monastery. Ahead, the Potter could make out the five gilded bulb-shaped domes of the Virgin of Smolensk Church.

An image of Piotr Borisovich leapt to his mind. He had been standing next to an open hotel window staring out at Moscow his last night in the country. He had gotten roaring drunk on French champagne, and had started to sing snatches of Moussorgsky's *Khovanshchina*, an opera that recounted the story of Czar Peter's revolt against the Regent Sophia; Peter banished her to the Novodevichy Monastery, lynched three hundred of her *streltsy* under the windows of her cell and nailed the hand of Prince Khovansky, her principal ally, to her door. Piotr Borisovich's voice had been pitched low and surprisingly on-key. Then, suddenly sober, he had stopped singing and cocked his head and smiled the way he always smiled—with his eyes, not his mouth. Little wrinkles had formed at the corners of his eyes, making him appear older than he was. Violence is in our blood, he had said, looking out at Moscow but thinking of America. Violence and a passion for plotting. You and I, the Potter had agreed, are the last practitioners of a dying art.

The way he said the sentence had made it seem as if they were on a holy crusade.

"End of the line, comrade fur cap." The driver braked to a stop in front of the gate leading to the Novodevichy Cemetery.

The Potter noticed the meter wasn't running, so he nodded and let himself out of the taxi. It roared off. The Potter stood a moment on the sidewalk savoring the cold—the taxi had been overheated, but in Moscow no one ever complained of being subjected to too much heat—then turned and made his way into the heart of the cemetery, past rows of eroded tombstones. The paths, as far as he could tell, were deserted. In matters like this, the Potter knew from experience, no one hurried. When they were absolutely sure he wasn't being followed, they would come for him. He wandered past a stand of graves—Gogol's, Chekhov's,

Mayakovsky's, Esenin's (the last two were suicides; the violence, the plotting had been too much for them). His feet were beginning to feel numb again; if the cold snap kept up he would have to start wearing his wool-lined slippers inside his galoshes, as he did at the height of winter. He paused before the glistening white marble bust of Stalin's beautiful young wife. She had stormed out of a Kremlin dinner party one night in 1932, gone home, put a pistol to her head and, as Piotr Borisovich once quipped, introduced a foreign object into her brain. Another suicide! More violence! "To Nadezhda Alliluyeva," the inscription on the bust read, "from a member of the Communist Party, J. Stalin."

"Psssssst!"

The Potter turned to see a little man with shirred skin squinting at him from several meters away. He must have stepped from behind a tombstone, because he hadn't been there a moment before. The man beckoned with an emaciated finger. The Potter approached. The man removed his hat, an unexpected sign of deference considering who they were and what they were up to. "I have confirmed," he announced, nodding a very bald head, "that you are alone. Down that path, through that gate, you will discover another taxi waiting for you."

"Where will it take me?" the Potter asked, knowing the question would never be answered.

"Anywhere!" replied the little bald man with a mischievous wink, and planting his hat squarely on his head, he darted with unexpected sprightliness between two tombstones and disappeared.

7

Atop the great baroque belfry in the center of the monastery grounds, two men dressed in ankle-length mink coats and mink hats stood with their backs to the wind. Because they were vaguely related (one's mother's brother had been the other's uncle by marriage), because they directed Department 13 of the First Chief Directorate, the sabotage and assassination unit of the Komitet Gosudarstvennoy Bezopasnosti, better known by its initials KGB, their subordinates referred to them as the Cousins. The younger of the two, in his early forties, stared down at the cemetery through binoculars. The other, who was blind, the result of being tortured by the Gestapo during the Great Patriotic War, asked, "Is the bald man one of ours or theirs?"

"Theirs. Oskar must have pulled him out of a hat for this operation," the younger man answered.

"We should remember to log him," the blind man said.

"Small fish, big pond," the man with the binoculars replied. "Oskar will make us a present of him if we ask. In any case, we must be careful not to frighten any of them off before this whole thing becomes history."

The man with the binoculars watched the Potter enter the second taxi. "I will tell you the truth," he admitted. "I didn't think he would go for it."

"Did you know him personally?" inquired the blind

man. He used the past tense, as if he were speaking about someone dead and buried.

"I met him years ago just after he came back from New York," the younger man replied. "He was a great hero to us all then." He fitted his binoculars back into their leather case. "He had served Mother Russia well. We looked up to him."

Below, the driver gunned his motor and the taxi lurched away from the curb. The blind man bent an ear toward the sound, then tapped his long, thin white baton several times on the ground in satisfaction. "He is still serving Mother Russia," he said thoughtfully, and he pressed his lips into what, on his scarred features, passed for a smile.

8

⚜

The *yafka* (Russian for "safe house") turned out to be on Volodarskaya Street, down the block from the Church of the Dormition of the Potters.

When he discovered Feliks' hobby was throwing pots, Piotr Borisovich, sporting an ancient fedora that had seen one too many rainstorms, had hauled him off, one sparkling Sunday before he graduated to the "field," to see the mosaics and decorative brickwork of the church. What do you think? Piotr Borisovich had demanded, delighted to have come up with something in Moscow that the *novator* didn't know about. What I think, the Potter had responded, is that religion is the opiate of the people. Piotr Borisovich had laughed like a schoolboy. But what do *you* think? he had persisted, trying as usual to get past the cliché. Speaking as an atheist, the Potter had observed, I think that no amount of mosaics can obscure the fact that a church is essentially a lie. Piotr Borisovich had shaken his head. You forget what Spinoza said, he had remarked, his voice unaccustomedly moody: there are no lies, only crippled truths.

Crippled truths, the Potter reflected now, making his way up a dark staircase, the stench of urine drifting past his nostrils at each landing, may be better than no truths at all. In what sense? he could imagine Piotr Borisovich inquiring encouragingly. In the sense, he could hear himself replying, that if something is worth doing, an argument can be made that it is worth doing badly.

The Potter struck a match and peered at the number on the door. It was missing, but the outline of where it had been was unmistakable. The Potter shook out the match and deposited it in a trouser cuff and knocked lightly on the door.

"Come."

The room had two windows with their shades drawn and an uncomfortably bright electric light and two folding metal chairs and a calendar on a wall set to the previous month.

"We are September, not August," the Potter observed. He walked over and tore off August and crumpled it into a ball and tossed it onto the floor. As an afterthought, he glanced behind the calendar. All he found was more wall.

"So," said the man sitting on one of the two folding metal chairs. He was of medium height, unshaven, with a silver-rimmed pince-nez wedged onto the bridge of a long, lean Roman nose. "I thank you for taking advantage of our taxi service."

"Your precautions were impeccably professional," the Potter said.

The man accepted this with a nod. "Coming from the *novator,* I take that as a compliment. I shall pass it on to my associates, yes? They too will take it as a compliment."

He was being buttered up, the Potter realized, by the man with the accent he couldn't quite place. There was a hint of German in it, a hint of Polish; a Ukrainian, perhaps, who had spent his formative years in a German concentration camp in Poland. Or a Pole who had been pressed into the Red Army. Or a bilingual German.

"So," the man began again, clearing his throat nervously, "for the purpose of this conversation, it may be useful for me to have a name, yes?"

"It would be useful," the Potter agreed.

"You will call me Oskar. So: my associates and I are prepared to get you out of the country—"

"I have a wife," the Potter said stiffly.

"When I speak of you, it goes without saying I mean you and your wife."

"Such details go *with* saying," the Potter corrected him grimly.

"I take your point," Oskar acknowledged affably.

"You talk of getting us out of the country. Out of the country where?"

"Initially, you will go to Vienna, yes? The debriefing will be conducted there. In pleasant surroundings, it goes without . . . it goes *with* saying. The representatives of several intelligence services will want to buy time with you. After all, it is not every day that we can come up with a *novator*, yes?"

"Yes," the Potter agreed. Buy time. That made Oskar a free-lancer. Though in all probability he was a free-lancer on a leash. But whose leash? "It is not every day."

"After Vienna," Oskar continued, "we will supply you with identities, with a legend, with bank accounts, with a modest business even. A pottery studio might be appropriate. You can live where you want."

"Could we go to Paris?"

Oskar smiled for the first time. "You have been to Paris, yes?"

"Yes." In fact the Potter had passed through Paris on the way back from his tour of duty in New York. "My wife dreams of it."

"Paris is entirely within the realm of possibility," Oskar said with the tone of someone who considered the matter settled.

"How do you plan to get us out of the country?" the Potter wanted to know.

Oskar permitted himself a gesture of impatience. The Potter politely retracted the question. Oskar said, "That brings us to the part of the conversation where you suggest what, specifically, you can offer to us to justify our efforts, not to speak of our risks."

The Potter suppressed a faint smile. " 'Justify' in the sense of provide financial profit?"

Oskar knew he had to choose his words carefully. "If we decide to get you out, we will want to be rewarded for our efforts. It is a fact of life that there are organizations in the West that will pay generously for your information. But you misjudge us if you think the money is for us. It will fund projects designed to undermine a regime, a system, a philosophy that we consider odious." Lowering his voice to a whisper, Oskar intoned Dostoevsky's famous phrase, "Where there is sorrow and pain, the soil is sacred, yes?"

"Yes," the Potter remarked dryly. Somehow he believed Oskar. He had the look of an idealist, which is to say the look of someone with a short life expectancy. "My having been a *novator*—doesn't that, in itself, justify your efforts, your risks?"

Oskar shrugged.

"There were circuits in New York," the Potter said softly. He had been trained to keep secrets; giving them away didn't come naturally. "There was an entire *rezidentura*. There was an *istochnik*—a source of information—in the United Nations Secretariat."

"So: that was all some time ago," Oskar noted. "And you have been out of circulation for six months now."

"Try it out on your principals," the Potter insisted. "In any case, it is all I have to offer."

"Of course I will try it out," Oskar said. "But I suspect that your *rezidentura*, your *istochnik*, are what the Americans call"—here he switched to English—"old hats." Speaking again in Russian, he added, "You are familiar with the expression, yes?"

"Yes," repeated the Potter, remembering Piotr Borisovich's ancient fedora, wondering what he had gotten himself into; wondering if in the end they would get out of him the thing he valued more than the pupil of his eye. "I am painfully familiar with old hats."

9

❦

Oskar inserted a key and let himself in the service door. It was a little-used back entrance to a stuffy transit hotel on Sushchevsky Bank Street, behind the Riga Station. The narrow service stairs hadn't been swept in years, but then the few people who used it generally had other things on their minds besides cleanliness. The doors on all the floors except the fourth were bolted shut. Upstairs, Oskar felt his way along the pitch-dark corridor, one hand on the wall, the other raised protectively before his eyes. It occurred to him that the people who frequented the fourth floor could easily afford to supply light bulbs, but probably felt more comfortable in the dark. At the third door along the corridor wall, Oskar knocked and then entered without waiting for an invitation. He stuffed his scarf into the sleeve of his raincoat, and hung it on the clothes tree alongside the two mink coats. So: if the Cousins were wearing their mink coats now, when it was not even freezing out, God knows what they would do in January when the temperature could drop to minus thirty. Well, everyone had his threshold of pain, or cold, or corruptibility, yes? It remained to be seen what the Potter's was.

The blind man recognized Oskar's footfall. "You're early," he called, "which means things went badly."

"Things went quickly," Oskar corrected him. "It would have been very curious—suspicious even, yes?—if he had offered us precisely what we wanted the first time around."

"He needs to marinate," agreed the other man in the room.

The blind man tapped his baton against his shoe impatiently. "He should be pushed," he insisted. "You could play the tape recording of the meeting back to him. He has already done enough to merit a firing squad."

"With all respect," the younger Cousin said—he was, after all, dealing with someone who, on paper at least, was his superior—"he needs to be pulled, not pushed."

"He has a violent temper, yes?" Oskar noted. "If he crosses frontiers, whether physical or psychological, he must have the impression that he is controlling his own destiny."

"What will you do now?" the blind man asked, conceding to the others the question of pace.

"So," Oskar said, "I will report back to my German Merchants. Then I will sit by the phone and reflect on what the peasants say—that all things come to those who wait, yes?"

10

❦

Carroll and Francis were confirmed bachelors. It wasn't that they didn't like women; they just didn't trust them. And what sex drive either came equipped with at birth had long since been channeled into other pursuits. Carroll lived with an unmarried sister in a rented apartment in Georgetown. Francis lived alone in a downtown residence hotel with a kitchenette crawling with cockroaches. He sprayed once a week, ironed his own shirts, darned his own socks and except on Tuesdays and Fridays made his own dinners. On Tuesdays he grabbed a bite in a delicatessen and went to a motion picture; to a spy film whenever possible. On Fridays he dined out with Carroll. They had been meeting Fridays more or less to review their week's work since they began sharing an office, some twelve years before. For eight of those years they had been faithful to a particular Chinese restaurant. Then they discovered the chef sprinkled monosodium glutamate on all his dishes. Now they ate Chinese health food.

Francis lifted the metal lid on his dish from Column B and sniffed suspiciously at the contents. The gesture annoyed Carroll. "I don't know how you can be so calm," he whispered fiercely. His own face was a mask of frustration. "After what's happened . . ."

"Nothing happened that wasn't expected," Francis said.

"What if he doesn't have what we want?" Carroll whined.

For a moment Francis thought his partner might actually burst into tears. "The Potter was the *novator*," he reminded Carroll. "He was in charge of the sleeper school. He has it."

"Imagine offering us a ten-year-old *rezidentura*, or an *istochnik* at the United Nations! What does he take us for, amateurs?"

"You act as if he meant it as a personal insult," Francis reproached Carroll. "He's dealing with free-lancers, remember, not us. He was simply testing the temperature of the water."

"I hope to God you're right," Carroll said. The muscle in his cheek twitched several times, then stopped of its own accord. "Our whole scheme depends on him."

Francis' eyes narrowed; some music was forming in the back of his brain. "I'm just thinking out loud, but it might not do any harm to shake him up a bit. . . ."

Carroll snapped his fingers; lyrics had leapt into his head. "What if we sent *him* the names of the *rezidentura* and the *istochnik*!"

"I knew you'd come up with something," Francis remarked, and he tucked the corner of his napkin into his collar to protect his taxicab-yellow bow tie and attacked the plate of whole-wheat noodles, Chinese cabbage and steamed shrimp.

11

⚜

"Svetochka," moaned Svetochka, kicking off her worn suede boots, collapsing into an easy chair that badly needed recovering, "is dead."

She had just come back from the store with two tins of salted fish, a kilo of onions, a box of rice. "Seven lines," she moaned, feeling very sorry for herself. "One for the fish, one for the onions, one for the rice. That's three. Then one to pay the cashier. That makes four. Then back to the first line to collect the fish, another to collect the onions, a third to collect the rice. That's seven. You know your Lenin, Feliks. Is there something in it about Communism needing *lines*?"

The Potter smiled for the first time in days. "There are lines because there are shortages," he explained.

"And why," Svetochka demanded, massaging the balls of her feet, "if everybody is working according to their ability, do we still have shortages?"

The Potter helped himself to some more vodka. "In the old days, before the revolution, they used to say that the shortage would be divided among the peasants. Now we are fairer—we divide the shortage among everyone. That's Communism."

"Well," she replied with a sigh, "Svetochka preferred it when you had your ration privileges at the food center. The people who work there are much more polite." A faraway look crept into her eyes; she might have been talking about heaven. "They even have someone who opens the door for you when your arms are loaded. They *recommended* things. The lettuce is especially fresh, they say." Tears spilled from her eyes. "Lettuce in *winter*! God knows where it came from. The okra is from Central Asia, they say. The oranges from Cuba. Try—"

"Enough." The Potter cut her off with an impatient wave of his hand.

"You have one answer for everything, Feliks. Enough! *I've had enough of your enough!* When we first met you had a ration at the food center and a *dacha* and a chauffeured automobile when you phoned up for one. You came home from that warehouse of yours with something for Svetochka almost every day. I wore lipstick colors nobody in Moscow ever saw before."

"Enough," muttered the Potter. He felt as if he were being tuned too high.

"You said you would take your Svetochka to Paris one day," she taunted him. "You said we would take the elevator to the top of an enormous steel tower and look out over the world and laugh our heads off."

The Potter tilted his head onto the back of his chair and closed his eyes tiredly. "What if I told you I would still take you to Paris?" he asked quietly.

She flung herself at his feet, hugged his knees. "Oh, Feliks, if only you could! Svetochka doesn't want to grow old without making love in Paris. We'd make love *before* dinner, the way we used to. Do you remember what an appetite you had afterward?"

"I still have an appetite," the Potter commented bitterly. He opened his legs and felt her nestle between them. "I lost my job and my ration and my *dacha* and my chauffeured automobile, but I never lost my appetite."

12

⚜

The second meeting took place in the second taxi. Oskar was driving. "So: I passed your offer on to my potential clients," he announced, concentrating on the road, his voice drifting back over his shoulder. "Here is their response."

He handed a note back to his passenger as he accelerated past a long line of people waiting in a corner taxi queue. A young woman in a tattered fur coat and fur hat leapt after him, desperately waving a ten-ruble note. In the back seat, the Potter unfolded the piece of paper. There were two columns, one marked A, the other B. Nine names were listed under Column A—the entire New York *rezidentura*. One name, that of an African diplomat who had spent his formative years at Patrice Lumumba University in Moscow, was listed under Column B—the *istochnik* at the United Nations.

"In America, Chinese restaurants have a Column A and B on their menus," the Potter noted absently. "They certainly went to a lot of trouble to say no."

"I interpret it as a sign of personal respect for you, yes?" Oskar remarked.

They were passing the zoo, and the Potter thought he could make out the bleating of some frustrated animal coming from one of the buildings; then it occurred to him that the sound might have originated in his own imagination. He leaned forward so that his mouth was close to Oskar's ear. "I have given the matter a great deal of thought," he told him.

"So: I suspected you would."

Oskar was beginning to get on the Potter's nerves. "You are very sure of yourself," he noted.

Oskar shrugged. "You were the *novator*. If you really want to get out of Russia, you will come up with something to pay your way, yes?"

Behind the taxi, a siren wailed. Oskar pulled the car over sharply to the right. A Zil limousine with lace curtains on its rear windows raced down the middle lane toward the Kremlin. Up ahead, a policeman held up cross traffic until the Zil had passed.

"That's probably—" Oskar named an alternate member of the Politburo, an expert on agriculture whose star was considered to be on the rise. "I hear he has a mistress stashed away in one of those new buildings behind the zoo. So: where were we?"

The Potter said, "I lost three sleepers in six months. One of them simply disappeared. He was a physicist by training. He was inserted into America so that he could eventually take over a network of subagents working at various atomic installations. With his background in physics, he would have been in a position to evaluate their information, direct them to fill in gaps in our knowledge, that sort of thing. Four of the subagents were eventually caught and put on trial in America. Two others were never identified. I don't know the names of the two, but I could supply enough information about them—where they worked during what years, their professional qualifications, a description of the family of one, the sexual preferences of the other, so that your clients can identify them."

Oskar pulled up at a red light. Just abreast of them, a man and a woman in a Czech Skoda were arguing bitterly. "I go over it again and again," the Potter could hear the man yell, "and I can't find the beginning."

"The beginning of what?" the woman cried.

"The beginning of where it went wrong," the man replied. "The beginning of—" The light changed and the Czech car raced off.

Oskar threw his taxi into first and started down the street after the Skoda. "So: it went wrong," he called over his shoulder, "right after the Bolshevik revolution when some comrades proposed opening a special restaurant for members of the Party. Those who were against it argued that Communists should starve along with the working classes. Those who were for it argued that they couldn't lead the working class to paradise if they didn't have the physical strength. The matter was brought to Lenin. You know the story, yes? Lenin ruled in favor of establishing a special restaurant. Things were never the same after that, yes? I will let you off in front of the Hotel Ukraina. So, enter the lobby and buy a newspaper from the kiosk, then go on about your business."

"What about my offer?" the Potter asked.

"I will call you when I get a response, yes?" Oskar said without noticeable enthusiasm.

13

❦

The blind man's white baton came down like a whip against the legs of his chair. "So much for your *pulling*," he announced in a voice that left no room for discussion. "Now we will do some *pushing*!"

14

❦

The Deputy Assistant Procurator, a burnt-out middle-aged time-server with long clumps of hair pasted across his scalp like fingers, kept the Potter waiting ten minutes before he even looked up. There was a chair in front of the polished table that served as his desk, but he never offered him the use of it. "You have been summoned," the Deputy Assistant Procurator eventually said—it was at this point that he glanced at the Potter for the first time—"summoned, eh, in accordance with—" He named an article of the penal code. The Deputy Assistant Procurator shuffled through a sheaf of official-looking papers with seals and signatures on the bottom of each one. "You are informed . . ." He removed his eyeglasses and cleaned them with the tip of his tie, then carefully hooked them back over his ears. ". . . informed, eh, that criminal proceedings have been opened against you in connection with charges of, eh, pilfering state property from the warehouse annex of the state security institution that you were formerly in command of." He lost his place and peered at the paper he was reading. "Eh, in command of. You are advised to retain a lawyer. You are further advised that the penalty, if convicted of violating the particular article of the penal code with which you are charged, is ten years at a strict-regime labor camp, confiscation of all personal property, annulment of pension and, eh, voting rights." The Deputy Assistant Procurator looked up. "Do you have any comment to make?"

The Potter said in English, "I hear it was charged against me that I sought to destroy institutions."

"What does that mean?" snapped the Deputy Assistant Procurator in annoyance.

"It is a line written by the American poet Walter Whitman."

"It doesn't help your case to be quoting an *American* poet."

"He is considered to be very progressive," the Potter said sarcastically.

The Deputy Assistant Procurator pushed a paper across the table toward the Potter, and held out a ball-point pen. "Sign your full name at the bottom to indicate you are familiar with the contents."

The Potter accepted the pen and looked down at the paper. It was all a mistake, of course. He had served the state too long and too well to be accused now of swiping the odd bit of clothing or an occasional lipstick from the American warehouse. Compared to some of his colleagues or superiors, the Potter's acquisitions had been extremely modest; a senior section chief had once trucked out painters and carpenters and electricians employed by the Center and set them to work rebuilding his *dacha*, and nobody had uttered a word. The Potter forced himself to focus on the paper. Over "Name of accused" someone had typed in "Feliks Arkantevich Turov." So it wasn't a mistake after all. Over "Race" it said "Jew." In what sense is a Jew always, ever a Jew? Piotr Borisovich had once laughingly asked, and then, suddenly serious, he had answered his own question: In the sense that every ten or twenty years, the state will go out of its way to remind him. But why was the state, which in the Potter's experience never did anything haphazardly, choosing this particular moment to remind him of his racial roots? And why was the state suddenly concerned with his penny-ante pilfering?

"I haven't got, eh, all morning," said the burnt-out Deputy Assistant Procurator, who had precisely that.

The Potter reached down and scratched his signature across the bottom of the sheet, acknowledging that criminal proceedings had been opened against him; acknowledging also that his life, or what was left of it, was spiraling out of control.

15

❦

Svetochka turned up the volume on the radio so that their neighbors couldn't eavesdrop. "What did he want?" she demanded, though she could tell by his face that she might be better off if she didn't know.

"They are looking into irregularities," the Potter said vaguely. He would never survive a strict-regime labor camp; if he were tied up to the pier of old age now, imagine what he'd be in ten years. And if, by some miracle, he lived through it, Svetochka certainly wouldn't be waiting for him when he got out.

"What kind of irregularities?"

The Potter gripped his glass of tea in both hands to warm his fingers. "There was some pilfering at the warehouse while I was the *novator*." Lipsticks, makeup, earrings, perfume, cigarettes, cigarette lighters, underwear, nylon stockings, records, cinema magazines, once a dress, once a pair of women's blue jeans, all manufactured in America, had disappeared.

"How can they prove it was you who took them?" Svetochka asked.

"When they are at the appropriate stage of the investigation," the Potter said numbly, "you will tell them."

Svetochka reacted as if she had been slapped across the face. "How can you bring yourself to say such a thing? Svetochka would never do anything to hurt her Feliks."

"You will be offered the opportunity to save yourself," the Potter explained with a calmness he didn't feel. "You will hesitate long enough to convince yourself of your loyalty to me, but in the end you will do what has to be done."

"Oh, Feliks," she cried. "You can't let them do this to Svetochka."

The words seemed to echo through the Potter's head. To Svetochka! He would lose his pension and wind up in a strict-regime labor camp for ten years, and they were doing this to *her*. Stirring a spoonful of jam into his tea, he smiled grimly.

"You must give them what they want, Feliks."

He shook his head. "I am in a difficult position," he said. "I am not yet sure who wants what."

Svetochka nervously uncrossed and recrossed her legs, giving the Potter a glimpse of garter belt, of thigh. Once, when she had drunk too much vodka, she had admitted that, as a young girl, she planted herself in front of a mirror and practiced crossing her legs in a way that would permit the men facing her to see up her skirt. Later, when he had reminded her of this, she had denied it indignantly. But the perfection of the gesture spoke for itself.

"There was a phone call for you while you were out," Svetochka announced absently. "Someone named Oskar . . ."

He stopped stirring his tea. If he could give Oskar what *he* wanted, there still might be a way out. "What did he say?" the Potter asked.

"It was a funny message. He said to tell you he is in possession of a piece of paper, that it is divided into two columns, one marked A, the other B. He said there was one name in each column."

"One name in each column?"

Svetochka nodded. "He said you would understand. Who is this Oskar?"

"He is a middleman," the Potter answered. "He brings buyers and sellers together."

Svetochka wasn't listening. "There must be a solution," she blurted out. "It is only a question of finding it."

"There is," the Potter said quietly.

"Then take it!"

"It would mean betraying a friend." The Potter had known all along it would come down to this. He tried to imagine what advice Piotr Borisovich would give him. We are in a ruthless business, he could hear Piotr Borisovich saying. We are not humanists, so why pretend to be? Save yourself, he could hear Piotr Borisovich saying. If I were in your shoes, I certainly would.

On the radio, the Moscow Symphony Orchestra reached the end of one movement and began tuning up before starting another. In the audience, people coughed. Svetochka breathed a name into the silence. "Piotr Borisovich?" The orchestra launched into the new movement.

The Potter looked quickly away, confirming her guess.

"If you give them Piotr," she plunged on, thinking she was talking about the Deputy Assistant Procurator and warehouse pilfering, "they will leave you and Svetochka alone?"

"If I give them Piotr Borisovich"—the Potter felt as if he were finally getting the spiraling clay under some kind of control—"we can go to live in Paris."

Svetochka's eyes widened. "Paris," she repeated. She didn't hesitate. "He betrayed you," she spat out. "You can betray him!"

The Potter's hand shook; tea spilled onto his trousers. "What do you mean, betrayed me?"

She avoided his eye. "When you started bringing him around, he was very polite, very respectful at first. Later, when he didn't think you would notice, he would look up Svetochka's skirt, brush the back of his hand against Svetochka's breast. Svetochka knew what he was thinking. You went off once, you said it was to

Poland. Remember? You were away for ten days." She appeared to run out of words; out of breath too.

"Go on," the Potter ordered weakly.

"Ten days you were away. He dropped by. He said he was looking for you, but we both understood that he knew you were not in Moscow. We drank some vodka. Svetochka was lonely without her Feliks. Before she knew what had happened, we were in—" She burst out furiously, "Does Svetochka have to draw you a picture?"

"I don't believe you," the Potter cried. "You are lying."

"If Svetochka is lying," she retorted, her voice barely audible above the music, her eyes flashing, "how would she know that Piotr Borisovich was circumcised?"

16

❦

"So: you got my message?"

"I got it."

Oskar seemed just as tense as the Potter. "You understood it, yes?"

"I understood it," the Potter acknowledged. He watched the trolley cars slide noiselessly past in the street below. What sound they made was dampened by the storm windows fitted over the regular windows. Someone had been very lazy. In summer such windows were usually taken off. Maybe it wasn't a question of cold, though. Maybe it was a question of security. Cotton had been stretched along the sill between the windows to absorb the condensation, and moss had been placed on the cotton—a touch that indicated that the regular resident of the apartment had peasant roots. "Your potential clients already knew the identities of the people in question," the Potter continued tonelessly. "They were not buying."

"So: I assume you have come up with another proposition," Oskar remarked casually, "or you wouldn't be here, yes?"

The Potter wondered if Oskar was as sure of himself as he sounded. "Another proposition, yes."

Svetochka had been right, of course, about Piotr Borisovich. On several occasions the Potter and his pupil had visited the Sandunovsky Bathhouse together. There, stark naked amid the smoke screen of steam and the stale smell of sweat and birch bark, they had nibbled on sticks of salted fish and talked in undertones about the idealism that somehow had gotten lost in the shuffle in Russia. Glancing down, the Potter had noticed that Piotr Borisovich was circumcised. "It is a rare thing in Russia," Piotr Borisovich had commented, his eyes following the Potter's gaze. Indeed it was! Since the revolution, even Jews hesitated when it came to having their children circumcised. The Potter had been born before the revolution, but his parents had seen the handwriting on the wall. His father had decided that with all the anti-Semitism in Russia, the day might come when the boy's safety would depend on his *not* being circumcised. Piotr Borisovich's father, curiously, hadn't even been Jewish. But he once came across a pamphlet describing the medical advantages of circumcision. Practicing what the author-doctor preached, he had himself circumcised though he was already a grown man, and his son circumcised at birth. The circumcision had almost been the undoing of the father. Trapped behind German lines at one point during the war, he had been taken for a Jew. He had been awaiting execution in a cell when the Red Army counterattacked and liberated the town.

It struck the Potter, who had an inner ear permanently tuned to pick up such details, how ironic it would be if the circumcision turned out to be the undoing of the son.

The Potter turned to confront Oskar. "The last sleeper to pass through my school while I was the *novator*," he briskly informed him, "was named Piotr Borisovich Revkin." He could see interest burning, like a pilot light, in Oskar's normally masked eyes. "He was inserted into America two years ago. He lives in a section of New York under deep cover, waiting for the signal indicating his controllers have decided to give him a mission."

Oskar couldn't suppress the note of excitement

that crept into his voice. "You know the name under which he operates, yes? You know *where* he is?"

The Potter nodded.

Oskar took a step in the Potter's direction. "You are familiar with the signal that can awaken this sleeper of yours, yes?"

"Yes."

"So: my clients will want to know how you came into possession of this information," Oskar said.

"His cover name is part of the legend we worked out together at the sleeper school," the Potter explained. "The location I know because, for personal reasons that had to do with an affinity we shared for a certain poet, he sent me, in violation of standing rules, a picture postcard of the house he lives in."

"And the awakening signal?"

"When we selected an awakening signal, I always made it a point to choose a phrase that was already embedded in a sleeper's memory—a familiar motto, a line of a song or a poem he had known since childhood. There was a line of poetry that we both knew . . ." The Potter's voice choked for an instant. Did one betrayal inevitably lead to another? What level of Dante's hell was he sentencing himself to? He drew a deep breath. ". . . knew and appreciated. I wrote out the awakening signal in my own hand in his dossier."

"If my potential clients accept and you don't have the information you claim to have . . ." Oskar left the sentence hanging.

The Potter said softly, "I am not an idiot. I know the rules of the game." Against his will, a brittle laugh seeped from the back of his throat. "I helped write them."

17

⚜

The younger Cousin helped the blind man off with his coat. Tapping his white baton before his feet, the blind man made his way into the hotel room. "Well, Oskar," he called out, uncertain where in the room Oskar was, "in the end pushing him didn't do any harm, did it?"

Oskar said, "So: it is my opinion he would have come around eventually."

The younger man waved Oskar off. He had once seen the blind man lash out with his baton at the legs of someone who crossed him.

Oskar shrugged. "The important thing," he told the blind man, "is that he has come through with what you wanted. It is true what he said about the awakening signal, yes?"

The blind man found the seat with his baton and settled into it. The younger man extracted a red file from a briefcase and opened it on the table. The blind man ran his fingertips over several pages as if they were written in braille. "Of course the awakening signal is in his handwriting," he said. "That's how we first discovered that he knew it."

"If he had typed in the signal," said the younger man, "it might never have occurred to us to use him. He'd still be bringing home American mascara to that bitch of a wife of his."

"What about the postcard?" Oskar asked. "It is conceivable that the Americans will administer truth drugs to him. Every detail must check out if they are to swallow the whole story."

"There was a postcard," the younger man confirmed. "Only the sleeper in question never sent it."

"We arranged for it to be sent," the blind man confessed smugly, "to fill in the single gap in the *novator*'s knowledge. Since he and this sleeper of his aren't going to meet again, he will never find that out."

"So: all that remains to be done now is to convince my clients to accept the deal, and then ship the *novator* and that whore of his out of the country, yes?"

"Your clients will agree to the deal," the blind man announced in a tone that left no room for doubt. And with a laugh that contained no trace of humor, he added, "I was never more sure of anything in my life."

18

Francis had come down with a head cold. It was serious enough to make him skip his Tuesday-night film. Wednesday morning he telephoned Mrs. Cresswell to say he had a fever and would not be coming in. She put him on hold for a moment, which irritated Francis because it conveyed the impression that he required *permission* to stay away from the office. Then Carroll came on the line. "Mrs. Cresswell tells me you are under the weather," he said. Something in Carroll's voice made Francis suspect that his cheek muscle was atwitch.

"I have a hundred and one," Francis informed him as if it were an accomplishment.

"A hundred and one *what*?" Carroll's mind was on other things.

"A hundred and one degrees of fever!" Francis cried into the mouthpiece. "I can't see to drive."

"It's not enough," Carroll retorted. "Grab a cab." And lowering his voice to a hoarse whisper, he confided, "We are starting to haul in our fish."

Francis swallowed. *We are starting to haul in our fish!* It was the most original operation he had ever been involved in in his career. If it succeeded, history would be diverted as if it were nothing more than an inconvenient stream!

"Did you hear what I said?" Carroll hissed into the phone.

"I shall be right in," Francis said with great dignity. "I only need to put on an appropriate tie."

19

For eighteen excruciating days, the Potter didn't hear a word from Oskar. After the first week went by in sinister silence he broke down and dialed B one-forty-one, twenty-one, but almost had his eardrum shattered by the peculiar whining sound that in Moscow indicates the number is out of order. Had it all been a hoax? Someone's idea of indoor sport? Or even worse, a trap designed to test his loyalty? But if it were a trap, why would they wait to spring it?

In the state he was in, throwing pots was out of the question. They spiraled off into lopsided shapes that had nothing in common with the conception in his head. So the Potter paced: the attic, the bedroom, the corridor, the streets around the apartment building in which he lived. Nine days after his last session with Oskar, the Potter was prowling around the attic when he heard the phone ringing underfoot. He raced downstairs, but Svetochka beat him to it. "I understand," she was saying into the mouthpiece. Her posture was rigid, her face frozen in an expression of a sullen child. "We will both be there. You will be able to set your watch by our arrival."

The call turned out to be a summons from the Deputy Assistant Procurator's office for a groundbreaking session. Svetochka astonished the Potter by scrubbing every trace of makeup off her face, wearing her lowest heels and her drabbest clothes—until it dawned on him that it was her idea of how to impress Deputy Assistant Procurators with one's innocence. At the interview, Svetochka rose to the occasion and denied everything, starting with her age. "I happen, Comrade Procurator," she announced, baring teeth that looked as if they had been *sharpened*, "to be twenty-nine years of age, and not thirty-one."

The Deputy Assistant Procurator peered at a photocopy of her internal passport through a magnifying glass. "It says here in black and white that you were born in . . ." He read off a month and a year. "Subtract that from today"—he began counting on his fingers—"and you are left with thirty-one."

Svetochka's jaw angled up in displeasure. "The woman who issued me the passport wore thick eyeglasses. She made an error when she copied the date off my birth certificate."

"And where, if I may make so bold as to pose the question"—the Potter recognized this as a standard bureaucratic effort at irony—"is this, eh, birth certificate?"

"My mother had it."

"And where"—bureaucratic exasperation now—"is your mother?"

"In a coffin, underground, in row seven, aisle D of the municipal cemetery of Smolensk."

"I see," moaned the Deputy Assistant Procurator, though of course he didn't see at all. For thanks to Svetochka, he got so bogged down with inconsequential matters (height, weight, color of eyes, Party background, education, date of marriage, et cetera, et cetera) that he had to schedule a second session to attack the question of pilfering from the warehouse of a state institution. And by that time, Oskar had gotten back to them.

He called from a public phone one midnight. So: if the Potter would go down to the corner, a taxi would pick him up. Do you know what time it is? the Potter asked, relieved to have finally heard from Oskar but anxious, for tactical reasons, not to let him know it. Ignoring the question, Oskar said only that the Potter was to bring his wife with him, yes? Why bring my wife? the Potter was on the verge of demanding, but Oskar had clicked off the line.

Svetochka relished the envious stares of the others in the taxi queue when the first cab that came along refused everyone except them. The little man with shirred skin, the one who had popped up near Nadezhda Alliluyeva's tomb in the Novodevichy Cemetery, was planted behind the wheel. "Still going *anywhere*?" he asked, and he laughed a madman's laugh. He eventually deposited his passengers before a drab prefabricated apartment house on Krasnaya Street, a stone's throw from the planetarium.

Did every site in Moscow hold memories for the Potter? When Piotr Borisovich discovered that the Potter had never been to a planetarium, he had immediately arranged a visit. Revolutions had been the theme of the day. They had served up on the overhead dome, as if it were a meal, the sky as it looked over Petrograd the night the Bolsheviks stormed the Winter Palace in 1917. Then they projected the sky as it looked over Philadelphia after the signing of the Declaration of Independence, July 4, 1776. Walking back to the hotel afterward, Piotr Borisovich had started rambling on about American history. Did the Potter know, he had asked, that both Thomas Jefferson and John Adams died within hours of each other, on July 4, 1826, fifty years to the day after they signed the Declaration? James Monroe, another signer and the last President to have been forged by the American Revolution, died five years to the day later. In the decades before the Civil War, the veterans of Bunker Hill, Lexington, Valley Forge, gradually died off. In the end, Piotr Borisovich had said, the Americans and the Russians were confronted by the same problem: how to transmit the idealism of the founding revolutionists to the generations that came after them. The Americans, according to Piotr Borisovich, had never solved the problem. And we Russians, the Potter had asked, have we solved it?

Piotr Borisovich had glanced sideways at the Potter, calculating how frank he dared get with the *novator* who controlled his life as surely as a puppeteer controls his marionette. It is my opinion, Piotr Borisovich had finally said—he appeared to be avoiding the question, but of course he wasn't—that revolutions don't so much change things as *rearrange* them. The Potter had accepted the statement for what it was: in the Soviet context, people consecrated friendships by uttering things which, if reported to the authorities, could get them fired or jailed or, occasionally, shot. And the Potter had responded in the same currency. I agree with you completely, he had said in a formal voice he normally reserved for oaths or rites. The people who made our revolution, theirs too, dreamed bigger dreams than we dare dream today.

The moment had contained something of the aura of an exchange of rings at a marriage ceremony. But then Piotr Borisovich, who had become the son the Potter could never father, had betrayed him. And now he, in turn, would betray Piotr Borisovich. It would end, the Potter could hear Piotr Borisovich saying with that bitter laugh of his that sounded like steam escaping from a partly open valve, in night, in death. And he remembered the line of Walter Whitman's that he had started to quote in reply and Piotr Borisovich, his head cocked quizzically, had completed.

" '. . . the hands of the sisters Death and Night,' " the Potter had recited.

Piotr Borisovich had picked up where he left off: " '. . . incessantly softly wash again, and ever again, this soil'd world.' "

"So," Oskar was saying—he had been waiting in the shadows of the first-floor landing—"we meet again." He reached for Svetochka's hand and bent his lips to the back of it, which made the Potter think that Oskar's accent was Polish after all. "Your husband, dear lady, calls me Oskar, and there is no reason under the sun why you should not do likewise, yes? Meeting you makes my day."

No one had ever kissed Svetochka's hand before, and it went to her head. "The pleasure," she chirped, adopting airs the Potter never knew she was equipped with, "is mutual."

Using a latchkey attached to a thin gold chain, Oskar let himself into an apartment on the fifth floor. The three of them groped their way along a darkened hallway toward a door. Light seeped from under it. A soft whirring sound came from beyond it. "Let me do the talking," Oskar cautioned as he ushered them into the room.

A Jew wearing an embroidered skullcap and peering through incredibly thick eyeglasses sat bent over a pedal-operated prewar Singer sewing machine. Oskar muttered something in Yiddish, and the young man nodded shyly at the Potter and Svetochka. "You are the fortunate ones," he said in Russian. He stood up and came around in front of his Singer and squinting professionally through his thick lenses, sized them up. "They will look perfectly American when I am through with them," he promised.

"American!" Svetochka's eyes cocked open.

The Jew, who was in his early twenties, handed Oskar a pad and a pencil, then produced a measuring tape. "Arms up, if you please," he instructed the Potter, and he began calling out measurements—neck, shoulders, chest, waist, inseam, sleeve. "You wear your skirt too low on your hips," he commented to Svetochka as he moved around her taking measurements. To Oskar the Jew said, "What will you do for shoes?"

"Only give me the sizes, I will provide them."

Later, outside the building, the Potter took Oskar aside. "What was all that about?" he demanded.

"So: you will be leaving the country in five days' time under valid American passports," Oskar explained. "It is a crucial part of the operation that you pass in every detail for Americans, yes?" And he went on to explain when, and how, they would get out of Russia.

"It is that simple?" the Potter asked in amazement.

"You would be happier crossing the border in the Arctic Circle on snowshoes, with dogs barking in the distance, yes?" Oskar emitted the only laugh the Potter was ever to hear from him. "So: it is my opinion that you have read too many cheap spy novels."

The next afternoon Svetochka withdrew two hundred rubles from her bank account and spent every last kopeck of it at the ornately decorated Gastronom No. 1 on Gorky Street, popularly known as Yeliseyevsky's after the owner of the delicatessen before the revolution. Rubbing elbows with the Gastronom's regular clients, the wives and daughters of Central Committee members, leaving large tips on every counter that she came to, Svetochka managed to get out of the store with a supply of blinis, a package of salted crackers, a container of thick cream, a tin of Beluga caviar, several fresh Norwegian herrings and two bottles of Polish Bison vodka.

"What have you done?" the Potter groaned when he saw her purchases set out on the small table in their bedroom.

"We won't need rubles in Paris," Svetochka announced innocently, "so Svetochka decided to spend as much as she could here before we leave."

"You idiot! The last thing we want to do is attract attention to ourselves." He collapsed into a wooden chair and stared at the display of luxury that any other time would have set his mouth to watering.

Crestfallen, Svetochka spread some caviar on a salted cracker, poured some vodka (which she had put outside a window to chill) into a glass and offered them to the Potter.

"I am not hungry," he grumbled.

Svetochka planted herself in a chair facing him. "What if we stimulate your appetite?" she asked suggestively, and she slowly, deliberately crossed, and then recrossed, her legs.

They made love with the light on, something they hadn't done in months. Working the Potter's dwarfish body as if she were preparing a field for planting, faking an orgasm (and when she finally had one, exaggerating its intensity), Svetochka caused him to forget, if only for a moment, Piotr Borisovich and Oskar and the pier of old age to which he felt moored. Later, munching on biscuits coated with caviar, washing them down with chilled vodka, Svetochka blew lightly into his ear and whispered, "That is only a sample of what Svetochka will do to her Feliks when we get to Paris."

20

⚜

Two days before they were scheduled to leave Russia, the Potter decided the time had come to pay a last visit to Piotr Borisovich's father. Not only did he want to see the old man before he left; there was also the practical matter of recovering the package he had carefully stashed away in a secret compartment under the floorboards of his house.

The day of the visit the Potter spent several hours doing some elementary street work to make sure he wasn't being followed. It had been quite a while since he had practiced tradecraft, but the gestures he had learned as a young man, and had perfected during his four years as *rezident* in New York, came back fairly easily. He used reflecting surfaces—doors of polished cars, buses—as mirrors to observe what was going on around him in the street without appearing to. He made it a point to be the last one to board a trolley, and the last to leap off before it started again. He lingered in front of store windows on the Arbat and looked in them to see who else might be lingering in front of other store windows. He ducked into an underground tunnel that pedestrians used to cross October Square, hurried halfway down it and then suddenly doubled back on his tracks—and watched to see who else might double back on his tracks. He entered GUM, the archaic bazaarlike department store across Red Square from the Kremlin, through one door, allowed himself to become caught up in a mob stampeding for a counter that had just put East German umbrellas on sale, and then made his way out of another door. He ducked into a prewar apartment building near Pushkin Square, climbed to the sixth floor, where the corridor connected with an adjoining building, and emerged from an entrance of a different building on a different street. It was midafternoon before he decided his wake was clean. He caught a taxi to the Central Depot and boarded a bus for Peredelkino, a village about forty kilometers from Moscow.

In the half year since his last trip to Peredelkino, Moscow had sprawled, like a lazy lady, farther into the countryside. Prefabricated concrete apartment buildings had sprouted on either side of the road; to the Potter's eye they had the aesthetic appeal of pillboxes. Streets that had been bulldozed into existence, but not yet paved, ran off like rivulets in every direction. Beyond the last building, in still-unleveled fields covered with corn stumps, the skeletons of giant cranes, some on their sides, some upright already, hinted at the further expansion of the city limits. "There are no limits to cities," Piotr Borisovich had once remarked as he and the Potter drove through what was then the suburb into the countryside. He had thought a moment and then revised his sentence: *There are no limits*, he had said, though at the time the Potter hadn't been sure what he was getting at.

Now he thought he understood. And he wondered, not for the first time, whether he had been Piotr Borisovich's teacher, or Piotr Borisovich had been his.

Outside of Moscow, the first peasant cottages, looking distinctly one-dimensional through the dirty window of the bus, appeared on either side of the Minsk highway. With their painted, carved wooden shutters and carefully tended vegetable gardens—in Russia, something like half the fresh vegetables came from these tiny peasant plots—they provided quite a contrast to those pillboxes that would eventually rise in their places.

In the old days, before the revolution, the peasants going off to the fields used to leave their doors unlocked and food set out on the table in case anyone happened by. But then the Bolshevik grain-confiscating squads had happened by, and the peasants had started locking their doors. Probably because of his peasant roots, Piotr Borisovich had talked a great deal about the subject during his stay at the Potter's school. The trouble, he would say, his voice reduced to the soft purr he used when he felt deeply about something, was that the Bolsheviks, being city-bred and city-oriented, never quite knew what to do with the eighty percent of the population that lived outside the cities. The peasants were the enemy, the Potter would explode. In their heart of hearts, they were all capitalists—they wanted to *own* the land they worked. What they wanted—Piotr Borisovich would shake his head in disagreement—was to *own* the *crop* they harvested, and not have it carted off without compensation to feed the workers in the cities.

They hadn't seen eye to eye on everything, the Potter and Piotr Borisovich, but their differences only seemed to bind them closer together—to reinforce the notion, foreign to Soviet Russia, that holding different opinions was perfectly normal.

Arriving at Peredelkino, the Potter walked the four kilometers along a rutted road from the depot to the peasant's cottage the old man had moved into. "I always wanted to water, and be watered," he had said then, but he had been exhibiting symptoms of senility already, or at least that's what they had claimed when the theoretical journal for which he worked decided it was time for him to retire. The Potter himself had never been convinced that the old man's wandering mind—he alighted on subjects like a butterfly, and left a butterfly's imprint on them—was worn thin. It might just as well have been his way of coping with a world glued together by a peculiar attitude toward power: confronted by hypocrisy, people simply shrugged.

The old man, whose name was Boris Alexandrovich Revkin, had had a good run for his money. He had worked his way up to become a division propagandist in the Red Army during the Great Patriotic War, and had gone to work after the war as an editor for a well-known theoretical journal. One of his early articles dealt with something called "left deviationism." In it, Revkin had used the expression "political narcissism" to describe the Chinese Communist leadership. When asked, at the weekly editorial meeting, where he got the expression, he had replied, "Why, where else, I invented it!" The chief editor, who had made his reputation by taking a single line from Marx and writing a four-hundred-page book on it, had laughed outright. "If all you want are lines out of Marx and Lenin," Revkin had cried indignantly, "get someone else to do it." Assuming that his audacity indicated he had friends in high places, the chief editor shipped the article over to the Central Committee for a decision. When it came back, four months later, it contained a handwritten notation in the upper-left-hand corner. "Publish," it read, followed by an initial: "S."

Which is how Boris Alexandrovich Revkin became the Soviet Union's resident expert on "left deviationism."

His spine curved into the shape of a parenthesis by his years of harvesting cotton, the old man was on his hands and knees weeding between the green peppers in his vegetable garden when the Potter, his collar open, his suit jacket slung over his shoulder, finally arrived. The sun, sinking through a stand of white birches, dispatched slats of yellowish light across the ground. Revkin looked up, squinting into the light, and spotted the Potter mopping the perspiration off his neck with his handkerchief. "Contrary to appearances," the old man cackled, struggling to his feet, wiping his palms on his overalls, masking behind a studied briskness his pleasure at seeing the Potter, "sunsets don't grow on trees. What brings you all this way, Feliks? You have news of Piotr, maybe?"

"No news," the Potter said quickly. "What brings me all this way is you." He fished one of Svetochka's bottles of Bison vodka from his jacket pocket and handed it to Revkin. "A small present," he mumbled in embarrassment.

"Ha! Now I know you want something!" cried the old man, hopping over a row of baby cabbages, snatching the bottle from the Potter. He led the way to his cottage, lighted the stove, put some water to boil on it. When it grew dark he closed the shutters, served tea (which he himself drank, peasant-style, through a lump of sugar wedged between his teeth), eventually reheated some cooked cabbage with chunks of meat in it, on the assumption, which the Potter never challenged, that his visitor would stay the night. In time the vodka, served with the meal, loosened the old man's tongue and he began to reminisce, his words slurred, his voice hoarse, about what he called the bad old days: the Big Mustache (Stalin) and the Little Mustache (Hitler); the exhilarating struggle against the *Nemtsi*, the tongueless ones, the Germans; the endless double lines of beardless farmboys in gray caps with thick winter longcoats rolled and strapped on their backs making their way through ruined villages as delayed-action mines exploded in the distance; two teenagers with signs around their necks saying they had been collaborators, hanging by their twisted necks from tree limbs. The end of one story tugged at the beginning of another. His well of memories had no bottom.

Stretched out on a battered couch, the Potter nodded off, then woke with a start to hear the old man droning on. "I knew the Germans would lose the war," he was saying, "but not because of the reasons we used to give in our newspapers. They were going to lose the war—are you paying attention, Feliks?—because their ultimate goal wasn't to win it, but to fight it. Do you follow the distinction, Feliks? If they had wanted to win the war, you see, they would have mobilized everybody who could have helped, instead of eliminating them in death camps. To me it was always as evident as the nose on your face, Feliks. They wanted to lose the war and bring the world crashing down on their heads like dishes spilling from a shelf. They were acting out myths"—the old man poured the last of the vodka into his glass and tossed it off—"but then, in one way or another, all of us are acting out myths. You. Me." A distant look came into his ancient eyes. "Piotr even. Even Piotr." The old man cackled gleefully. "Especially Piotr. I always said he was meant to be a prince, or to kill a prince. I was never sure which. What do you think, Feliks? . . . Feliks?"

The old man gently drew a cover over the Potter, stoked the fire, carefully allotted two more logs to it, and shuffling off to his bed in the far corner of the room, drew the Army blanket that served as a curtain and went to sleep himself.

The Potter woke up in the pitch darkness and heard the old man snoring from behind the curtain. Moving quietly, he struck a match, lighted a candle and made his way into the unheated room that Revkin used to store his vegetables for the winter. He found the loose floorboard without any trouble, pried it up with a kitchen knife and retrieved the package wrapped in a woman's kerchief. He unfolded the cloth and examined the contents. It was all there. He had hidden it away years before, when he had returned from his tour in New York. At the time he had been riding high, and the precaution had been a professional reflex; an act of tradecraft that wasn't spelled out in any of the textbooks; a hedge against difficult times that was second nature to people in his business. Later, when he had been obliged to retire as *novator* and move into a small apartment with another family, he removed the package from its original hiding place and stashed it away under the floorboards of the old man's cottage.

The Potter had started to slip the floorboard back into place when he noticed the second oval of flickering candlelight superimpose itself on the first. He turned to see the old man standing in the doorway, the hem of his nightdress brushing his bare feet.

"I knew it was there," he snapped, inclining his head toward the package. "And I know what brings you all this way."

"I would have come anyway—" the Potter started to protest, but the old man, smiling sadly, interrupted him.

"What brings you all this way, Feliks," he said, blinking away the film of moisture forming over his eyes, "is to say good-bye."

The Potter couldn't, didn't, deny it.

And then the old man astonished the Potter. "If you can get out the way Piotr got out," he whispered fiercely, "more power to you. My future is in my past. For you, for Piotr, there is still life before death."

The Potter was up and dressed at first light; he wanted to get back to Moscow as early as possible. He looked around for a scrap of paper on which he could jot a note. His eyes fell on the Army blanket that screened off the old man's bed from the rest of the room. It seemed incredibly still, as if there were no life beyond it. . . . The skin tightened on the Potter's face. He tiptoed to the curtain and peeled back an edge. The old man lay on his back, his mouth gaping open, his eyes, unblinking, fixed on the ceiling over his head. The Potter stepped up to the bed and placed a palm on Revkin's chest. He felt his rib cage under the quilt. It was deathly still.

Another myth acted out! And what timing. For the old man had been the hostage that kept Piotr Borisovich on the straight and narrow. With him gone, the Potter would be free to betray his last, his best sleeper—and then, if he moved rapidly, save him from the results of that betrayal.

21

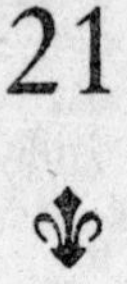

Carroll's cheeks were swollen from having swallowed a candy with finely chopped walnuts in it, and Thursday had trouble making out what he said. Francis provided a running translation. "He says you are to touch base with the West Germans. He says it is a matter of protocol."

Carroll said, ". . . eason hem ang ound en u alk otter."

"He says there's no reason for them to hang around when you talk to the Potter."

"In other words," Thursday said, "I'm to skim off the cream, as we say in the trade, and leave the milk for them."

"Ite," Carroll mumbled.

"Right," Francis repeated.

"I'm to get three items from him," continued Thursday. He wanted to show that he had memorized his instructions. He ticked off the items.

". . . r ack eeee oes," said Carroll.

"Or back he goes," translated Francis.

"If he doesn't come across with the aforementioned items," repeated Thursday, "back he goes, on the next plane out, wife and all."

"Ite." Carroll nodded, touching an inflamed cheek with his fingertips to make contact with his twitching nerve.

"Right," Francis interpreted.

"Un ore ing," muttered Carroll.

"I got that," said Thursday, smiling brightly. "He said, 'One more thing.' "

Carroll glared at him over his half-empty box of candy. In the Company's early days, a good man Friday was seen and not heard. Still, they were lucky to have one as thick as Thursday. If anyone could carry out instructions without really understanding what he was doing, it was him. "Ve ev-ing," Carroll said, "u unicate ith *obody*, ot ven ector, out is."

Francis raised a pencil and tapped Thursday on the shoulder as if he were knighting him. "He says, above everything, you communicate with *nobody*, not even the Director, about this."

Thursday giggled excitedly. "Mum's the word," he said.

22

❦

"You what?"

"Svetochka couldn't abandon them like that, Feliks," she pleaded. "They would die of dehydration."

The Potter strained to control himself. No matter how many times he went over it with her, she still didn't seem to grasp the situation. They had to walk out of the house as if they were coming back in two hours, and avoid at all costs making it appear that they were going away for a long time. Not to mention forever! "What exactly did you tell them?"

"Svetochka didn't tell them anything," she insisted, fighting back tears. "Svetochka only asked them to water the plants."

Above all, he must not make her nervous, he reminded himself. "It is not serious," he told her. "They may think we are going to visit the old man in Peredelkino for a day or so."

Svetochka breathed a sigh of relief. "About my sister," she started to say, but the Potter cut her off.

"Not a word," he ordered. "News travels fast. If you tell her, she will phone up her husband, and his brother works as a Merchant for the Center and will immediately suspect something if he hears I am leaving the country. You can always send her a picture postcard from Paris," he added.

"Paris," she repeated wistfully, her round face relaxing into a distant smile. "Will she be jealous!"

It wasn't the easiest thing in the world to turn your back and walk away from everything you had, you knew, you were. The Potter understood this more than most people. He had discussed it at great length with Piotr Borisovich before he had turned *his* back (albeit on assignment). They had come to the conclusion that you had to bring something with you from your past, no matter how insignificant it was, in order to get a hook into the future. It provided a transition. It helped you keep your sanity when you finally realized that none of what was happening to you was a dream—or a nightmare. When his time came to leave, Piotr Borisovich had taken with him a small, well-thumbed American paperback edition of Whitman poems, with the lines they both loved, the ones about the sisters Death and Night, underlined in pencil.

The Potter too had given in to the temptation of traveling with a security blanket. Locking up his attic workroom, he had treated himself to a last look around. It had meant a great deal to him, his workroom, especially since he didn't have an office to go to anymore. If he took something with him, he decided, it would come from here. He was sorry to leave his wheel behind—he had constructed it himself from a kit imported from Finland—but there was nothing to do about that. He would buy a new wheel in the West, an electric one maybe, whose speed was controlled with a pedal. His eye had fallen on the length of wire he used to cut his pots off the wheel. Piotr Borisovich had made it for him with a middle A string from an old piano, and a thick piece of bamboo at each end to grip it with. On the spur of the moment, the Potter had pocketed the wire, switched off the bulb and left.

"You are absolutely positive there is no danger?" Svetochka asked him for the hundredth time as they prepared to leave the apartment. She was wearing her highest spikes and her shortest skirt, which was her idea of how women looked in Europe.

"There is no danger as long as you do precisely

what I told you," the Potter promised her. He wondered, even as he spoke, if it were true.

"Paris," Svetochka repeated under her breath, as if the mere mention of the word could still her doubts, calm her nerves, give her the nervous energy she needed to cross thresholds. And the Potter understood that what she carried with her from her past in order to get a hook into the future was her longing for something that, until now, she could never have.

The little man with the shirred skin was waiting behind the wheel of the taxi parked in front of their door. Seeing the Potter and his wife, he crooked his emaciated finger in their direction. When they had settled into the back seat, he tipped his hat to them in the rearview mirror. The last time the Potter had seen this gesture, the little man had accompanied it with a mischievous wink. Now he exhibited all the formality of an undertaker. "I am told," he said over his shoulder, throwing the taxi into gear, drifting out into traffic, "that you are going to the Holy Land."

Svetochka glanced quickly at the Potter, but he cut off her protest with a warning look.

"We are not paid for what we do," the little man continued intently, "we are volunteers. Getting Jews out of Russia is God's work. I take it as an honor to be part of Oskar's organization."

"How many have you gotten out?" the Potter asked politely.

The little man preened behind the wheel of the taxi. "I myself have been involved in fourteen confutations before you two." He laughed self-consciously. "For reasons I have never fathomed, that is what Oskar calls it when we smuggle someone out of the country. A confutation."

The little man's use of the word "confutation" had a calming effect on the Potter. It was a professional term, and reinforced the impression that Oskar was the professional he claimed to be. And getting out of Russia would very much depend on Oskar being a professional.

The little man maneuvered the taxi through afternoon traffic. He drove slowly, cautiously, observing every sign, signaling every turn until he came to a light turning red. Accelerating sharply, he shot across the intersection.

"Nicely done," the Potter observed, and he turned to look at their wake. Nobody was following them.

The Potter noticed that they were heading in the opposite direction from Moscow Airport, but he said nothing. "Listen carefully," the driver called back over his shoulder. "There is a pedestrian island ahead, where the peripheric becomes Valovaya." He glanced at the dashboard clock. "We are right on schedule," exclaimed the little man. "I will pull over. You will get out and jump across the island into the taxi you will find waiting on the opposite lane."

The pedestrian island came into view ahead. "I wish you both Godspeed," the little man cried in an excited, high-pitched voice as he braked to a stop next to the island. The traffic piled up behind the taxi. Drivers leaned on their horns in annoyance. The Potter jerked open the door on his side, pulled Svetochka from the back seat and practically dragged her across the island into the back seat of the taxi that was headed in the opposite direction. Without waiting for the door to close, the driver—it was the squirrellike man who had kept a scarf over his lower jaw the first time the Potter had set out to meet Oskar—floored the gas pedal and propelled the taxi into the traffic flowing through the peripheric.

The Potter twisted in his seat to look behind them. The tradecraft was fairly elementary, but extremely efficient. One instant you were going in one direction. The next instant you were off in the opposite direction. If someone were following you, he'd have to make a highly visible U-turn.

Nobody did.

"We are as clean as the freshly scrubbed ass of a baby," the driver, who had been studying his rearview mirror, said after a moment. He turned south at the next crossroad. The taxi passed under a sign that indicated the airport was dead ahead.

They crossed a circus caravan heading into the city, with several overweight lions lazing in cages in flat trucks, and the head of a giraffe projecting over the cab of a large van. Several dozen open trucks filled with cabbages and early apples from nearby collective farms were backed up behind the caravan. The highway widened as they got closer to the airport. It was six lanes, three in each direction, when they finally spotted the hangars and control tower and radars and turned off onto the flat approach road.

"The meter is running," the driver reminded them in a tight voice. He adjusted his scarf so that it covered the lower part of his face. "Be sure to pay me when I let you off—it looks more natural that way. And for God's sake don't forget the two valises in the trunk compartment."

"Svetochka is frightened," Svetochka suddenly whispered in the Potter's ear. She looked as if she were ready to throw up.

"Think of yourself as an actress playing a role—two roles, actually," he whispered back. "You had the makings of a great star once. You can do it."

Svetochka swallowed. "Svetochka will try," she murmured.

The taxi slowed as it entered the circular driveway in front of the terminal and pulled up before the main doors. "Remember," the Potter instructed Svetochka, "you are a happy Russian wife off with her husband to the Black Sea for some sand and sun."

Svetochka drew a deep breath. Then, moistening her lips, flashing her most superior smile, she slipped into the role. "Do pay the man, Feliks," she ordered in a loud voice. "I don't want to miss a minute more of sun than I have to."

The Potter glanced at the meter and counted out some rubles. Then he went around to the trunk compartment and removed the two valises in it. The taxi roared away from the curb before the Potter could close the lid of the trunk compartment. A uniformed policeman farther along the curb called after the squirrellike driver, but he never looked back and he never slowed down.

Standing in the gutter, the Potter stared after the departing taxi, then started to carry the valises toward the door. From the curb Svetochka berated him. "Darling, there are porters who do that sort of thing."

The Potter dropped the valises and signaled with a forefinger. A porter strolled over and placed the two valises onto his dolly. "Domestic or foreign?" he asked in a sullen voice.

"Domestic," Svetochka told him. The porter nodded and wheeled his dolly off. The Potter and Svetochka fell in behind him.

Oskar's scheme was elegantly simple. Using their own internal passports and a set of genuine Aeroflot tickets for a flight about to leave for the Crimea, they would pass through the cursory checkpoint at the "Domestic" entrance. At some point two Americans (hired for the occasion by Oskar) with reservations and tickets for an Austrian Airlines flight to Vienna would pass through the door marked "International" twenty meters farther down the driveway, where the control was more strict. There, frontier officers who spoke several languages not only checked passports and visas and currency forms, but cast an experienced eye over the traveler's valises and clothing; if there was any doubt, the passenger would be engaged in conversation.

Smiling broadly, chatting away as if she had nothing more on her mind than whether she had taken along enough bathing costumes, Svetochka presented their internal passports and their airline tickets to the guard at the door. He glanced at the photos on the internal passports and then looked up at the faces in front of him, lingered for a moment more than he had to on Svetochka, checked the date on the tickets, put a tick next to their names on a boarding list, and waved them through.

The Potter had the same relationship with airports that he had with telephones: he used them without enthusiasm. Once inside, he paid off the porter and retrieved their valises. Carrying one in each hand, he led Svetochka through the crowded hall toward the staircase that descended to the toilets. Downstairs, a janitor in overalls was backing toward them mopping the linoleum as he went along. Svetochka said, "Excuse me, can we pass?"

The janitor turned. It was Oskar. Svetochka gasped in surprise, then, recovering, started to bring her hand up so that Oskar could kiss the back of it, but abandoned the idea when she saw the frown of disapproval on his face.

The Potter had half-expected Oskar to turn up; he knew from personal experience that there was an irresistible urge to hover in the wings during any delicate operation. It was not so much a matter of making sure it went off without a hitch as of *taking pleasure* from its going off without a hitch. In Oskar's shoes, he would have done the same.

"So," Oskar said quietly, "you have only to follow me." He put aside his mop and led them to an unmarked, unlocked door. "Five minutes, yes?" he reminded them as they ducked into the small room in which the janitors stored cleaning products. "I will rap twice when the coast is clear." So saying, he let himself out the door on the other side of the storage room—which led to the toilets on the "International" side.

Svetochka and the Potter snapped open their valises. Inside each was a second, smaller valise, this one of American manufacture and plastered with old stickers in English. Inside the second valises were several sets of clothing with American labels sewn into them. They had been made to measure by the Jewish tailor that Oskar had taken them to. "Look at this underwear," Svetochka whispered as she stripped off her Russian garments. "It is genuine nylon!"

They quickly dressed in the new set of American clothes, fitted on their American shoes, pocketed their American passports and Austrian Airlines tickets to Vienna, and packed their old clothing away in the valises they would leave behind in the room. As a final touch, the Potter slung an American camera over his shoulder.

"How does Svetochka look?" Svetochka demanded, adjusting the pleats in her navy-blue skirt.

"You look, as they say in America, like a million dollars," the Potter told her. And he meant it. The Jewish tailor had dressed her better than she normally dressed herself. "Are you ready to play your second role?"

Svetochka nodded, and repeated the English phrases he had made her memorize. "What does he say? With his accent I can't understand a word." She smiled and asked in Russian, "How was that?"

"Excellent."

The Potter transferred the length of piano wire with the bamboo grips on each end to the pocket of his American suit jacket. While Svetochka put the finishing touches on her makeup, he checked to make sure the package he had recovered from the old man's cottage was securely wedged between several shirts at the bottom of his American valise.

There were two soft raps on the door leading to the "International" toilets. Oskar squeezed into the small storage room. "So: it is time to go," he said. He inspected them from head to toe. "You will easily pass for Americans. The plane for Vienna is boarding now. Surveillance is light. The two frontier specialists on duty are posted, as we knew they would be, at the front gate. The people at the Austrian Airlines desk will assume that if you got past the frontier specialists, you are the genuine article." To Svetochka he added, "If someone talks to you in English, just smile and repeat what Feliks taught you to say. Feliks will answer in English if he has to."

Oskar opened the door a crack to make sure that the hall outside the "International" toilets was empty. Then he motioned them out of the room. Carrying the smaller, American valises, the Potter and Svetochka climbed the stairs toward the main "International" hall. At the top step the Potter paused to look back. Oskar had turned away and was rinsing a mop out in a pail of water. There are no good-byes for people in our line of work, Piotr Borisovich had noted when the Potter accompanied him to the airport on the first leg of the voyage that would take him to his assignment in New York. The Potter had felt a lump mounting to his throat; he couldn't have said anything if he had wanted to. Piotr Borisovich had emitted a thin, brittle laugh and had stalked away. The Potter had stared after him for a long moment, wondering if they would ever meet again, then had turned back toward his limousine.

In the main "International" hall, the Potter led the way toward the Austrian Airlines boarding gate. From invisible loudspeakers a crisp voice announced in Russian, and then in German, that the flight to Vienna was now boarding. In the "Domestic" half of the terminal, Oskar's Americans, who had entered the airport through the guarded "International" door on one set of documents, would be boarding the plane to the Crimea using duplicates of the internal passports of the Turovs, Feliks and Svetlana, and a second set of tickets. When the boarding lists of the Crimea and Vienna flights were checked by the frontier police, everyone would be accounted for.

The Potter and Svetochka were passing the counter where babushka dolls of all sizes were being sold. The Vienna gate loomed ahead. Suddenly the Potter felt a hand on his shoulder. "Feliks?" a voice asked quietly.

The Potter turned and found himself looking into the unsmiling face of the dapper flaps-and-seals man from the sleeper school. He wore pointed Italian shoes and sported a hairline mustache on his upper lip. His real name was Grishka something or other, but everyone had called him Starets, or Holy Man, because he happened to have been born in the same village in the remote Tobolsk Guberniya of Siberia as the original Starets, Rasputin. It had been a standing joke at the sleeper school to cross yourself when you passed the Starets in a corridor. The last time the Potter had seen the flaps-and-seals man was during the sleeper school ceremony at which the Potter was handed an inscribed Czechoslovak wristwatch.

"Grishka," the Potter spluttered, mustering all the enthusiasm he could. He had never really liked the flaps-and-seals man; he was too obvious a Party hack, too ready to report snatches of idle conversation he may have overheard. "What on earth are you doing here?"

The Starets lowered his voice. "I am off to Vienna for a flaps-and-seals job." The Starets had been farmed out to local *rezidents* quite a few times during his years at the sleeper school. A local agent would want to get into a letter or a valise without the owner becoming aware of it. The Starets would be called into town for a one-shot assignment, opening and closing the flaps and seals so perfectly that nobody would know they had been broken into.

"And you?" the Starets asked. He nodded at Svetochka over the Potter's shoulder. They had met at various social functions held during the Potter's tenure as *novator*. To the Potter he said, "I thought you were on the Center's shit list."

"I am on assignment too," the Potter said quickly. The words just came out. He couldn't think of anything better to say.

By now the Starets was studying his clothing and his valise with its American stickers. His eyes narrowed. When he spoke, his tone of voice was guarded. "You are going to Vienna with *her*?"

The Potter had the sinking sensation experienced by cornered animals. He might have been able to convince the Starets that *he* was going to Vienna on assignment. But Russians in his position—Russians in *any* position!—were never allowed out of the country with their wives. The wives were kept back as hostages against their return.

"Last and final call for Austrian Airlines flight 407 to Vienna," the voice on the loudspeaker system announced.

"I am under orders to the Vienna *rezident*," the Potter said quietly. "We are supposed to look like American tourists arriving from Moscow."

The Starets was openly suspicious now. "I don't believe you," he said flatly. "If what you say is true, I would have been instructed not to engage you in conversation and jeopardize your cover."

The Potter smiled thinly. "You are in the process of blowing an operation that has been in the works for a long time," he informed the Starets. "It was to make this operation credible that I was retired as *novator* of the sleeper school. If all this preparation is wasted, it will go hard on you."

The Starets insisted stubbornly, "I must check what you tell me with the Center."

The Potter came to a decision. "I will show you my orders," he said. "It will save you from looking like a fool." He turned to Svetochka. "Wait for me here," he instructed her. Motioning with his hand, he indicated that the Starets was to follow him. He led him down the stairs to the "International" toilets. Oskar, dressed in street clothing, was emerging from the janitor's storage room. "I need to use the room for a moment," the Potter told him. Oskar glanced sharply at the Starets. "It is all right," the Potter said, as if he were anticipating a question other than the one in Oskar's eyes. "I can vouch for him. He is the flaps-and-seals man from the sleeper school. I want to show him my Vienna orders."

Without a word, Oskar stepped aside and allowed the two men to enter the small room. The Potter went in first. The Starets followed. It never occurred to him to worry about his safety. He was a head taller than the Potter, and a good deal huskier; on top of everything, he was a member of the Moscow Center's amateur karate team. Inside, the Potter removed his ticket pouch from his breast pocket, took out the ticket, and handed it to the Starets. "Hold the next-to-last page up to the light," he ordered him. "There is a travel authorization, an unlimited-funds authorization, an access-to-codes authorization. You will recognize the signature."

The Potter said it all with such authority that the Starets began rehearsing what he could say to explain his interference in an ongoing operation. The *novator* had been fired from the sleeper school, not transferred to another directorate, he could argue. He was traveling with his wife, a point that would be in the Starets' favor; nobody traveled abroad with a wife. It wasn't his fault if someone at the Center had failed to alert him that they were booked onto the same flight. The Starets held the ticket to the light and squinted up at it. Just as it dawned on him that no secret writing was emerging, he felt the strand of piano wire slip over his head and settle around his neck. He started to reach for it as the incredibly strong hands of the Potter, straining against the bamboo grips at each end of the wire, tightened it across his Adam's apple. The Starets attempted to scream, but all that emerged from his throat was a strangled gasp. There were karate movements that might have saved him: an elbow to the solar plexus, a foot lock that could send an attacker plunging sideways. But these were things remembered during intraservice matches. With the wire vise tightening on his neck, every instinct screamed out to him to wedge a finger between the wire and the throat, to alleviate the horrible pressure that was building up in his lungs.

His sight went first; suddenly he was blind. Then he lost control of his bowels. Then his muscles went limp.

The Potter let the lifeless form settle slowly to the

floor, where it lay in a heap like dirty laundry. He reached for a limp wrist and felt for a pulse. Finding none, he retrieved his plane ticket, stared for an instant at the corpse, then let himself out of the storage room.

Oskar had disappeared. The Potter didn't hold it against him. Oskar had counted on getting the Potter and his wife out of the country without leaving a trace. No matter how things turned out in the small janitor's room, it wouldn't be healthy for him to stick around. For the Potter, everything now depended on when they found the body. If the Vienna-bound plane was still in Soviet air space, the Chief Directorate of Border Guards, a KGB department, had the authority to order it back to interrogate the passengers. If that happened, the Potter was doomed.

"You look as if you've seen a ghost," Svetochka whispered when the Potter returned. "What happened to your friend?"

"I made up a story about us being authorized to leave the country."

"And he swallowed it?"

The Potter nodded grimly.

"Then why are your hands shaking?"

"Come on," the Potter snapped. He hefted the two valises, one in each hand. At the counter, Svetochka presented their American passports and tickets as the Potter deposited the valises onto the scale.

"You are traveling light," the woman behind the counter said pleasantly in English, which she spoke with a thick German accent.

Svetochka smiled nervously at the Potter and articulating carefully, said, "What does he say? With his accent I cannot understand a word."

The woman behind the counter was too busy tagging the valises to catch Svetochka's mistake. She pushed a foot pedal and the conveyor belt started up, carrying off the valises. "Have a good flight," said the woman, handing the tickets and passports, and a pair of boarding passes, back across the counter.

"We will try," the Potter replied.

They boarded the plane, found their seats, strapped on their seat belts—and waited. "What if he comes on the plane and speaks to you in Russian?" Svetochka whispered worriedly.

The Potter stared out of an oval window at the uniformed border guard at the foot of the ramp. A civilian walked up to the guard and together they double-checked the manifest. One of them tapped the paper with the point of a pencil. A passenger was missing. Would they allow the plane to take off without him?

Svetochka plucked at the Potter's sleeve. "What if?" she demanded. "What if? What if?"

"He will not board the plane," the Potter replied woodenly.

"How can you be sure?"

The Potter avoided her eye. "I *am* sure."

Outside, one of the uniformed frontier officers who had been stationed at the "International" entrance trotted up with a list of his own in his hands. The three men compared lists. The civilian shook his head in puzzlement. Why would someone check in through the main entrance and then not show up at the plane? The pilot of the Austrian Airlines plane descended the stairs. There was a hurried conversation among the four men. The pilot glanced at his wristwatch several times. The civilian hurried over to the terminal door and plucked a telephone off its hook. The pilot boarded the plane and said something to one of the stewardesses, who walked down the center aisle counting noses. She reported the results to the pilot, who descended the stairs again. The civilian returned to the ramp. Gesturing toward the control tower, the sky, his wristwatch, the pilot argued with the three Russians. They listened, exchanged looks, raised eyebrows in indecision. Finally the civilian shrugged and signed the manifest; allowing a plane to take off with one passenger too few was not as serious as allowing it to take off with one passenger too many. The pilot bolted up the stairs and tugged the plane door closed after himself. Workmen in green overalls pulled the stairs clear of the plane. A moment later one of the engines coughed into life. And then a second.

As the plane started to taxi toward the end of the runway, the Potter reached into his jacket pocket to grasp his hook into the future—his potter's wire. It wasn't there! He patted the other pocket. It too was empty. His body melted into the seat. In his hurry to board the plane he had left his signature on the Starets' body.

At the end of the runway, the engines revved up. The plane's vibrations reached the Potter's bones. He gripped the armrest until his knuckles turned white. Looking out of the window, he caught sight of a red-and-white-striped wind sleeve dancing in crosscurrents of air. It looked obscene, first inflating and then going limp, then inflating again. He wished he could make love to Svetochka, and then was struck by the fact that each time in his life he had killed someone, his mind had turned to—taken refuge in—the thought of love-making. Perhaps murder and copulation were related in the same way that death and night were related. Perhaps they were sisters!

The plane lurched down the runway, and the Potter had the terrible sensation that his presence on board would prevent it from taking off. Had the Russians invented the ultimate method of keeping people in the country? Their guilt at leaving made the plane *heavier* than air! Just as he convinced himself that it was scientifically possible (people who are very frightened, Piotr Borisovich once observed, usually experience a moment of madness), the Austrian plane groped its way off the runway, sank back again, then lifted off for good. Under his feet, the Potter felt the comforting crunch of the wheels folding into the fuselage.

Now there was nothing left to do but watch the minutes tick by—and wait.

23

⚜

The blind man examined the corpse with the tip of his thin white baton. "Strangled, you say?"

"With a length of wire," the police officer said brightly. As the local Ministerstvo Vnutrennikh Del (MVD) man, he had been summoned by the janitor who discovered the body. Now he was more than a little awed to find himself in the presence of two directors of the KGB's Department 13.

"So: strangled with a length of potter's wire," Oskar added pointedly.

"How can you be sure it is potter's wire?" the blind Cousin inquired.

"Because of the bamboo on either end," the younger of the two Cousins explained. "Potters use such pieces of wire to slice their pots off the wheel."

The blind man tapped his cane against the MVD man's leg. "That should narrow the problem down considerably," he noted. "The killer is obviously a potter. Moreover, to strangle someone of this size, he would have to have incredibly strong hands."

The younger Cousin saw what the blind man was driving at. "Potters have strong hands from wedging clay," he told the MVD man.

The police officer said, "The airport doctor who examined the victim estimated that he had been dead about half an hour. We've had two planes take off during that time—one to the Crimea, one to Vienna.

Our potter might be on one of them. The plane to Vienna is still in Soviet air space and subject to our orders. I suggest we recall both planes immediately."

The blind Cousin snapped, "Out of the question." He offered no explanation. The MVD man knew better than to seek one.

The younger Cousin asked the MVD man, "How long before the Vienna plane is out of Soviet air space?"

"I would say"—he made a quick calculation—"another hour and a half."

"Here are your instructions," announced the blind man. "You are to lock up this room and forget about the corpse for another two hours. Then you will note in your call book that the janitor has just informed you of the presence, in his supply room, of a dead man. You will investigate immediately. You will issue a report saying that he was strangled with a length of potter's wire, and you suspect he was part of a ring of smugglers that had a falling-out. Only that."

The local MVD man saluted the blind man and left the room.

The stench was becoming overpowering. The blind man found the door with his baton and ducked through it. The younger Cousin and Oskar followed him out.

Oskar quietly told the Cousins, "The Potter identified the victim as the flaps-and-seals man from the sleeper school. He was apparently booked on the Vienna flight, recognized Turov and became suspicious."

"No matter how meticulously you plan an operation," the younger Cousin said philosophically, "you can't foresee everything."

"It is precisely our business to foresee everything," the blind man snapped in irritation. His baton beat out an angry rhythm against a radiator. One year of planning had almost been ruined by a coincidence. "Still, this may work for us in the end," he said. He turned toward the younger Cousin. "I want you to make sure word of the crime appears in *Pravda*. Bury it in the middle of a story on the airport police so it won't be too conspicuous—a passing reference to a body found strangled yesterday in a storage room. Mention the only clue—a length of potter's wire." The blind man turned away and stared off into space with his sightless eyes. Revenge, the peasants said, was a dish that tasted better cold. He had waited long enough, and plotted carefully enough, and he would have his meal. "The fact that the Potter murdered a man in order to get out of the country," the blind man mused out loud, "will be useful to us when the time comes to go public."

24

⚜

Under the silver wing, the high Carpathians gradually flattened into rolling foothills. The plane banked and then leveled out over a vast plain. A meandering river came into view. The Potter pressed his cheek to the inner window; there had been moments right after the takeoff when its coolness against his skin had been the only thing that kept him sane. "That must be the Danube," he muttered.

Svetochka free-associated. "The waltz," she said in an awed voice.

"The river," the Potter corrected her.

The plane banked again, maneuvering into its landing pattern. Vienna tilted into the frame of the oval window like a lopsided photograph. Every time the plane banked, it slid back into view, nearer, more distinct: cathedral spires, university towers, Hapsburg palaces, the famous Rathaus; a potpourri of styles (neo-Gothic, Italian Renaissance, modern Gothic, Greek); and one or two prominent buildings that Piotr Borisovich, who always averted his eyes when he passed any of Moscow's seven grotesque Stalin Gothics, would have laughingly referred to as neoridiculous.

Svetochka drank it all in over the Potter's shoulder—the terminal, its roof garden with people waving happily, the planes with exotic markings parked along the tarmac—as they touched down, taxied and then braked to a stop. Her eyes were misty with emotion, and she blew her nose noisily into a handkerchief that she plucked from the Potter's jacket pocket. "What happens when we get off the plane?" she whispered.

"What happens when you go into the sea?" he replied cryptically. "You get wet."

Svetochka tossed her head in exasperation. "Will we be met is what Svetochka wants to know."

"We will be met," said the Potter, who knew the mechanics of things like this the way a watchmaker knows the inside of a timepiece, "by someone who will invite us to pay for our passage."

Sensing a storm building up in him, Svetochka nestled close and said very softly, "Svetochka is very glad to be here. Soon she will show you how glad she is."

The sun was sinking below the rim of the runway as they left the plane. The Potter spotted the welcoming committee the instant he stepped onto the top of the ramp. Any idiot could have. One was a little man who gripped a black umbrella by the middle and pinned his black homburg to his head with the curved handle so the hat wouldn't be carried off in the wind. The second, probably the junior of the two, judging by his position several steps behind and to the left of the little man, wore a long trench coat and black galoshes. The passengers filing off the plane were steered toward a waiting bus. When Svetochka and the Potter reached the tarmac, the little man with the homburg pinned to his head by the umbrella handle stepped forward. "Delighted you could come," he announced in an English thick with a guttural Bavarian drawl.

"What does he say?" Svetochka asked, dutifully pronouncing her memorized lines. "With his accent, I can't understand—"

"He wants us to follow him," the Potter whispered in Russian. Steering Svetochka by an elbow, he followed the little man toward a small pickup truck parked on the other side of the plane.

The procession passed under the plane. Water glistened on the silver belly; to the Potter, it looked as if the plane was sweating. Two other Germans in trench coats were waiting next to the open rear doors of the small pickup truck. The Potter and Svetochka climbed into the back and sat down on a low metal bench. Outside, the man wearing the homburg and the two others talked in undertones. Ten minutes went by. Eventually Galoshes arrived and hefted the two American valises plastered with labels into the pickup. Then he and Homburg took their places on the metal bench across from the Potter. Nobody said a word. The rear doors were slammed closed and locked. The other two Germans climbed into the front seats. The motor turned over. The pickup was thrown into gear and began to crawl across the runway toward the other side of the airport.

They rolled along for several minutes. They must have passed close to the end of the runway, because they heard the stutter of propeller engines revving up for a takeoff, and saw, through the small scarred rear window, the flashing green of a starboard wing light. After a while the pickup came to a stop. The Potter could make out men talking quietly in German, then the sound of an entrance in a chain-link fence being pulled back.

Svetochka looked at him in bewilderment. "And Paris?" she asked plaintively. Inhibited by the silent stares of the two Germans, she shivered and drew closer to the Potter.

The pickup stopped before the giant doors of an enormous hangar. The driver came around and opened the back door. Svetochka started to slide out, but Galoshes put a restraining hand on her arm. "Only him," he said. Looking the Potter in the eye, Homburg nodded toward the open door.

"You will wait for me here," the Potter told Svetochka in Russian. He patted her knee on his way out of the pickup.

"What is happening?" she called after him in fright. "Why can't Svetochka come with you?"

Dusk was settling over the distant runway like soot. Some mechanics in overalls were working on the motor of an airplane nearby, but they didn't look up. The driver put his shoulder to the giant door and rolled it back enough for the Potter to slip into the hangar. Then he pulled the door closed with a resounding clang.

The hangar was empty; not a person, not a plane, not a vehicle of any kind was in sight. The Potter had a sudden urge to yell and hear his voice come back at him from a far corner. A narrow steel staircase climbed up one wall to a balcony with half a dozen small offices on it. The doors of the offices were made of frosted glass. A light burned in the second office. Mounting the steps, listening to his own footfalls echoing through the hangar, the Potter homed in on the light. He reached the door, pushed it open and entered.

Hunched behind a metal desk, a thin young man with protruding amphibian eyes peered up at the Potter through round steel-rimmed eyeglasses. He seemed to be on the verge of giggling, which made the Potter wonder if he had somehow missed the humor in the situation. Beware of people who laugh in the wrong places, Piotr Borisovich had once quipped; they are more dangerous than those who don't laugh in the right places.

"You will be the American," the Potter said in Russian.

The thin young man was in fact the Sisters' man Friday. "What makes you think I am American?" he asked. He spoke fluent Russian, but with a pronounced Brooklyn accent.

"There is always an American at the end of the line," the Potter said moodily. "Besides, Oskar spoke about his people collecting money for the information I would provide." The Potter lowered himself into a folding metal chair. "The only ones with money to spare these days are the Americans."

Thursday didn't find this comment to his taste. "You miss the point if you think of this in terms of money," he observed. "We are fighting atheistic international Communism—"

The Potter cut him off with a wave of his hand. "Spare me, if you please, your Sermon on the Mount."

The skin on Thursday's neck reddened. "Your kind could do with a little bit of Sermon on the Mount!" He burst out giggling. "Suppose," he suggested in English, a gleam in his protruding eyes, "we talk turkey."

"Suppose," the Potter agreed, though he was not quite sure what the expression meant. Reluctance welled up in him like bile. Betraying Piotr Borisovich into the hands of this giggling preacher who sat across the desk from him seemed . . . *grotesque*! If he could stall long enough, he still had the package he had recovered from the old man's cottage.

"As I understand it," Thursday continued, switching back to Russian, leaning across his desk, flicking his tongue over his lips in expectation, "you are to show your appreciation for your deliverance by giving me three items of information."

"That is not the order of things I had in mind," the Potter said. "Before I pay my way, I will want some indication from your superiors"—his way of saying that he considered Thursday too junior to deal with—"concerning my and my wife's future." ("My future," Piotr Borisovich once exclaimed in a moment of intense depression—he had been quoting the poet Akhmatova at the time, and his words had made a deep impression on the Potter—"is in my past." Curiously, the old man had used the same expression the night he died.)

Thursday started to giggle again when a telephone hidden away in a desk drawer rang. He yanked open the drawer and placed the telephone on the desk. It was one of those old-fashioned European models, black, with a second earpiece that you could unhook and hold to your free ear. "Yes," Thursday said into the mouthpiece in English, staring all the time across the desk at the Potter with his goiter eyes. He listened to the voice on the other end of the line. "I see," he said slowly. "Really," he said. "With a length of potter's wire?" he said. He clucked his tongue. "I wonder who could have done such a naughty thing," he said. "I appreciate the call," he said. He dropped the receiver onto its cradle and hooked the earpiece back into place. "Well," Thursday observed, "that more or less changes everything, doesn't it?"

There was a commotion in the hangar below. Svetochka's stiletto heels beat out a panicky rhythm as she raced up the steel staircase. Homburg and Galoshes pounded up the steps after her. All three burst into the room. Svetochka lurched into the Potter's arms. Homburg, his face beet red from exertion, said, "She started to scream something about wanting to see him. There were workers around. I didn't want to attract attention, so I let her come in. She saw the light and ran up before we could stop her."

Thursday waved Svetochka to another of the folding metal chairs. She sat on the edge of it and crossed her legs. Thursday was distracted by the glimpse of thigh. "To pick up where we left off," he told the Potter, slipping into his Brooklyn-accented Russian, "you were on the verge of disclosing to me three items of information."

The Potter felt as if the four walls were pressing in on him. Voices suddenly reverberated. The bulb overhead seemed unbearably bright. These were things that happened in nightmares. If only this *were* taking place in a dream; in a nightmare even! "I am ready to cooperate," he replied carefully, feeling his way, "as soon as we have established the framework within which each increment of cooperation is compensated by an increment of . . ."

Thursday was giggling excitedly. "You sound like a lawyer playing for time, but that is the one thing you don't have. Time, friend, is what you've run out of. An Aeroflot flight for Moscow leaves here in"—he peered at his wristwatch—"twenty-seven minutes. You and the young lady will be placed on that plane by my associates here unless you supply me with the information I want."

It dawned on Svetochka that the young man leering at her through round lenses was proposing to send them back. "You know, Feliks, you must tell him," she whispered in the voice of a schoolteacher instructing a stubborn pupil.

"Our Russian friends," Thursday continued, "will be only too happy to get their hands on you. It seems that they are investigating a murder that took place in the airport just before the plane you were on departed. A man was strangled to death in a storage room near the toilets. The only clue was a length of potter's wire found next to the body. During the war, if I remember correctly, strangling was your trademark—"

"Feliks!" Svetochka breathed. She sat back on her folding metal chair and stared at the Potter. She was very frightened. "If you go back," she moaned, "they will say that I was your accomplice. They will put both of us up against walls and shoot us!"

Thursday sensed the moment had come to mix in a carrot or two. "As soon as you've given me the three items that were agreed upon," he told the Potter in what he thought was a soothing voice, "we will arrange for you to be taken to a small hotel in Vienna. You will be very comfortable. You will undergo the usual debriefing. At the same time, concrete arrangements will be made for your future. It is understood by everyone concerned that you will eventually want to settle in Paris." Thursday waved an arm at Homburg and Galoshes, and they backed out of the room, closing the door behind them. "Paris," Thursday added, as if it were the detail that could tip the scale, "is supposed to be beautiful in the fall."

"For God's sake," Svetochka cried, "for *Svetochka's sake*, tell him what he wants to know."

Thursday fought down an urge to giggle; his face contorted as if he were suppressing a yawn. He spread his hands awkwardly, palms up, as if to say: It is up to you, friend.

25

Carroll's cheek muscle had gone on another rampage. Francis felt giddy, as if he had flown too high without oxygen, or drunk too much champagne.

Carroll read what Francis had written on his yellow legal pad: "He is living under the assumed name of Peter Raven."

Francis reached for the pad and added, "The Potter would know the name because he was the one who worked out the legend with the sleeper."

Carroll brought a damp palm to his cheek to pacify the twitching muscle. "The awakening signal," he scribbled on his pad, "is a line from Walt Whitman: 'The hands of the sisters Death and Night incessantly softly wash again, and ever again, this soil'd world.' The i in 'Night' is to be dotted with a microdot containing the location of a dead-letter drop. The dead-letter drop will have in it an innocent-looking advertisement containing numbered microdots that give the details of the mission he is assigned."

Francis wrinkled up his face as if he had swallowed something bitter. "Thursday says the Potter selected as an awakening signal a line of poetry that both he and his sleeper admired," he wrote. Out loud he added, "Shows he had bad taste. Personally I never liked Whitman. All those unbuttoned shirts! All that hair on his chest! He was a poser. It follows that his poetry is a pose."

Carroll looked at the deciphered cable again. "The sleeper is living in a brownstone at number 145 Love Apple Lane in Brooklyn Heights," he wrote.

"Do we know exactly how the Potter knew that?" Francis asked.

Carroll carefully wrote out, "Thursday says the Potter received a picture postcard in the mail one day, with a photograph of the house on it, from his sleeper. Walt Whitman once lived in the brownstone. There's a bronze plaque next to the door. 'Here lived—' That sort of thing. The sleeper couldn't resist telling the Potter he was living in Whitman's house. So he sent him a picture postcard with some banal message on it."

Francis snickered. "Having a great time. Wish you were here," he said out loud.

Carroll did something he rarely did—he looked directly at the person he was speaking to. "We have gotten our hands on a perfect criminal," he said.

"I suppose we have," Francis agreed in a voice that held more than a trace of awe in it.

26

⚜

Carroll was ignoring forests and lingering over trees: what form the awakening signal would take; how it would be delivered; where the first dead-letter drop would be (Francis was partial to country drops, which is to say places rarely frequented, while Carroll, who saw safety in numbers, favored city drops); how much money should initially be given to the sleeper (Carroll and Francis planned to finance the venture on a fifty-fifty basis); making arrangements at the inn in Pennsylvania (they had already procured the rifle; one of them would have to drive out and plant it there before the sleeper arrived). Nuts and bolts. Details. The kind of thing that bored Francis to death, but gave Carroll an orgasm.

As it was a Tuesday, Francis had stopped by his apartment long enough to change into more casual clothing, then had driven downtown to his favorite delicatessen for a hot roast-beef sandwich on rye with half sour pickles on the side. Later he walked over to the movie theater two blocks farther east and bought a ticket to see Elizabeth Taylor and Laurence Harvey in *Butterfield 8*. He had missed the film when it first came around, and was delighted to have a chance to see it. He got there early and had no trouble finding a good seat in the smoking section. The house filled up, the lights went out, the film flashed on. Not surprisingly, Francis had difficulty concentrating on the movie. Too many thoughts competed for attention in his head. Normal intelligence activities involved, at best, small triumphs—"taste treats" is what Carroll, thinking no doubt of his candies, called them—which gave the illusion of having some impact on current events. But only one in ten thousand—a Sorge, for instance, whose information from Tokyo permitted Stalin to thin out his defenses against the Japanese and concentrate on the Germans—really affected the course of history. Well, Francis too was going to affect history.

The music built to a crescendo. The image on the screen began to fade out. Francis extracted a cigarette from a pack and reached into his jacket pocket for a book of matches. He had given up smoking years before on medical advice, and only treated himself to a cigarette at the end of his regular Tuesday-night film. As always on these occasions, there was a single match left in the book. Francis used it to light his cigarette, inhaled, tossed the empty matchbook under his seat, and smiling as if he had nothing more weighty on his conscience than the death of a rodent, headed for the entrance and the warm, moist September air.

27

❦

The first people to arrive for the ad-hoc Damage Control Board meeting at the retired general's house were the Center's handymen. Wielding odd-looking devices that they plugged in and maneuvered like vacuum cleaners, they proceeded to "clean" house. What they were looking for were magnetic fields, the kind given off by hidden microphones. What they found was one earring, lost by the general's wife months before, and several coins that had slipped behind the cushions of a couch.

The general's study, on the second floor of a private house on Lenin Hills, had a splendid view of the city, and the guests who had never been up to the room before made appropriate noises of appreciation. A soccer match was in progress in the Lenin Stadium, across the river, and every once in a while a roar, not unlike the sound of surf pounding against a shore, wafted up.

"Does anyone happen to know the score?" the GRU man asked.

"One–zero in favor of Dynamo," announced the Central Committee representative, "but that was as of fifteen minutes ago."

"Did you catch the move the Bulgarian wingback put on the Dynamo goalie last week?" asked the lieutenant colonel representing the Party Control Commission. "His hips went one way and his body the other."

The KGB's Second Chief Directorate man offered around his pack of Chesterfields. "Will someone please tell me why is it we have a defection every time Spartacus has a home game? I'd like to know if there is a connection between the two."

"It's an American plot," quipped the GRU man, "to drive us crazy."

There was the sound of a thin baton tapping along the wooden floor. The people at the window exchanged glances. Department 13 of the First Chief Directorate usually sent someone over to these postmortem sessions in case of a decision to eliminate the defector. But for one of the Cousins to show up meant that they were dealing with no ordinary defection. "This could turn out to be more interesting than the soccer game," the representative from the Politburo whispered to the others.

The blind man found a seat at the long table with his baton and settled into it. The others in the room followed suit. The general, wearing well-tailored civilian clothes with an Order of Lenin conspicuous on his breast, limped into the room and took his place at the head of the table. "The score is one–one," he announced in a gruff voice. "Zhilov scored with a bullet from thirty meters. Anyone wants mineral water, help yourselves. Don't stint. I don't pay. The state does. What's on our plate today?"

The KGB's Second Chief Directorate man, the specialist on defectors, pulled a dossier from a plastic portfolio. "Turov," he read, "Feliks Arkantevich."

The general's eyebrows arched up. "The old *novator* from the sleeper school?"

"The same," acknowledged the KGB man. "He and his wife were booked onto a flight to the Crimea two days ago. Instead they wound up on a scheduled flight to Vienna. It all looks as if it was very well organized. It may have been the Israelis; Turov is a Jew. It may have been one of the émigré groups working on a German leash. Whoever it was supplied him with false papers, reservations, even two people to take their places on the Crimea flight."

"I assume you are looking into *how* he got out,"

the general interrupted. "The special area of interest of this board is what he took with him."

The KGB man shrugged. "Turov's been out of circulation for six months."

The lieutenant colonel from the Party Control Commission said, "He can tell them almost everything there is to know about our sleeper school—how we recruit candidates, how we train them, how we inject them into America—"

"It is unlikely he can tell them anything they don't already know," insisted the KGB man. "About twelve months ago one of Turov's sleepers went over to the Americans when he received his awakening signal. You chaired a damage-control session on him, General."

"If Turov has nothing of value to offer, why did someone go to all that trouble to get him out?" the blind man, sitting on the right hand of the general, inquired quietly.

"A pertinent question," acknowledged the general.

From across the river, a hollow roar drifted up from Lenin Stadium. A young aide in uniform dashed into the study and whispered something in the general's ear. "Two–one, Dynamo, on a penalty shot by Misha Tsipin," the general announced gleefully. He turned to the KGB man. "Why *did* they go to all that trouble to get him out?" he asked with exaggerated politeness. He had developed a theory when he received his first star that politeness, out of context, was appropriately menacing. "Surely he had something of value to offer them."

The KGB man turned a page in his dossier. "There is still one sleeper on the active list who was trained by Turov while he was *novator*. He is planted in America, awaiting the signal that will activate him."

"Does Turov know the identity under which the sleeper operates?" the General asked.

The KGB man nodded gloomily. "In the sleeper's dossier, the legend was typed. But the awakening signal was written in ink. We have ascertained that the handwriting is Turov's."

"To sum up," said the general, shifting uncomfortably in his chair because of his gout, "we must assume that the defector Turov is familiar with the identity under which the sleeper is operating, as well as the coded signal that will convince him he is being activated to perform a mission for Moscow Center."

There was dead silence around the table. The Central Committee representative poured a glass of mineral water and sipped it thoughtfully. The KGB man pulled his Chesterfields from his pocket. "Does the General object if I smoke?" he asked in a subdued voice.

"I most emphatically do," snapped the general. "Cigarette smoke stimulates bile, which poisons the blood and leads to attacks of gout. Ten minutes in a room with cigarette smoke and no amount of acupuncture can alleviate the pain."

The pack of cigarettes disappeared back into the KGB man's pocket.

The Party Control Commission representative remarked, "What good would all this information do Turov, or the Americans, assuming, as we must, that he conveys it to them, unless he knew *where* to find the sleeper? Before I was posted to the Party Control Commission, I was assigned to the KGB's Second Chief Directorate. I remember how these things worked. Once the sleeper passed out of the *novator*'s hands—once he graduated from the school to fieldwork—his dossier was taken over by the particular Merchant at Moscow Center who would run him. The sleeper's location in America would be known to the Merchant, but not to the *novator*—especially not to a *novator* who had been put out to pasture and no longer had access to dossiers of his graduates."

The KGB man nodded. "Our comrade from the Party Control Commission is quite correct. There is no way that Turov could be familiar with the sleeper's location in America. He could be anywhere, for all he knows."

The blind man tapped his baton against the leg of his chair. "Turov knows where the sleeper is," he stated flatly.

"That is simply not possible," the KGB man insisted in a nervous voice. "There is no way he could have had access to that piece of information."

The blind man reached into his breast pocket, extracted a brown envelope and offered it to the general. From beyond the window there was another roar, but nobody paid attention to it. The general pulled two pieces of paper from the envelope. "Photocopies," he said.

"Two sides of an American picture postcard," the blind man acknowledged. "These were picked up as part of a regular intercept program on foreign-source mail passing through the Central Post Office. The picture postcard in question was sent to Turov from Brooklyn, New York, several months after the sleeper was inserted into America. The awakening phrase in the sleeper's dossier, the one in Turov's own handwriting, happens to be a line taken from the works of the revisionist American poet Whitman."

"And the picture on the postcard," announced the general, examining it closely, "shows the facade of a house in Brooklyn Heights that Whitman once lived in."

"The message on the picture postcard," continued the blind man, "is not important. But the handwriting is—it's definitely that of the sleeper. He was informing his *novator*, despite express rules which forbid this kind of communication, that he had rented rooms in a building once occupied by Whitman."

"If Turov knows where the sleeper is in America," said the Party Control Commission representative, "this is very bad news indeed."

"It opens the possibility," said the blind man, staring sightlessly in the general's direction, "that the *novator* will convey to the American Central Intelligence Agency information that will permit its operatives to activate and control a Soviet agent in place. Once awakened by the proper coded signal, the sleeper will assume he is being run by his superiors in Moscow, and carry out his orders. Which means that the Americans have the potential of committing a crime—any crime—and then arranging for the blame to fall on us."

"The ideal solution to the problem," the general mused—he appeared to be talking to himself—"would be to eliminate the sleeper before the possibility you raise becomes a reality."

The blind man scraped his chair back from the table and crossed his legs. "We have two Canadians on tap in Toronto for an eventuality such as this. But the chances of their getting to the sleeper before the Central Intelligence Agency activates him are almost nonexistent. The CIA has had Turov for two days already. They will recognize the obvious advantage, the necessity even, of moving rapidly."

"Which leaves us with a potentially explosive problem on our hands," the general noted. His voice had turned polite again; he was extremely irritated.

"We are not without potential solutions," suggested the blind man.

The Politburo representative leaned forward. He was a classic case of someone whose importance derived from the fact that he reported back to important people. "Would the director of Department 13 care to be more specific?" he asked in a way that left the blind man little choice.

In his eagerness to know the answer, the general reiterated the question. "What are the potential solutions?"

"Like any good lawyer," explained the blind man, "we must construct our case proving that the CIA is responsible for the crime, always assuming one will be committed. To begin with, we have the defection of the *novator* of the sleeper school, the awakening signal, the legend, the copy of the picture postcard, all of which tend to support our story that the control of the sleeper was exercised by the CIA, and not Moscow Center."

"We will have a hard time convincing the world of that," the Politburo man said dryly.

"When the time comes to convince the world," the blind man said matter-of-factly, "we will arrange for someone inside the American intelligence community to testify on our behalf."

"This is within the realm of possibility?" the general asked, making no effort to mask his astonishment.

"It is within the realm of certainty," announced the blind man.

Later, while various participants were waiting in the foyer for their limousines to be summoned, the general hobbled over to the blind man and the KGB's Second Chief Directorate man. "I neglected to ask you whether there were any ongoing operations that were likely to be jeopardized by the defection of the *novator*. It is something I should include in my postmortem report."

The KGB man shook his head. "We have no problems," he said.

The general directed his voice at the blind man. "How about Department 13?"

"Actually, we have one operation under way in America," he said. "We are running an agent, via a Cuban cutout. His principal mission is to neutralize some of the more outspoken anti-Castro people in the country."

"Wetwork?" asked the general, an eyebrow dancing up in interest.

"Wetwork," acknowledged the blind man, using the professional term for assassinations. "The agent is listed in your current operations portfolio under the code name Khanda, which is Hindu for 'double-edged sword.' As far as I can tell, the defection of the *novator* will have no effect on Khanda."

Another roar drifted up from Lenin Stadium across

the Moscow River. The general's young aide came trotting into the foyer. "Dynamo scored again in the final seconds," he cried. "It's all over, with Dynamo on top three–one."

The general's face relaxed into one of those famous sour smiles he was noted for using when he appeared on television. "Let us hope," he remarked, "that all of our games end on a similar note."

28

⚜

Outside it was night; inside too—a "Ninth-month midnight," in the words of Whitman.

Mesmerized by the headlights, Svetochka had stared for the better part of an hour at the traffic on the Ringstrasse, the boulevard that circled the inner city. Suddenly she had drawn the thick curtains across the bay window with an angry jerk, cutting off the noise of traffic so abruptly it seemed as if a needle had been lifted off a phonograph record.

She had been pleased at first with the small hotel on the quiet side street off the Ringstrasse; with the subtle click of the desk clerk's heels; with the three-room top-floor suite; with the four-poster bed; with the cream-colored sheets and the enormous fluffy square pillows in lace cases. She had stripped to the skin in the white-tiled bathroom and soaked in the high tub for the better part of an hour, and then phoned down for tea and little cakes the size of fingernails. But when they arrived, lined up in rows on an oval silver tray, she discovered she was unable to swallow. Her throat had constricted, her stomach had knotted up.

"In fear," she burst out when the Potter insisted on knowing why. "Svetochka can't eat, Svetochka can't shit, Svetochka can't think straight because Svetochka is *afraid*!"

"Afraid of what?" the Potter pleaded with her. "We are safe here. The hotel is guarded. The top floor is sealed off. The Austrians, the Americans, they will not allow anything to happen to us."

It was at this point that Svetochka became mesmerized by the headlights on the Ringstrasse, and then jerked closed the thick curtains, creating a night inside the room to match the night outside.

"The Austrians, the Americans," she spat out, "can't protect Svetochka from *you*!"

"From me?" The Potter moved toward her, intending to take her in his arms, fumble for a breast, apologize profusely for existing.

Svetochka shrank back against a wall. She had always been aroused by the Potter's potential for violence; aroused even more by her ability to control it, tame him. But she had lost the thread of confidence. She stared across the room, imagining the Potter's hands molding themselves around her neck. Now that she knew they had been used to strangle someone, her skin crawled, her heart ached at the idea of being caressed by them. "Don't come near Svetochka," she whispered fiercely.

"What do you think I will do to you?" the Potter demanded.

Svetochka's breath came in short, desperate gasps. She fumbled for words. "I think maybe . . . you will . . . *hurt* . . . Svetochka."

The Potter's voice filtered out of the darkness as if it were a faint suggestion of light. "Are you afraid of night, Svetochka? Are you afraid of death?"

From the shadows along the wall, Svetochka moaned. "Aren't you?"

The Potter felt for the wall switch, found it, illuminated the filaments in the tiny flame-shaped bulbs in the overhead chandelier. In his official capacity as *novator*, he had once asked Piotr Borisovich the very same question. I live by Jung's dictum, his last, his best sleeper had replied without hesitation. Jung's dictum? (The Potter hadn't been familiar with it, Jung being *persona non grata* in the Soviet Union.) That the second part of life is ruined, Piotr Borisovich had explained, his head cocked, his eyes studying the *novator*, unless we are prepared to welcome death. "I welcome death," the Potter told Svetochka now, "as another in a long line of possible solutions to my problem."

After a while Svetochka calmed down, though she grew tense when he got up to turn out the overhead bulbs; the filaments of light had become linked to the filaments of Svetochka's sanity. Seeing the expression on her face, the Potter left the light on.

Thursday rang up on the house phone to see how they were getting along. The Potter told him they were getting along nicely, thank you. Thursday asked if they lacked anything, anything at all. All they had to do was name it, he insisted, giggling nervously through the phone. You are too kind for words, the Potter responded in the tight voice that indicated he had taken an important decision. When Thursday hung up, the Potter announced he was going to shower, and beckoned Svetochka to follow him. In the bathroom he turned on the hot and cold taps full force to mask his voice from the microphones that were bound to be planted. He brought his lips close to Svetochka's ear. "I am leaving," he told her.

"Leaving?"

"Leaving you. Leaving here."

Relief swept through Svetochka's body at the thought of being rid of him. "Where will you go?" she whispered back.

The word emerged from the back of the Potter's consciousness. "*Anywhere*," he said.

"You said the hotel was guarded," Svetochka said. She was desperate for him to be gone. The idea of being touched by him sent pulses of fear up her spine. "You think they'll let you simply walk out of here?"

"I have a plan," the Potter confided, and drawing her closer to the water gushing from the ornate taps, he told her what it was.

Her first screams, hollow shrieks that sounded as if

they had originated in a tunnel, echoed through the corridor shortly after midnight. Thursday, barefoot, wearing a flowery silk ankle-length robe, scampered over from his room down the hall and pounded on the door. The Austrian squad leader and the four heavies on the night shift turned up moments later. All five had drawn their pistols. Svetochka, still screaming, threw open the door. She was stark naked. "We were making love," she gasped, flinging one hand modestly over her full breasts.

Thursday's eyes bulged even more than they usually did. "Calm yourself," he shouted excitedly in his Brooklyn-accented Russian.

Svetochka, the amateur actress, got a grip on herself. "I went into the bathroom to perform an act of feminine hygiene," she said with dignity. "When I returned to the bedroom—" She began sobbing, abandoning her breasts and covering her eyes with her hands to hide the lack of tears.

Thursday brushed past her into the bedroom. The Austrians crowded in after him. The bay window was wide open, the curtains billowing inward in the night air. "The son of a bitch jumped!" Thursday exclaimed. He gripped the sill and leaned over it. The gutter was illuminated by an old-fashioned curved lamp protruding from the wall of the hotel. Thursday stared at the street, trying to make out the spread-eagled body on the cobblestones. He wondered how the Sisters would take the news of the death of the Potter. The Austrian squad leader, leaning out of the window next to Thursday, muttered, "*Est niemand unten.*" He's right, Thursday realized. There was no body to be seen in the street below. He and the Austrian squad leader turned back to the room to question Svetochka.

Six floors below, the heavy front door of the small hotel on the quiet street opened, and a short, thick-set, dwarfish figure emerged. He was carrying a small American valise in his right hand. He appeared to hesitate for the barest fraction of a second, angling up his face to the night as if it were tangible, like rain; as if he intended to quench a thirst from it. Then he turned on his heel and strode off briskly up the incline toward the all-night taxi ramp at the edge of the Ringstrasse.

BOOK II

Death

Of course I can, Appleyard asserted. I can do anything. I can do snow falling. I can do smoke rising. I can do the sun setting. I can do someone dying. The last two are actually very similar. . . .

1

The American agent known to the Cousins by the code name Khanda picked up his visa from the Mexican consulate in New Orleans the last week in September, on the day the newspapers first ran the item about the forthcoming visit of the Prince of the Realm to a particular city. Traveling under the alias of Alek James Hidell, he set out by bus for Laredo, Texas, then strolled across to Nuevo Laredo and continued on in a Mexican bus.

Once in Mexico City, Khanda made contact with his Cuban cutout. Normally all contacts between Khanda and his Merchant were handled by the Cubans. But because the assignment was so sensitive, the rule was ignored and the Cuban set up a treff *with the Russians. There were two of them. The first, named Vladimir Volkov, was the Department 13 man in Mexico. The other, the younger of the two Cousins who ran Department 13, had flown to Mexico especially for this meeting.*

The first session took place in a seedy motel near the city's airport. The Cubans provided warm bodies to seal off the area. The Russians turned up with a bottle of decent Polish vodka and a five-hundred-gram tin of black beluga caviar. Khanda had grown particularly fond of caviar during the two years he had spent in Russia, so the meeting got off on the right foot.

Khanda was five feet, ten inches in height, lean, wiry even, with a look of grim determination etched into the thin lines of his mouth. He impressed people as being sulky, but the very few who knew him more than casually saw him as someone with a permanent chip on his shoulder, a score to settle.

Speaking Russian, the three chatted about Khanda's life in America. The Russians asked whether his wife had any idea of what he was up to. He assured them she didn't. She knew about the clip-fed rifle, fitted with the telescopic sight, that he had bought from a mail-order house in Chicago, but she believed his story that he used it for target practice. The Cousin broached the delicate subject of what had gone wrong the previous spring when Khanda tried to assassinate an outspoken anti-Castro military officer. "It was night," Khanda told them with a nervous shrug. "I couldn't see too well. I missed."

The Russians, both of whom were experienced in handling Department 13 field men, were careful not to bruise his ego. "It could happen to anyone," the Cousin said sympathetically.

Khanda produced the article he had clipped from the newspaper, and they talked at length about the Prince's forthcoming visit. Volkov flattened a detailed map of the city on a table, weighing down the corners with ashtrays. The three of them pored over it. Experts had studied the situation, the Cousin said. They had decided that there were two ways for the Prince to reach the luncheon site from the airport. He traced the routes with his thumb. The Prince could go down Main Street, turn onto the boulevard and proceed directly to the site. Or he could jog right off Main onto Elm Street, then head for the freeway and the site. "What you must do," the younger Cousin said, "is go there and study the two routes carefully."

Khanda, who had been trained at Department 13's secret espionage school outside of Minsk, squinted at the map as if it were a landscape and he was a gardener. "I have to find work in a building that will give me a clean shot at him no matter which of the two routes he chooses," he said.

They discussed, in very general terms, angles of fire, distances at which the Italian rifle fitted with the telescopic sight could be considered accurate, how many shots Khanda might reasonably expect to fire, escape routes from the scene of the crime and, eventually, from the country.

The room grew dark as the sun disappeared behind the airport hangars. Volkov drew the shades and switched on several lights. The younger Cousin handed Khanda an envelope filled with American money. "There's not too much in it because we don't want you to draw attention to yourself," he explained.

Khanda smiled faintly. "I don't need much," he said.

Volkov said, "You have two months to organize things."

Khanda said, "That should give me enough time."

The younger Cousin said, "We all know you're the best man for the job."

"If anybody can pull this off," Volkov chimed in, "it's you."

"I'll do my best to justify your confidence," Khanda said.

The younger Cousin accepted this with an appreciative nod.

2

❦

It had been a long time since the Potter's last, best sleeper had been called by his Russian name; so long, in fact, that to his own ear it didn't seem to refer to him anymore. His papers referred to him as Raven, a name that the Potter hadn't liked at all (even though it had the advantage of being close to his real name of Revkin) when they were working up his legend back in the sleeper school in Moscow. I would prefer something more common, the Potter had said, by which he meant a name that filled several columns, several pages even, in the local phone book, and he had come up with half a dozen suggestions: Carter, Jackson, Livingstone, Parker, Taylor, Turner. But Piotr Borisovich had insisted. It's me who has to live with the name, he had argued, so it's important I feel comfortable with it.

In the end the Potter had agreed reluctantly to "Raven," the name of the killer in Graham Greene's *This Gun for Hire*. To Piotr Borisovich, Greene's Raven had something of a fallen angel about him, which is roughly how he saw himself; like the Greene character, he fancied he came equipped with a sense of morality that belonged to another time, another place, which was a roundabout way of saying that he couldn't control what century he happened to have been born in, that it wasn't his fault if morally speaking he had to improvise.

For a long time Piotr Borisovich had been delighted with his new name, and the fallen-angel status that went with it. "Peter Raven," he would introduce himself boldly to women, doffing his hat, cocking his head, smiling with his eyes until little fanlike wrinkles formed at their corners. In recent weeks, though, for reasons he had not yet put his finger on, he had taken to whispering his old name to himself when he was alone, like some high priest murmuring the sacred name of God in the holy of holies so that the correct pronunciation would not be lost to posterity.

"Piotr Borisovich Revkin," the Sleeper whispered now, articulating each syllable.

"What was that?" Kaat called down. She was leaning over the banister at the top of the stairs, a forefinger nervously curled through the necklace of worry beads dangling from her neck. The blue point with the gray nose and gray paws sprawled at her feet, peering down, looking from one to the other as if she could follow the conversation.

"What are you doing here?" the Sleeper demanded. "You're supposed to be at work." He looked at her sharply. "Are you spying on me?"

"I thought I heard you say something," Kaat explained. She began to nibble on a fingernail.

"You're biting your nail again," the Sleeper told her.

"I'm hungry," Kaat said.

"You're nervous," the Sleeper corrected her.

"Have it your way," Kaat said. "What *were* you saying?"

"If it makes any difference, I said you were particularly imaginative last night," the Sleeper said. Again little wrinkles spread out from the corners of his eyes.

"Liar!" Kaat shot back. Then, "You think so?"

"I think so," the Sleeper acknowledged.

"How did you find Millie?" Kaat challenged.

"Millie I found . . . conventionally violent," the Sleeper replied thoughtfully.

"You like violence, don't you?" Kaat commented in a melancholy undertone.

"I like sex," the Sleeper corrected her, "and to the degree that violence is related to it, I *appreciate* violence."

The Potter, too, probably because of his own relationship with that bitch of a wife of his, had several times, in his conversations with the Sleeper, referred to the relationship between sex and violence. It turns you on, he had once suggested. (He had arranged for one of the Center's female stringers to come up to the Sleeper's apartment the night before, and was surveying the damage the morning after.) You mean violence turns me on to sex? the Sleeper had asked. I mean sex turns you on to violence, the Potter had said. The Sleeper had nodded moodily, acknowledging the insight. I'd give my right arm to know why you recruited me for the sleeper school, he had said suddenly; it was not something they had talked about before. I recruited you, the Potter had informed him, because you are a man of strengths. The Sleeper couldn't restrain a snicker. I see myself as a man of weaknesses, he had said, surveying the apartment in disgust. But the Potter had only shaken his head knowingly. Your principal strength, he had remarked, is that you are aware of your weaknesses.

"God knows why I go on living with you," Kaat called down from the banister.

The Sleeper shrugged. "Nobody's forcing you."

"Here's the thing," Kaat burst out. "I like the sense of mystery you convey. That's what drew me to you in the first place, the feeling that I could peel layers of you away, as if you were an onion, and never get to a center. But I admit it: sometimes you drive me straight up the wall." She started to bite a nail again, caught his look and stopped.

Wearing Indian sandals, a copper-colored miniskirt and a tie-dyed T-shirt with the word "Maybe" stenciled across the front, Kaat scooped up her cat (which she called Meow) and came tripping down the stairs. "I'm off to the mortuary," she announced, massaging her forehead with her thumb and third finger as if she were keeping a migraine at bay.

"Why don't you leave the cat home for once?" the Sleeper asked.

Kaat shook her head. "She doesn't like to be separated from me. You know that."

The Sleeper said, "I don't know how you do what you do."

"It's a job like any other," Kaat said. "Setting the hair of dead people pays better than setting the hair of the living. And it's a great comfort to the relatives to see their loved ones looking lifelike. Besides, I don't consider dead people dead. They're just in passage between two incarnations." Kaat turned back at the front door. The cat, nestled in the crook of an elbow, purred with a dignified rolling of R's. "I almost forgot," Kaat said. "A letter came for you this morning. I left it in the salad bowl in the kitchen on top of Millie's birth-control pills." She smiled hesitantly in the Sleeper's direction. "I passed my ring over your horoscope again," she told him.

"And?"

"It's pretty much what I told you last night. From the twenty-seventh of this month until the thirteenth of October, you are particularly vulnerable to anaxiphilia—"

"Another one of your A words," he moaned.

"Millie gave it to me last week. She found it in a movie-magazine horoscope. It means the falling in love with a *schnook* by someone who ought to know better."

"I don't see myself falling in love with anyone," said the Sleeper.

You will never fall in love, the Potter had once told Piotr Borisovich after they had had a bit too much vodka at a private military restaurant. Falling in love is needing someone, and the only person you need is yourself.

"I don't see you needing anyone either," Kaat told him now. He glanced quickly at her, but she was already changing the subject. "As for your physical safety, you should be particularly prudent on the ides. This month's are past, happily for you. October's come on the fifteenth. November's are on the thirteenth. Also, watch out for vicious circles."

"How can you tell a vicious circle from a normal circle?" the Sleeper asked sarcastically.

"All circles," Kaat snapped with a flash of temper—how could he be so thick as not to see it?—"are potentially vicious." Smiling vaguely at a fleeting thought, tucking the cat firmly under her arm, she disappeared out of the door.

The Sleeper shook his head in frustration. She wasn't the easiest person in the world to live with, this catlike Kaat with her collection of words beginning in A and the sunken eyes that stared out with an almost mystical intensity at the world she could never quite get a handle on. She had been violated once, the Sleeper knew; violated again when the man she loved at the time refused to have anything to do with a violated woman. More than once the Sleeper had seen her wince at what he took to be the memory of pain. The thing she valued most in lovers these days—she made no bones about it—was kindness.

It was the thing the Sleeper gave her the least of.

The letter was where Kaat had tossed it. The address on the envelope had been typed out on a typewriter with a red ribbon. Peter Raven, 145 Love Apple Lane, Brooklyn, New York. The postmark indicated it had been mailed in New York two days before. There was no return address. The Sleeper held the envelope up to the light filtering through the kitchen window. He could see the outline of a folded piece of paper inside.

He didn't like the look of it. At all.

It flashed through his mind that maybe they had gotten wind of his living arrangements, that they were furious with him for drawing attention to himself when he should have been melting into the foliage of what people considered a more conventional sexual arrangement. Yet the Sleeper's *ménage à trois* provided the ultimate cover, in the sense that it went against preconceived notions. Who would ever believe that a man living with two women was in reality a Soviet agent?

The Sleeper laughed out loud. He was jumping at shadows. It was ridiculous to think they could have learned about his roommates. Or that having learned of the situation they would risk communicating with him about it. The letter was probably nothing more than the announcement of the opening, on Pierrepont Street, of a new coffee shop where the local talent could read aloud poetry at night. Or another reminder from the Keep Brooklyn Heights Clean Committee to curb the dog he didn't own.

The Sleeper slit open the envelope with a kitchen knife, extracted the folded piece of paper and opened it. And the words, typed on the same red ribbon, leapt off the page at him.

. . . the hands of the sisters Death and Night incessantly softly wash again, and ever again, this soil'd world

So it had finally come! It was only now, reading and rereading the words, that he realized that in some distant reach of his brain he had nursed the faint hope that they might have forgotten about him; misplaced his file; restaffed the appropriate department with technocrats who preferred electronic gadgets to flesh-and-blood sleepers. Yet he was too rational a creature not to know that what had happened was inevitable. They hadn't brought him in from Frunze in Central Asia, educated him at Moscow University, trained him for nineteen solid months at the Potter's school, and then gone to all the expense and trouble of inserting him in America to forget about him.

Dazed to the point of dizziness, feeling as if he were groping his way across the vaguely familiar terrain of an unpleasant dream, the Sleeper took the letter upstairs to his attic workshop. He thought of the Potter kicking away at his Finnish wheel in *his* attic workshop. He wondered if he still used the piano wire the Sleeper had fashioned for him to cut his pots off the wheel. He wondered too if the Potter had managed to hold on to Svetochka; during the week they had made love together, she had told the Sleeper that she didn't plan to hang around forever with "the Jewish dwarf," as she called him.

Someone—probably Kaat, because she made a fetish of breathing fresh air—had left an attic window open, and the dozen or so mobiles that the Sleeper had in stock were all spinning wildly. It was strange, he was the first to admit, how he had been drawn to the business of finding fulcrums. The Potter had suggested it as one of many possible professions that would give him the independence he needed to function as a sleeper. The Potter had even offered to teach him how to throw pots, but from the moment the wild-eyed Uzbek had shown him what a fulcrum was, and taught him to weld, he had been hooked. Aside from its other advantages, being an artisan of some sort meant he wasn't on any payroll and attracted little attention from the government agencies that thrived on Social Security numbers, tax forms and the like.

He retrieved the flamethrower cigarette lighter from the cigar box full of old lighters, unscrewed the back and pulled out the thin cylindrical microdot reader. Working with an Xacto blade and a tweezers, he carefully pried the microdot away from the dot over the i in the word "Night" and deposited it on the lens of the reader. Then he angled the cylinder up to the desk lamp. What emerged was a negative in which the printing appeared in white. "Piotr Borisovich," it said. (Had some sixth sense caused him to start pronouncing his Russian name out loud so that when he came across it in print he would know instantly that it referred to him?) The microdot went on to describe the location of a dead-letter drop in an alleyway around the corner from the old Brooklyn Eagle Building in Brooklyn

Heights. (Whoever was getting in touch with the Sleeper obviously preferred country drops to city drops, a detail that the Sleeper took as a sign of high professionalism.) The message wound up with the words "much luck" and a postscript that read, "The Potter sends you his personal wishes for the success of your assignment."

So the Potter had a finger in the pie! It was a reassuring thought to the Sleeper, whose comfortable world of fulcrums had just been shattered. It meant that his father was still alive in Peredelkino. And it guaranteed that whatever it was they wanted him to do would be doable; the Potter would not have put his seal on the letter if it weren't. Spying, the Potter had drummed into the head of his last, best sleeper, was an exploration of the art of the possible.

The Sleeper went over to close the attic window, but instead found himself gazing out moodily over the carriage-house roofs on Love Apple Lane. He remembered staring out over Moscow from the open hotel window his last night in Russia. He had gotten roaring drunk on French champagne, and surprised himself by dredging up from some corner of his memory snatches of Moussorgsky's *Khovanshchina*. The opera had made him think of the three hundred *streltsy* lynched by Peter the Great on the monastery wall, and he had turned to the Potter and (suddenly emotional, though the Potter never sensed it, he was sure) had said: Violence is in our blood, violence and a passion for plotting. You and I, the Potter had agreed, are the last practitioners of a dying art. Funny how the dwarfish *novator* had gotten under his skin; funny also how he had made the filthy business of spying seem like a holy crusade.

It was curious he should think of the Potter now. Curious, too, that it should occur to him for the first time that the Potter had never held out the promise of a holy grail at the end of the holy crusade.

3

❦

For Piotr Borisovich Revkin, life had more or less begun with a holy crusade (the Great Patriotic War) and a holy grail at the end of it (to find himself, amid incredible slaughter, still alive). Revkin had been a strapping curly-haired fifteen-year-old who already shaved with his father's pearl-handled straight-edge when the local Party recruiters in Frunze, scraping the bottom of the manpower barrel, called up youngsters who *looked* seventeen. When the one-armed sergeant major who filled in the forms found out that Revkin spoke fluent English, there had been some talk of sending him to Moscow to translate the operating manuals that came with American Lend-Lease equipment. But then the sergeant major discovered why Revkin spoke English. His mother, it turned out, had been an American feminist in the mold of Emma Goldman who had emigrated to Russia in the early thirties to construct the future. She had been arrested and tried as a Trotskyite "wrecker" during one of the mid-thirties purges. Convicted of the specific charge of throwing sand into the gears of some factory equipment in order to sabotage Stalin's five-year plan, she had been dispatched to a Gulag camp, from which she had never returned. (Her last words to her son as she was being led from the courtroom had been an old Russian proverb: "To dine with the devil," she called in English over the heads of the guards, "use a long spoon!") Eventually a package of thick socks and lard that her Russian husband, Piotr Borisovich's father, sent her came back with "VMN," the Cyrillic letters for "Highest Degree of Punishment," stamped on it, indicating that the idealistic feminist had finished up in front of a firing squad.

To make sure that the same fate didn't befall the rest of the family—in those days, simply being related to a condemned person was *prima facie* evidence of anti-Soviet intentions—Piotr Borisovich's father had abandoned his job as a journalist, his apartment, his stamp collection, his hand-carved chess set (the last two were sold to raise cash), and had gone into hiding with his son on a cotton collective, where the work of harvesting was so backbreaking that the manager didn't ask too many questions of those willing to do it. In the course of four harvests the spine of the father took on a permanent curve. When Piotr Borisovich watched his father, bathed in sweat, bending under the weight of the bales of cotton, he swore to himself that one day he would make it all up to him.

In the end it was the war that "saved" them from the long arm of the vengeful Bolsheviks. The elder Revkin, making use of his journalistic credentials, went off to serve as a propagandist with a newly formed division. And the younger Revkin wound up as a front-line combat soldier.

About the war, Piotr Borisovich never said a word. Not one. To anybody.

After the fall of Germany, Piotr Borisovich, by then a war-weary veteran of seventeen, returned to Frunze, a sprawling city of low buildings and wide streets with narrow canals through which icy mountain water was circulated to bring temperatures down during the hot summer months. He was something of a local hero, which qualified him for a place in the reviewing stand during the May Day parade. On the breast of his worn Army tunic he wore the Order of the Red Banner, which made him, according to the Frunze Party newspaper, one of the youngest soldiers in the

Red Army to possess the medal. He had earned it, the story explained, because of his exploits as a sniper; he had been officially credited with the deaths of one hundred and forty-four fascists, which didn't take into account the twenty-two for which he had no corroboration. The newspaper added the enticing detail that the young fascist-slayer always sighted on the jugular—and rarely missed.

For the next several years the Army sent Piotr Borisovich, by then a teenager with a ready, if somewhat sardonic, smile, around Central Asia giving marksmanship demonstrations to new recruits. He might have ended his days as a rifle instructor if it hadn't been for a sharp-eyed State Security talent scout who, one fine day, saw Piotr Borisovich place twenty-five bullets into a bull's-eye at a hundred meters and decided to take a look at the boy's dossier. When he discovered that Piotr Borisovich spoke fluent English, his interest turned to enthusiasm.

But in those days State Security did not simply approach a potential recruit and make a pitch. For reasons that had to do with the deep sense of insecurity of all successful revolutionaries (what would prevent others from following in their footsteps and toppling them?), the elders in the organization preferred to get a hook into a candidate first. The obvious hook in Piotr Borisovich's case was his father, who by that time was working for a well-known theoretical journal as its resident expert on left deviationism. The senior Revkin was suddenly arrested on the charge that he had failed to include in his dossier the pertinent detail that the enemy of the people to whom he had been married was American. It was at this point, with his father cooling his heels in Moscow's Lubyanka prison, that the younger Revkin was summoned to the local State Security headquarters for what he later laughingly referred to as a "friendly chat."

The three men and one woman who faced Piotr Borisovich across the table didn't mince words. With his war record, above all with his knowledge of English, the interviewers pointed out, Piotr Borisovich could eventually render considerable service to the Motherland. And the rewards, they made it very clear, would be generous: he would never have to worry about material things for the rest of his days. The young Revkin, anxious not to fall into the same trap as his father, said that there was no way he could accept an appointment with State Security, because he was the son of a convicted enemy of the people who had suffered the highest degree of punishment. One of the interviewers waved a hand. "We know all about that," he said. "Did you know that my mother was American?" Piotr Borisovich asked. "That too, that too," he was assured. "Did you know that my father is at this very moment in prison?" The interviewers exchanged looks. During the period of collectivization of agriculture in the early thirties, one of them said, his eyebrows arched to indicate he was conveying important information, all relatively well-off peasants were rounded up and shipped off to Siberia—their land, their animals, their houses, their equipment confiscated. The only exceptions were *kulaks* who had sons serving in the Red Army. The principle was established then: a son's service to the Motherland can mitigate a father's sin.

Piotr Borisovich signed on the dotted line, then raised his right hand and swore an oath of allegiance to the Motherland and the father figure who presided over it. Two days later he received a telephone call from *his* father. He had been released from jail, welcomed back to work at the theoretical journal, even given a small raise. And mystery of mysteries, a brand-new refrigerator that he had neither ordered nor paid for had been delivered to his tiny apartment. Was he going crazy? Or had Communism, in the form of a refrigerator for everyone, finally come to Russia?

Without even applying for one of the coveted places in the school, Piotr Borisovich received written notice that he had been accepted in Moscow University. He was assigned his own room in an apartment on Lenin Hills within walking distance of the university. Each month he found in his mailbox an envelope with one hundred rubles in it, an enormous sum by student standards. On the eve of school vacations, the amount was always doubled. Little was asked of Piotr Borisovich in return except to educate himself in the ways of the world. Every six months or so he was summoned to appear before a review board which met in an apartment in downtown Moscow (Piotr Borisovich never again set foot in a State Security building) to give an account of what he was doing. Why had this trimester's grade in the origins of Marxism-Leninism fallen below the previous trimester's grade? he was politely asked, as if his tutors had nothing more in mind than the sharpening of his intellect. What did he think of the three African students in his advanced English class? he was asked, as if his tutors were simply checking on the company he kept. Only once did Piotr Borisovich have reason to believe that the State Security organs were watching him more closely than he imagined. Did he ever hear anyone criticize the Soviet leadership? he was asked. No, he replied. Did the words "Russia is an intellectual wasteland" strike him as being familiar? He may have heard words to that effect, he admitted. Where? He didn't remember. Who uttered them? He didn't remember that either. Wasn't it the young professor of American poetry, the one who read Whitman aloud to his class all the time, who the previous week had said this to several students during a coffee break in the cafeteria? Now that they mentioned it, admitted Piotr Borisovich, it may have been. Then why hadn't he reported this anti-Soviet remark to the authorities? Because, Piotr Borisovich explained lamely, it had seemed inconsequential at the time. Don't let a lapse like that happen a second time, one of the tutors warned.

That night Piotr Borisovich got a phone call from his father. An odd thing had happened that day, he said. Two burly men had turned up at his door, flashed a paper he never got a chance to read, and removed his refrigerator. With all his food still in it!

Several days later, mumbling vaguely about how they had mistaken the number on the apartment door, the two moving men returned Revkin's refrigerator. The next time Piotr Borisovich heard an anti-Soviet remark, he reported it immediately to the authorities.

What with his hundred-ruble stipend and his apartment on Lenin Hills, Piotr Borisovich had no problem attracting a steady stream of women to his bed. No sooner had one affair ended than another was under way. At times, affairs overlapped; at times all three shared the same bed. During his last year at the university, Piotr Borisovich fell in love with an older woman whose husband, a doctor, had been arrested in what would turn out to be Stalin's last purge. Piotr Borisovich managed to talk her into going to bed with him, but when he phoned her to arrange a sequel, she refused. Furious, Piotr Borisovich began calling her up while he was making love with other girls and describing in precise detail what they were doing. He even passed the phone to his bed partners and had them describe events from their point of view. The doctor's wife wasn't turned on—but Piotr Borisovich was. Phoning up one lover while he was making love to another became his fetish.

If the tutors knew about it—and it was unthinkable that they didn't—they never brought up the subject at the semiannual review.

Why they had turned a blind eye to his fetish became clear after Piotr Borisovich was graduated from Moscow University. The Moscow Merchant who became his control obviously considered his sexual prowess to be a major part of his qualifications. Coached by his Merchant, Piotr Borisovich assumed the role of a young dissident writer living illegally (without a resident's permit) in a garret off Gorky Street in downtown Moscow. He would hang around the restaurants and hotel bars frequented by Western tourists, coming on as a frustrated literatus famished for any contact with the West, whether in the form of books, records, blue jeans or warm female bodies doused with French perfume. More often than not, within three days of meeting a single woman, Piotr Borisovich had an intense love affair going. The inevitable partings, with Piotr Borisovich vowing to smuggle love poems out of the country and the women promising to smuggle Western novels back to him, were arranged to give the female tourist the sense that she was running risks for love, not to mention puncturing holes in the infamous Iron Curtain. Weeks or months later, the unsuspecting women would receive a note, smuggled out of Russia by a "friend" of Piotr Borisovich's, saying that he had been arrested by the authorities because of his clandestine contact with the recipient of the letter; that they were now demanding that she cooperate with the Russians by providing relatively inconsequential scraps of information that she might stumble across at work; that he, Piotr Borisovich, preferred to suffer in a damp prison cell than have her run any risk for him; that his love for her would not be affected in the slightest when, as he thoroughly expected, she told the Russians to go to hell.

The ploy didn't always work, but it brought positive results often enough to provide Piotr Borisovich with a unique career in the KGB. When he wasn't operating out of his garret, with its mattress on the floor and its piles of well-thumbed American and English paperbacks strewn haphazardly about, he lived in a well-furnished three-room apartment across the Moscow River from the Kremlin, owned a secondhand Volkswagen, even had the use of a *dacha* set in a stand of white birches in a bend of the Moscow River an hour and a half down the Smolensk highway from the capital. He had girlfriends galore (who thought he worked as a courier for the diplomatic service, which accounted for the periods when he dropped from sight), more money than he could spend, access to the KGB's department store with its shelves full of Chivas Regal and Chanel No. 5 and Lucky Strike cigarettes (he ordered by phone; unmarked packages were hand-delivered to his door). The months, the years ticked pleasantly, painlessly by. It was difficult to see how life could have been better.

And yet in a remote corner of his consciousness, in a part of himself he had never dared expose, there was a hesitation; a shadow of a doubt; a vague feeling of having missed a boat. The uneasiness was especially strong when, on the rare occasions Piotr Borisovich found himself alone, he thumbed through an American paperback edition of Whitman poems and came again across the lines about the sisters Death and Night. Surely there had to be something more to it all before Death and Night rang down, like a fire curtain, on his life.

It was at this point in Piotr Borisovich's gloriously dull existence that he received the summons to report to a military hotel. It specified a date, an hour, and was signed with the word "novator," the one in charge. A sergeant in civilian clothes led him up to the third floor and opened what looked like a broom closet. It turned out to be the entrance to a secret staircase that led to a spacious apartment on the hotel's top floor. Finding himself alone in the apartment, Piotr Borisovich took a look around. In the middle of a coffee table was a bowl filled with American candy bars. An American record player, a Magnavox, stood on a shelf, along with an enormous collection of American records, everything from Nat King Cole to the latest Broadway musicals. Bookshelves were stacked with American magazines—*Newsweek*, *Time*, *Life*, *Esquire*, *Coronet*, *The Saturday Evening Post*—and copies of *The New York Times*, which (judging from the wrapper) were flown in daily from Helsinki.

Whoever lived in the apartment was obviously quite an Americanophile.

Piotr Borisovich was surveying the view from the apartment's windows—he could see the Kremlin towers, and Saint Basil's Cathedral rising above the Kremlin wall across the Moscow River—when he heard someone at the door. He turned. A man so short he appeared almost dwarflike threw the bolt on the inside of the door and then faced Piotr Borisovich. The man squinted at him for a moment, then said in English, "Could I trouble you to step away from the window. All I can see is your silhouette. It is not enough." When Piotr Borisovich hesitated, he added, "If you please."

Piotr Borisovich walked to the middle of the room. The newcomer made no move to shake hands. He motioned his guest to a chair, pulled up another one so that it was facing him and sat down. Their knees were almost touching. "I am not a devotee of Dostoevsky," the newcomer announced forthrightly. "But he has had a great influence on me. It happened this way: several hours after Nicholas I countermanded Dostoevsky's death sentence, Dostoevsky wrote a letter in which he said, 'Life is a gift.' With your combat record in the war, this is something that is surely embedded in the marrow of your bones. All life is a gift, and you are wasting yours."

"You think so?" Piotr Borisovich retorted belligerently. He was put off by the frankness of the approach.

"I know so," the visitor insisted passionately. "I know because I have been watching you—literally watching you!—for the better part of two years now. You are one of those people who thrive on tension; you are addicted to it, as if it were a drug and you needed a daily fix. I suspect that that is what got you through the war in one piece. You are uneasy unless you are living on a limb that could break at any moment. You are not too imaginative, not at all fanatical; you are a plodder who sees things through once he starts something." The Potter paused for breath. "Because of the execution of your mother, because of your experiences in the war, you tend to ignore the past and live in the present, though to keep your sanity you occasionally throw little hooks into the past—I am referring to your habit of phoning up a previous bed partner while you are making love to someone new." An apologetic grimace deformed the Potter's face. "You see, I have made it my business to figure you out. I know everything there is to know about you. I know about your father; I know how he acquired his refrigerator, and how his spine got that curve in it. And knowing all this, I am going to make you an offer. I am going to propose to you a way of life in which you will do what you do *well*, not for material rewards, not for the Motherland or the cause, not for the sex, not even for your father's continued well-being, *but in order to earn my approval.*"

Piotr Borisovich stared with new interest at the speaker, who was gripping the arms of his chair with hands that appeared to be incredibly strong. He was no youngster. But there was a steadiness to his regard, a flame in his eyes that commanded instant respect; instant allegiance even.

"I accept," Piotr Borisovich blurted out before he knew he intended to respond.

The other man didn't smile. "This has been a wretched century," he noted, and then he said something that made their line of work seem like a crusade. "You and I are going to try to make the next one better." He stood up and offered Piotr Borisovich his hand. "My name is Feliks Arkantevich Turov," he said formally. "I am the *novator* of the sleeper school, in which you are now enrolled."

For the next nineteen months, the period during which Piotr Borisovich was under the Potter's wing, he lived in the top-floor apartment of the military hotel. The workload was unrelenting—six days a week, ten hours a day, which didn't include the Sleeper's "free" time, during which he was expected to become acquainted with American popular music (there was usually a disc playing in the background) or dip into the library to familiarize himself with Steinbeck, Hemingway, Dreiser, Jack London, Mark Twain and F. Scott Fitzgerald. Formal classwork—courses given by the Potter himself or one of his assistants—generally took up the mornings. These included the theory and practice of espionage, the philosophy of Marx, Engels and Lenin as it applied to intelligence activities, and an intensive study of every facet of the United States: its history, geography, political development, military establishment, FBI organization and methods of law enforcement. There were daily classes given by the Potter on spoken English, which concentrated on polishing the Sleeper's knowledge of colloquialisms; he learned how to curse like a stevedore and to charm someone with slightly off-color jokes. He studied the intricacies of baseball and football from films until he knew what a balk was, and could predict with considerable accuracy whether a quarterback would run or pass.

The thread that ran through all the courses was to develop the Sleeper's professionalism. He memorized the standard operating procedures for sleepers until he could rattle them off in his sleep. Once awakened, for instance, a sleeper must ignore all communications that arrived out of prearranged channels and pretended to come from friends and relatives. The logic for the rule was obvious: informal messages from friends or relatives might actually have been sent by the enemy in an effort to confuse a sleeper or divert him from his mission. The Americans had succeeded in doing just this in the mid-fifties: an agent received a written message from his wife saying she had defected; when the agent went to meet her, he found the FBI (which had forged the letter) waiting for him. It was a point that the Potter put a great deal of emphasis on.

"What would you do if you were on a mission and got a message from your father?" the Potter asked.

"I'd ignore it."

"What if you got a message from, say, me?"

"I'd ignore that too."

"What if you heard a voice you knew on the phone? My voice, for instance, telling you a mission had been canceled?"

"I'd assume someone in the American intelligence

establishment knew of the connection between us and was imitating your voice. I'd interpret it as a danger signal and take steps to make sure the person pretending to be you couldn't communicate with me again."

Afternoons at the sleeper school were usually devoted to technical subjects. Piotr Borisovich learned microphotography, regular photography, secret writing, how to communicate through dead-letter drops, how to surveille others, how to detect and evade the surveillance of others. Once a week he was driven out to a remote KGB rifle range to familiarize himself with pistols and rifles available in America, and perfect his marksmanship on these unfamiliar weapons.

For every hour of classwork, there was an hour of tradecraft in the streets. Under the watchful gaze of the Potter, who was something of an expert on the subject (he was something of an expert on *every* subject, Piotr Borisovich would say), the Sleeper, among other things, learned how to scout the route a dignitary would take in order to select the best site from which to assassinate him.

Evenings the Potter personally projected American movies—the sleeper school had an enormous library of Hollywood films that had been captured from the Germans during the war—for the Sleeper in the top-floor apartment of the military hotel. Everything that dealt with police or law-enforcement agencies was generally shown twice. One night they would watch Yul Brynner heading a ring of narcotics smugglers. The next, a police thriller starring Alan Ladd or Edward G. Robinson.

The last months at the school were spent working up the Sleeper's legend—the identity under which he would penetrate and live in the United States. (It was at this point that the wild-eyed Uzbek took the Sleeper in hand and taught him how to make mobiles.) Together the Potter and the Sleeper pored over source books compiled over the years by KGB agents in the United States, working out addresses where the Sleeper had lived as a child, places he had vacationed at, descriptions of his parents and the location of their tombstones, the names and descriptions of neighbors, of schools he had attended, of jobs he had worked at, of his bosses and coworkers, even of girls he had dated. No item was too small to include in the Sleeper's biography; it was the odd detail, the Potter stressed again and again, that would convince an interrogator that a suspect was telling the truth. The fact that someone lisped when he talked, that a girl wore padded brassieres, that a drugstore where the Sleeper had worked as a fountain clerk specialized in egg creams (which the Sleeper learned how to make in case anyone should ever ask him), were priceless pearls in the necklace of the Sleeper's new identity.

Through it all the two men developed a relationship that provided the Potter with the son he had never been able to father, and the Sleeper with a surrogate father. As the Potter had predicted, the Sleeper found himself attacking his studies with an ardor designed to impress his mentor and earn his approval. And the Potter discovered in his last, best sleeper the rarest of Soviet birds—a kindred spirit.

From the moment that they consecrated their budding friendship—when each, in turn, uttered something which, if reported to the authorities, could get him fired or jailed or even shot—there had been an unspoken complicity between them. For each of them, the part of their relationship that had to do with friendship outweighed the part of their relationship that had to do with work.

Eventually the Potter took the Sleeper to the American warehouse located in the basement of one of the KGB's safe houses, which is the point at which Piotr Borisovich understood that school was almost out. The Potter supplied him with American clothes, and instructed him to wear them so that when he was infiltrated into America they would no longer be new. Cracking open a bottle of Bison vodka that night, the Potter presented to his pupil a scroll announcing that he had been appointed a lieutenant colonel in the KGB. The Sleeper was touched, not so much by the rank, but by the fact that he owed the appointment to the *novator*.

When it came time to leave, the Potter accompanied the Sleeper to the airport in his chauffeured limousine. In the parking lot near the terminal, they both became tense. They started off toward the terminal together, not daring to look at one another, the Potter walking as if he were following a coffin. The Sleeper indicated with a gesture that it would be better if he went on alone. He could see that the Potter was at a loss for words; was fearful that if he found them, whatever he said would sound foolish. The Sleeper emitted a thin, brittle laugh and turned on his heel and stalked off. He could feel the Potter's eyes boring into him; could sense the depth of the affection in the Potter's regard. But when he gave in and glanced back, the Potter had already turned toward his limousine.

The Sleeper understood that both of them suspected their paths would never cross again.

4

That there was a Man Friday network was due to a peculiar quirk of office egos. The young assistants had the security clearances of their masters, but the status of field mice, which meant that they didn't have the rank to take meals in the senior dining room, or the grace to eat with the groundlings. The result was a cozy Man Friday clubroom on the fourth floor, with a soft-drink vending machine in one corner and a pool table on which many a man Friday sharpened his eye.

"Eight ball in the side pocket," said the Deputy Director's man Friday, whose name was Harry. "What's this about your Potter skipping town before the farmers could milk him?"

Thursday watched with bulging eyes as Harry drew a bead on the eight ball. "How did you hear about it?" he asked.

Harry dispatched the cue ball into the eight ball, and the eight ball into the side pocket. "Four ball straight in," he said. "The Sisters' Op Proposal updater passed through the Deputy Director's in basket, which just happens to be on my desk." With a flick of his wrist, he sank the four ball.

"Yeah, well, the Austrians were about as amateur as they come," Thursday explained. He giggled at the thought of how amateur they had been.

"And the Potter, obviously, was an old pro," Harry

added with more than a trace of arrogance as he surveyed the table for another shot.

"That was it exactly," Thursday agreed quickly. "The amateurs versus the old pro."

"Seven ball is dead in the corner," announced Harry.

Thursday squinted at the seven ball. "I've got five bucks says it's not."

"You're on." Leaning over the table, the Deputy Director's man Friday sent the cue ball into the one ball, and the seven, which was touching the one, was propelled straight into the corner pocket.

"Shit," said the Sisters' man Friday.

"You were in Vienna, weren't you?" Harry asked casually. "Fourteen in the side."

Thursday sensed that some of the blame for the loss of the Potter's warm body might rub off on him. "It was a German show," he said defensively. "I was only there to skim off the cream."

"Oh?" Harry seemed mildly surprised. "There was no mention of any cream in the Sisters' updater." He shot and missed.

Thursday shrugged. "I don't know what's in the updater," he said, "but I got what I was sent to get." He studied the table for a shot, but couldn't find one. "I'll play safe," he announced.

"And what is it you were sent to get?" Harry asked.

"Listen," Thursday said uneasily, "I work for the Sisters."

"Just between us," Harry coaxed, "I'm curious to know what the cream was."

Thursday tapped the cue ball lightly, burying it behind a group of balls next to the cushion. He giggled with pleasure at the shot. "If it'll get no further than this room," he said.

5

❦

Two old hags lugging enormous plastic shopping bags were systematically searching through garbage cans in the alley behind the Brooklyn Eagle Building, and the Sleeper had to wait until they finished their scavenging before he could approach the dead-letter drop. He counted down four garages from the corner, then slipped between the wooden fence that marked the limit of the garden behind the Eagle Building and the side of the garage, and began searching for the brick with the word "Mother" chalked on it. It will all boil down, the Potter had once told him with an embarrassed smile, to whether, when you search for your first set of instructions, you do so with a sense of urgency. The Sleeper had been struck by the Potter's choice of words at the time. Why urgency? he had asked curiously. Because urgency, the Potter had replied, is what modern war has lost. My principal task as *novator*, as I see it, is to instill in my sleepers the sense of urgency that was present when the person you were shooting at was also shooting at you.

The Sleeper found the brick, opened his pocketknife and began to pry it out with the blade. To his satisfaction, he discovered he *was* working with a sense of urgency; his pulse pounded, his skin tingled with urgency. For a fleeting moment he thought he might lose control of his bladder in his desire to get to the heart of the dead-letter drop. He worked the brick free and bent to peer into the hole. There was nothing in it; no instructions, no war to go to, shooting or otherwise. He reached in and searched the drop with his fingertips—and found the small, squat metallic capsule wedged into a crack at the back of the opening. The capsule had been dulled with black shoe polish so as not to attract attention. The Sleeper replaced the brick, unscrewed the capsule, removed the scrap of paper and threw the capsule into the space behind the garage full of bottle shards and rusted tins.

At first glance, the message looked like a printed advertisement for a Brooklyn firm specializing in cleaning coal furnaces. But the paper felt odd to the touch—probably because it had been coated with potassium permanganate, a normal precaution to make sure it would ignite when exposed to the slightest heat.

Back home in his workshop, the Sleeper examined the leaflet with a magnifying glass, spotted three i's with dots that looked suspiciously thick, and went to work. He carefully pried the dots off with an Xacto blade, then deposited them one at a time on the lens of his microdot reader.

Once again his skin tingled with a sense of urgency.

The microdots were numbered. The first instructed him to pack a bag and leave home within one hour of having read the order. It listed an interim destination, and told him what kind of transportation to use. It also told him what kind of weapon he would find at the interim destination.

The second microdot identified his ultimate destination, and specified his itinerary and the pace at which he should travel in order to arrive there on a specific day. It cautioned that he was not to arrive early.

The third microdot identified the target, listed the day and hour of his arrival in the city, traced the routes he could take to get from the airport to the luncheon site, discussed in very general terms angles of fire, distances at which the weapon could be considered accurate, how many shots the Sleeper might reasonably expect to fire, escape routes from the scene of the crime and, eventually, from the country. On completion of the mission, the microdot added, the Sleeper would be repatriated to the Motherland and sent into luxurious retirement. This was to be his first, and last, assignment.

The Sleeper read the name of the target again to make sure he had gotten it right. Any levelheaded person would panic at the idea; panic, it seemed to him, was the only sensible response to such an order. Did he really believe that he would go through with it? But if he didn't at least *try* to obey his orders, his father would suffer. So, too, would his surrogate father, the Potter; for it was a principle of the sleeper school that the Potter's career was tied to the success or failure of his students.

Overhead, one of the Sleeper's mobiles swayed gently in currents of air. The beak-shaped end of it dipped like a duck drinking from a puddle, until the fulcrum worked its magic and the beak lifted. The whole business of spying, the Sleeper realized, was a kind of mobile: the Potter, his wife, the Sleeper, his father, the Merchants in Moscow who thought up projects for him. But where in all this was the fulcrum to be found?

The Sleeper struck a match and brought the flame near the edge of the printed leaflet. The paper exploded into flame with a whooshing sound and he had to drop it in the sink to avoid being singed. A stinging odor filled the attic. The Sleeper opened a window to air it out.

"What's that smell?" Millie called from the upstairs bedroom. "Kaat, something's burning in the attic. Come quickly! Kaat!"

Kaat and Millie came racing up the stairs to the door of the attic workshop, Kaat with her soft sandal tread, Millie with her spiked heels stabbing the floorboards. "Peter?" Kaat called through the locked door.

"Open up," Millie chimed in. She banged a fist against the door.

"I'm coming," called the Sleeper. He quickly copied off his itinerary on the back of an envelope, put his microdot reader away, ran some water in the basin and washed the three microdots and the ashes down the drain. Then he opened the door for the two women.

"What's up?" Kaat said, sniffing away as if she were hunting truffles, relieved to see that the entire attic was not going up in flames.

"He's not up!" Millie joked, glancing lewdly at the Sleeper's crotch. "I suppose there has to be a first time for everything," she added with a sigh.

"Don't be vulgar," Kaat snapped at Millie.

Millie, who was four years younger and a head shorter than Kaat, pouted. "What's vulgar about an erection?" she demanded. Her nostrils, which were large to begin with, flared. "Vulgarity is in the ear of the be-listener. Anyway, that's what my math teacher always used to say."

"Your math teacher said that?" asked the Sleeper.

Millie shrugged innocently. "After class. In bed," she said.

Kaat had the impression that Millie knew just what effect she was creating. "I thought you suffered from aculculia," Kaat remarked.

"Another one of your A words," the Sleeper groaned in despair.

"I love her A words," Millie declared with passion.

"Aculculia is a mental block against arithmetic," explained Kaat.

"I did have a block against arithmetic," Millie said. "That's why I slept with the teacher."

Kaat had to laugh at that.

Millie laughed too. "Do you have any new A words?" she asked.

"Two," replied Kaat. "I found out that I'm an aelurophile, which means cat lover. And that I'm amphierotic, which means I can be aroused by members in good standing of either sex."

Millie said, "You're too much, Kaat. Don't you think she's too much, Peter?"

The Sleeper nodded dutifully. "I always thought Kaat was too much," he agreed.

"I'm not sure it sounds like a compliment when you say it like that," Kaat noted.

"Listen, it's only two-thirty," Millie pointed out. She slipped into what she thought of as her Katharine Hepburn voice. "What if we all moseyed on down to the master bedroom for a roll in the hay?"

"What does that mean, 'moseyed'?" asked the Sleeper.

"I'm only good at A words," Kaat observed maliciously.

"You don't know what 'mosey' means?" Millie asked incredulously.

The Sleeper shook his head.

"It means to sort of stroll, to meander, to make your way slowly. It's a cowboy word. You do know what 'roll in the hay' means?"

The Sleeper laughed. "I know what it means. But I haven't got time. I have to go on a trip."

"Go where?" Kaat wanted to know.

"You never said anything about going on a trip," Millie muttered. She clearly had her heart set on a roll in the hay.

"I had a call this morning," the Sleeper improvised. "An old friend of mine, someone I knew in the Army, invited me down to his place in Pennsylvania."

"How long will you be gone?" Kaat asked quietly. She brought a fingernail to her mouth and began to nibble on it.

"Ten days. Two weeks maybe."

"Two weeks!" Millie exploded. "What are we going to do for sex?"

"You can always fall back on Kaat's amphieroticism," the Sleeper said.

"It's not the same without a man," Millie said sulkily.

Kaat asked, "Where exactly are you going?"

"I already told you," the Sleeper said vaguely. "Pennsylvania."

"Will you call us?" Millie asked. She batted her eyelashes suggestively. "You know. Like you did when you went to Denver to show your mobiles."

The fanlike wrinkles formed at the corners of the Sleeper's eyes. "You liked that?" he asked. "Hearing me describe what I was doing to another woman?"

"Personally," confessed Millie, "I liked hearing her describe what she was doing to you."

"How about you?" the Sleeper asked Kaat.

The cat named Meow nosed open the door to the attic and padded silently into the room to arch her back against the side of Kaat's calf. Kaat scooped up the cat and stroked her under the chin. "Here's the thing . . ." she began.

"Why do you always begin your improtant sentences with 'Here's the thing'?" the Sleeper asked.

"Always," Millie agreed.

"Here's the thing," Kaat said, ignoring them both. "In one of my previous incarnations I must have been a member of a harem, because I like sharing my lovers, which is to say that I'm mildly jealous but not possessive. If it turns you on to phone up while you're making love to someone else, that's just another way of sharing, as far as I'm concerned."

"I love you, Kaat," Millie said in a soft voice. "I mean it. I really do."

Kaat smiled at her, and kissed her lightly on the lips. Then they both set to packing the worn leather valise that Peter kept in the back of an upstairs hall closet. Passing the kitchen on her way down to the basement laundry room to collect his socks, Kaat heard Peter talking on the phone. "Where does it leave from?" he was asking. "Is that 'gray' as in the color gray?" He listened for a moment. "How long will I have to wait for the connection in Scranton?"

Half an hour later, Kaat and Millie zippered up Peter's valise and wrestled it downstairs, which was difficult because Millie was so unstable on her heels that she tottered from side to side. The Sleeper (having collected false driver's licenses and Social Security cards, along with a supply of cash, from a hiding place in his attic workshop) sauntered down after them. Kaat noticed that he was carrying his copy of Walt Whitman.

The Sleeper noticed her noticing it. "I'm taking it to read on the train," he explained.

"On the train," Kaat repeated.

"What's wrong with going by train?" the Sleeper asked.

"I love trains," Millie declared. "I love to pee while they're in stations."

"Well," said the Sleeper, at a loss for words.

"Well," Millie ventured. "I guess this is where someone says the thing about parting being such sweet sorrow, or whatever."

"I guess," Kaat agreed.

The Sleeper glanced at Kaat and saw her studying him from the depth of those sunken eyes that always made her look as if she knew more than she said. He would miss Millie's body, he decided, but he would miss Kaat; all of her. It suddenly occurred to him that he didn't even have a picture of Kaat. And he knew from experience that after a week or two he wouldn't be able to remember what she looked like. He never seemed to remember what the women in his life looked like once they were out of sight.

"See you," Millie said, and she reached out and rubbed his crotch playfully.

"Good-bye," Kaat said solemnly.

Millie laughed nervously. "Jesus, you'd think he was going forever."

"I'm sorry," Kaat blurted out, "but I'm only good at arrivals."

The Sleeper came up with the thin, brittle laugh that summed up his attitude toward the business of parting forever from people he liked. He grabbed his valise, and plunging past the plaque indicating that Whitman had once lived here, disappeared from view.

"Hey," Millie said to Kaat with as much enthusiasm as she could muster. "What about that roll in the hay?"

6

The man bolted to a sitting position in the bed. Sweat drenched his undershirt. For a long, terrifying moment he didn't know who he was. Fighting back a pervasive panic, he tried to figure out *where* he was. He could hear the whine of a machine, and he remembered having to summon the night clerk to show him how to work the air conditioning. He was in a hotel, that was it. Slowly he began to reconstruct what he was doing there. He had been in Canada but he had left there. By train. Going south. To New York. Of course! To New York to save someone. Someone he had betrayed. To save his last, his best sleeper!

And then it all came flooding back, like a high tide, until he was awash in damp, chilly memories. He was trying to get to Piotr Borisovich before he could carry out the orders he was certain to receive; to tell him of his betrayal and the death of his father; to free him. The Potter permitted the air to seep from his lungs in relief. He finally knew who he was, and where he was, and what he was doing there.

None of the information was very comforting.

He got out of bed and stumbled through the half-light to the washbasin in the corner of the room. He turned on one tap. A gurgling sound, extraordinarily human, came from it. But no water. He tried the other tap. It coughed several times, then emitted a thin stream of rusty, lukewarm water. The Potter splashed some of it on his face. It tasted stale. He glanced at himself in the tarnished mirror over the basin. He thought of Svetochka, and tried to summon up her face, her voice, a particular mannerism; anything at all. But all he managed was her pubic hair, which was curly and wiry, like steel wool, and the tiny mole on the inside of her right thigh, and the hair under her arms and on her legs. He had failed to memorize the rest of her.

The Potter went over to the window, which was almost opaque from decades of dirt and rain, and studied the street below. A garbage truck was making its slow way down the block. Two garbage men wearing overalls and thick gloves hefted metal garbage cans onto a churning mechanism in the rear of the truck, then sent the empty cans clattering back to the sidewalk like spent projectiles ejected from a cannon. The Potter had arrived in New York after midnight, and had decided to pass what was left of the night in a cheap hotel near the docks below Brooklyn Heights that he remembered from his days as *rezident* in the city. He had been tempted to go directly to the Whitman house, on the theory that the shortest distance between two points was a straight line. But the shortest route wasn't necessarily the safest. For the people who had gotten the Potter to betray the Sleeper, the people who had presumably awakened the Sleeper, might very likely be keeping tabs on him. Having crossed a continent and an ocean, having made his way to within a long stone's throw of the house on Love Apple Lane, the Potter had to tread now as if he were crossing a mine field. For that he needed daylight. He had been so impatient for it to come that he had imagined it, and the light in his mind's eye had kept him from falling asleep. When he finally drifted off, he had woken up without the slightest idea of who he was. Amnesia, of course, was an obvious, even convenient form of flight from reality. Looking out now at the street, the Potter was almost sorry he had reconstructed his identity.

Almost.

Prowling around the room impatiently, the Potter forced himself to wait until the streets of Brooklyn Heights were crowded with people rushing off to work. They seemed to have a reasonable amount of enthusiasm for getting where they were going, but the Potter attributed this to capitalism's ability to buy off the proletariat with the equivalent of an extra wet dream a week. Love Apple Lane, with its neat brownstones and miniature gardens, went off at right angles from Henry Street. If number 145 (the Potter could see the brass plaque glinting near the front door) were staked out, it was not visible to the naked eye. But it wouldn't be. Someone (with a camera fitted with a telephoto lens to record comings and goings) could be watching from behind any one of a dozen curtained windows across the street. To know for sure, the Potter would have to stake out the block, observe the men, and even the women, who came and went, establish a pattern that might give away a change in shifts. But the Potter knew he didn't have a day or two to spare for that. There was an alley lined with private garages behind Love Apple Lane, and he decided it offered the best avenue of approach. Several men in business suits were backing their cars out of garages. Nearby, a teenage boy in blue jeans and a sweatshirt sat cross-legged on the ground pumping up the wheels of his bicycle.

"If you please, how can you tell which one of these houses is number 145?" the Potter asked.

The boy looked up, then went back to his pumping. "You can always go around the front where the numbers are," he said.

"I am allergic to streets," the Potter told him. "I am more comfortable in alleys."

This seemed to amuse the boy, because he smiled up at the Potter. His mouth was metallic with braces. "One-forty-five is the guy with the two girls," he said. "The guy that makes those floating mobiles."

"That is the one," the Potter agreed.

"It's down there," said the boy. He pointed with his chin toward the far end of the alley.

The Potter said, "If I wrote out a note, would you deliver it to the door for me? I would be willing to compensate you."

"Compensate?"

"Pay. Money."

"How much?"

"How would three dollars be?"

The boy stopped pumping abruptly. "Why not?" he said.

The Potter pulled a piece of paper from his pocket, and bracing it against a garage door, scribbled a note. He knew that the Sleeper wouldn't respond to a personal note; he had been trained not to. So he wrote out several lines that the Sleeper would think only the real Potter would know. He folded the note several times, counted out three dollars and handed it to the boy. "Take a good look at me so you can describe me to the man who makes the mobiles," he said. "Tell him the person who gave you this note is waiting for him in the coffee shop in the lobby of the St. George Hotel. You think you can remember all that?"

"The lobby of the St. George Hotel," the boy repeated brightly.

He packed away his pump, climbed on the bicycle and pedaled off toward the end of the alley. Leaning his bike against a fence, he looked back and waved, then disappeared into a garden. The Potter left the alley and headed in the opposite direction from the St. George for several blocks. When he was sure he wasn't being followed, he doubled back on his tracks.

He was working on his third cup of coffee in a corner booth of the coffee shop when the boy appeared outside the door. He was walking his bike because he was with someone—a woman in her thirties, the Potter quickly calculated, though it would have been impossible to say if it was her early thirties or her late thirties. The boy put his face to the window of the coffee shop and spotted the Potter. He turned his back toward him and said something to the woman, who stared over his head at the corner booth. She spoke to the boy, then came around the shop to the door and walked directly up to the booth in which the Potter sat. She opened the note that he had sent over with the boy and read what he had written aloud.

"The lines about the sisters Death and Night—they were favorites of his." She stared at the Potter intently, waiting for him to react. "He even has them underlined."

"In pencil," the Potter added, feeling his way. "We both like very much the poetry of Walter Whitman."

She felt awkward standing there, looking down at him. "Do you mind if I join you?" she asked.

"If you please," the Potter said, motioning her toward the bench. He signaled with his finger for another cup of coffee.

They surveyed each other across the gulf of the unwashed table as the waiter brought the coffee. It was served in a cheap, thick cup. Some of the coffee had spilled onto the cheap, thick saucer. The woman plucked a napkin from a metal dispenser and carefully fitted it into the saucer so that it would soak up the spilled coffee. "Funny," she observed absently, "how people always talk about how you shouldn't cry over spilled milk, but they never think about spilled coffee."

"You should always cry over spilled milk," the Potter told her. "Spilled coffee also, if it seems appropriate."

"Peter called him Walter too," she noted. She nibbled nervously at a fingernail.

"I beg your pardon."

She looked up quickly. "Peter always referred to Whitman as Walter, the way you did a moment ago."

"That was his name, Walter. Walter Whitman."

The woman shook her head. "Everyone calls him Walt. He called himself Walt."

The Potter lifted his shoulders in a vague shrug.

"He's left, you know," the woman said. Her body

was just across the table, but her voice seemed to come from far away. "Forever. He's not coming back."

So he had arrived too late. "Did he tell you that?" the Potter asked, a note of desperation seeping into his tone.

She shook her head once, angrily. "He didn't have to. It was evident. He took his copy of Whitman with him. *Walt* Whitman. It's probably the only thing—the only material thing—he really gave a damn about." She studied the Potter from the depth of her sunken eyes.

"Here's the thing. He talked about a teacher he once had, someone who was tied up to the pier of old age. I never forgot that phrase. He talked about someone who made him think he was on a crusade. He said his teacher was an amateur potter with powerful forearms and hands." She reached across the table and ran the tips of two fingers along the Potter's forearm. Her touch was so light it made him shiver. "He talked once about showing the mosaics of a church to someone, and driving out to the countryside to visit his father with someone. If he told one story, he told a hundred. And I understood, although he never said so specifically, that these weren't different *someones*, but one *someone*. He even described, in great detail, making love to the wife of someone." Her eyes flashed up. "I was a fool to tell you that. Maybe you didn't know it."

The Potter couldn't bring himself to speak.

"My name is Kaat," she said to change the subject. She spelled it for him.

"What kind of name is Kaat?" he asked.

"It's my maiden name," she explained. "I was married once, when I was nineteen. I got divorced a year later. I didn't want to wear the name of a man I didn't live with, didn't love, so I went back to my own name. My first name I detest. So I call myself by my maiden name, Kaat. Everyone else does too." She smiled at a memory. "The first time I told Peter about Kaat being my maiden name, he said something that made me wonder who he really was."

"You wondered who he was?"

"My maiden name reminded him of someone else who went by her maiden name, a woman called Krupskaya. She was Lenin's wife. Nobody called her Nadezhda, which was her first name, or Mrs. Lenin. They called her Krupskaya. But you know all that, don't you?" She smiled across the table at him, and the Potter noticed, for the first time, that she had a way of smiling with her mouth and taking it back with her eyes. "Admit you know who Krupskaya was," she insisted. She pulled the coffee cup closer and tried to see her reflection in the muddy liquid. "There were things—little things—that gave him away."

All those months, those years, of creating a legend; of piling up details, as if they were bricks, until they constituted an impressive building; of training the Sleeper to fit inconspicuously into a society, the Potter thought. And this girl comes along out of nowhere and sees right through him. "What do you mean, gave him away?" he asked, and was astonished to recognize in his own voice a note of professional curiosity. He had thought he was through with all that.

"More coffee?" the waiter called over from the counter. The Potter waved a finger no.

"He never drank coffee," Kaat remembered. "He drank tea, and once, when he thought nobody was around, I caught him straining it through a sugar cube clutched between his teeth. Russians do that, don't they?" She tilted her head and angled up her chin, as if challenging him to contradict her. "Peter was Russian. I bet you are too."

The Potter could either deny it and lose her, or admit it and use her. She knew the Sleeper had left. She knew him well enough to sense that he had left for good. Maybe she knew where he had gone. The Potter drew a deep breath. "His name was Piotr Borisovich Revkin."

"And who are you?"

"I was the teacher. My name is Feliks. Feliks Turov."

Across the table, Kaat pressed her eyes shut, obviously relieved, then opened them and for lack of anything more original to say fell back on the standard formula for meetings, "How do you do?"

"How do you do," the Potter replied, inclining his head formally, and he remembered Piotr Borisovich exploding into laughter during one of their early sessions on the top floor of the military hotel and sputtering: What a curious thing to say when you meet someone—how *do* you *do*?

"Now that you've told me this much," Kaat ventured, "you might as well tell me everything." And she encouraged him with one of those smiles that she took back with her eyes.

And so the Potter, calculating that he had very little to lose, lowered his voice and told her what seemed safe to tell her: about the Sleeper working (as he discreetly put it) for the Soviet government; about how he had learned the Sleeper had been betrayed; about how he had used the false passport and the American money he had stashed away years before to cross Europe and the Atlantic to Canada, and then made his way to New York, to Brooklyn Heights, to Love Apple Lane—to warn the Sleeper, to tell him of the death of his father; to free him.

Kaat, in turn, described the departure of the Sleeper four days earlier. He had received a letter in the morning mail (no, she hadn't noticed the postmark) and announced, in midafternoon, that he was going to visit an old Army friend in Pennsylvania. On her way down to the basement laundry room she had overheard him on the kitchen phone inquiring where something left from, inquiring also how long he would have to wait for a connection in Scranton. "He asked the person on the other end if it was 'gray' as in the color 'gray,' " Kaat remembered. "Later he made a point of saying he was going by train, but I knew he was going by Greyhound." When the Potter looked confused, she added, "Greyhound is the name of a bus company."

"Of course! He went to Scranton by Greyhound. But where did he go after Scranton?"

"I can always ask him where he is when he calls up," Kaat said.

The Potter stared at her. "What makes you think he will call you up, if you please?"

"Here's the thing," Kaat began, flustered. "Peter—how can I explain this?—Peter's not exactly like other men. Sexually, I mean. He's anfractuous." She spotted the puzzled look in the Potter's eyes. "You won't know what 'anfractuous' means. It's one of my A words. It means full of windings and turnings."

"An—"

"—fractuous. When I first met Peter—I lived in an apartment farther down Love Apple Lane, and my cat, whose name is Meow, escaped into his backyard—he was living with Millie. We hit it off, the three of us, and they eventually invited me to join them."

"The boy with the bicycle said there were two women living with Piotr."

Kaat nodded. "Everybody on the block knows about us. We're something of a vicious triangle. She likes me, I like him and he likes—liked—her."

"You said something about him phoning."

"I was getting to that," insisted Kaat. "One of Peter's sexual windings and turnings is that when he's away from home, he makes love to other women. And he likes to phone us up and describe it while he's doing it. Sometimes he even puts the woman on and makes her describe it."

The Potter recalled the Sleeper's sexual habits from Moscow, remembered analyzing his fetish of phoning up previous bed partners while making love to someone else as his way of throwing little hooks into the past; remembered also concluding that the Sleeper's strength was that he knew his weaknesses. "You like this sort of thing?" he asked Kaat now.

Her eyebrows shot up. "Of course I do. Doesn't everyone?"

He avoided the issue. "You think he will call up from Pennsylvania while he is having sex with someone?"

"He has every time he went away before," Kaat pointed out. "He was in Denver last February to show his mobiles and called up three times."

Kaat studied the Potter with her deep-set eyes. "When he phones up," she explained to the Potter excitedly, "I can tell him that you're here, that you want to see him—"

The Potter shook his head. "He will not believe you," he said flatly. "He has been trained *not* to believe you. He has been trained to disregard all contact that appears to originate with friends. He will think the Americans put you up to it. He will suspect the call is being traced and hang up on you. He will never call back again."

"What can I tell him, then?" Kaat asked in despair, chewing again on a fingernail.

"You cannot tell him anything," the Potter instructed her. "You can only listen to what he says and try to figure out where he is. And then let me know."

The Potter glanced at the coffee-shop window and saw that the boy with the bicycle was still there, staring at them through the glass. "What does he want?" he asked Kaat.

"I wasn't sure what I'd find when I got here," she explained, "so I asked him to hang around just in case I needed someone to scream for help." She waved to the boy, who waved back and leaping onto his bicycle, pedaled off.

"Assuming we do find out where Peter is," Kaat concluded thoughtfully, "the trouble is, he may no longer be there by the time we arrive. Pennsylvania is a big state, you know," she added gloomily.

"What do you mean, 'when *we* arrive'?"

"I'm going with you," Kaat announced.

The Potter waved a hand in frustration. "That is out of the question," he declared.

Kaat squinted at him across the table. "Then when I find out where he is, I'll go without you!"

"Why do you want to go?" the Potter demanded in exasperation.

"I have nothing to stay here for now," Kaat fired back. For her the couple (or "triple," as Millie liked to call it) was essentially a conspiracy; an "us" against a "them"; something to help her survive endings, which were invariably unhappy. She sensed that she had lost Peter forever. What was more normal than to be drawn to a new mystery, a new conspiracy? She stared at the Potter for a long moment. Then he lowered his eyes. "So that's settled," Kaat said. Before he could argue, she added, "I've had an anacalypsis. That means 'revelation,' as in 'brilliant idea.' Peter's obviously somewhere around Scranton. Why don't we rent a car and drive to Scranton? Millie can hold the fort on Love Apple Lane and record the conversation if Peter phones up. Millie's a model, you see. She has one of those tape machines hooked up to the phone so she won't miss a booking. We can call her up from Scranton and get her to play the conversation back to us. That way, Feliks—you don't mind if I call you Feliks, do you?—there'll be less time between his phone call and our arrival; there'll be more of a chance of still finding him there." She noticed the expression on his face. "Don't worry," she whispered. "I'm not a political person—I have no ideological ax to grind." She raised her right hand as if she were taking an oath. "I promise to be a noiseless patient spider seeking spheres to connect." And she added, "That's another line from your *Walter* Whitman."

The Potter had to admit that Kaat's scheme was as good as any he could devise. And traveling with the girl, unorthodox as it seemed, offered certain advantages, from a professional point of view. For one thing, he would be less likely to stand out in a crowd. He could use her to rent cars and buy train tickets and reserve hotel rooms, thus exposing himself less. More important, she would be the one to call the Sleeper's number in Brooklyn Heights, a fact that would arouse less suspicion if, as he suspected, the phone were being tapped by the people who had awakened the Sleeper.

"I accept your proposition with pleasure," the Potter announced with irritating politeness.

"You are bowing to the inevitable," she noted, "but you are bowing gracefully. And gracefulness, in my book, is next to cleanliness. And everyone knows what cleanliness is next to." She reached across the table for his hand. The Potter was familiar with the American habit of shaking hands to conclude a deal, and he offered his. But she didn't want to shake hands; she wanted to study his fingernails. She brought his hand across the table and leaned over it. "Do you believe in reincarnation?" she asked. She didn't wait for him to reply; somehow she knew what he would say. Like Peter, he had the look of someone rooted in reality. "I do," she insisted. "I've had four lives already that I remember. This is my fifth." She studied his fingernails, touched one as if she were testing its texture, then turned his hand over and peered at his palm. "You've had at least two previous incarnations," she said. "You were a victim in both—that much any idiot can see."

"That," the Potter told her with undisguised sarcasm, "should give me a certain amount of training for my present incarnation."

7

The Potter lingered in the shadows of the warehouse across the street from the pier waiting for Kaat to pass. She was driving one of those ridiculous American automobiles with shark's fins rising in the back and chrome everywhere. When she failed to find him, she followed his instructions and circled the block. He let her come around three more times to make sure she was not being followed—or hadn't betrayed him!—before he stepped out under the streetlight and flagged her down.

"I was beginning to think you'd never turn up," she groaned as the Potter tossed his valise into the back and slid into the passenger seat. She sounded winded, as if she had been running; tired, as if she hadn't had a good night's sleep for some time.

A cat, rolling its R's in a mixture of pain and frustration, howled in the back seat.

"What is that?" the Potter asked, startled.

"That," announced Kaat, throwing the car into gear, "is my cat. She is in heat—"

"What does that mean, in heat?"

Kaat looked quickly at the Potter. "It means she's having her period. She wants a male of the species, is what it means. She howls for days when she's in heat. Millie refused to keep her, but I don't hold it against her. Millie is basically a dog person. I don't mind dogs personally as long as they have the sense of independence of a cat. The female of the species is especially independent. Having a female cat has advantages and disadvantages, but males are impossible unless you fix them, and that's one thing I could never bring myself to do. I mean, can you imagine the *guilt* you must feel living with an anorchous cat—"

"That must be one of your A words," the Potter noted.

Kaat maneuvered the rented Chevrolet onto the ramp leading to the Brooklyn Bridge and Manhattan. "You catch on fast," she said. "It means without testicles."

"You are talking a great deal," the Potter said in a voice so utterly calm that Kaat found it irritating.

"That is because I am appropriately nervous," Kaat admitted. "My mouth is dry. My pulse is racing. I am suppressing the desire to scream. All that business about going to the other end of Brooklyn to rent a car, of circling the block until I found you. You will have to understand that this is the first genuine nonsexual adventure of my life, and I am taking it very seriously."

The Potter studied her out of the corner of his eye as she steered the car through evening traffic, across Manhattan toward the Holland Tunnel. She gripped the wheel with both hands, which he noticed now were long and exceptionally pale, with a ring on every finger except her thumb. Several of the nails were bitten down to the quick. It occurred to the Potter that she drove well, working the clutch and the gearshift effortlessly, weaving in and out of lanes, leaning on the horn in exasperation when the car in front went too slowly for her, all the while keeping up a steady stream of conversation. "I studied art," she was saying, "because I was convinced I'd been a painter of still lifes in one of my four previous incarnations. I actually went to Florence for a year to learn how to restore still lifes. Did you know that it's easier to restore very old paintings than relatively new ones? That's because it takes a hundred years before paint is really dry on a canvas." Kaat sighed. "There's a certain symmetry to my life, I have to admit it. I began with still lifes and wound up with still lives," she plunged on, casting an occasional sideways glance at the Potter to make sure he was paying attention. "I started restoring paintings for a living and wound up restoring corpses."

The Potter, who had had a good deal of experience with death in his day, asked how she felt in the presence of death.

"Here's the thing," she answered as the cat leapt with a sour howl onto the back of the driver's seat and stretched out behind Kaat's neck. "Since I believe the spirit of the dead person is merely in a limbo between two incarnations," Kaat continued, arching her neck against the cat, "I guess I don't feel sad, if that's what you mean. How about you? How do you feel in the presence of death?"

The Potter turned away to stare out of the side window. "It has been my experience," he observed with a certain melancholy, "that being in the presence of night, of death, loosens one's bowels, dulls one's appetites, dampens one's enthusiasm, since it demonstrates in an unforgettable way how that fragile thing called life will inevitably end."

Kaat shook her head vigorously. "When all is said and done, we haven't got much in common, you and I," she told him. Ahead, the streets were crammed with cars and trucks approaching the Holland Tunnel tollbooths. She shrugged fatalistically. "I suppose we are antiscians. That refers to people who live on the same meridian, but on either side of the equator, which means that at high noon their shadows fall in opposite directions."

The Potter nodded in agreement. "We come from different planets," he said. "When you were in school, your mother gave you a sandwich and sent you off on a bus."

"Something like that," Kaat agreed.

"My mother gave me an ear of corn. A plowhorse came by to take us to school. There was nobody to help us climb up on him. So we would drop the ear of corn on the ground, and when he lowered his head we would grab his ears and shinny up his neck. I remember that there were seven of us crammed onto the back of the horse by the time he got to school. And we considered it luxurious not to have to walk, because the roads were a sea of mud."

Kaat rolled down her window, paid the toll and maneuvered the Chevrolet into the lane of traffic that seemed to be going through the tunnel the fastest. The Potter sank deeper into his seat. He disliked tunnels passionately; it wasn't so much that he felt trapped in them as physically squeezed by them. During the Great Patriotic War, he had spent several weeks hiding in an abandoned mine while Waffen SS squads combed the countryside, shooting partisans and Communists on sight. In the night, when the wind was right, he had been able to hear the shots reverberating through the valley.

From some backwater of his mind, he dredged up memories. "It was during the war," he said out loud, though he wasn't sure why he wanted to tell her this, "that one of my comrades, a university professor, took to referring to me as the ascian. How is that for an A word?"

"Ascian." Kaat tried it out. "It has a very soothing sound. What does it mean?"

"It refers," the Potter told her, "to someone who doesn't cast a shadow at all in sunlight."

Kaat looked at him curiously. "And you don't cast a shadow in sunlight?" she asked sharply.

"In those days I didn't. I don't know about now."

They talked about more down-to-earth matters after that. The Potter directed Kaat into a labyrinth of narrow back streets on the Jersey side of the river north of the tunnel. It was an area he had come to know during his tenure as *rezident* in New York.

If Kaat was curious how the Potter came by his experience—"Left at the next corner, left again, right at that warehouse"—she never let on. Following his instructions, she eventually brought the Chevrolet to a stop in a deserted alleyway down the block from an all-night bar with a broken neon sign sizzling over its door. When she cut the motor she could hear the faint sound of a tide lapping against pilings, and make out the outline of several freighters tied to piers beyond a chain-link fence at the end of the block.

"You will wait for me here," the Potter instructed her.

"You actually expect me *not* to go with you?" She shivered at the idea of remaining alone in the car.

She must have transmitted her alarm to the cat, because it began emitting that throaty howl again.

"Can't you keep the animal quiet?" the Potter demanded.

"No," Kaat said flatly. "What do I do if you don't come back?"

"If I am not back in, say, twenty minutes, go home and forget you ever met me."

The cat perked up behind Kaat's neck. Kaat seemed to perk up too. "Go home, he says," she told the cat. "What home? I have no home; I have only a former home. Even if I had a home to go home to, how in God's name would I find my way out of this maze? What are we doing here anyway, if you don't mind my asking?"

The Potter rummaged in his valise for something, found what he was looking for and slipped it into his jacket pocket. "I used up all the money I had getting myself to New York," he told her. "I need more. There used to be people here who bought things of value without asking questions."

"You could have asked me if you needed money."

"I need other things too."

"Like what?"

"I need bullets. Also a gun to put them in."

"Why do you need a gun?"

"I need a gun," the Potter explained patiently, "because I am beginning to be frightened. I will tell you something you will probably find amusing. If I had to do it all over again, I wouldn't." He opened the door. "Lock this after me. Keep the cat quiet if you can." He laughed under his breath. "If anything happens to me, perhaps we will meet in another incarnation."

Kaat grabbed his sleeve. "Here's the thing: you're frightened. Fear is contagious. I've caught it. Me also, if I had it to do over again, I wouldn't."

They exchanged gentle, conspiratorial smiles. "That," the Potter told her quietly, "may be the first sensible thing I have heard you say."

At the end of the alley the Potter turned, and for an instant Kaat thought he was going to wave, but he only shook his head in confusion and continued on toward the all-night bar.

The bartender was the only one who looked up when the Potter came through the door, though the dozen or so men scattered around the booths appeared to suspend all conversation. The Potter hefted himself onto a stool and eyed the collection of baseball bats in an umbrella stand near the cash register. The bartender, a heavyset, balding man in his forties who looked as if he might have once been a baseball player, eyed the Potter suspiciously.

"Why are you looking at me like that?" the Potter finally asked.

"Well, now, someone who didn't know better might say I was sizing you up," the bartender replied.

A sailor in one of the booths snickered.

"I would like a drink, if you please," the Potter ventured.

"You have definitely come to the right place," the bartender said. "Don't tell me what you want—let me guess." He squinted at the Potter, screwed up his beefy lips, rubbed a forefinger along the side of his bulbous nose. "Vodka!" he exploded. "Bison vodka when you can get it. Am I right or am I right?"

"How do you do it?" the Potter asked.

The bartender leaned across the counter toward the Potter until their faces were inches apart. "No offense intended, but you talk with some kind of foreign-type accent, so I figured you must be off the Polak ship three piers down. And any idiot knows that Polaks drink vodka. Good vodka when they can get their mitts on it. Any vodka when they can't." He laughed at his own joke.

"A glass of Bison vodka would certainly be welcome," the Potter acknowledged.

The bartender leaned back. "Don't have Bison vodka," he said. "But I can give you a shot of good old New Jersey vodka."

"I never heard of New Jersey vodka," the Potter admitted.

"That don't surprise me none," said the bartender. "New Jersey vodka is what's left over when they finish refining petroleum." Several of the sailors in the booths laughed out loud at that. Smiling maliciously, the bartender poured out a shot glass full and set it before the Potter.

The Potter raised the glass to his nose and sniffed the contents. It smelled vaguely like glue. Then he brought it to his lips and drank a small quantity. It seared the back of his throat. He gasped. The bartender slapped the bar in pleasure. "Moonshine," he explained when he stopped laughing. "Good old hundred-proof New Jersey moonshine."

At the booths the sailors resumed their conversations. Nodding toward the moonshine, the bartender said, "No harm intended."

"No harm done," the Potter said amiably. "Listen, I have been here before. To this bar. Years ago."

The bartender's attitude changed. His eyes appeared to cloud over. "You don't say," he muttered guardedly.

"I do say. There used to be a narrow staircase back there that smelled of urine. It led to a corridor that also smelled of urine. At the end of the corridor was a room in which men played cards for big stakes. They were usually Italians, though there was an occasional Jew. The Italians all wore diamond cufflinks, I remember."

"You have a very good memory," the bartender conceded grudgingly. "Be careful it don't get you in no trouble."

"I also remember that there was a button under the bar that you pushed when someone started up the back stairs."

"Say, you really are one smart cookie. What ship did you say you were off?"

"I didn't say," the Potter said. "Why don't you reach under the counter and ring the bell now." With that, he slipped off his stool and headed toward the back of the bar and the staircase. It still smelled of urine. Ahead, the Potter thought he could make out the distant sound of a buzzer. The upstairs corridor had been painted recently, and the smell of paint overpowered the smell of urine that had almost asphyxiated him the last time he had come through it; he had been in the market for a rifle equipped with a new U.S. Army night sight at the time. The door at the end of the corridor had been fitted with a peephole. The Potter knocked politely and then stared up into the peephole so that whoever was on the other side could get a good look at him.

Eventually a bolt was thrown, then a second one. The Potter tried the knob. The door clicked open. He entered the room. There were five men seated around a glass-covered table, with colored chips and cards scattered around it. All of them were in their shirtsleeves. Four of the five wore diamond cufflinks. Another man, with his jacket on, sat on a windowsill. Still another, wearing a raincoat, lounged with his back to a wall. The Potter closed the door and stepped boldly into the room. The man lounging against the wall shifted position so that his back was pressed to the door.

"Do you have a name?" This from the man without diamond cufflinks.

"I have an occupation," the Potter announced. "I am a seller."

"A traveling salesman has found his way to our door," quipped the man on the windowsill.

One of the Italians peered up at the Potter through thick eyeglasses with gold rims. "We have met maybe before," he suggested.

"It is possible," the Potter agreed, although he couldn't place the face.

"And what treasure is it you are selling?" the same Italian inquired with infinite politeness.

The Potter reached into his jacket pocket and took out a package wrapped in an old kerchief. He undid the rubber bands that bound it and removed the cloth. Then he stepped forward and deposited two engraved plates on the table.

The player without diamond cufflinks whistled through his front teeth. "Twenty-dollar plates!"

He passed the plates to one of the Italians, who held them up to the light and studied them. He must have been something of an expert, because the others seemed to be waiting for his verdict. "The engraving is first class," he finally announced. "Where did he get these?"

"Where," the Italian without diamond cufflinks repeated the question, "did you get these?"

"How I came by them does not concern you," the Potter replied evenly. (The man lounging against the door straightened up, but one of the Italians shook his head imperceptibly, and the man relaxed again.) "They are of German origin," the Potter went on. "They were made by the same artist who engraved the Third Reich's deutsche-mark plates. The original intention was to print up a supply of funds for German agents working out of Mexico during the war. But the Russians reached Berlin before the plates could be put to use."

"And wound up in your hands," said the Italian who thought he recognized the Potter. "Which means that your accent must be Russian."

One of the players studying the plates whispered, "These are worth a fortune."

"What if we are not buyers?" another Italian said. "What if we are takers?"

"If you are takers," the Potter pointed out, "it follows that you will have to spend a certain amount of money to dispose of a body. The sum of money I want from you is so modest that it will be cheaper for you to pay me than to kill me."

The man lounging on the windowsill grunted. "Maybe we won't see the situation the way you see it," he warned.

"I am betting that you will."

"You are betting your life on it," suggested the Italian holding the plates. He looked up. "How much is modest in your book?"

The Potter took a deep breath. "I require five thousand dollars in small bills," he said. "I also require a handgun. Any one will do as long as it is in working condition."

"He needs five thousand dollars," the man without diamond cufflinks repeated with a laugh. "He needs a handgun. So what else does he need?"

The Potter remained silent.

"A guy with an accent waltzes in off the street—how do we know this is not a setup?" the man lounging against the door demanded.

"You will never in your life get another opportunity to come into possession of plates of this quality," the Potter said. "You are all gamblers, aren't you?"

The man without diamond cufflinks scraped back his chair, walked over to a buffet and picked up the telephone. "Charlie, do me a favor, huh," he said into the receiver. "Duck outside and take a good long look around. Then come back and let me know what you see."

The Potter retreated to a wall. The men at the table passed the plates around and talked Italian in undertones. After a while the telephone sounded. The man lounging on the windowsill sauntered over and picked up the receiver. He listened for a long moment. "Okay," he said, and hung up. "There's a Chevy parked in the alleyway. There's a girl and a pussycat in it. The doors are locked. The girl refused to open. Nothing else is in sight."

The men around the table exchanged looks. "Well," said the man without cufflinks, "do we buy from him, or do we bury him?"

The man with the gold-rim glasses burst into guttural laughter. "For five thousand dollars, we can't go wrong." He gestured to the man on his right. "Pay him, Frankie. Eugene, remove the bullets from your gun and give it to him."

Eugene didn't like the idea of parting with his pistol; it was an Italian Beretta, .22-caliber, that he had won in a crap game the previous year, and he had become attached to it. "Why does it have to be my gun?" he whined.

The Italian who held the plates looked up sharply. Eugene puffed up his cheeks and let out the air in an annoyed burst. Then he removed the clip from his Beretta and thumbed the bullets out of it into his palm before reinserting the empty clip back into the pistol.

The Italian who thought he recognized the Potter was staring at him curiously. Suddenly his face brightened. "I know where I seen you before," he said. "It was here, in this room. Seven, maybe eight years ago. You were a buyer then, not a seller. How the mighty have fallen."

Pocketing the money and the pistol, the Potter turned toward the door. Eugene still blocked his way, and seemed in no mood to move.

"He is a Russian secret agent," the man who recognized the Potter announced to the others.

"Get out of my way," the Potter ordered Eugene in a low voice that he hoped was full of menace.

"Maybe you think you can make me," Eugene shot

back, caressing the knuckles of one hand with the palm of the other.

"Leave him leave," the man who had identified the Potter ordered.

Eugene reluctantly stepped to one side. With a last look over his shoulder, the Potter left the room. He fled along the corridor, down the staircase through the bar—the bartender was nowhere in sight—into the street. The neon sizzled over his head like the rattle of a snake. The night air sent a chill through the Potter, and he realized he had been sweating profusely—from fear, probably, though he hadn't been aware of it at the time. Fear to him implied that there was hope. This was an illusion he didn't harbor.

He ducked into the alleyway and saw the Chevy and waved to Kaat. She waved back, though her waving had an agitated aspect to it, and then the Potter realized she wasn't waving, but pointing, and he turned back to see the hulking figure of the bartender advancing toward him in a shuffling step used by wrestlers when they stalk an opponent. He was gripping one of those American baseball bats in both hands, and thrashing it about in front of him with short snaps of his thick wrists. "What I am going to break first is your ankles," he called in an excited voice. "Then I am going to break your kneecaps. Then your rib cage. Then your wrists. Then your neck. Then your skull." He laughed hysterically, shuffling forward all the while. "You were wrong about how much it costs to bury someone. I work cut-rate. A package deal is what I offer. The body, buried, for twenty-five hundred dollars. Niggers, foreigners, I do for the fun of it."

The Potter backed away until he was up against the front grille of the Chevrolet. Swinging the baseball bat, grinning into the darkness, the bartender closed in on him. A loss of nerve hit the Potter—it manifested itself as a sudden weakness in his knees, a ringing in his ears. It was not only a question of the violence that would be done to him, but to the girl in the car behind him:

having disposed of the Potter, the bartender would then feel obliged to attend to the eyewitness. The bartender was so close now that the Potter imagined that he could feel the rush of air that preceded the swishing bat. The Potter knew he had to move, to do *something*, but for the life of him he couldn't see what he could do. The bartender was too big, too methodical. And then Kaat, behind the wheel of the Chevrolet, switched on the car's high beams and leaned on the horn. Startled, blinded, the bartender jerked an arm up in front of his eyes. The Potter stepped forward and kicked him sharply in the crotch. The big man groaned and doubled over. The bat clattered to the pavement. The Potter moved around behind the kneeling figure, took a grip on his thick neck and began to squeeze. Gasping, the bartender tried to pry the Potter's fingers loose, but the years of kneading clay had strengthened them into a vise. After a while the bartender went limp in the Potter's oustretched arms. He let the corpse slip to the ground. Kaat flicked off the high beams, and the Potter could see her peering out at him from the window of the Chevrolet. Violence is in my blood, he wanted to tell her, but the pale mask of a face that stared back at him seemed to say that that was something she knew already.

8

Khanda arrived in the designated city at the end of the first week of October, and using the alias O. Lee settled into a one-story rooming house in a run-down section of town. One block away, past a yellow-brick self-service laundry and a pharmacy with a parking lot next to it full of pickup trucks, he could make out the center of the city rising from the flat like a wart. He had bought a street map of the city and had traced the two possible routes from the airport to the luncheon site, one in blue, one in red. In the days that followed, he went over the routes again and again, and eventually compiled a list of buildings from which he could get a shot at the target no matter which of the two routes was finally selected. Several of the possibilities he ruled out because of the nature of the business conducted in them; he stood precious little chance of getting a job in a bank, or an insurance company, for instance. Eventually he narrowed the possibilities down to two buildings. On the thirteenth, he put on a tie and jacket and presented himself at the employment office of a lumber company whose top floors dominated the route between the airport and the city proper. He was interviewed by a wispy woman with a harelip who became suspicious at his failure to produce references from previous jobs. His application was turned down.

On the fifteenth of the month he made an application for work in his second choice, a rust-colored brick warehouse on the corner of Houston and Elm that dominated a roughly diamond-shaped plaza through which the target would have to pass on his way to the luncheon. The building had been constructed at the turn of the century as railroad offices, had been turned into a branch office of a plow company, and only recently been converted into a warehouse. Khanda, again wearing a tie and jacket, sensed that he was making a good impression on the woman who interviewed him this time. He explained away his lack of references by saying that he had attempted free-lance journalism since his discharge from the Marines. The interviewer asked when he could start, assuming his application for employment was accepted. Khanda flashed a boyish smile and replied eagerly, "First thing tomorrow morning." The interviewer smiled back. And Khanda knew he had the job.

9

❦

Thursday spotted the item in the New York *Daily News*, to which he subscribed at office expense so he could follow the comic strips. A minor-league left-fielder who had made it up to the majors for three months and four days almost two decades before had been found murdered near the New Jersey docks. "It's the *way* he was killed," Thursday told the Sisters when he showed them the item.

Francis, who was wearing a new orange polka-dot bow tie that seemed almost fluorescent, screwed up his nose in disgust. "I abhor physical violence," he observed. He handed the newspaper, with the item circled in red, across to Carroll, who was spitting a piece of caramel laced with pistachio into his palm. Carroll read the article casually. Then his brow furrowed, and he read the article a second time. "You don't think it's him?" he asked Thursday, staring at a point on the wall over his right shoulder.

"During the war," Thursday recounted in that smug way he had of offering up footnotes to history, "he left a trail of strangled German corpses. The British claimed there were eight. The Germans—our Germans—listed eleven in his dossier. Then there was the little matter"—here Thursday capped a giggle before it could leak to the surface—"of the man who was strangled in the airport just about the time our friend the Potter enplaned for the Free World."

Francis waved a hand vaguely, as if he were trying to discourage a fly from touching down near him. His wrist was limp, a sure sign that he was not convinced.

Thursday seemed offended. "I took the initiative of phoning a lieutenant in homicide whom I had some dealings with, the one who was assisting us in our inquiries, as the British like to say, when we tried to make the suicide of the Bulgarian diplomat's wife look like murder in order to hook the diplomat. Anyway, my source says that the late left-fielder worked as a bartender in a watering hole frequented by members of the Mafia; that the man who killed him had been dealing with the very same mafiosi; that one of them, known to the imaginative New York City Police Department as Luigi the Lean, recognized him as a Russian who had been around years before trying to purchase a rifle with a U.S. Army night sight on it. Luigi also told my source that the Russian's car was parked in a nearby alleyway, exactly where the body of the late left-fielder was eventually discovered; that the car had two passengers, a young woman and a pussycat."

Carroll astonished everyone in the room by *whinnying*. "It's the Potter, all right," he concluded.

"How on earth did he get from that hotel room in Vienna to the docks of New Jersey?" Francis wanted to know.

"The Potter has always been a resourceful man," Carroll pointed out. He turned on Thursday with such ferocity that the poor man had the urge to duck. "Did you body-search him when he arrived in Vienna?" Carroll demanded. "Did you at least go through his belongings?"

Thursday grimaced. "I assumed our German friends would tend to routine matters like that," he replied lamely.

"You *assumed*," Carroll sneered.

Francis said stoically, "A man like the Potter would have squirreled away a supply of Western currency, spare passports, a kilo or two of cocaine even, for that proverbial rainy day."

"That's probably what he was doing down at the docks," Carroll concluded. "Trading in his cocaine for greenbacks."

"And the late left-fielder made the mistake of trying to increase his employers' profits," Francis guessed.

Thursday eyed Carroll's box of candies; considering that he had been the one to spot the crucial item in the newspaper, he thought that Carroll might break with tradition and offer him one. But Carroll had other things on his mind. "You can slink back to your cubbyhole," he instructed Thursday. "We'll whistle when we need you."

As soon as the door closed behind their man Friday, Francis said to Carroll, "What do you think?"

"What I think . . ." he began, and then, motioning with his head toward a wall, he reached for pencil and paper. "What I think," he scribbled on a legal pad, "is that he came to warn the Sleeper and found him gone."

"What if," Francis wrote, "he tracks the Sleeper down?"

"The only people in the world," Carroll wrote, "who know where the Sleeper is going, and what route he is taking, are in this room. How could he track him down?"

"How could he get from Vienna to New York?" Francis wrote in turn—and Carroll could almost *hear* his exasperation. "He is a resourceful man, you said it yourself," Francis wrote. "What if the Sleeper told someone where he was going? What if he left footprints?"

Carroll shook his head. "The Sleeper's not one of those who leaves traces everywhere he crawls—like a snail does when it crosses a leaf. You are jumping at shadows," Carroll concluded.

Francis took the pencil, hesitated, then bent his head and wrote, "You are sure?"

Carroll, staring at the wall over Francis' shoulder, nodded. "I'm sure," he said out loud.

Francis waved a hand vaguely. Once again his wrist was limp; once again he was not convinced. He began collecting the leaves of yellow paper with the intention of shredding them before he left the office.

Carroll turned his attention back to the box of candy. "Damned pistachios will be the death of me," he muttered under his breath as he fumbled with the tinfoil of another candy.

10

❦

It was not Francis' usual night to take in a film, but a nagging doubt lurking like a migraine behind his forehead persuaded him he ought to. Francis liked neat packages. The Potter turning up in America represented a complication. People had to be notified. Contingency plans had to be drawn. Precautions had to be taken.

Later, Francis wouldn't even remember what film he had seen that night, so deep was his absorption with the problem at hand. He stared at the screen in the filtered darkness without registering the images. He listened to the dialogue without making any sense of the words. When the final freeze frame faded and the houselights came up, he had more or less put everything into perspective. He reached into his pocket for the cigarette he ritually smoked at the end of a film. He used the single match left in the book to light it and discarded the empty matchbook under his seat. The sweepers could clean up after him, he reassured himself. Taking a deep, distasteful drag (how he longed to give up smoking entirely), he casually sauntered (Francis prided himself on his ability to saunter; he thought of it as a dying art) up the center aisle toward the exit.

11

Killers, the Potter liked to tell his student sleepers when he was initiating them into the theory and practice of espionage, almost always came in twos. Which was another way of saying that if someone was worth killing, he (or—why not?—she) was worth killing well. If one assassin failed, so the conventional wisdom went, the second might be able to profit from the confusion caused by the first attempt and carry out the assignment. The classical example of this, of course, was the assassination of Czar Alexander II in 1881. The first bomb thrower managed to wound some guards and horses. When Alexander made the mistake of stepping out of the carriage to survey the damage, the second bomber nailed him.

Both the Soviet and the American espionage services tended to have their killers work in tandem. Two of the best in the business, known in professional circles as the Canadians because of their nationality, were vacationing in Ottawa after successfully carrying out an assignment from the Romanian counterespionage service to "neutralize" a Romanian exile. The man in question had published details of the sexual dalliances of members of Bucharest's ruling circle. Marriages had broken up. Careers had been ruined. The Canadians had been contacted. They had gone to London, tracked their victim until they had become familiar with his routines, then dispatched him at high noon in Piccadilly

Circus by jabbing him in the groin with the poisoned tip of an umbrella as he waited impatiently for a bus.

The Canadians had completed three assignments since the first of the year and complained openly of "metal fatigue," but their Merchant, thinking they were referring to the aluminum castings of their gyrojet pistols, promised to supply new ones. Left with no choice, the Canadians, posing as homosexuals, made their way to Niagara Falls, wandered arm in arm across the border as if they had nothing more on their minds than sightseeing, picked up the new gyrojet pistols, false identifications, a supply of cash and two valises full of clothing at a safe house in Buffalo, then rented a black Dodge and headed southeast toward Lancaster, Pennsylvania.

The Canadian who wore a tiny woman's watch on his wrist and traveled under the name of Ourcq did most of the driving. He was in his middle forties, balding, bloated, effeminate, with the beginnings of a paunch that no amount of Canadian Air Force exercises could get rid of. The other Canadian, a rail-thin man with wavy hair who was using the name Appleyard, passed the time working on a crossword-puzzle paperback. He had spent several years as a soundman on radio soap operas, and could imitate almost anything. Whenever he was stumped over a word, he would purse his lips, fill his cheeks with air, produce a scrap of tinfoil or sandwich wrap, bring a palm up to his lips, stare off at some middle distance—and come out with noises: horses' hooves, a door opening, a kettle boiling, the whine of a jet engine starting up, static on a radio, fire in a chimney. He claimed he could do snow falling, smoke rising, the sun setting, the sound of someone dying; the last two, he said, were indistinguishable from each other. He was imitating a train pulling into a station when Ourcq glanced at him and said, "What the fuck's the name of the fucking place in Lancaster again?"

Appleyard reached into the inside pocket of his jacket for the itinerary they had picked up at the Buffalo safe house. "It's called 'Seventh Heaven,' " he replied presently, and puckering his lips, he produced a perfect imitation of surf lapping against a shore.

After a while Ourcq shook his head in despair. "It's a shit assignment," he decided. His brow wrinkled up in disgust. "Asking us to be fucking sweepers! There are fucking professional sweepers for fucking sweeping."

"Maybe the professional sweepers were off killing, so they sent the professional killers to sweep."

Ourcq was not amused. "What if the fucker who is following the other fucker isn't following the other fucker after all?" he moaned. "Then we come all this fucking way for nothing."

"Maybe he's not as much of a dwarf as they say he is and we won't recognize him," Appleyard added. "Maybe he is not accompanied by a woman with a pussycat."

"Me, I don't see why they couldn't let the fucker who is the fucker who's being followed take care of the fucker who is doing the following," Ourcq insisted.

Appleyard, who sometimes had trouble following Ourcq's sentence structure, clucked his tongue to imitate the sound of tumblers falling in a combination lock. "Maybe," he offered, "they didn't want the follower and the followee to meet."

"It is no fucking way," Ourcq muttered, "to run a fucking cold war."

Appleyard nodded in vague agreement and went back to his crossword puzzle.

12

The walls, it seems, did have ears.

"I'm just thinking out loud," Francis' voice came from the tape. "What if . . ."

"You bastard," Carroll spat at the interrogator without ever looking him in the eye. He brought several fingers to his cheek to deal with his twitching muscle, and arched his neck to take the pressure off the welt under his starched collar.

"What if *what*?" Carroll's voice on the tape prompted impatiently.

"What if we were to put our man Friday onto someone with Mafia connections?" Francis said on the tape recording.

The interrogator, whose name tag identified him as G. Sprowls, depressed the Stop button on the tape recorder. He had a conspiratorial half-smile installed on his otherwise impassive face—a half-smile which looked as if it had been recently taken from a deep freeze and not yet defrosted. "Now, why," G. Sprowls inquired gently, trying as usual to imply that there was some sort of complicity between the questioner and the person he was questioning, "was Francis suggesting that your man Friday contact the Mafia?"

"In the course of any given day," Carroll replied loftily, "we throw around dozens of ideas. That's what we are paid to do, in case you don't know it. We think up angles, avenues of approach—"

"I am fully aware of what you are paid to do," G. Sprowls said. The half-smile glistened on his lips like dew on a petal. "But you haven't answered my question, have you? Why the Mafia?"

"I don't remember," Carroll maintained, a muscle twitching quietly in his cheek. He longed to plunge his hand into a box of candy, but decided the interrogator would interpret it as a sign of weakness if he asked for one. "We'd have to go over any jottings Francis or I made to see what we were onto at that moment."

"Francis shreds the notes at the end of each workday," the interrogator reminded Carroll. He smiled pleasantly. "You've already told me that." He depressed the Fast Forward button until the tape reached number one-forty-eight, then put it on Play again. "What we will need"—it was Francis' voice again—"is someone who can carry out an assignment without knowing it came from us."

G. Sprowls pushed the Stop button. "Exactly what assignment were you talking about?"

The interrogation of the Sisters was in its fourth day. It began at the end of the first week of November on the express order of a very nervous Director of the Central Intelligence Agency when Thursday's indiscretions on the Man Friday network filtered up to the Athenaeum. G. Sprowls, the Company's utility infielder who specialized in tying up loose ends, was summoned back from Mexico where he was finishing the interrogation of a junior code clerk who seemed to have an endless string of mistresses. (G. Sprowls's tentative conclusion was that the code clerk was nothing more sinister than an accomplished lover.) The first thing G. Sprowls did on arriving in Washington was to isolate the Sisters; they were installed in separate but equal apartments in a safe house in Wilmington, Delaware, and brought out, one at a time, into the Grill Room, as G. Sprowls liked to call it, for their daily four-hour sessions.

Another, less experienced interrogator might have

started the ball rolling by hooking each of the Sisters up to a lie-detector machine and then confronting them with the discrepancies between their version of events, contained in the Sisters' formal Op Proposal updater, and Thursday's version, passed on to the Deputy Director's man Friday over a pool table. But G. Sprowls knew the discrepancies were too vague, too undefined, to get a handle on. Did Thursday really skim off some cream when the Potter came across in Vienna, for instance, or did Thursday, in his eagerness to appear important, merely convince himself that he had? Did the Sisters set out to lure the Potter to the West in order to get access to someone who could carry out an assignment without knowing it came from them? If so, what assignment had they invented for him to carry out? Did they think they had authorization? Did they actually have the authorization they thought they had? If they had received orders, had they interpreted them correctly?

All of this, to G. Sprowls's jaundiced eye, represented the proverbial can of worms. What he needed to do was question the Sisters at great length in order to be able to compose the right questions. That was the process he had used to break the Soviet sleeper in the CIA ranks whom the Sisters themselves had unmasked not long before. The disadvantage of working this way was that it was slow. The advantage was that it was sure.

"What we need—" Carroll was saying on the tape.

"What we need," Francis' voice repeated eagerly on the tape.

"What we need—" Carroll, from the tape recorder, whined.

The tape continued to run through the playing head, but there was no sound for roughly three minutes. Then Carroll's voice, distant, hollow, could be heard saying, "He might just do it."

G. Sprowls stopped the tape recorder. "Who might do what?" he inquired.

Carroll shook his head. He didn't remember.

"What were you doing during the long silence?" G. Sprowls asked.

"Thinking."

"Not writing?"

"We may have been jotting notes to ourselves," Carroll conceded.

"If there were notes," G. Sprowls remarked, flashing his half-smile as if it were a storm warning, "Francis would have shredded them at the end of the workday?"

Carroll's cheek muscle twitched once. "That's correct," he said.

"What was it," G. Sprowls wondered out loud, "that was so important you couldn't say it—you had to write it?"

When his turn came, Francis took a slightly different tack. "Of course I understand you are going through the motions," he confided to G. Sprowls at one point. An angelic smile took up a defensive position on his face to deal with the conspiratorial half-smile confronting him. "The last thing in the world you really want is for me to tell you what we are up to."

To G. Sprowls, it seemed almost as if Francis were daring him, inviting him even, to discover it. "So you are up to something?" he inquired.

Francis spread his hands innocently. "Josef Stalin started out his professional life as a seminarian," he retorted, "which explains why he was obsessed with confessions. What is your excuse?"

"Assuming you are up to something," G. Sprowls persisted, ignoring the historical diversion, "do you have authorization?"

"As a general rule," Francis noted, "Carroll and I are pointed in the right direction by our betters."

"Then perhaps you can explain why the Director himself authorized this interrogation?"

"That is clearly a matter you will have to pursue with the Director."

G. Sprowls selected another tape from his collection and played it for Francis. His voice could be heard saying, "Shows he had bad taste. Personally I never liked Whitman. All those unbuttoned shirts! All that hair on his chest! He was a poser. It follows that his poetry is a pose." There was a moment of silence, after which Francis asked on the tape, "Do we know exactly how the Potter knew that?" Then there was a very long stretch of tape without anything. Finally Francis' voice was heard again. "Having a great time. Wish you were here," he snickered. Carroll's voice, faint, said, "We have gotten our hands on a perfect criminal." To which Francis, a bit awed judging from his tone, replied, "I suppose we have."

G. Sprowls glanced at his wristwatch. They had been at it for more than three hours. Francis showed not the faintest sign of fraying at the edges. "Why," G. Sprowls tried, "were you discussing Whitman?"

In all his life Francis had never smiled more innocently. "Don't tell me, let me guess. You are one of those Whitman hysterics who can't put up with the slightest criticism of the master."

If G. Sprowls came equipped with one thing for the business of interrogation, it was a thick skin. "What could Carroll have meant," he went on as if Francis' response had not registered, "when he said that you had gotten your hands on a perfect criminal?"

"I would have to refresh my memory from my notes to answer you," Francis said.

"And the notes—"

"—were shredded," Francis finished the thought for him, "at the close of every workday."

"By you."

"By me."

"I see."

"Do you?"

13

The Sleeper was tired: of spending his evenings alone in his room; of taking his breakfast while it was still dark outside; of trudging off into the fields every morning with the rifle slung over his shoulder and two sandwiches (the Hunter's Special, prepared by the inn's chef) in the pocket of his brand-new Sears, Roebuck bush jacket; of working the bolt until his fingers blistered; of waiting; most of all, of waiting. But he had a fixed schedule, and a fixed itinerary, and there was no question of deviating from it. An order, the Potter had drummed into his head at the sleeper school, is to an agent as commandments one through ten are to an Orthodox priest. It was a matter of the Sleeper's being patient one more day. Tomorrow he would be off and running again, and anything, including a cramped, smoke-filled Greyhound bus, would be better than being cooped up in the phony luxury of Seventh Heaven, an inn just outside Lancaster with its birds wheeling freely through the lobby and the corridors, the birdshit stains on the furniture, the traditional Pennsylvania Dutch meal with its seven sweet and seven sour courses at every dinner.

Again and again, the Sleeper's thoughts drifted, almost against his will, to the mission. If his father's well-being, and in a sense the Potter's too, didn't depend on his performing well, he doubted if he would go through with it. One prince more or less in the world wouldn't change anything as far as he could see. But he had been backed into a corner; the one luxury he no longer had was choice. He imagined the moment when he would reach his ultimate destination, and wondered what his chances were of succeeding; he guessed they were quite good, or he wouldn't have been sent out in the first place. He wondered too what would happen to him after the mission. He wouldn't be returning to his comfortable life in Brooklyn Heights, of that he was certain. If he managed to survive, his masters would surely repatriate him to some corner of the Soviet Union remarkable for its remoteness.

If he was suddenly lonely, if he ached above all for just one more night in the same bed as Kaat, he could take comfort from the fact that he had accomplished what he came for. On the first day, he had zeroed in the rifle, bracing it on the elbow of a dead maple tree, aiming through the four-power telescopic sight and firing at a homemade bull's-eye. The rifle had been firing low and to the left. Using a small screwdriver, the Sleeper gradually adjusted the sight. After that he went to work recapturing the talent he had had when he served as a sniper during the Great Patriotic War.

It came back fairly quickly. In the beginning, he had trouble concentrating and felt unsure of himself. He missed more things than he hit. By the third day, however, he was beginning to get his concentration—and his confidence—back. He started once again to think of the rifle as an extension of his arm, and aiming became just a matter of pointing. He had been told in his instructions that he would be firing at a slowly moving target, but the possibility existed that it might be moving rapidly. So the Sleeper fired mainly at moving targets—rabbits, birds, ducks skimming the surface of ponds. He had always had a sixth sense for leading a target; an almost Zen feeling that all he had to do was point at the place where the target would be when the bullet got there. By the afternoon of the fifth day, and all during the sixth, he was snapping off shots and hitting practically everything he aimed at.

"So how'd it go today?" the wife of the inn owner asked when the Sleeper showed up at the bar for the Seventh Heaven Happy Hour. She was a handsome woman in her late twenties, married to a grouchy man a good deal older than she was. Her name was Marjorie, but the waiters and several of the inn's regular customers called her Sergeant Major, as if it were a rank; one of the younger, more insolent waiters even saluted her when he delivered a check to the cash register. "What did you bag?" she wanted to know.

"Everything I aimed at," the Sleeper replied testily. A bird flew in from the lobby and plunked down on the bar nearby.

"You're that good?" Sergeant Major asked, smiling suggestively.

The Sleeper stared at her curiously. "Why don't you put me to the test?"

"Maybe I'll do just that," she shot back, and she dispatched a damp palm down her thigh to smooth out an imagined wrinkle in her tight skirt.

It was after eleven when she scratched her long fingernails on his door. He let her in and locked it after her. She had brought a bottle of cognac and two glasses, but the Sleeper made it clear he didn't go in for preliminaries. He asked her what she was wearing under her dress. Instead of answering, she bent and caught the hem and peeled it over her head. Underneath, she was naked, round, in places as soft as a sponge. She had hair under her arms and legs, which reminded the Sleeper of the women he had made love to in Russia; he liked hair on the female body. Somehow it seemed to make them less abstract, more real. Sergeant Major stretched out on the bed and parted her legs and raised one knee and moistened her thumb and forefinger and pinched her nipples to make them erect. "Now," she announced with a nervous laugh, "we'll see how good a shot you really are."

Some time passed. Neither of them had any idea of how much. Eventually Sergeant Major rolled off the Sleeper's body and laced her fingers through her hair. The Sleeper had the impression she was surfacing, like a deep sea diver. "I've read about that," she whispered hoarsely, "but I've never actually tried it—I wasn't sure I'd enjoy it."

"Did you? Enjoy it?"

Sergeant Major smiled a faraway smile; she was coming up, but she had not yet reached the surface. "Do you know any other tricks?" she asked.

The Sleeper nodded lazily. He reached for the phone. Sergeant Major was intrigued. "Who are you calling at this ungodly hour?"

The night clerk who doubled as a switchboard operator came on. "I want a number in Brooklyn," the Sleeper told him. "After you get it for me, I want to hear the click you make when you get off the line."

The number rang a long time before anyone picked up the phone on the other end. "Yeah?" Millie finally said, suppressing a yawn. "Who the hell is it?"

"It's me," the Sleeper said.

Millie came awake instantly. "You know what time it is, for Christ's sake?"

"What are you wearing?" the Sleeper demanded.

Millie's tone changed. "A T-shirt."

"Take it off."

After a moment she said, "Okay, it's off."

"Take the phone over to the couch and curl up," the Sleeper instructed her. "You're going to hear a bedtime story."

Millie purred like a cat. "It's one of *those* phone calls," she said. "I can't wait!"

14

At the foot of a bed, the cat angled a paw over its head to keep the light out. Kaat kicked off her shoes and stretched out on one of the twin beds. They had just come back, the three of them, from a diner across the street from the motel. The desk clerk had given them a mimeographed street map of Scranton. Kaat removed the antique gold ring, which she wore around her neck attached to a length of silk string, and dangled it over the map.

"If you please," the Potter asked, "what are you doing?"

"I'm trying to find out where he is in Scranton," she told him, her eyes concentrating on the ring.

"And the ring is going to tell you?"

"If it does tell me," she retorted, "you'll be an autologophagist."

"Which is?"

Kaat glanced up from her pendulum. "An autologophagist is someone who eats his words," she said.

The Potter settled onto the edge of the other bed. "What made you become interested in words beginning with A?" he wanted to know.

Kaat shrugged defensively. "Everybody who collects things specializes," she explained. "Stamp collectors collect art stamps or French stamps or whatever. Antique dealers collect porcelain. Kids collect matchbooks. I collect A words. I suppose you could say I'm basically an A person. It's no accident that Kaat has two lovely A's smack in the middle of it." She nibbled thoughtfully on a fingernail.

"Try phoning again," the Potter advised her. He busied himself loading the Beretta with the bullets she had bought for him that afternoon. Normally the clip held eight bullets, but the Potter squeezed ten in. Giving yourself an extra margin was what separated the professionals from the amateurs. He wondered how professional he really was in the end. The whole idea of going out on a limb with this odd girl who nourished herself mostly on her own fingernails and passed pendulums over maps seemed more ridiculous than ever. To begin with, the chances were that the Sleeper would never call Millie in Brooklyn Heights. Even if he did, there was only a remote possibility that he would tell her where he was. The Americans, he remembered from his days as *rezident*, had an expression that perfectly described what he was on: they called it a wild-goose chase.

The girl, moreover, was beginning to get on his nerves. She had carried on a running monologue during the ride down to Scranton, almost as if she dreaded silence, as if only a string of words could keep her phantoms at bay. (Silence, the Sleeper once laughingly told the Potter, was a gift two people could offer each other only after they were intimate.) The Potter had discovered a great deal about Kaat during those hours in the car. She shivered before it got cold, she admitted; according to her, the chills originated in her imagination. She liked making love and being made love to, she said; she relished the sensation of not knowing where her body ended and a lover's began. When the street (as she called real life) got too rough for her, she sought refuge in her mind's eye, which she sharpened, she said, as if it were a pencil.

"Call her up again, if you please," the Potter repeated now.

Kaat put aside the map and pendulum, picked up

the phone and gave the number to the receptionist. A moment later she could hear the telephone in Brooklyn Heights ringing. Instead of Millie's recorded voice coming on as before, Millie herself snatched up the receiver. "Kaat, is that you?" she cried.

"Where have you been?" Kaat demanded.

"She is in?" the Potter asked. He came around to sit next to Kaat on the bed.

"Thank God it's you," Millie cried. "Peter phoned."

"He's called," Kaat whispered triumphantly to the Potter.

"Who are you talking to?" Millie asked.

"Nobody. What did he say?"

"Wait a sec. I'll play the tape for you."

"She's playing the tape for me," Kaat whispered. She and the Potter bent their heads so they could both listen to the voice coming from the earpiece.

The Sleeper's voice came over the line. "You're going to hear a bedtime story," he said.

"It's one of *those* phone calls," Millie's voice replied. "I can't wait!"

A woman's voice could be heard. She was breathing hard. Kaat and the Potter exchanged looks. "I don't have the vaguest idea what to say," the woman pleaded.

Fainter, the Sleeper's voice: "Tell her what we're doing. Describe it."

The woman laughed uneasily. "You want me to tell her everything?"

"Absolutely everything," Millie insisted on the tape.

"Well," the woman began, talking between gasps, "I'm lying on my stomach . . . on my stomach, see, with my ass more or less, eh, elevated"—the woman giggled hysterically here—"holy shit. 'Elevated' is the right word, and he's, eh, he's—" She stopped abruptly, almost as if she were too preoccupied to talk.

"He's *what*?" Millie prompted on the tape.

The real Millie came back on the line. "Are you catching all this, Kaat? Are you turned on?"

"I'm catching it," Kaat said. "I'm suffering from

apodysophilla—that's a feverish desire to undress," she explained.

"He's"—it was the woman's voice on the tape again—"oh, Jesus." She expelled a lungful of air, and what began as a husky sigh wound up as a throaty scream.

The Potter turned his head away so that Kaat couldn't see his expression.

"He's inside me now," the woman continued, her voice weaker than before. "He's reaching under my stomach with a hand and rubbing my clit." She gasped as if she were in pain.

"Keep talking," the Sleeper's voice ordered in the background.

"He's . . . behind me . . . not moving . . . perfectly still," the woman said more calmly now. "It's me that's . . . doing . . . the moving. When I . . . when I back up I get . . . his dick going . . . deep. When I move forward . . . I get his finger." She giggled again. "I can pick my poison!"

On the tape, Millie could be heard moaning. The real Millie came back on the line. "That's me moaning," she laughed.

"As if I couldn't tell," Kaat retorted. She sounded annoyed. "Did you ask him where he was, for Christ's sake, or did you just beat off?"

"I asked him, I asked him," Millie assured Kaat.

"Say, where are you two?" Millie said on the tape.

"She wants to know where we are," the woman told the Sleeper.

"Don't tell her," the Sleeper could be heard saying.

"We're in a bed," the woman told Millie between gasps.

"Give me a little hint," Millie begged on the tape.

The woman giggled again. "We're in a . . . hotel in Holland," she told Millie. "We're in seventh heaven, with birds flying through the corridors—"

There was a click on the tape. Millie came back on

the line. "He hung up before she could say any more," she said.

After Millie had hung up, Kaat and the Potter sat on the edge of the bed staring at the floor. Kaat chewed on a fingernail. Eventually the Potter said, "The phone call didn't tell us very much."

At the foot of the bed the cat stretched, then coiled again. Kaat said, "We know he's somewhere in Pennsylvania. What did the woman say? A hotel in Holland. Seventh heaven, with birds—"

"—flying through the corridors," the Potter remembered.

Kaat snapped her fingers. "My ex might be able to help us," she announced brightly.

"What is an ex?"

"My ex. My first husband."

"Did you marry again after you left him?" the Potter asked.

Kaat shook her head no.

"Then why do you call him your first husband?"

Kaat shrugged. "Even when I married him I thought of him as my first husband," she said, suddenly melancholy, suddenly distant. "He had the look, the smell, of a first husband. He was much older than me," she said as if it explained everything, which made the Potter wonder if Svetochka had referred to him, behind his back, as her first husband. "He was a country singer," Kaat plunged on. "Still is, I imagine, though his voice was beginning to go the last time I heard him. He spent twenty-three years wandering around the back roads of America, with his beat-up guitar in the trunk of a beat-up station wagon. That's how I met him. It was in Oklahoma. I was sixteen going on twenty-five, if you know what I mean. I heard him sing in a bar in Wetumka, Oklahoma. My ex, whose name is W. A. Henry Oaks, though everyone called him W.A., my ex claimed that every town was famous for a different position."

"Different position?"

"Different *sexual* position. Wetumka, according to W.A., was famous for the Wetumka. The next day we drove north to Weleetka, where W.A. was playing a bowling alley, and I discovered the Weleetka. After that there was the Okmulgee, which only thin people can do. Thank God we were thin! Later, when we wanted to use a certain position again, we referred to it as the Wetumka, or the Weleetka, or the Okmulgee." Kaat began chewing wistfully on a fingernail.

"What was the Okmulgee?" the Potter asked, not sure whether he believed the story—or whether he wanted to know.

"You're sure you want to know?"

"I take back the question."

She laughed and told him. "You're blushing," she said when she had finished.

The Potter went back to his own bed. "If you think your first husband can help us, phone him up," he said moodily. He didn't know how he got into these conversations with her. He seemed to follow her wherever she led. He would have to concentrate on the problem at hand; use her if there were ways she could help him; discard her when it became clear that she could serve no purpose. All this talk of sexual positions just blurred the picture. He would have to make a greater effort to keep things in focus.

Kaat eventually got her ex husband on the phone. "What time is it on the Coast?" she asked him. "Then I didn't wake you?" she asked him. "No, I'm not sorry I didn't wake you," she snapped. "Listen, W.A., don't start on me, all right?" She listened to the voice on the phone for a moment, shook her head and planted her eyeballs in the tops of their sockets. "Here's the thing, W.A.," she said when she could get a word in, and she went on to tell him why she had called. For reasons she couldn't explain just now, she and a friend were trying to track down another friend in a hotel somewhere in Pennsylvania. The only clues they had came from a woman who said that the hotel was in Holland, that they were in seventh heaven with birds flying through the corridors.

W.A. let out a howl at the other end of the phone. "Heck, I played that joint three, four years ago," he cried. "The owner is a certified maniac about birds. He has got dozens of them zooming around the halls. One of them even shat on my guitar while I was singing. Got me such a laugh I tried to incorporate it in my act, but I couldn't get the goddamned bird to shit twice in the same place."

"You actually know where this hotel is?" Kaat asked.

" 'Course I know. Holland is the nickname of a county outside of Lancaster, in the heart of Pennsylvania Dutch country. The hotel is called Seventh Heaven."

15

❦

"Can you do someone going to a refrigerator for a glass of milk?" asked Sergeant Major.

"He can fucking do anything," Ourcq, in a sour mood, muttered under his breath.

They had arrived at Seventh Heaven just as the Sleeper was checking out. Ourcq took one look at the birds perched around the lobby and the birdshit stains on the carpets and announced he was ready to follow the Sleeper. Appleyard had to remind him of the pertinent rule in the standard operating procedures for sweepers: when you are sweeping someone's wake, you have to linger twenty-four hours after he leaves to make sure he is clean.

Appleyard took a sip of his Scotch on the rocks to moisten his lips. Drumming the balls of his fingers on the top of the bar, he produced footsteps approaching the refrigerator. With a sharp cluck of his tongue he made the sound of the door being opened. He snapped his fingernail against the whiskey glass to duplicate the sound of the milk bottle being taken out. Blowing through puckered lips, he imitated milk being poured into a glass. Sucking in air, he produced the sound of drinking. And he capped it all with a genuine belch of pleasure.

Sergeant Major and a young couple at the bar applauded. "He's really good," the woman insisted to her husband. "He could be on television."

Ourcq looked at the time on the woman's watch on his wrist, then glanced through the arch into the lobby and spotted the girl at the front desk. She had a pussycat tucked under her right arm as if it were a rolled-up newspaper. "Imitate the sound of a fucking pistol with a fucking silencer attached going off," Ourcq instructed Appleyard, and he gestured with his eyes toward the lobby.

Appleyard peered over Ourcq's shoulder—and with a spitting sound produced the effect Ourcq had asked for.

In the lobby, the desk clerk brushed away a bird that had landed on the register and shook his head. Are you sure? the girl seemed to be saying. Even at this distance, it was evident that she was disappointed. The desk clerk shook his head again. He was probably telling her that the person in question hadn't left a forwarding address. Ourcq laughed to himself. Some people didn't like pussycats following them.

The cat, surveying the world from under the girl's arm, stared wide-eyed at a bird that planed past its head. The cat's tail spiraled up playfully. The girl snapped at the cat and turned back toward the front door.

"It is time for us to leave this fucking Seventh Heaven," Ourcq told Appleyard. He peeled off some bills and deposited them on the bar.

"Can you do a deep-sea diver surfacing?" the woman at the bar asked Appleyard.

"Can you do a bird pulling a worm from its hole?" asked Sergeant Major.

"Of course I can," Appleyard asserted. "I can do anything. I can do snow falling. I can do smoke rising. I can do the sun setting. I can do someone dying. The last two are actually very similar. Only I don't maybe have time right now." With that, he gulped down the rest of his Scotch, set the glass back on the bar and trailed after Ourcq toward the door.

16

The Potter, not Kaat, happened to be driving, which is what saved their lives. He had been watching the headlights overtaking them in the rearview mirror. For some reason it made him think of Oskar's taxi worming its way along Zubovsky Boulevard from the Krimsky Bridge. When the car that was overtaking them pulled abreast on a straight stretch of road, and then stayed abreast, the skin on the back of the Potter's neck crawled; once again his body knew before he did. He glanced sideways and noticed it was a black Dodge with two men in the front seat. One of them was pointing at him, and then the Potter knew what his body knew. "Sweepers!" he muttered as his foot shot out and jammed down on the brake.

He never heard the shot. The only evidence that one had been fired was the neat hole that appeared in the window on the Potter's side of the car, and an instant later a second hole that turned up in the window on Kaat's side, inches in front of the Potter and Kaat. The Potter, behind the Dodge now, swerved to the left just as a second bullet drilled a small hole in the front window and buried itself in the rear seat above the head of the sleeping cat.

Kaat gasped and brought a fingernail to her lips. "What's—" (Later, when she recalled what had happened, she would comment on the Potter's ataraxia—utter calmness.)

The Potter accelerated and brought the Chevrolet hurtling up to the Dodge, and into it. The man twisting in the passenger seat trying to squeeze off a shot through his own rear window was flung sideways against the door. The driver spun his steering wheel to the right and braked in order to skid his car to a stop and block the road. He would have succeeded, except that he skidded half a yard too far. The Potter spotted a gap between the back of the Dodge and the nearest trees and drove his Chevrolet through it. The left wheels climbed up onto a shoulder, the car teetered, Kaat screamed. In the back seat the cat landed on all four feet on the side window. Then the Chevrolet sank back down on its four wheels and hurtled away from the Dodge behind them.

The Potter, leaning forward, peering into the night, gripping the wheel intently, tried desperately to sort things out. He had a short lead on the Dodge, but they would back and fill and start after him in a matter of seconds, and he had no doubt that the Dodge could outrun the Chevrolet. Ahead, on the farthest edge of his high beams, he caught a glimpse of a narrow bridge and a highway marker indicating that an intersection was coming up right after it. The next instant the Chevrolet was rolling over the bridge, and the intersection was looming ahead. In his rearview mirror the Potter caught sight of two dancing pinpoints of light. His hand shot out and pushed in a knob, cutting his own headlights. Night enveloped them, shrouded them, smothered them. Kaat whimpered some words, but the Potter didn't try to understand what she was saying. When he judged that they were almost up to the intersection, he braked and spun the wheel to the right and then speeded up again, expecting any instant that the Chevrolet would come crashing to a stop against the trunk of a tree. Through the front window he could make out a faint ribbon of grayness stretched ahead; under the wheels he could feel the smoothness of a road. He cut the engine and braked, more gently this time, and brought the car to a dead stop.

"Don't make a sound, don't move, if you please," the Potter whispered fiercely, and flinging open the door, he plunged from the car. He tugged his Beretta from his jacket pocket and pulled back the slide on the top of the barrel, chambering a round, and started back up the road toward the intersection. Thoughts, plots, plans, possibilities raced through his mind; his life, Kaat's also, would depend on his calculations being correct. Ahead, the Dodge squealed to a stop at the intersection. So far, so good. The two men in it would cut their engine and turn off their own headlights and get out of the car, each on his side, and peer in the three directions the Chevrolet could have gone for a glimpse of a taillight, the sound of a racing motor.

Suddenly a single powerful beam stabbed out into the night from the Dodge, and the Potter realized with a start that the car was equipped with a spotlight. It swept the road ahead, then swiveled past nearby tree trunks and bushes and leapt forward to illuminate the road to the left of the Dodge. The Potter knew he had only a few seconds left before the spot stabbed down the road he was on and pinned him in its beam. He lurched forward a few paces, then sank heavily to one knee, and gripping the Beretta with both hands, aimed. The spotlight began to swivel past trees in his direction. Squeeze, don't jerk the trigger, he shouted at himself in his head, and he willed his muscles to go through the motions *slowly*. Just as the light blinded him, he fired two quick shots. Glass shattered. Light ceased to exist. The Potter fired twice more at the part of the Dodge's silhouette where the front wheel would be, and heard a soft hissing sound. At the front door of the Dodge, several small sparks, as momentary and as bright as flashing fireflies, speckled the darkness, followed by spitting noises, and there was a scratching in the road just to the Potter's left, as if someone were trying to strike a safety match against it. The Potter leapt to one side and lumbered back along the soft shoulder away from the Dodge and its fireflies, toward the Chevrolet. Behind him doors slammed. Someone kicked a tire and cursed. The Potter could hear footfalls as two men started trotting down the road after him.

Winded, the Potter came up to the Chevrolet and dived into the driver's seat and hit the starter. The motor coughed into life. Grinding the Chevrolet into gear, the Potter let the car leap forward. Something punctured the car's trunk compartment with a whine. Then the Potter was in second gear and the car was rolling smoothly and the gap between the fireflies in his rearview mirror and them widened. The Potter sucked air into his bursting lungs and looked at Kaat to see if she were all right, but she was trembling and staring back over her shoulder with an infinitely sad look in her eyes. Following her glance, the Potter caught sight of the small bloodstained body of Kaat's Meow lying like a discarded fur mitten on the rear seat.

"I wonder," Kaat said in an almost inaudible voice, "what she will turn up as in her next incarnation."

17

Khanda slid into the booth across from the portly man whose name was Rubenstein. They were about a mile and a half from the downtown wart, in a zone where an ordinance was in force banning liquor that was paid for by the drink. Hence the charade that this was a private club, and the people in it regular members. In fact, anyone could buy a membership at the door for an evening, and the price translated into a certain number of free drinks. The police gave the club a wide berth (except when they changed into civilian clothes and turned up for some drinks on the house) because Rubenstein had a reputation for being generous when it came to slipping small envelopes into jacket pockets at police headquarters.

Eyeing Khanda across the table, Rubenstein mumbled something about his not being at all what he expected.

"What did you expect," Khanda asked.

"Considering what you are going to do, someone a bit older, more worldly," Rubenstein admitted.

Khanda shrugged. Rubenstein asked how much progress he had made. Khanda told him about the job he had gotten in the warehouse. He had scouted the upper floors, he said, and he thought he had found the perfect sniper's nest, one that would give him at least three shots at the target as the limousine was moving almost directly away from him.

"What about the getaway?" Rubenstein inquired.

"What about the getaway?" Khanda shot back. "That's supposed to be your bailiwick."

"If you can get out of the building, I can get you out of the country," Rubenstein promised.

Khanda said he thought there would be enough confusion after the shooting for him to make it down a back staircase to the street before the police could figure out where the shots had come from and seal off the building.

"Have you timed it?" Rubenstein asked.

"Not yet," Khanda admitted. "But I figure if I abandon the rifle instead of trying to hide it, I can be out of there in a matter of minutes."

"You have to walk out so you don't attract attention to yourself," Rubenstein cautioned.

"I'm not stupid," Khanda said.

Rubenstein asked what kind of rifle Khanda planned to use. He had been associated with the Chicago underworld before he was recruited by the Russians, and knew a thing or two about firearms.

Khanda told him about the rifle he had bought through a mail-order house. "At the distance I plan to shoot from," he said, "I'll have trouble missing."

Rubenstein nodded. "In the right hands the rifle should be deadly," he agreed. He pushed aside the Scotch glasses and unfolded a small map of the city on the table. "After the shooting, you board a bus here," he said, pointing to an intersection not far from the assassination site. "You get off here. Then you walk toward my apartment, which is here. I'll pick you up in my car and drive you to a private airport outside the city. Our mutual friends will have a small plane waiting to take us to Mexico. I've dealt drugs in Mexico. I know my way around there. From Mexico, our Cuban friends will get you by boat to Cuba, and from there, by an Aeroflot flight, to Moscow."

Khanda studied the map. "It looks good," he said, nodding. "It looks very good."

"It always looks good," Rubenstein said moodily, "until something unexpected happens. The main thing is for you not to panic. If you can make it to where I can find you, I can guarantee I'll get you to Moscow."

Khanda sipped his drink. Rubenstein asked Khanda if he had any other questions. "This is the moment to ask them," he said, "since it would be wiser if we never met again."

"When I was in that school of theirs in Minsk," Khanda ventured, "we learned that assassins always work in pairs. Have you heard any talk about someone else having the same assignment as me?"

"As far as I know," Rubenstein assured Khanda, "you're all alone in this."

Khanda seemed relieved. "Well," he said, "I guess that covers just about everything," and he smiled boyishly and spread his hands.

To Rubenstein he looked like a traveling salesman who had wound up his pitch. "Good luck and all that sort of thing," he told him.

They shook hands. Khanda slid out of the seat, and hiking up his trousers, strode through the semidarkness of the club toward the street door. Rubenstein stared after him. He had to admit it, he didn't much like the look of him. There was an arrogance to his eyes, an iciness to the set of his lips that disturbed Rubenstein, left him with a bad taste in his mouth. Well, so much the better. It would only make carrying out his instructions that much easier.

If for some reason he couldn't organize Khanda's escape, he was under orders to organize his death.

18

G. Sprowls was not a happy man. Normally his superiors left him with a free hand when it came to conducting interrogations. He set the pace; he delivered the goodies. This time, however, they were putting pressure on him. Nobody came right out and told him to speed things up. Rather there were subtle hints—delivered almost daily—that speed was essential. Various highly placed people would phone to see if progress had been made. There would be pregnant pauses on the other end of the line when G. Sprowls hedged. The impression would then be conveyed that time was of the essence. If, as the superficial facts seemed to suggest, the Sisters had set in motion an operation on their own, the aristocrats in the Company's front office wanted to know about it, and fast. The point being that they could then exercise the option of either canceling it—or taking credit for it.

Which is why G. Sprowls decided, several days before he was as ready as he would have liked to be, that the time had come to hook Francis up to a lie detector.

"I thought you said you wouldn't get around to this until the end of the week," Francis remarked absently as the technician inflated the rubber tube around his chest that would measure his breathing rhythm. Francis might have been getting his annual electrocardiogram for all the attention he paid.

G. Sprowls disregarded the comment, as usual. "Is that too tight?" he asked, his half-smile frozen on his face.

"Not at all," Francis said politely.

The technician, a man in his early sixties, hovered over the black box so that he could read the trace produced by the three styluses. "Anytime you are, I am," he told G. Sprowls.

"For what it's worth," Francis said pleasantly, "I am ready too."

G. Sprowls turned to the first page in his loose-leaf book. He studied what he had written for several minutes, then nodded at the technician, who threw a switch setting the styluses in motion. "We'll begin with some control questions, if you don't mind," G. Sprowls said. "Would you be so kind as to state your full name as it appears on your birth certificate."

"Francis Augustus," Francis said, and he added his family name.

"State your marital status."

Francis adjusted the knot of his mauve bow tie. "Happily, blissfully, single," he replied.

"State your age, your home address, the model of the car you drive."

"I am, at last count, forty-four years of age. I live at—" He gave the address of his downtown residence hotel. "I am the proud owner of a rather beat-up but serviceable fifty-nine Ford."

The technician looked up from the trace and nodded.

"We will turn now," G. Sprowls said, "to the details surrounding the defection from Russia of Feliks Arkantevich Turov, known also as the Potter."

"By all means," Francis agreed heartily.

"Will you tell us where the idea that the Potter might want to defect originated?"

"Either Carroll or I, I forget who, noticed an item in one of the West German Y summaries that mentioned that Turov had been put out to pasture. We had more or less followed his career; we were, you might say, fans of his. We knew he had suffered a series of setbacks in recent months."

"Can you be more specific?" G. Sprowls ordered.

"I can try to be," Francis agreed, flashing an innocent smile. "Three of the sleepers that Turov had trained had bitten the dust, as they say in the wild west. Turov was bound to be blamed for their loss."

"You and Carroll contributed to the Potter's downfall when you ferreted out one of his sleepers, I remember."

"So did you," Francis shot back. "We exposed him, you broke him."

G. Sprowls ignored him. "Aside from the loss of the three sleepers, and the subsequent disgrace of the Potter, was there any other reason to think he might be ripe for defection?"

Francis swallowed a yawn. "We knew in a very general way that he was married to a woman much younger than he was who was likely to put a great deal of pressure on him."

"What kind of pressure?"

"The money that had been available, the apartment overlooking the Moscow River, the chauffeured limousine, the access to Western products, all of these would disappear. If he wanted to keep the woman, and we suspected he did, he would have to come up with the equivalent."

G. Sprowls glanced at the technician, who lifted his eyes to gaze through the upper part of his bifocals. "So far, so good," he said.

"Let's talk about authorization for a moment," G. Sprowls suggested.

"Let's," Francis repeated amiably.

"The effort to get the Potter to defect was authorized, according to my notes, by the Deputy Director for Operations. Is that your understanding?"

"We proposed, he disposed."

"When you proposed, as you put it, did you also

tell the Deputy Director precisely what you expected to get from the Potter if he could be induced to defect?"

"Absolutely," Francis replied.

"His version is that you said you expected to get odds and ends."

"Odds and ends are what we thought we would get," Francis agreed. A smile of transparent innocence spread across his features. "You are not thinking this through," he chastised G. Sprowls. "If we had been operating behind the Deputy Director's back, why would we have sent our man Friday to Vienna to skim off the cream? Surely one of us would have gone in his place."

G. Sprowls leaned forward. It was precisely this point that baffled him. "The fact of the matter is that your man Friday did skim off the cream," he went on. "The fact of the matter is that he was acting on your specific instructions. The fact of the matter is that you wound up with more than odds and ends."

Francis shook his head in mild frustration. "The Potter trained sleepers. What could have been more logical than to ask him, at the moment he came across the frontier, if he would have the kindness to give us, as a token of his good faith, the names and addresses of any sleepers who might still be in circulation?"

"You acknowledge that that was the cream that your man Friday was sent to skim off?"

"We would have been idiots if we hadn't sent him to try," Francis insisted.

G. Sprowls flipped to the next page in his looseleaf book and studied it for a long moment. "Your man Friday," he said without looking up, "has told us that the Potter gave him the name and address and awakening signal of a Soviet sleeper living in Brooklyn Heights, and that he passed this information on to you. Is his version of events correct?"

"Perfectly correct, yes."

"Yet your Op Proposal updater filed with the Deputy Director, a photocopy of which I have before me, contained no mention of the fact that you had come into possession of this information," G. Sprowls drawled.

It struck Francis that G. Sprowls tended to slip into a drawl when he thought he had a nibble and was starting to gently reel in the line. "No mention at all," he acknowledged cheerfully.

"Of course you can account for this discrepancy," G. Sprowls said in his slow drawl.

"Of course."

G. Sprowls looked up from his loose-leaf notebook and issued a formal invitation. "Feel free to do so," he said.

Francis actually sighed here. "We naturally attempted to verify the information when our man Friday—our *former* man Friday is probably more accurate—passed it on to us," he said. "There was a person by that name living at the address in Brooklyn Heights specified by the Potter. Except that he had decamped. Skedaddled. Flown the coop. A discreet phone call elicited the information that he was off somewhere on a business trip. Quite obviously, there were only two ways of confirming the Potter's information. We could have hooked the Potter up to one of these contraptions"—Francis cast a benign smile at the black box behind him—"over in Austria. Except the Potter had slipped through our man Friday's not very sticky fingers and was no longer available. Or we could wait for the alleged sleeper to return to his nest in Brooklyn Heights, then send him the awakening signal, along with an order or two—tell him to scratch his ass in front of the information booth at Grand Central station at high noon, for instance—and see if he responded. In any case, it would have been ridiculously premature for us to have put any of this into our Op Proposal updater—surely even you can understand that. People of our caliber only deal with confirmed information. Consider this: perhaps the Potter was not a defector, but someone planted on us in order to make us swallow false information. Perhaps he was a genuine defector who, once across, decided to give us bubbles that burst when you tried to get a grip on them. Perhaps our *former* man Friday was inventing the whole thing."

G. Sprowls looked Francis in the eye. "And you are willing to state categorically that neither you nor Carroll awakened the alleged sleeper and sent him on his merry way?"

"Categorically, yes."

The technician shrugged uncertainly. "Could he make a positive declaration? 'I state categorically that neither I nor to my knowledge Carroll'—that sort of thing."

G. Sprowls focused his half-smile on Francis.

Francis exhaled sharply through his nostrils and nodded. "I state categorically that neither I nor to my knowledge Carroll awakened the alleged sleeper residing in Brooklyn Heights and dispatched him on a mission. Does that do the trick?"

On the spur of the moment (the question was not in his loose-leaf book) G. Sprowls asked, "Have you had any contact with agents or representatives of another country?"

Francis' face glistened with innocence as he replied, "I have not had any contact with agents or representatives of another country."

G. Sprowls glanced at the technician, who bent over the styluses scratching away in the black box. Finally the technician looked up. "He's telling the truth," he concluded.

"All of it and nothing but," Francis added cheerfully, "so help me God." And he added mischievously, "You are barking up the wrong tree."

Carroll didn't fare as well as Francis when G. Sprowls put him through his paces that very same afternoon. "He's lying," the technician announced evenly, staring at the telltale traces through the bottom half of his bifocals.

G. Sprowls cleared his throat. Curiously, he seemed embarrassed for Carroll, almost as if he had stripped him of his clothing. "So you are up to something after all," he said.

A muscle twitched in Carroll's cheek. "We are not up to anything we should not be up to," he declared.

"Whatever you're doing," G. Sprowls filled in the gap, "you have authorization to do it?"

"We are good soldiers," Carroll insisted, his eyes staring vacantly at some point on the far wall. "We are patriots—the word is not used lightly. We serve the best interests of our country in ways that our superiors indicate to us." Unable to control himself any longer, Carroll burst out, "The first war I fought in was the wrong war. The next one will be the right war. We must at all costs be prepared for it."

"I see," G. Sprowls said, although he didn't see at all what Carroll was getting at. He decided to let the business of wrong wars and right wars go for the moment, and concentrate on the question of authorization. If he could discover who Carroll thought had given him authorization, perhaps he could uncover what Carroll felt authorized to do.

"It is fairly simple," Carroll replied in answer to another question. He seemed eager to justify himself. "Things were said by highly placed people in public places—at in-house pours, at a reception for a British colleague, at a medal-pinning ceremony honoring the fellow down the corridor from us who was retiring."

G. Sprowls appeared to sympathize completely with Carroll. "You read between the lines," he suggested in a slow drawl.

"The Director was obviously in no position to give an explicit order," Carroll said. "So he did the next best thing. It is out of the realm of possibility that he would have said what he did if he hadn't expected someone to take his words to heart; and if he hadn't expected someone to act on them." He arched his neck to relieve the pressure from his starched collar. "We are, Francis and I, old hands. We were, as Francis likes to say, pointed in the right direction. Where is the crime if we marched?"

"When you marched," G. Sprowls drawled softly, his half-smile inviting confession, offering absolution, "you mean that you organized the defection of the Potter in order to get access to the identity and awakening signal of a Soviet sleeper; that you then used this signal to awaken him and send him off on an assignment that you knew your superiors would approve of."

For an endless moment the styluses scraped noisily away in the black box. Again a muscle twitched in Carroll's cheek. "That's roughly it," he acknowledged wearily.

On a hunch, G. Sprowls slipped in a question. "Have you had any contact with agents or representatives of another country?"

Carroll closed his eyes in frustration. "You don't understand anything I've told you, in the end," he said.

"Would you like me to repeat the question?" G. Sprowls asked.

"No contact with agents or representatives of another country," Carroll said in a dull voice.

The technician looked up at G. Sprowls and nodded. Carroll was telling the truth.

"And Francis is involved in this with you?" G. Sprowls wanted to know.

"Francis speaks for Francis," Carroll snapped. "I speak for myself."

"About the assignment you gave to the Soviet sleeper," G. Sprowls said casually.

"When he carries it out," Carroll replied carefully, self-justification unfurling across his face like a flag, "you will know it instantly. Everyone will know it instantly. People we don't even know will stop us in the corridor and shake our hands."

The technician tried to catch G. Sprowls's attention; to indicate to him, with a roll of his eyes, that Carroll was stark raving mad. But G. Sprowls was concentrating on making Carroll think he sympathized with him. Exaggerating his drawl, he started to pose another question.

Carroll cut him off. "I can't tell you any more than I've already told you," he said curtly. And he closed his mouth in a way that indicated he had no intention of opening it again in the immediate future.

19

G. Sprowls ate cold sandwiches in his office that evening, and worked late into the night. Seeing the light through his transom, the night security officer knocked on the door to make sure he had authorization. G. Sprowls, irritated at the interruption, showed him a chit signed by none other than the Director himself.

The thing that was baffling G. Sprowls as he pored over the printouts, notched with numbers to indicate what question was being asked at any given moment, was how Francis and Carroll, who worked together, could be telling completely different stories, with no trace that either one was lying. Had Carroll gone off on a tangent of his own? The routine tape recordings of their office chitchat made this seem unlikely. Whatever they were doing, they were obviously doing together. Yet Carroll had admitted they were up to something. And Francis had denied it.

And they were both telling the truth.

G. Sprowls removed his eyeglasses and massaged his eyes with a thumb and forefinger. His lids felt inflamed, his eyes more comfortable closed than open. He was tempted to lean his head on the desk, to doze off, dreaming, no doubt, of styluses scratching away on paper and a dwarflike figure pinned, like a gypsy moth, to a piece of cork in a collector's case. As usual, G. Sprowls resisted. With a determined gesture he fitted his eyeglasses back over his rather oversized ears and started where he always started when he couldn't put his finger on something he suspected was there: at the beginning. "We'll begin with some control questions, if you don't mind," the transcript read. "Would you be so kind as to state your full name as it appears on your birth certificate."

G. Sprowls glanced across at the stylus traces that corresponded to the answer. There wasn't a waver in them. "Francis Augustus," Francis had replied, adding his family name.

His name!

G. Sprowls's brow furrowed thoughtfully. A conversation in the lunchroom some four or five years before came back to him. Several middle-echelon ex-field hands responsible for funneling money to friendly trade-union people in Latin America had been talking about a wild scheme that had circulated in the form of a lemon-colored Op Proposal, only to be shot out of the sky by a prudent department head. The scheme called for bribing the captain of a supertanker to run his ship onto some rocks off Cuba, causing an enormous oil spill that would pollute the coastline, ruin Cuba's fishing and tourist industry, and in general divert economic resources away from Castro's military and industrial buildup. "Sounds like something the Sisters might have thought up," one of the ex-field hands had said, and when G. Sprowls, just back from an overseas tour and new to Washington, had asked who the Sisters were, he had gotten the full description. There was Carroll with his three-piece suits and red welts around his neck from the starched collars which, so it was said, he wore to atone for unspecified sins; and there was Francis, who sported outrageous bow ties, an expression on his face midway between curious and reluctant and a Cheshire cat's innocent smile—so innocent, in fact, that he regularly lied about his *name* during the annual lie-detector tests and managed to fool the black box.

G. Sprowls reached into a drawer and took out Francis' service file. He thumbed through the sheets in it until he came to the one he was looking for—a photocopy of Francis' birth certificate. The name listed on it was Francis Algernon. Not Francis Augustus.

So he had lied, while hooked up to the black box, about his name.

G. Sprowls gazed up from Francis' service file, the half-smile warped into a grimace of satisfaction. He had heard about people who could beat the black box, but he had never come across one before. The box registered stress that someone would feel when he didn't tell the truth—moisture on the palms, a slight change in pulse rate or respiration. But Francis was obviously one of those extremely rare individuals who didn't feel stress of any kind when he lied. And if Francis was able to lie about his name, he would have been able to lie about the Potter and the Sleeper.

20

Almost everything the Sleeper knew about tradecraft he had learned from the Potter. During the first months at the Moscow sleeper school, the Potter had concentrated on sharpening his student's powers of observation. Piotr Borisovich would be dispatched to spend an afternoon in the lobby of a large tourist hotel, with instructions to note everything that happened and report back to the Potter. "You omitted the arrival of the fat American woman carrying a shopping bag from a Paris department store," the Potter would say after debriefing the Sleeper. "Also the Intourist woman who had a dispute with someone on the phone and burst into tears when she hung up. Also the man in the wheelchair who asked you for a match. The man in the wheelchair, in case you are curious, works for me. He was there to watch you."

So it went. One day Piotr Borisovich would be assigned to follow a junior diplomat from a junior country—but always from in front, since people seldom suspected anyone in front of following them. Another time the Sleeper would be sent across the city and back, and then asked if anyone had been following him. At the beginning, there might be no one, but his imagination would get the best of him and he would think there had been someone. On still another occasion there might be someone, but the Sleeper would not spot him and would report back that his wake had been clean. Slowly, however, he began to get the hang of it. He had a natural instinct for the streets, a good memory for faces, sharp eyes and a knack for improvisation, which in the end is the hallmark of a good agent. As the Potter drummed into his head: there were no rules. He himself, he explained by way of giving an example, had once hobbled after an Israeli agent in New York for the better part of an afternoon, on the theory that the agent would never suspect a crippled man of following him.

In time the Sleeper's tradecraft became as good as the Potter's. He too learned how to take advantage of the reflecting surfaces in the street to keep track of everything that was going on around him; not just store windows, but doors of cars, windows of buses, distant mirrors on the walls of department stores. It was a rare event when he couldn't pick out of a crowd the man or woman, and once, a teenager on roller skates, whom the Potter had put on his tail. (One tip the Sleeper never forgot: if you spot someone following you and don't want him to know he's been spotted, pick your nose.) It became a standing joke between them that once the Sleeper had identified the tail, he bought him a vodka if he was a man, and seduced her if it turned out to be a woman.

Now, whiling away two and a half days between buses in a small town in Ohio, the Sleeper, without consciously thinking about it, found himself scanning the rush-hour crowd for that telltale jerk of a head that turned away when he looked at it; for the glimpse of someone who didn't move through the streets at the rhythm of the crowd around him, but seemed to linger at store windows studying objects that, judging from appearances, he seemed unlikely to buy. The last thing the Sleeper expected was to spot anyone—which is why he felt shaken when he spotted two shadows. The first one, in his middle forties, balding, bloated, effeminate, was in a telephone booth, dialing as if his life depended on it. What gave him away was that the Sleeper remembered seeing him twice before earlier in the afternoon, both times in telephone booths dialing like mad. The second man, rail-thin, with wavy hair and lips that seemed to be pursed and producing sounds, the Sleeper noticed because every time he saw him he was gazing up at street signs as if he were lost.

The Sleeper immediately dismissed the possibility that they were two local hoodlums who had spotted a stranger in town and were planning to roll him. If they had followed him for any length of time, they would be aware that he had arrived by Greyhound bus and was staying in a not very luxurious hotel near the station—hardly the mark of someone who might be carrying a good deal of cash on him. (Ironically, the Sleeper did have more than six thousand dollars in small bills, most of which he had stuffed into the top half of the viola-da-gamba case in which the rifle, broken down into component parts, fitted.) Which narrowed it down to people who were in the same business he was in.

But on which side was the irritating question.

Forcing himself to act as if nothing unusual had happened, the Sleeper caught his bus early the next morning and, following his itinerary to the letter, headed farther west. The two men—he had nicknamed the one with the pursed lips Whistler, and the effeminate one Whistler's Mother—weren't in the bus with him, nor did he spot them trailing after him in automobiles, nor were they around when he touched down that night in a motel on the outskirts of Indianapolis. Walking through the city the next morning, the Sleeper used every reflecting surface he could find, but the two men were nowhere to be seen. He was beginning to think he might have imagined the whole thing when, thirty-six hours after he had left the small town in Ohio, he saw them again. When he turned to look over his shoulder, he spotted Whistler gazing up at a street sign at an intersection. Half an hour later he saw Whistler's Mother squeezed into a phone booth in a drugstore, dialing away as if he were reporting a fire.

The Sleeper thought he could perceive a time pattern in the movements of Whistler and Whistler's Mother. Like him, they would have taken roughly twelve hours to get from the small town in Ohio to Indianapolis. Yet he hadn't spotted them for thirty-six hours. Which meant that they had not bothered to tail him for twenty-four hours. And that little detail told the Sleeper two things: they were most likely professional sweepers who lingered for a day after he moved on to ensure that nobody else was following him; and they obviously had a duplicate of his itinerary.

The theory was easy enough to verify. The next day the Sleeper boarded a bus that would take him across Illinois to St. Louis. Two blocks from the Greyhound terminal he let out a cry of panic and went racing up the aisle to the driver with a story about having forgotten the valise that had all his music in it. The driver shrugged a pair of fat shoulders, swung the bus over to the curb, opened the doors with a rush of air and let the Sleeper off. "You can catch another bus around noon," the driver shouted down, "but you'll have to buy another ticket 'cause this one's been punched, and there ain't no way in the world I can unpunch it."

Doubling back on his tracks, the Sleeper returned to the motel on the outskirts of Indianapolis. He made his way down a long, narrow alley past several overflowing garbage cans to the kitchen door. The only person in the kitchen was a black dishwasher wearing pink rubber gloves that reached to his elbows. He was finishing up the breakfast dishes. Depositing his viola-da-gamba case and his worn leather valise under a table, the Sleeper walked over to the swinging doors and looked through the small porthole into the dining room. An elderly waiter was setting the tables for lunch. Beyond the dining room was the bar. Two men sat on stools in front of it, sipping drinks, glancing occasionally at the check-in desk, which they could see in the mirror behind the bar.

The two men were Whistler and Whistler's Mother.

Which meant that they were sweepers: *nash*, literally *ours*, sent by the people who had drawn up his itinerary, his masters in Moscow.

But why did his masters in Moscow feel he needed sweepers trailing after him? What did they know that he didn't know? Had there been a leak that could compromise his mission, not to mention his life? Were they afraid that he would lose his nerve? Had they sent the sweepers after him to make sure he went through with it? He was tempted to stop them on the street, invite them—in Russian; would they be embarrassed!—to a bar for a glass of vodka, the way he did in Moscow when he spotted the man whom the Potter had put on his tail.

But this wasn't Moscow, and he wasn't a neophyte sleeper learning the fundamentals of tradecraft. This was America. And he was on a mission that would end, if he was successful, in someone else's death; in his own death if he was not.

Mulling over the various possibilities, the Sleeper retraced his steps and caught the noon bus to St. Louis. There was a half-hour holdover at Terre Haute. When he got back to the bus, he found a woman sitting in his seat. She was wearing blue jeans and white ankle-length socks and high heels. She was chewing gum and reading an old issue of *Vogue* and shaking her head in despair, activating long pendulum earrings that the Sleeper expected to chime the hour. "Hey, you don't mind none if I take the window?" she asked, looking up with a faint smile. "Buses give me claustro-whatever."

Depositing his viola-da-gamba case in the rack overhead, the Sleeper slid wordlessly into the aisle seat next to her. "That's very gentlemanly of you," the woman said. "There are not many gentlemen around these days. Say, what did you say your name was?"

"I didn't say what my name was," the Sleeper answered. "But I will be glad to tell you." He gave her the name he was traveling under.

"My name is Orr," she said, "with two R's. Geraldine Orr. My friends call me Jerry."

"I am extremely happy to make your acquaintance," the Sleeper told her, his appetite whetted by the curve of her breasts inside her black turtleneck sweater.

"Likewise, I'm sure," said Jerry Orr.

It came out in conversation that she had been offered a job checking hats and selling cigarettes in a nightclub in St. Louis. She had worked there several years before, but had left to live with a garage mechanic in Terre Haute. That had ended badly when he went off with his childhood sweetheart, a Wave stationed in Norfolk. "Couples are basically collisions," Jerry Orr said with a sigh, and the Sleeper agreed heartily. Couples, in his experience, were unnatural combinations, something people created for economic or logistical reasons. But when you came right down to it, after the newness wore off, living as a couple was like condemning yourself to permanent house arrest; you limited your possibilities, and hence your potential. Even Millie's "triple," which at least had the saving grace of offering variety, had begun to feel like a prison of sorts. The Sleeper thought of Kaat. There had been something unusual about her, he had to admit it. If you had to be trapped in a couple, it was better to be trapped with someone like Kaat in the end.

"I don't ever want to get involved again," Jerry Orr was saying, "because it takes too much out of me. Emotionally, I mean. I like people who are just passing through, if you see what I mean."

The Greyhound picked up speed as it crossed the high plateau on which Terre Haute was planted. Long fields stretched off like religious wafers to the horizon. It occurred to the Sleeper that if the world were really flat, the horizon he could see from the window of the bus might be the bitter end of it. Soon after, the Wabash was behind them and the bus was heading down Route 70 into Illinois. The Sleeper thought about the man he was traveling across the country to kill. He had seen a photograph of him in a copy of *Newsweek* discarded on a bench at the bus terminal. He seemed like a decent enough man, fiddling with the button of his suit jacket, eyeing the camera with sardonic detachment. The Sleeper shrugged away the image of the man he would see, if all went according to plan, through the telescopic sight on his rifle. He felt devoid of energy; of hope. He remembered another snatch of Walter Whitman. "The past and present wilt . . . I have drained them." Which left the future. To get his mind off it, he reached across and brushed the back of Jerry Orr's wrist with his fingertips. "I'll be in St. Louis for two days and two nights," he told her. And he added pointedly, "I'm just passing through, if you see what I mean."

The faint smile on Jerry Orr's face brightened. She saw what he meant.

21

Kaat had gone into mourning for her dead cat. "Why would they want to kill her?" she cried, biting furiously on a fingernail. The Potter's answer—that they hadn't wanted to kill her cat; they had wanted to kill *them*! —didn't diminish her sense of loss. The fact that the cat was dead and buried (in a trench by the side of a back road, covered with gravel and dead leaves) and they were alive seemed to impress her more than anything the Potter could offer her in the way of comfort. Then, almost six hours to the minute after the bullet pierced the back of the car and lodged by pure chance in the cat's body, she shook herself the way a dog does when it comes in out of the rain. "Here's the thing," she said in a serious voice, and it was evident to the Potter that she had stopped thinking about the cat and started thinking about herself. "I want out. I'm not made for this kind of adventure. I have butterflies in my stomach just thinking about what happened."

She saw the confusion on the Potter's face as he tried to figure out how someone could have butterflies in the stomach. "It means I'm nervous," she explained in exasperation. "It means I have gas. It means I fart all the time."

The Potter had seen people crack before, and with less cause; had been surprised that she had not cracked sooner. "A night's rest, perhaps," he muttered, as if sleep could solve her problem, could dissipate the gas, could restore her sense of her own dignity, could give her the courage to go on.

"Park me somewhere," she pleaded, and her voice had the unmistakable vibrations of fear in it. "Park me anywhere."

"And Piotr Borisovich?"

She avoided his eye and concentrated on a fingernail.

"Look," he said finally—the Chevrolet's headlights had just picked up a sign indicating they were crossing the border into Indiana—"if I can catch up with Piotr and talk to him, maybe I can save his life."

"Why is someone trying to kill him?" Kaat asked in a voice so devoid of inquisitiveness it was obvious she would have been just as happy if he didn't answer.

"Piotr Borisovich is an espionage agent," the Potter said in a whisper, as if he were afraid of being overheard. "He has been sent on a mission, that much is obvious. This is what I think: whoever sent him on this mission wants Piotr to be caught, so that the blame for the mission will fall on the Russians."

"What am I doing here?" Kaat mumbled, staring out of her side of the car.

"It was your idea to come," the Potter blurted out. "I need you. Believe me, if you please. If you please?"

The Potter was squinting into the headlights of an oncoming car. When it passed, he glanced quickly at her. "It is important for me," he said suddenly. "I must save him." And he repeated, "If you please? He is the son I never had."

Kaat looked straight into his eyes as if she could see through them to some dark center, some remote corner where he would not give any more of himself away.

The moment passed. He turned back to the highway. "Stay, please, at least until he makes one more phone call to your friend in Brooklyn, New York," he said in a flat voice.

"Why not?" she replied, moved by his physical

ugliness; by his need for her; above all by the difficulty he had expressing it.

After she agreed, the Potter broached the subject of the car. "You want me to steal an automobile that belongs to someone else?" Kaat exploded when he first raised the possibility.

"We cannot keep driving around in this one," the Potter insisted, and he explained some of the facts of life to Kaat. There were two men behind them who would presumably mount a spare tire in place of the flat tire with the bullet hole in it, and start out after them. If they managed to catch up with them they would kill the Potter, and then feel obliged to deal with any witnesses in a similar way.

Kaat asked how the two men in the Dodge could possibly find them, given the twists and turns the Potter had taken in the hour after the incident at the crossroad. "We don't have any idea where we are going," she pointed out with irreproachable logic, "so how can they know where we're going?"

It was a reasonable question, to which the Potter offered a reasonable explanation. They had run into the two men in the Dodge right after they had almost caught up with the Sleeper; they had most likely been spotted making inquiries at the inn with the curious name of Seventh Heaven. Which meant that whoever had awakened the Sleeper and dispatched him on his mission had been covering his tracks with what the professionals called sweepers. And that, in turn, meant that every time they managed to get close to the Sleeper, they risked a new run-in with the men in the Dodge. Driving around in the Chevrolet would only make matters easier for the sweepers.

Kaat still wasn't convinced about the need for a new car until the Potter told her *how* she would steal it—at which point she made a hundred-and-eighty-degree turn and waxed enthusiastic about the idea and began peering eagerly through the front window looking for a suitable location. On the outskirts of a small town in southern Indiana they found what they were looking for: a low, modern circular structure with pulsating neon arrows pointing the way from the main road, and raucous rock music filling the night around it.

The parking lot in back of the nightclub already held more than three dozen cars. The Potter drew up on the far edge of the lot, near a line of trees, and cut the motor. He rummaged around in the trunk for the tool kit that came with the tire iron, found a screwdriver in it and began to remove the Chevrolet's license plates. Once he had them off he told Kaat he was ready if she was. She took a deep breath to calm her nerves, unbuttoned, at the Potter's suggestion—he had a mania for details like this—another button of her shirt, and went around to plant herself on the curb near the front door of the nightclub.

Within minutes a red two-door Ford pulled up and two girls spilled from its doors. The Potter, watching from the corner of the nightclub, waved Kaat off; he wanted a newer, heavier car, also one that was more subdued and less likely to attract attention. The boy who was driving the Ford honked his horn at the girls as they disappeared through the door of the nightclub, and gunning his engine, raced off to park in the lot.

The Potter let four more cars go by before he found one that appealed to him. Eventually a blue four-door Chrysler eased to a stop in front of the entrance. A girl and a boy emerged from the back seat, a second girl from the front seat. They were well dressed, slightly older than the other clients of the nightclub; they gave the impression of college kids who had borrowed a car from one of their parents for a night of slumming.

The Potter pointed at the car and nodded vigorously. Kaat mustered a toothy smile and trotted around to the driver's side. "There's a new service starting tonight," she informed the driver. "We park your car for you, and bring it around when you're ready to leave." And she added, "There's no charge, but if you'd like to give me something for my trouble, I won't say no."

The boy behind the wheel hesitated, then caught sight of his girl observing him. Not wanting to appear unsophisticated, he climbed out of the car, fished a dollar bill from his shirt pocket, handed it to Kaat with a nod and went off to join his friends. Kaat slid in behind the wheel and drove the Chrysler over to where the Chevrolet was parked. The Potter appeared a moment later and began attaching the license plates from the Chevrolet.

"I don't believe it!" Kaat exclaimed as they sped away from the nightclub in the Chrysler. "I actually did it. Me! I stole a car!" She pressed her hands to her ears in exhilaration. "In my next incarnation," she abruptly announced, her eyes pressed shut as if she were visualizing it, "I want to do that kind of thing more often. I want to *not* suppress farts and *not* set the hair of dead people and *not* obey the law all the goddamned time." She slid down in the seat so that her head rested on the back of it, kicked off her shoes and propped her feet up on the dashboard. "Do people steal cars in Russia?" she asked after a while.

"There aren't that many cars in Russia to steal," the Potter replied with a laugh. "There is very little crime in the ordinary sense of the word—muggings, bank robberies, burglaries. On the other hand, everyone steals from the state whenever they can. People work less and accept their full salary. They take bribes for doing what they are supposed to do anyway. You might say that we have no crime, but more than our share of corruption."

The way he said it made her turn her head toward him. "Why do you serve the state if there is so much corruption?" she asked softly.

The Potter waved a hand in irritation; she didn't understand at all. He was a Chekist from the old school; he had made his commitment to Leninism early in life, and stuck to it even when the excesses of the cult of the personality became apparent. If there had been a viable alternative, he had never been aware of it. Western democracies were decadent; they weighed competing philosophies rather than deciding where the rights of the matter lay. Stalinism, moreover, was not the inevitable result of Leninism, but an aberration. Mankind's best—for the Potter, its only—hope rested in the idealistic seeds buried within Leninism. But how could he explain all this to her? He decided to try; it suddenly seemed important to tell her *who* he was.

"The roots of the Russian state are idealistic," he said. "Because things have taken a bad turn is no reason for someone to abandon the original dream. All dreams turn sour at some point. Only the faint of heart, or those whose original commitment was self-serving, lose faith. That is something you, being American, should understand better than most people. Your country started out with idealistic roots too, but your 'All men are created equal' didn't include Negroes. It took a civil war to bring them into the mainstream of the country's idealism. You still haven't solved the problem completely. But the important thing is that you are evolving. My country will evolve too. It will move closer to a situation in which its actions match the idealism of its founders."

"You believe that? You believe Russia will rediscover its idealistic roots?"

The Potter said quietly, "I am obliged to believe it."

"What about Peter?" she asked after a moment's reflection. She appeared to wince at the memory of a pain when she pronounced his name. "Does he believe in Russia? Does he think what he is doing will help it evolve?"

"We both of us thought that what we were doing would help it survive," the Potter replied, thinking of the unlaundered years, "and as long as it survived, it would evolve."

Kaat reached over to rest her hand on the Potter's,

but he jerked it away. It wasn't that he was afraid of physical contact with her; it was more a matter of wanting it too much.

They continued on in a westerly direction, one of them driving, the other dozing in the passenger seat. They stopped at an all-night diner next to a drive-in movie, and Kaat phoned Millie back in Brooklyn, but she hadn't heard anything more from Peter. The Potter was afraid they had lost him forever, but Kaat remained hopeful. She found a road map and spread it across her knees and dangled her grandmother's ring over it, and announced that they should continue west. They stopped in a cheap motel, slept four hours, ate breakfast at a truckers' watering hole, then continued on west. By noon they had made it as far as Indianapolis. Kaat disappeared into a telephone booth while the Potter downed a cheeseburger, and emerged a few moments later shaking her head in disappointment.

They slept outside Indianapolis that night in a motel with a sign that said "No dogs" and had yellowish powder sprinkled on the sides of the cabins to discourage the strays that did show up. As soon as they settled into their room, Kaat phoned Millie, but all she got was the tape-recording machine. "It's me again," she said into it. "I'll call back." She wandered into the bathroom and the Potter heard her drawing a bath, heard also (his ear was fine-tuned to such things) that she didn't throw the lock on the door. Could he—dared he—take it as an invitation? In their cheap motel the night before, he had dreamed that his bed was a raft tossing about on a turbulent sea, surrounded by a circular horizon as sharp and as menacing as a razor blade. His mouth had felt parched, and it was only when he looked over, still in his dream, at the next raft and saw the naked woman clinging to it that he identified his thirst. What he wanted, he had realized with surprise, was to take her in his mouth as if she were a wet sponge, to suck the last drop of moisture from her. Now, listening to her in the bathroom—the toilet flushed, the water stopped running in the tub, a body settled gingerly into it—he permitted himself the luxury of imagining Kaat's body; of composing it the way a police artist puts together a composite portrait of a criminal: pointed breasts with insolent nipples, a visible rib cage, lean thighs, a soft bed of pubic hair, a flat backside that arched smoothly up to thin, bony shoulders. He felt the stirring of an erection—but only the stirring! He was, he reminded himself with a tired shrug, tied up irrevocably to that pier of old age.

He slipped off his jacket and loosened his tie, wedged the back of a chair under the doorknob as a precaution, removed the clip from his Beretta and then reinserted it, savoring the metallic sound of its being wedged home, and put the pistol under his pillow. He walked over to the bathroom door, listened for a long moment, then rapped lightly on it with his knuckles. "Did you say something?" he called, hoping she had; hoping she would.

"No," she answered. He could hear her splash in the water. He put his hand on the knob and silently turned it and felt it give way. And he realized that there was nothing to stop him from opening the door except his own view of himself as someone Kaat would not voluntarily choose to make love with.

It was enough. He let the knob ease back. It closed with an audible click.

"Are you still there?" Kaat, suddenly alert, asked from the bathroom.

The Potter listened to his own breathing until it was regular again. "No," he replied, and he went over to the bed and pulled off his shoes and stretched out on it.

She emerged from the bathroom a quarter of an hour later dressed in an ankle-length printed woolen nightdress that she must have owned since she was a teenager. She peeled back the blanket of the other bed and slipped between the coarse sheets. "You wanted to ask me something?" she said, looking across the room at him from the other raft. When he didn't answer, she said, "Before, when you were at the door of the bathroom. What did you want to ask me?"

"I wanted to ask you what it was like . . ." he began, and he left the rest of the question hanging.

She regarded him for a moment with her deep-set eyes. "Here's the thing," she said matter-of-factly. "With two, it is very often heavy, pompous, weighed down with appropriate sentiments, impossibly serious. But with three it has the saving grace of at least being humorous. Something funny is always happening. All the ridiculous things we do to each other, the way we attack each other's bodies, the awkward angles our limbs make as we flail away at each other—it's all very comic really. Have you ever looked at dogs copulating and not laughed? Watching humans make love is pretty much the same. Being watched too." She smiled across at the Potter, adrift on his raft. "Does that answer your question?"

He nodded in a distracted way. "Excuse me, if you please. I didn't mean to . . ."

"It's all right," she said, and he glanced sharply at her and realized it was.

Kaat tried Millie once more before they went to sleep. She answered on the second ring. "He called," she cried in an agitated voice. "Half an hour ago. You want to hear the tape?"

Kaat motioned to the Potter and held the earpiece so they could both listen to it. "Of course I want to hear the tape," she told Millie.

The Sleeper's voice could be heard on the line. "Are you in the mood for a bedtime story?" he asked Millie. He must have been in a public place, because from the background came the sound of people talking, of dishes being rattled.

"Am I ever," Millie said gleefully on the tape.

A woman's voice asked, "Why are you giving me that?"

"So you can say hello," the Sleeper told her.

"Hello," the woman said into the phone without much enthusiasm.

"Hello," Millie answered on the tape.

"All those hellos!" the real Millie complained to Kaat.

"You want *what*?" the woman could be heard asking the Sleeper. She laughed uneasily. "You have got to be kidding." The woman said to Millie, "Are you still there?" Then she gasped.

"Am I ever," Millie told her. "Where are you?"

"I remembered to ask her right off where she was," Millie told Kaat.

"Well," said the woman, and then she gasped again and was silent for a time.

"Old Peter must be shoving it right in," Millie whispered to Kaat. She spoke quickly, as if she were afraid of interrupting the tape recording.

"This is crazy," the woman could be heard saying. She must have brought the telephone close to her mouth then, because her voice became very distinct. "We're in this restaurant on top of the hotel. The view's terrific, though to tell you the honest-to-God truth, I haven't paid much attention to it. He doesn't want me to tell you the name of the hotel, or the name of the city we're in. We're over the river now, but we—" She gasped, then laughed weakly.

"Go on," the Sleeper could be heard encouraging her.

"—we won't be over the river for long. We made love in the hotel before we came up here to eat." Her voice became muted; she was holding a hand over the mouthpiece. "Do you want me to tell her about that part?" She came back on the line to Millie. "Okay. What he wants me to tell you is what we're doing now. Here's what we're doing now," she began in a singsong voice, as if she were starting a composition on how she spent her summer vacation. "The restaurant is kind of dark, see, and the tablecloth comes down low over the edge, and we're sitting on a banquette-type bench with our backs to the river, only the river isn't there anymore, see, the river has moved on and the city is there now, and I'm not wearing any underwear, right—" She stopped talking for a long moment. "Oh God." Another pause. "Yeah, well, like I was saying, I'm not wearing any underwear, see, and your friend here has disappeared under the table because nobody's looking our way, and even if they were looking our way it is much too dark for them to see anything, and me, I am just sitting here with my back against this banquette-type bench with my legs apart talking to you on this phone they plugged in, looking as if nothing . . . nothing out of the ordinary is going on, only it is. If you ask me, something very out of the ordinary is going on." Suddenly the woman hissed in panic, "The waiter's heading this—"

And then the phone went dead on the tape recording.

Millie giggled and told Kaat, "I'll say something out of the ordinary is going on. Jesus! You got to hand it to him, does he have his nerve!"

This time Kaat woke W.A. up when she phoned him on the Coast. "What are ex-husbands for if you can't ring them any hour of the day or night," she told him.

"You exaggerate," W.A. reproached her. "You always did. Maybe that's what was wrong between us."

"What was wrong between us," Kaat fired back, "is that there was nothing but sex between us."

"You used to think the sex was pretty damn good," W.A. muttered unhappily.

Kaat's voice softened. "It was more than pretty damn good," she said. "I just wanted more than sex, W.A."

"Have you found the more with somebody else?"

"Not yet, W.A. But I'm still looking."

"Break your heart," W.A. said gruffly. "What's it to me? Why'd you call?"

Kaat told him. The friend they were trying to catch

up with was in a restaurant on top of a hotel. Apparently it had a great view. It seemed to be situated over a river, too, except the river moved on, whatever that meant, and the city took its place.

"Whatever game you're playing sure sounds like fun," W.A. said. "Call me back in fifteen minutes." And he hung up.

"What did he say?" the Potter asked.

"He said for me to call him back in a quarter of an hour."

"Why?"

"He probably wants to look something up in his diary," Kaat said.

A feeling of frustration consumed the Potter. Here they were waiting for Kaat's ex, as she called him, to look up something in his diary! It was the kind of thing that happened in spy stories, but not in real life. It went against every instinct in his body, against every experience he had ever had, against everything he had taught the sleepers who passed through his school in Moscow. Yet what choice did he have? And he had always said there were no rules.

"You're sure she said the river moved on and the city took its place?" W.A. asked Kaat when she called back.

"That's what she said," Kaat insisted. "Does it make any sense to you, W.A.?"

"The river has got to be the Mississippi," W.A. said. "The city has got to be St. Louis. The restaurant has got to be the revolving restaurant over a hotel named the Riverview. They wanted me to play there right after they built it, but I got seasick because of the motion and vomited and couldn't perform."

"W.A., if I were in L.A. right now, you know what I'd do?"

"Heck, let me guess," W.A. said, shifting his voice into what he considered to be his seductive register.

"You've got one dirty mind," Kaat chastised him.

"That's not what I'd do. What I'd do is give you a kiss on the lips."

"I'll take whatever I can get," W.A. said.

Kaat hung up the receiver and regarded the Potter, who was already shoving the few things he had into his small overnight bag. He straightened, his eyes closed of their own accord and he found, to his astonishment, that he could *remember* Kaat, remember what she looked like, and with his eyes still closed he said in a hollow voice, "I am still needing you."

Kaat spoke slowly, discovering herself in every word, in the spaces between the words. "I still need to be needed."

Within twenty minutes they had woken up the night clerk to pay their hotel bill, loaded the little they had in the Chrysler and started west on Route 70 toward St. Louis. The road was still wet from a late-night cloudburst, and the occasional car or truck passing in the opposite direction sent pinpricks of light spitting up at them from the rain-soaked highway; the effect, Kaat said, was like watching fireworks burst under them. First light, seeping over the brim of dark clouds stretched along the horizon, caught up with them as they crossed the Wabash. By the time sun popped up behind the brim of clouds, almost like a target in a shooting gallery, they had taken a good bite out of southern Illinois. They stopped at a service station for gas and paper cups filled with muddy coffee dispensed from a bright red vending machine. The Potter went around back and urinated at the edge of a clearing rather than use the rest room, which smelled as if it hadn't been hosed out in years. On their way out of the service station, they passed a hand-lettered sign that wished them "Happy Motoring," "an example," the Potter noted in annoyance, "of the curious American idea that motoring involved something more than getting from one place to another."

Gazing out at farmers already perched on their tractors, at the furrowed fields that looked as if giant fingernails had been scratched across the surface of the earth, Kaat remarked that getting from one place to the other, for her at least, had never been accompanied by a feeling of pleasure. "I suppose you have to want not to get where you're going in order to really enjoy the trip," she said thoughtfully.

They passed through a series of villages masquerading as towns, and towns with all the trappings of cities except size, and the Potter commented that every town and village in Russia had its Communist Party headquarters, whereas in America the thing they all had in common seemed to be the funeral home, usually Colonial or at least neo, always sober, with a gleaming black hearse with lace curtains on its windows stationed in the driveway, nose outward, as if ready for a fast getaway. "From a business point of view," Kaat noted absently—she had had a certain amount of experience with funeral homes—"you can always rely on people dying."

They spoke in undertones about the institution of death; of how some people avoided the notion of its being an end by visualizing it as a beginning; of how others, tired of beginnings, took comfort in anticipating the closing of the curtain, the end of the act. At one point the Potter said he thought it was a phenomenon peculiar to America that the approaches to its great cities were more often than not lined with used-car lots and cemeteries. In the chaos of the inner cities there was barely room for automobiles or the living, and the Potter considered there was a certain logic to the used and the dead setting up camp on the periphery. It was where they belonged, he said; it left the center of the cities reserved for the living, he said, and he thought to himself: for the killing also.

St. Louis turned out to be no exception—though the cemetery that filled the fields on either side of the road was a graveyard not for people but for cars. They were piled on top of each other, silent, solemn leaning towers of rust, monuments, the Potter said, to the two unpardonable transgressions of people and machines: growing old and growing obsolete.

The Potter pressed his foot down on the accelerator and sped past the gateway of the city toward the rendezvous with the living, the killing at its center.

22

❦

Ourcq was stretched out on the bed, his scuffed black oxfords still on his feet, inflating and deflating his stomach in one of the Canadian Air Force exercises designed to strengthen abdominal muscles. Appleyard stood gazing out of the window, listening to the rain beat against the panes, memorizing the sound. Moistening his lips, pursing them, he began to imitate the rain, and when he had gotten it just right he slowly turned up the volume until it sounded as if it were raining *inside* the room. Ourcq's head snapped around in Appleyard's direction. "Can't you imitate the fucking sun shining for a change?" he flared.

With a shrug, Appleyard cut off the sound of rain. "I can do the sun setting, but not shining," he said.

Ourcq sat up in bed. "How much fucking longer we got to stay cooped up in this fucking pigeonhole?"

Appleyard glanced at his wristwatch. "He checked out four hours ago. We should hang around for another twenty hours if we go by the book."

"Twenty fucking hours!" Ourcq groaned. "Fucking sweeping is fucking impossible."

"You want me maybe to get some magazines up here?" Appleyard offered.

"Something with a lot of fucking ass in it," Ourcq agreed. "Get a receipt and we'll put it on the fucking expense account."

Appleyard started to slip into his suit jacket. Just

then the phone next to the bed purred. Appleyard, struck by the sound, imitated it.

Ourcq said, "Who the fuck would be calling us?" as he reached for the receiver. He listened for a moment, then muttered to the person on the other end, "You don't fucking say," and hung up.

"It's the fucking girl," Ourcq told Appleyard. He looked around for his suit jacket. "She doesn't have the fucking pussycat under her fucking arm, but he's sure it's her."

Two minutes later Ourcq and Appleyard arrived in the lobby. Separately. Ourcq, who hated stairs, had taken the elevator; Appleyard, who suffered from nosebleeds in elevators, had taken the staircase. Ourcq nodded toward the desk clerk who had tipped them off. The desk clerk nodded toward a door behind the newspaper stand. Ourcq and Appleyard wandered casually across to the door and stood with their backs to it for a moment, surveying the lobby. Ourcq said, "The fucking dwarf's still unaccounted for. You stay here and keep a fucking eye peeled for him. I'll go find the fucking girl."

"Why don't I maybe go find the girl for once?" Appleyard complained.

"Because it is me who gives the fucking orders," Ourcq whined. "Besides, I am a better fucking shot than you are."

"I missed," Appleyard explained, obviously not for the first time, a pained expression clinging to his face, "because he jerked the car when I pulled the trigger. It could happen to anyone."

"But it fucking happened to you," Ourcq insisted without a shred of sympathy. He opened the door a crack, saw that the long corridor on the other side of it was empty, and ducked through, closing the door behind him. He kept his right hand on the butt of his pistol in its shoulder holster as he moved along the corridor, trying doorknobs on either side. They were all locked. Which left the door on the far end of the corridor. Ourcq approached it without a sound, tried the knob with his left hand, realized that this door wasn't locked. He withdrew his hand, pulled a handkerchief from his trouser pocket and went back along the corridor unscrewing the three overhead bulbs. Then he felt his way back along the wall to the unlocked door. He drew his pistol from its holster, took the silencer from his jacket pocket and screwed it into the tip of the pistol. Flattening himself against the wall, he again reached for the knob and softly eased open the door.

The area beyond, a large storage room stacked with round banquet tables of various sizes standing on their edges, along with hundreds of folded chairs, was totally dark except for the eerie red halo above the "Emergency Exit" sign at the far end. Ourcq, still flattened against the wall on the corridor side of the door, strained to catch the faintest sound in the storage room. Hearing nothing, he bent his body until he was doubled over in a crouch, then sprang over the threshold and straightened with his back flat against the wall inside the room. Barely breathing, he devoted another long minute to listening. It was Ourcq's theory that he had a fixed amount of time to spend when stalking a target; that half of it should be spent on his own safety, and the other half on the target's death. Having used up the portion for himself, Ourcq stepped off smartly from the wall and headed down the aisle formed by the stacked tables toward the emergency exit. He was halfway across the room when he heard a scraping sound ahead. He stopped in his tracks.

"I know you are fucking there," Ourcq called. "Come out where I can fucking see you and nothing will happen to you. I just want to ask you a few fucking questions."

In the dull glow of the "Emergency Exit" sign, Kaat moved into his field of vision farther along the makeshift aisle. "Why are you following me?" she asked.

Ourcq could see her outline, but not her features.

He had to make sure it was the right woman. Keeping his pistol parallel to his leg so that she wouldn't notice it, he said, "I'm the fucking house detective. You asked at the fucking desk about one of our clients. The clerk said there was no one registered under that fucking name. Then you fucking described who you were looking for."

Kaat said, "Are you really incapable of saying a sentence without using the word 'fucking' in it?"

"I can fucking well say a sentence without the word 'fucking' in it if I fucking want to. But I don't fucking want to. Now, how about if you describe for me the fucking man you were looking for."

Kaat described Peter Raven to Ourcq.

"That is who I fucking thought you were looking for," he said. He took a step in Kaat's direction. "You were looking for him in the fucking Seventh Heaven, too, weren't you?"

"And you were one of the two men in the Dodge who shot my cat," Kaat said.

"I definitely did not shoot no fucking cat," Ourcq contradicted her. "Appleyard shot the fucking cat. Where is the fucking dwarf who was traveling with you?"

It was at that instant that Ourcq felt the icy burn of metal against the nape of his neck. "The dwarf is right behind you, if you please," the Potter said with quiet passion. "Far enough so that if you kick a foot back or try to catch me in the stomach with an elbow, you will come into contact with nothing but air. Near enough so that I can put a twenty-two-caliber bullet through your neck the instant I feel you move. Listen to me carefully. I am now going to count out loud to three. If you move before I reach three, or if I do not hear your gun fall to the floor, I will pull the trigger. I do not have a silencer. My Beretta makes a soft coughing sound. But you will not hear a thing. So. One. Two."

Ourcq's pistol clattered to the floor.

"Kick it away. Slowly. Good. Now undo your belt and let your trousers drop to your ankles. Good. Now turn very slowly to your right, facing the table, and reach up with your hands and grip the top edge of it, and lean your forehead against it. Very good. You have saved your life. For the moment." The Potter took a step backward. "You can turn on the lights now," he called to Kaat.

She found the switch, and the storage room was bathed in light. "Move your head so I can see your profile," the Potter instructed Ourcq.

Ourcq did as he was told.

"I have seen you before," the Potter announced.

Kaat came up behind the Potter. "In the Dodge," she suggested.

"I have seen him before the Dodge," the Potter said. "In Moscow." To Ourcq he said, "When were you in Moscow, if you please?"

Ourcq turned back to the table. "I have never been in Moscow in my fucking life," he said.

The Potter smiled faintly. "If you do not understand what I am now saying to you," he told Ourcq in Russian, "I am going to shoot you through your spinal column."

"I understand, I understand," Ourcq answered in Russian, which he spoke with a Canadian accent. In English he added, "We are both of us on the same fucking side!"

"You are sweepers," the Potter said.

"Fucking sweepers, yes," Ourcq agreed enthusiastically.

"Dispatched by a Soviet *rezident* to sweep the trail of an agent on a mission?"

"You know as much as I fucking do," Ourcq said. "Can I take my fucking hands down and pull up my fucking pants now?" And he added in a low voice, "In case you didn't notice, there's a fucking lady present."

"No," said the Potter.

"But I told you," cried Ourcq, his voice suddenly hoarse with emotion, "we are on the same fucking side."

"I think I know whose side you are on," the Potter said, "but I am not yet sure whose side I am on."

"What are you going to do with him?" Kaat asked.

"I am going to bombard him with questions. And I am going to shoot him if he does not answer them."

"All you can fucking talk about is shooting people," Ourcq complained.

"I did see you in Moscow, didn't I?" the Potter demanded.

"How should I fucking know if you saw me in Moscow? I was there three fucking years ago. There was a fucking medal ceremony. There was a fucking cocktail party with some fucking department bosses. There was a fucking debriefing on a job I had pulled off for my fucking *rezident*. There was even a fucking orgy in a fucking *dacha* on the fucking Black Sea."

"I saw you at the cocktail party," the Potter remembered. "You spread caviar on a slice of toast as if it were butter. I was a *novator* at the time, which is why I was invited. Everybody loved your accent when you spoke Russian. You were a big success. It comes back to me now—you had a Canadian father and a Russian mother."

"A Canadian mother and a Russian father," Ourcq corrected him.

"You didn't say 'fucking,' " Kaat noted. "Keep up the good work."

"Fuck off," Ourcq snapped in irritation.

"Watch how you talk, if you please," the Potter warned sharply.

Ourcq laughed under his breath. "You going to shoot me because you don't like the way I fucking talk?"

"I may," the Potter said.

"He might," Kaat chimed in, though she doubted he would.

Ourcq laughed out loud this time. "Imagine getting wiped away because you talk fucking dirty!"

"You are not a regular sweeper," the Potter suggested. "You are a hit man. A specialist in wetwork."

"Wet fucking work," Ourcq agreed. "But they needed sweepers fast, and we were fucking available."

"You were given an itinerary," the Potter said quietly.

Ourcq didn't say anything.

"Here's the thing," Kaat said from behind the Potter. "We know where he's going. How do you think we found him at Seventh Heaven? How do you think we found him here?"

Ourcq grunted. "You fucking missed him at Seventh Heaven. You fucking missed him here too." He turned to look over his shoulder at the Potter. "You are a fucking professional. You and I talk the same fucking language. You know where he's going, my fucking ass! If you knew where he was fucking going, you wouldn't need to ask me. I can give you any fucking answer under the sun. Why are we playing this fucking game anyhow?"

Ourcq turned back to the table and took a deep breath, and wondered if it would be his last.

The Potter grabbed Kaat's arm and pushed her in the general direction of the door with the "Emergency Exit" sign over it. She took a few steps, then hesitated. The Potter, who was wrapping a handkerchief around the muzzle of his Beretta, waved her on impatiently. She turned and walked briskly away.

"Where is the fucking lady going?" Ourcq inquired nervously.

"Do not turn around, if you please," the Potter instructed him.

"Jesus fucking Christ," muttered Ourcq. His knees started to tremble.

"How many people have you shot in your day?" the Potter asked him.

"My fucking share," Ourcq admitted. His voice was pitched high, off its usual key.

"Did you enjoy shooting them?"

Ourcq shrugged, and for an instant it looked as if he were physically shaking off the question. Then he decided to answer it; maybe it would give him more time. "I did not fucking enjoy it. I did not fucking *not* enjoy it. It was what I did for a fucking living. We have all of us got to fucking eat!" He pressed his forehead to the table and closed his eyes and said in a harsh voice, "Do me a fucking favor, get it fucking over with."

The Potter glanced at Kaat, who was watching from the door. They looked at each other for a long moment. Then in one flowing gesture he bent and pressed his pistol to the toe of Ourcq's right shoe and pulled the trigger. The Beretta coughed discreetly, just as the Potter had said it would. Moaning softly, Ourcq sank to the ground. "Is that fucking all?" he asked in a weak voice.

"Isn't it enough?" the Potter asked. He felt very tired.

"It will definitely give you a fucking head start," Ourcq muttered. He was looking at his foot as if it belonged to someone else.

"That is all I will need," the Potter said.

"Do not waste any fucking moment of it," Ourcq advised him, and grimacing from the pain, he started to unlace the scuffed black oxford from which blood was seeping.

23

❦

Khanda knew the building inside out. On one errand or another, he had investigated every corner of it. At the very beginning he had toyed with the idea of shooting from the roof. He could keep out of sight beforehand behind the giant neon Hertz sign that flashed the time and temperature, or the enormous rusted boiler, abandoned when the warehouse switched from steam heat. But he had given up the idea because the police accompanying the target would be scanning, as a matter of habit, rooftops for the silhouette of a rifleman. Windows, because there were literally hundreds of them along the route, offered a much surer sniper's nest, he had decided.

Early on he had selected one, in the far corner of the sixth floor, which gave him the best vantage point. He stood motionless before it now, watching as the motorcade going through a dress rehearsal jogged right off Main Street and headed directly toward the warehouse in which he worked. Just below the warehouse the motorcade turned sharply left toward the railroad underpass and, eventually, the freeway that would take the target to his luncheon rendezvous. Squinting through an imaginary telescopic sight, Khanda went through the motions of working the bolt of his rifle twice and firing off three shots at the back of the Prince's head. It would be difficult to miss at this range, since his four-power scope would make it appear as if he were shooting at a target a mere twenty-two yards away. Then, too, his rifle had less recoil than the average military weapon, an advantage that increased its accuracy under rapid fire conditions. It also had a tendency to fire a bit high and to the right, a perfect defect when aiming at a target moving away and slightly to the right; it meant that he wouldn't have to make allowances for the apparent upward drift of the target due to the height of his sniper's nest.

Having fired off three shots in his imagination, Khanda punched his stopwatch, then trotted across the filthy warehouse floor toward the enclosed stairway in the northwest corner of the building. Taking the steps two at a time, he descended to the second-floor lunchroom, where he inserted a coin in the vending machine and bought himself a Coke. It was a touch Khanda was particularly proud of; someone wandering down the steps casually sipping a Coke would appear particularly innocent to a policeman racing up looking for a sniper. Then he made his way, Coke in hand, down to the main door and out into the sun-drenched street.

He punched his stopwatch and looked at it. Even stopping for the Coke, it had taken him three minutes from the time he fired the rifle until the moment he emerged from the warehouse. It was extremely unlikely that the police would be able to seal off the building in that time span. Hell, it would take them that long just to figure out where the shots had come from!

Sipping from his Coke, squinting this time because of the sunlight, Khanda surveyed the traffic passing the warehouse. A thin smirk stretched across his lips. In four days he would know if his calculations were correct.

24

❦

The Director, tall, thin, Midwestern in origin but very *nouveau* Georgetown in the way he dressed and carried himself, came around the desk and held out the box of chocolates toward Carroll. "The ones with the gold wrappers are filled with brandy," he told him. He flashed what had passed for an encouraging smile in the days when he had been an investment banker. "Two of them will ruin you for an afternoon. Three and you can testify before a Senate oversight committee and feel no pain whatsoever."

The Deputy Director, sitting on a couch made of leather as soft as kid gloves, chuckled appreciatively. G. Sprowls, leaning casually against a bookcase, looked on with his usual half-smile etched on his face. Carroll helped himself to a candy, undid the gold wrapper and popped it into his mouth.

"What did I tell you?" said the Director, settling back into his wicker swivel chair, a family heirloom that he had brought with him when he took the job.

Carroll swallowed. "Very good," he agreed. He arched his neck and wedged a finger under his starched collar. "You have done what you can to put me at ease. Now why don't we get on with it."

The Deputy Director leaned forward on the couch. "You are not going to be difficult, I hope."

Carroll concentrated on the wall above the Director's Toulouse-Lautrec, another family heirloom. "I'm not at all sure what I'm going to be," he admitted.

The Director tapped the eraser end of a pencil against his desk blotter. "If I understand you correctly," he told Carroll, "you take the position that I personally authorized an operation."

A muscle in Carroll's cheek twitched once as he nodded in agreement.

"Good. Fine," said the Director. "You are one of the old hands around the shop. I don't for an instant doubt that you and your colleague—what is his name again?"

"Francis," Carroll offered.

"Francis, exactly. I don't doubt that you and Francis are not motivated, like some people around here who shall remain nameless, by the current watchword, 'Don't do something, just stand there.' "

"We view the world situation as desperate," Carroll conceded. "We think it is—you yourself said it when you were pinning a medal on one of our neighbors recently—two minutes to midnight. If someone doesn't do something about it, and fairly quickly, time will run out on us."

"That is exactly how I see things," the Director, who had been well-briefed by G. Sprowls, insisted.

Carroll shrugged. "You spoke about the need for unleashing the Company."

"I have made no bones about where I stand," the Director readily agreed. "It is a matter of life or death, in my view."

"When you spoke at that reception for one of our British colleagues," Carroll continued, "you made a point of recalling Winston Churchill's preference, during the Second World War, for invading the Dardanelles before France."

"It would have changed the map of Europe," the Director pointed out. "It would have been the allied armies, and not the Red Army, that liberated the captive countries of Eastern Europe. We would have installed friendly democratic governments before they could have installed their dictatorial Communist regimes."

"Everyone understood what you were getting at between the lines," Carroll went on. "What we need in the Western world are leaders who are not soft on Communism."

"Leaders who are not afraid to bite the bullet," the Director offered.

"Who will stand up to the Communists," the Deputy Director added, "and not cut and run every time they confront them, whether at conference tables or invasion beaches."

"That's nicely put," the Director said approvingly. "I couldn't have phrased it better myself."

Everyone was staring at Carroll. Carroll was still focusing on a spot on the wall.

"So you see," the Director went on, "we are all of us in the same boat. If I authorized an operation, I won't back away from it now."

"Between us," the Deputy Director said, "what are you up to?"

"You can count on me to stand behind you," the Director vowed.

G. Sprowls straightened up at the bookcase. "You awakened the Soviet sleeper," he drawled, "and sent him off to kill someone whom you knew the Director wanted dead. That's it, isn't it?"

Again a muscle twitched in Carroll's cheek, only this time it wouldn't stop. He nodded imperceptibly.

"Who?" G. Sprowls asked quietly.

"Is it anyone we know?" the Deputy Director demanded. "The Russian ambassador, say, or that actor out in Hollywood who plays the Commie game by speaking out all the time against racism?"

"I have no doubt whatsoever that you have done the right thing," the Director observed. "But there may be loose ends to tie up. There may be ways we can enlarge the operation, or set in motion other auxiliary operations designed to take advantage of your"—he searched frantically for an appropriate word, and came up with—"initiative."

Carroll brought his fingertips up to his cheek to still the twitching. Then he quietly pronounced the name of the target of the operation that he and Francis had launched.

The Director stiffened in his wicker swivel chair as if he had received a heavy jolt of electricity. The Deputy Director's mouth gaped open and he collapsed weakly into the relative safety of the couch. Only G. Sprowls accepted the revelation with anything resembling equanimity. "Of course," he muttered to himself, "how could I have missed it!"

"You *what*?" the Director cried when he discovered how his vocal cords operated. "You had the audacity, the temerity, the *gall* to order the assassination of—" He couldn't bring himself to say the name of the target.

"I must be dreaming," the Deputy Director moaned from the couch. "I must be imagining things." He looked at G. Sprowls. "Tell me I am imagining things," he pleaded. "Tell me I will wake up at any moment and laugh at this whole business."

Carroll shifted his gaze from the wall to the window. "You authorized the operation," he reminded the Director. "You admitted as much a few minutes ago. There are witnesses . . . the walls have ears."

"My walls," the Director announced in an icy voice, "do not have ears. I authorized nothing of the kind. It never occurred to me that anyone would interpret my comments as an invitation to launch an operation. You and your friend are certifiably insane. Stark raving mad. My God, do you realize what has happened? If anybody in Congress or the press gets so much as a whiff of this, the Company will be ruined forever."

G. Sprowls came around behind the Director's desk and whispered for a moment in his ear. The Director appeared to calm down instantly. His eyes narrowed, and he began tapping the eraser end of his pencil thoughtfully against the blotter again. G. Sprowls looked at Carroll and asked in his slow drawl that suggested he knew the answer, "Who exactly knows about what you have done?"

"I know. Francis knows. Now you three know."

"If I can recapitulate," G. Sprowls said evenly. "You organized the defection from the Soviet Union of the Potter, who gave you the identity and awakening signal of a Soviet sleeper. You and Francis delivered the signal, activating the sleeper and dispatching him on a mission. Even as we speak, a Soviet agent—"

The Director saw what G. Sprowls was driving at. "Born and raised in Communist Russia, recruited and trained by the KGB and presumably—who could prove otherwise?—still under its operational control . . ."

The color had flooded back into the Deputy Director's face, and he leaned forward and finished G. Sprowls's line of reasoning. "A Soviet agent is traveling across the country to commit a crime."

Carroll leapt out of his chair. "Don't you see the infinite possibilities, the absolute beauty of the operation? If our sleeper succeeds, we eliminate someone who has hurt the United States more than any single person in recent history; someone who has sucked up to the Communists and tied the hands of those of us who are willing and able to fight them. If the sleeper is caught in the act, his identity will eventually come out, and the whole Soviet intelligence apparatus—"

"The whole idea that you can conduct business as usual with the Russians!" the Director interjected.

"—will be discredited," Carroll plunged on. "If, by any chance, the sleeper is not caught, we will identify him and place the onus for the assassination on his masters in Moscow." Carroll sank back into his chair, drained. "It is like a diamond with many facets—it is the most perfect, the most beautiful operation that has ever existed in the annals of intelligence work," he continued in an undertone. "The worst that can happen is that the sleeper will fail and the Russians will be blamed for the assassination attempt. The best that can happen is that he will succeed—and the Russians will be blamed for the death."

The Director regarded Carroll, then lowered his eyes to his blotter, then abruptly swiveled his chair around so that he could stare out the window. "I have to admit," he said after a moment, "it does have a certain—" He didn't finish the phrase.

G. Sprowls and the Deputy Director exchanged knowing looks. "If the Soviets are blamed," the Deputy Director offered from the couch, "Congress and the public will begin to see the world as we see it; as it really is! The Company will be unleashed to take its place in the front line of battle. We won't have to go begging hat in hand up on the Hill every time we need a few hundred million dollars."

The Director slowly swiveled back toward the room. It was apparent that he had come to a decision. "As far as I am concerned, gentlemen," he announced in a businesslike tone, "this meeting never took place."

The Deputy Director's eyes widened in complicity. "What meeting," he asked innocently, "are you talking about?"

25

⚜

There were loose ends. (There were always loose ends, the Potter would tell his students at the sleeper school; it was one of the few things people in their line of work could count on.) G. Sprowls was authorized to tie them up, a matter, he confided to the Director, of erasing footprints so that nobody could see who had passed this way.

Oskar, who happened to be recruiting for his network in East Berlin at the time, received a coded message summoning him West for an urgent meeting. Using one of his many aliases, he crossed through Checkpoint Charlie, took a taxi to a business district, and continued on foot to his safe house in West Berlin. He buzzed twice, sensed someone looking at him through the peephole, then heard the locks on the door being opened. He wasn't so much alarmed as annoyed when he didn't recognize the man who held the door for him; the fewer people he was exposed to, the safer he felt. But he became upset when the second man, waiting for him in the living room, turned out to be a stranger also. "So," Oskar said in German, sensing that something out of the ordinary was happening. "You must have a very important message for me, yes?"

The man Oskar spoke to was leaning against the wall next to a phony fireplace. He was wearing an overcoat and carrying a bouquet of plastic roses. The other man, the one who had let him into the apartment, came into the living room behind him and closed the door. "We are deliverymen," the man next to the phony fireplace told Oskar. He spoke German with a distinct Bavarian accent.

Oskar didn't like the look of him. "So what is it you are delivering?" he asked.

"Your body," the Bavarian replied just as the other man stepped forward and plunged a long, thin kitchen knife up to its hilt into Oskar's back.

"Why?" Oskar managed to gasp, as if it would be easier to deal with death if he understood the motives of his killers; as if his own fate, as long as it was logical, would be acceptable.

The Bavarian only shrugged. "They only told us who, not why," he informed Oskar.

The man behind Oskar caught him under the armpits and lowered him gently, solicitously even, to the floor. Oskar attempted to turn his face and get his mouth off the dirty carpet. But he couldn't move. He could feel the strength ebbing from his body. Someone was feeling for his pulse. He tried to open his eyes, to work his lips, to tell them to be sure not to bury him until they were positive he was dead, yes? Because he had a lifelong horror of waking up in a sealed coffin. But he was too dizzy to function. The carpet under his face was suddenly spinning; a whirlpool was sucking him into its center. Why? he thought to himself as he plunged head first toward it. At the last instant of consciousness, an acceptable answer occurred to him: Why not!

Within an hour of Oskar's rendezvous in the safe house, two middle-level West German intelligence operatives—the senior of the two habitually pinned a black homburg to his head with the curved handle of an umbrella, the junior trudged around in galoshes at the slightest hint of rain—were driving along an *autobahn* toward Berlin in response to a verbal summons from an American contact. They chatted about pay scales, and the political situation in West Germany, and whether they would live to witness the reunification of the two halves of their country. Galoshes told Homburg he was curious to know what had become of the dwarflike Russian defector and his floozy of a wife whom they had been assigned to welcome to Vienna several months before. Homburg shook his head. Curiosity, he informed his younger colleague, was what killed the cat. Galoshes took the hint and didn't pursue the subject.

Rounding a curve thirty miles from their destination, the Mercedes veered out of control. The steering pinion had snapped—at least that was what an in-house postmortem attributed the accident to. The car skidded off the highway, down an embankment into a ravine, where it burst into flame and exploded, killing the two men instantly.

The afternoon of Oskar's disappearance, Svetochka's body was discovered at the bottom of an elevator shaft in a downtown Vienna office building. There was a suicide note, written in her own hand, in the pocket of the used fur coat she had bought the previous week with the money she had wormed out of one of the Austrians in return for services rendered. "Excuse Svetochka," it read in English, "for the trouble she has caused. She is not wanting to stay here and she is not willing to go back, so she is going to put herself to sleep."

The Viennese detective who investigated the death was mildly curious how a woman could have pried open the doors to the elevator shaft. One of the uniformed policemen accompanying him managed to do it, but he was an amateur wrestler. The chief of detectives who read the preliminary report asked the detective to retype it leaving out his doubts about whether Svetochka had the strength to pry open the doors, or the ability to write a suicide note in English when she couldn't speak it. Quite obviously, the Viennese police were happy to accept the note, and the suicide of a recent immigrant from the Soviet Union, at face value. Why muddy the water? the superintendent in charge of homicides said when he closed the case.

G. Sprowls received reports of Oskar's disappearance and the deaths of the two Germans and Svetochka in the overnight pouch, shredded the only copies in existence, then dispatched Thursday's orders, in triplicate, through the interoffice routing system. The Sisters' former man Friday was cooling his heels in a basement cubbyhole, wading through piles of transcripts of obituaries from provincial Soviet newspapers and matching up the names with those of former members of the Politburo and Central Committee. The fact that he could discern no rhyme or reason in what he was doing didn't make the chore any easier, so that when the orders arrived sending him overseas, he barely glanced at the fine print to see where exactly he was off to. Anything, he decided, would be better than reading Russian obituaries in a stuffy basement cubbyhole. It was only after he had countersigned the orders, and returned the pink copy to the originating desk, that he bothered to identify his new post. "You will proceed, on a priority-one voucher via a military-air-transport flight out of Edwards Air Force Base, to Bangkok," the orders read, "where you will report to the adjutant station chief, Bangkok, for further assignment to listening post Echo-Charlie-Hotel, situated on the Cambodian–South Vietnamese frontier, 1.7 kilometers from the Ho Chi Minh trail. On arrival you will relieve the acting post chief, and file a full KIA report on the circumstances surrounding the death of your predecessor, as well as carry out to the best of your abilities the mission of the listening post as set forth in the listening-post operating-procedure annex to these orders."

Thursday's case officer, an older woman with a cigarette dangling from her lips and ashes dropping on the papers that passed across her desk, supplied him with a voucher for *per diem* funds to cover his travel expenses until his arrival in Bangkok. She also asked him to fill out and sign a standard next-of-kin form, and identify his beneficiaries in the event anything happened to him in the field. Thursday protested that he had never given the matter of beneficiaries much thought. The case officer brushed ashes off the appropriate form with the back of her hand and suggested that the time had come to do so. You are not going to a tea party, she informed him in a voice that was anything but motherly. The last two people we sent out to Echo-Charlie-Hotel came back in pine boxes.

In pine boxes, Thursday repeated, and he astonished the case officer studying him through a haze of cigarette smoke by giggling uncontrollably.

G. Sprowls's damp half-smile evaporated when the case officer phoned him to confirm that Thursday was off and running. He produced an index card with the words "Loose Ends" typed at the top, and carefully erased Thursday's name. Four other names had already been erased. All of them had "died of measles," Company argot for killing someone and making the death look natural. Which left three names on the card. The Potter, Feliks Arkantevich Turov, was the next on the list. G. Sprowls had put out discreet feelers. It was only a matter of time before his sources would locate the Potter. Then he would erase his name from the card too, and concentrate on the last two loose ends.

G. Sprowls looked up suddenly from the index card. A chilling thought had appeared on the horizon of his consciousness. He had caught sight of it while it was still a vague menace, too distant to define. He watched it draw closer. And then a shudder threaded its way down his spinal column as he identified it. If Francis could lie to the black box about his name, he could also have been lying when he claimed that he had not had any contact with agents or representatives of another country!

26

❦

The sign in the window of the Chinese health-food restaurant announced, in ridiculous lettering with Chinese curlicues, that it was under new management. "We should at least give it a try," Carroll insisted, and he led the way past the new owner, smiling uncertainly from his seat behind the cigarette counter, to their usual booth in the far corner.

They spent a long time studying the menu, made sure the waiter understood that they didn't want any monosodium glutamate sprinkled on their dishes, and then ordered, Carroll with undisguised enthusiasm, Francis with undisguised suspicion. Waiting for the food to come, they discussed the weather, the film Francis had seen the previous Tuesday, Carroll's sister's recent menopausal outburst when she discovered that he was throwing out socks instead of giving them to her to darn; in short, they discussed everything *but*. Until Carroll, midway through his plate of wild rice and steamed shrimp, slammed his chopsticks down on the table so loudly that the owner, watching them out of the corner of his eye for some sign that they were enjoying the food, looked over with an anguished expression on his face. Francis smiled innocently in his direction, and nodded encouragingly, and the owner, appeased, turned back to his abacus and toyed with it as if it were strung with worry beads.

"The way I see it," Carroll said quietly, staring off

into space, "is that what we had before was a brilliant operation for which we could never get credit. Now our masters are bound to see our talents in a new light."

Francis gestured with the back of his hand. "Raises, promotions, don't interest me anymore. I am too old to appreciate that sort of thing."

"I'm not talking about raises or promotions," Carroll hissed. "I'm talking about the plots we can hatch now that we have credit in the bank. The next time we come up with a scheme, the doors in the Athenaeum will open to us of their own accord. Listen to me, Francis. Between us, you and I can stop the hemorrhage that is sucking the lifeblood out of this country. America can return to being America the beautiful."

Francis toyed with his Chinese cabbage, which he found overcooked and underspiced. "What made you tell them?" he wanted to know.

"Pure instinct," Carroll replied without a trace of modesty. Modesty, in his book, was for people who had something to be modest about. "I knew the Director would have to be on our side." He leaned toward Francis. "I remember when you first noticed there was a pattern to his off-the-cuff remarks. That thing he said about it being two minutes to midnight, for instance. Or about the need for unleashing the Company. And how what the Director was really saying with the business about Churchill and the Dardanelles was that we desperately needed leaders who were not soft on Communism." In an unusual gesture that Francis found almost touching, Carroll shifted his eyes and actually focused on him across the table. "I have to hand it to you, Francis. You were the one who ignited the fuse. Without you, there would have been no scheme in the first place."

"You were the one who came up with the idea of using a Soviet sleeper," Francis said graciously. He had never been one to hog credit, and he wasn't about to start now.

"But you thought of getting the Potter to give us a

sleeper," Carroll reminded him. He shifted his gaze back to some undefined spot on the wall. "We are a perfect couple," he concluded. "We complement each other. Where you see forest, I see trees."

Francis nodded in agreement. "What we are," he said with a touch of pride, "is the sisters Death and Night."

Carroll leaned back in his seat and breathed in and out with evident emotion. "That's us," he said quietly. "The sisters Death and Night."

"That is certainly us," Francis agreed with an innocent smile.

27

❦

It was not the first time in his professional life that Francis was moved to reflect on the role that luck played in any operation. With good luck things could go right instead of wrong. With incredible luck they might go very right indeed. And a stroke of incredible luck, in the form of Carroll's "pure instinct" that the Director would go along with them, had just come Francis' way.

He looked up from his yellow legal pad and tried to recall the exact words Carroll had used to describe the meeting in the Athenaeum, then bent his head and continued writing. Not typing: he knew the day would come when handwriting experts would be called in to verify that Francis himself was the author of the notes in question. Carroll, he wrote, had delivered his report on the operation to the Director himself, in the presence of the Deputy Director and the Company's erstwhile utility infielder, G. Sprowls. Let them wriggle out of that when *they* were hooked up to the little black box, Francis thought. Carroll had reminded the Director that he had personally authorized the operation. "If I authorized an operation, I won't back away from it now," the Director had said. And the meeting had ended on a suitably conspiratorial note. "As far as I am concerned, gentlemen," the Director had announced, "this meeting never took place." "What meeting," the Deputy Director had asked innocently, "are you talking about?"

Francis felt a wave of exhilaration pass through his chest. For a moment he thought he might have trouble breathing, the sensation was so strong. The Athenaeum was locked into the conspiracy by a stroke of incredible luck. Now they would be trapped by the truth, as revealed by the scratching styluses of a lie-detector machine.

Francis dated the sheet of yellow paper, scribbled across the top, "Notes on conversation with Carroll in Chinese restaurant," then folded it in half and added it to the pile of office papers that he was supposed to have shredded. They were all stuffed into the false bottom of the kitchen garbage pail. The time was fast approaching, Francis realized, when he and his friends would have to organize his own death, along with a trail of evidence that led investigators to the treasure trove of incriminating notes in the bottom of the pail.

28

❦

For once, Francis enjoyed the Tuesday-night movie enormously. It was a musical comedy starring Judy Garland, for whom he had a lingering soft spot. She had a way of belting out songs that took his breath away; she conveyed the impression that she was ready to explode if she couldn't sing. When "The End" finally appeared on the screen, Francis was in love again, with the result that he almost forgot why he had come. Only when the people around him started to head for the exits did he remember to light up the cigarette. As usual, he used the last match in the book to do it, then casually dropped the empty matchbook under his seat and, still preoccupied with Judy Garland, headed up the aisle.

From his seat in the third row of the balcony, G. Sprowls observed the people on the main floor. A short man with wavy hair moved toward the aisle past the seat Francis had been in. Then a young couple. Then an older man with a young woman, probably his daughter, judging from the care they took to avoid touching. Then two middle-aged women, one with bleached blond hair piled in a knot on the back of her head, the second with short straight hair and an open handbag hanging from a strap over her shoulder. As the second woman came abreast of the seat Francis had used, the handbag slipped off her shoulder and fell to the floor, and several things in it spilled out. Laughing in embarrassment, the woman bent and stuffed the spilled items back into her handbag, and then hurried after her bleached-blond friend up the aisle.

As she passed underneath the balcony, G. Sprowls stood up and took a good look at the woman with the open handbag over her shoulder. All that remained for him to do now was attack the photo albums that the Company kept in the Identities Section, piled up on shelves as if some doting great-grandfather were keeping track of his progeny. Somewhere in one of those books G. Sprowls would come across the photo of the woman he had seen at the Judy Garland film. And then he would know what else Francis, his features frozen in an expression of pained innocence, had been lying about as the styluses scratched away in the black box behind his back.

29

⚜

To the Potter, it seemed as if America consisted of an endless string of small towns with curious names (Wishbone, Adam's Apple, Point Blank) and main streets inevitably named Main Street. Between towns there were billboards in the middle of nowhere advertising things he had no interest in: radio stations, beers, tractors, mobile homes, even advertising space on the billboard in question. Sometimes he and Kaat would pass a single home, hundreds of miles from open water, with a boat up on chocks in the yard. Once they spotted a run-down bar that advertised "bad whiskey," once a run-down church with a sign planted on the lawn that read, "Everybody *ought* to know Jesus." America, the Potter decided, was seeded with drive-in movies and trailer camps and baseball diamonds, and, most of all, discount stores; if you drove long enough and far enough, he commented to Kaat, you would get the impression that everything in the country was sold at a discount.

Kaat spent a great deal of time explaining things to the Potter: a sign that said "Soft Shoulders," for instance; or a Negro teenager overheard in the diner calling another Negro boy "Mother"; or an advertisement in front of a bank that said, "Throckmorton Savings and Loan Talks Turkey." The Potter remembered that Thursday had used the same expression in Vienna. How do you talk when you talk turkey? the Potter asked Kaat, and when she told him he broke into a smile for the first time since he had shot one of the sweepers in the foot. You should smile more, Kaat commented. The Potter asked her why, and she said the first thing that came into her head: that it made him look less arachnoid—another one of her A words, which meant "cobwebby." Which made him smile again.

They drove past sheep ranches and cattle ranches, and the Potter wondered out loud what it was that made one man raise sheep and another cattle; he guessed it was surely a preference that revealed a lot about someone's character.

At one point the highway climbed along a ridge and they could see a valley stretching out below them with dozens of neat farmhouses and sparkling white silos and manmade ponds and fences that always seemed to be in good repair. Perhaps there was something to be said for letting the peasants own the land they worked, or at least (here the Potter quoted what Piotr Borisovich had once told him back in Russia) the crops they harvested. At the mention of Piotr Borisovich, Kaat grew melancholy and began chewing on a cuticle.

The Potter realized he had said the wrong thing, and tried to distract her by asking her questions about herself. Where was she born? What had become of her parents? Did she have brothers? Sisters? What had she wanted to be when she grew up? And when she grew up, what had she wanted to avoid being? She answered, reluctantly at first, in abrupt phrases meant to discourage further questions. But the Potter would not be put off. What started out as therapy turned into thirst, as if knowing more about her would eventually give him access to her genitals.

Kaat was not misled. She understood enough about men to realize that he was trying to seduce her the only way he knew. Still, she found the questions irresistible. Neither W.A. nor the Sleeper, nor the dozen or so men who had played walk-in roles in her life, had ever asked her very much about the life that they had wandered into; the Sleeper—unlike the Potter now—had never even asked her what her first name was: Veronica.

They pulled into a motel on Route 35 outside Wichita, rented a room from a fat woman doing needlepoint in atrocious color combinations, and waited for the Sleeper to phone Millie again. There was no news that night, or the next day. The Potter and Kaat whiled away the time between phone calls to Millie walking in the woods behind the motel, or driving to a diner two miles down the road to get a bite to eat, or roaming around the streets of Wichita. During one meal, Kaat dangled her grandmother's ring over a road map and came to the conclusion that they should head south, but the Potter was not convinced; they would stay where they were, he decided, until they had something definite to go on.

Kaat fell asleep, fully dressed, on her bed in late afternoon, and woke to find the shades drawn and the Potter sitting on the edge of her bed, the palm of one hand resting tentatively on her breast. His desire, his need to touch her, was etched into the lines of his face. For a moment neither of them uttered a word. Then Kaat brought her hand to rest on the back of his, and ran her fingertips over his knuckles.

Taking the gesture as a sign of encouragement, the Potter buried his face in her crotch. Kaat stiffened and muttered, "Don't."

The Potter took the hint. "I am sorry, if you please," he said, sitting upright abruptly.

She regarded him with her deep-set eyes. "Here's the thing," she whispered. "I would if I could, but for it to work for me I need to feel like a co-conspirator." She tossed her shoulder in exasperation. "With you I don't have the sensation of sharing conspiracies. You have yours. I have mine."

The Potter closed his eyes and breathed deeply. "In the end everyone has his own conspiracies."

"Maybe another time," Kaat suggested gently. "Maybe when all this is over . . ."

The Potter elevated his chin and stared off into space. "All this"—he had in mind much more than she thought—"will never be over."

When Kaat phoned Millie after dinner, she came on the line in tears. "What's the matter?" Kaat demanded.

Millie was too choked up to answer. Instead she fumbled with her tape recorder and held the telephone to the speaker so that Kaat could hear for herself.

"Let me talk to Kaat," the Sleeper ordered on the tape. He seemed to be pressed for time.

"Kaat's not here," Millie replied. "I'm here."

"When is she coming back?" the Sleeper demanded.

"Where are you?" Millie asked. "When are *you* coming back?"

"That's just it," the Sleeper told Millie. "I'm not coming back. I called to say good-bye to Kaat."

"And me?" Millie burst out angrily.

"And you too, naturally."

"You bastard," Millie flared. "Where are you?"

"Tell Kaat," the Sleeper said. There was a long silence on the tape.

"Tell Kaat what?" Millie asked.

"I thought," the real Millie managed to say now between her tears, "that he was going to say he loved you."

"It would be totally out of character for him," Kaat told Millie.

"Tell Kaat that I met someone who wants to buy all the mobiles I can make," the Sleeper said on the tape. "I'm going to get rich," he added.

"You're not a capitalist," Millie told him. "You're an artist."

"I'm going to make a killing," the Sleeper said in a voice that had a bitter edge to it. "I'm going—" Then: "Shit." Then the line went dead.

"What does it mean in English?" the Potter asked Kaat when she had hung up on Millie. " 'I'm going to make a killing'?"

"It means he's going to make a lot of money," Kaat explained.

The Potter got up and began pacing the tiny room. "There is something I never told you about Piotr Borisovich," he said. "He is not an espionage agent in the ordinary sense of the expression. During the war he was a sniper, a crack rifle shot. Now he is a specialist in what we call wetwork—he is a professional assassin."

Kaat's eyes glistened, and she looked quickly away before the Potter could spot the tears. If someone had asked her, she would have sworn that she could never love someone who was capable of killing. Yet she had loved the man whom the Potter called Piotr Borisovich. She had sensed the mystery in him all along; it occurred to her now that she might also have sensed that violence was at the heart of the mystery. "It doesn't surprise me," she remarked. "Deep down I always saw him as an acutiator—in medieval times that meant a sharpener of weapons." A terrible possibility struck her. "You don't think . . ."

"He said he was going to make a killing," the Potter reminded her.

"Oh," Kaat breathed. "Whom is he going to kill?"

"If we knew the whom," the Potter said, "we might know the where."

They checked out of the motel and drove into Wichita for lunch. Afterward they ordered coffee. Almost as if they were putting off the inevitable, each ordered a second cup. "We've come a long way from that coffee shop in Brooklyn Heights," Kaat noted.

The Potter took a wad of twenty-dollar bills from a pocket and pushed it across the table toward her. "For your fare home." When she started to protest, he said, "If you please."

Kaat pocketed the money. "Where will you go?" she asked.

The Potter shrugged. "There are not many countries left for me to defect to," he answered. He thought a moment and said, "I will go to Canada. They say the climate is very close to Russia's. I like it when it is very cold because it gives me an excuse to drink a great deal of vodka."

They asked directions to the bus station, and the Potter drove her there. Kaat discovered she had an hour and a quarter until her bus left, so they settled down on a wooden bench to wait. A clock on the wall over their heads marked off the minutes with a loud clicking sound that resembled a door closing or a lock opening. After a while the Potter went over to a newsstand. The newspapers were arranged in two tiers, in-state and out-of-state. The Potter bought half a dozen out-of-state newspapers, carried them back to the bench and started going through them. "What are you looking for?" Kaat asked.

"The whom, the where," the Potter said without looking up.

He was reading an inside page of his fourth newspaper when his eye fell on a boxed item in the lower-left-hand corner. Once again the skin on the back of the Potter's neck crawled; once again his body knew before he did. (He could hear the squirrellike taxi driver with the worker's cap pulled low over his eyes calling, "And what about you, comrade fur cap?" almost as if the start of the journey had taken place that morning.) He ripped out the boxed item and reread it.

"What is it?" Kaat asked in alarm.

"Look at this," he instructed her. He handed her the clipping. It reminded readers of the impending visit to the city in which the newspaper was published of the Prince of the Realm, and announced the route he would take on his way from the airport to a luncheon at which he would speak.

"I don't—" she started to say.

"This is the whom," the Potter whispered fiercely, "and the *where*!"

It dawned on Kaat what he was talking about. "How could you know such a thing?"

"I know," the Potter insisted.

"You're guessing," Kaat said.

"I am guessing, yes," the Potter conceded. "But it all fits. Someone went to an enormous amount of trouble to organize my defection; to get the identity of a sleeper; to activate him and send him on a mission. They are not going to order him to hold up a candy store. The target has to be worthy of all this trouble. And then there is the matter of why they wanted Piotr Borisovich to commit the crime for them. There are local people, criminals, who do this kind of thing. But they wanted a Russian so that the crime would be traced back to Moscow, which would make it, from their point of view, a perfect crime." When Kaat stared at him, still not convinced, he added lamely, "You told me we should go south."

That made an impression on her. She brought a nail to her mouth and started biting on it nervously. "What if you're wrong?" she demanded. "What if this has nothing to do with him?"

"If I am wrong," the Potter said, "you will have lost three days and visited another American city." He added, "Have faith, if you please."

"All I come equipped with," Kaat said, "is a longing for faith." She got up and stalked off a few steps, stopped to think, then turned and came back to the Potter. "Let's say, for argument's sake, that you're right. How are you going to find Peter before he commits the crime?"

The Potter had an answer for that one too. "You forget that I trained Piotr Borisovich. What he knows, he learned from me. To find him, all I have to do is study the route through the city and calculate the best place from which to commit the crime. If Piotr Borisovich is half as good as I think he is, he will select the same place."

Kaat laughed under her breath. "All this is what we refer to in English as a long shot."

"It may be a long shot," the Potter said grimly, "but it is also our only shot."

30

If the Sleeper never saw the inside of another bus in his life, it would be too soon. The wrinkles in the countryside he had passed through the day before had been flattened out, like a shirt that had been ironed. The only thing to break the monotony was an occasional road sign indicating how far it was to the city. "This here ain't the real West," a man wearing blue jeans and tooled cowboy boots shouted across the aisle to the Sleeper. He leaned into the aisle, but he didn't lower his voice. "Hell, the real West don't start for another hundred or so miles. There the damn cities are so far apart you forget they exist by the time you get to one of them. Say, this your first time down to God's country?"

"First time," the Sleeper told him.

"Business or pleasure?"

"Both, I hope," the Sleeper said with a knowing smile.

In the back of the bus, a Negro woman scolded her eight-year-old boy for running in the aisle. "Thomas James, you get yourself right back here, hear?" she called. "Thomas James, you set yourself back down. What you got, ants in your pants? I don't want to hear another meow out of you, Thomas James."

"That there is the airo-port," the man across the aisle told the Sleeper in a booming voice, gesturing with his chin out the window. "Me, I'll take a bus over a plane any day of the week. Plain truth is that planes scare the pants off me. Afraid the damn things will come to a sudden stop—like against a mountain!" He howled at his own joke.

The bus driver (Safe-Reliable-Courteous, according to the plaque over his head) steered the Greyhound into Lemmon Avenue. Up ahead, through the front window, the Sleeper could make out the downtown area. "How long you say you were planning to stay?" the cowboy asked.

"Two days at the outside," the Sleeper told him.

The cowboy snorted. "First time I came down here," he recounted, "I was going to stay two days also. Came on down from Minnesota to visit an old lady who said she was my aunt. Wound up staying seventeen years. Ain't that something? I just plain liked the climate, is what kept me. They got themselves six weeks of what they call winter down here, but I sure as hell don't call it winter."

The Sleeper smiled pleasantly. Small wrinkles fanned out from the corners of his eyes. "In two days," he reassured the cowboy, and himself, "I will have accomplished what I came to do, and I'll be on my way."

"That's what they all say," the cowboy remarked with a wink.

The Sleeper turned to stare out of the window. The Greyhound was passing a small park with a statue of Robert E. Lee in it. A Mustang with its top sawed off wheeled past the bus. A girl was driving, another sat next to her. Looking down at them from the bus, the Sleeper noticed that their skirts had edged up along their thighs. He remembered the way Kaat had of planting herself in a chair with her legs spread and her skirt hiked up above her knees and dipping between them in a way that outlined her thighs. The Sleeper had always appreciated the innocence, the openness of her posture. Why, he asked himself, do my thoughts keep drifting back to Kaat? Is it because, as the Potter had noted back in Moscow, sex turns me on to violence, and I am getting close to the time and the place where I need to turn on to violence? I was a fool to phone her last night, he berated himself. What would I have said to her if she had been there? That I longed for her in ways that I can't explain, even to myself? That if things go badly in the next two days, reporters will be breaking down her door to get from her insights into the man she had lived with; had shared, along with Millie, a bed with? That if I manage to make my killing, I can retire to the relative luxury of a *dacha* on the Black Sea, and that I might ask her, once the dust has settled, to come live with me? Knowing Kaat, she would laugh in my face. She would produce an appropriate A word to sum up what she thought of the idea.

The Sleeper shifted into the window seat and pressed his forehead against the glass. The Greyhound was cutting across Main Street now, and the Sleeper, peering down it, was struck by how closely it resembled a canyon. Near the end of it several new buildings protruded, like new shoots in a hedge, from the mass of older ones. The modern steel-and-glass monsters reminded him of the pair of Polaroid sunglasses he had once bought and then thrown away because Kaat categorically refused to talk to someone if she couldn't see his eyes. I miss Kaat, the Sleeper admitted to himself. I miss her sadness and her insolence and her independence. I miss her telling me to watch out for ides, or who I was in a previous incarnation. I miss making love with her. Most women, in the Sleeper's experience, treated their lovers as fathers or sons, either snuggling into their arms or talking baby talk to them. Kaat treated hers as comrades, as someone she could share conspiracies with. And she gave and took pleasure according to a meticulously measured formula that never varied very far from fifty-fifty. Which was, when all was said and done, the way the Sleeper liked it.

"End of the line," the bus driver called as he swung the Greyhound into its berth and braked to a stop. The doors opened with a rush of air.

"See you in seventeen years," the cowboy told the Sleeper as he headed down the aisle.

Carrying his viola-da-gamba case in one hand and his worn leather valise in the other, the Sleeper turned his back on the downtown canyon and made his way toward a run-down section of town and the shabby one-story rooming house specified in the original orders he had recovered from the dead-letter drop in Brooklyn. Perspiring from the long walk, he eventually passed the yellow-brick self-service laundry and the pharmacy with a parking lot next to it full of pickup trucks. He stopped to loosen his tie and pass his handkerchief under his collar, and glancing back over his shoulder, took a long look at the center of the city rising from the flat like a wart. Tomorrow, if things went well, he would look back at the wart for the last time. If things went badly, he would be trapped in it.

Ignoring the "No Vacancy" dangling under the "Rooms for Rent" sign on the front lawn of the rooming house—his room would have been reserved for him by letter—the Sleeper cut across the front lawn to the porch. A cat with its head cocked, as if it expected the Sleeper to say something, stared impassively at him from the top step. "I am not a cat person," the Sleeper told the cat, but he knew he didn't mean it; given half a chance, he could become a cat person. He pushed open the screen door with his foot. A wiry young man was going out as the Sleeper entered. He held the screen door open so the Sleeper could pass, and nodded impersonally when he thanked him. Inside, the Sleeper found a room reserved in the name he was traveling under. "You must be a musician," the woman who ran the rooming house said when she spotted his viola-da-gamba case. "Don't get many musicians out here. More's the pity, 'cause if there's one thing I admire, it's music played by musicians." She reached under the desk blotter and produced a letter. "This here came for you. It was marked hold, so I went and held it."

The Sleeper deposited his belongings in his room,

locked the door from the inside and opened the letter the woman had given him. In it he found a street map of the downtown wart, along with an item, clipped from a local newspaper, giving readers the route that the target would take on his way from the airport to the luncheon the following day.

The Sleeper didn't have time to waste. "Going prowling so soon?" the woman who ran the rooming house asked in a singsong voice when she spotted him on his way out several minutes later. The Sleeper mumbled something about wanting to see the downtown area while there was still some light left in the sky, and the answer seemed to please her because she reeled off a list of the things in the city he shouldn't miss. He put several blocks between himself and the rooming house, then hailed a passing cab and instructed the driver to take him to the far end of the downtown wart. The Sleeper remembered the Potter's lessons well. There was no point in starting at the airport itself. Having just landed in a strange city, the people responsible for security would be at their sharpest there. On the roads leading from the airport to the wart, the motorcade would move at a brisk clip, and since there would be relatively few people lining the route it would be difficult for the Sleeper to judge from the cheers when the car containing the target was approaching. Even if he managed to get off a shot, the problem of escaping afterward would be compounded by the fact that there wouldn't be many onlookers.

You must start to look for a place to shoot from, the Sleeper could almost hear the Potter explaining in the patient voice he used when he was very sure of himself, where the crowds grow thick; where the cheers of the people lining the route announce the approach of the target; where the sound of a shot will send people scurrying in every direction, which means that you can run away from the scene along with everyone else without attracting attention. In the case at hand, the crowds would grow thick at the downtown wart, or more precisely at the point where the car containing the target turned into the Main Street canyon and proceeded through it at a leisurely pace so that the people lining the route could get a good look at him.

The Sleeper walked the route from one end to the other. He began at the city jail, where the motorcade was scheduled to enter the canyon, and wound up at the far end where the motorcade would jog right toward a warehouse and then left before turning up onto the freeway. Having gotten the general lay of the land, he flagged a taxi and returned to the city-jail end of the downtown canyon and started over the route a second time. There was a hotel situated at the corner where the motorcade would turn into Main Street, but hotels had house detectives who would be curious about a client carrying a viola-da-gamba case and asking for a room overlooking the route the Prince of the Realm would take. There was a mercantile bank building two blocks down the canyon from the hotel that attracted his attention. It wasn't so much the roof that interested the Sleeper (every policeman in town would be scanning roofs for the silhouette of a rifleman) as the upper-floor windows, which would give an excellent view of the canyon floor below. But when the Sleeper stuck his nose inside the lobby, he saw instantly that the mercantile bank building was not for him. Two uniformed policemen stationed behind a table were waving on the employees they recognized, and questioning everyone else. An hour before the motorcade passed, the Sleeper reasoned, it would be a risky business trying to talk his way past the guards.

There were several other buildings along the route that tempted the Sleeper, but in the end he dismissed them all: one because there seemed to be a series of factories on every floor, which meant the windows would be lined with workers; another because the lobby was plastered with "Wanted for Treason" posters carrying a photograph of the Prince of the Realm on them, and the local police would be sure to plant a handful of plainclothes detectives around the building the moment the motorcade passed; a third because a poster in the lobby announced that the pro-Prince contingent planned to rain confetti down on him from every window as he went by. The warehouse at the far end of the downtown canyon would have been an ideal choice, but the Sleeper decided it was so obvious—at one point the motorcade would jog directly toward it, and then move off obliquely away from it—that the building would certainly be crawling with police.

What you really want, the Potter had instructed him back in Moscow when they were scouting the route that the Indian Prime Minister would take from the airport to the Kremlin, is an open space. A window is an excellent place to shoot from if you have a great deal of time to prepare the assignment. You can select your building carefully, and even get a job in it so that it will seem natural for you to be there; natural also when you leave the building in the confusion that inevitably follows an assassination attempt. But for an assignment that you don't have weeks, or even months, to prepare, what you need is an open space, some place you can get to easily—and just as easily get away from afterward.

Several open spaces were scattered along the route that the Prince of the Realm would take. Two blocks down the canyon from the mercantile bank, there was a construction site with two cranes lying on their sides that might have provided excellent cover for a sniper. But workers wearing hard hats were installing the last segment of a chain-link fence that would make access to the construction site difficult. Farther along the canyon, on the right side, the Sleeper explored a small vest-pocket park sandwiched between two buildings. It had a patch of shrubbery in which a rifleman could hide as he waited for the motorcade to pass. But the park was set into a slight depression, and the Sleeper was afraid that the people lining the route would mask the target. Toward the end of the canyon, near the old courthouse building, there was a series of open plazas, but the areas were paved and didn't offer an obvious place to shoot from.

Which narrowed the choice of an assassination site down to the open space that the Sleeper had spotted the first time he had gone over the route of the motorcade. It had the advantage of being at the end of the downtown canyon, between the warehouse and the freeway, which meant that the people protecting the target would have passed the hundreds of windows on Main Street in a state of full alert, and with the freeway in sight just ahead would be breathing their first sighs of relief. It was a grassy area, elevated above street level, with a line of shrubs to obscure a rifleman, and a parking lot behind it to make access—and escape—relatively easy. There was one disadvantage: the target would be passing at practically right angles to the shooter, which would complicate the ballistic problem, but the Sleeper was confident of his ability to calculate lead angles.

He explored the site from every side; in the fading light he turned around it like a moth. There was an old man stationed in the parking lot behind the hedges, but he didn't appear to pay any attention to the Sleeper as he wandered through the area. From the street side the shrubs looked perfectly innocent, a small screen of decorative foliage that would be unlikely to draw more than a cursory glance from the people who were responsible for the safety of the Prince. At this point in their route they would be more interested in the windows of the warehouse behind them, and the overpass ahead.

"So," the woman who ran the rooming house asked when the Sleeper reappeared at the screen door, "what did you think of it?" She nodded toward the downtown wart. "The city, I mean? Some folks say it's pretty much like New York."

It dawned on the Sleeper that she seemed to be desperate for reassurance that she was not wasting her life in a backwater. "It would be difficult to tell them apart," he said, suddenly anxious to supply her with what she needed.

But the woman only turned away, shaking her head in disappointment, as if to say she knew a backwater when she saw one; as if to say she recognized an exaggeration when she heard one.

31

The Sisters arrived on the last flight that night, Carroll struggling to control a twitching facial muscle, Francis nervously fingering the knot of a taxicab-yellow silk bow tie and smiling angelically, as if he were going to officiate at a baptism. G. Sprowls, who had flown into the city the previous day, picked them up in a rented car and drove them into town, depositing them on the doorstep of a hotel overlooking Main Street, at the city-jail end of the downtown canyon. "I still don't see why we had to be here personally," Carroll complained as G. Sprowls pulled up to the curb.

"It's a matter of loose ends," G. Sprowls replied.

"That's what you told us over the phone when you asked us to come," Francis noted. "I wasn't sure what you meant by loose ends then. I'm still not sure."

G. Sprowls focused his half-smile on Francis, and the two men eyed each other for a moment. "There will be pieces to pick up after an operation of this kind," G. Sprowls finally drawled. "Depending on whether this sleeper of yours succeeds, depending on whether he is caught in the act or manages to elude capture, there will be clues to draw attention to, people to point in certain directions."

"That is the kind of thing you are supposed to excel at," Francis said. He tried to sound as if he were thinking out loud. "Carroll and I, on the other hand, have not operated in the field for years."

"If someone has to lend a hand, we thought"—G. Sprowls managed to put a subtle emphasis on the word "we"—"that it would be more discreet to call upon you two than to bring someone else into the picture."

"It was the Director's idea to have us come down here, then?" Francis asked. In his mind's eye he was already composing a memorandum on the conversation to add to the pile in the false bottom of his garbage pail.

"Trust me," was all that G. Sprowls offered, and he said it in a way that left them few alternatives.

32

There was no position that Ourcq could find to alleviate the pain that throbbed through his foot. "Maybe take another one of those painkillers," Appleyard, his eyes glued to the road ahead, suggested from the front seat.

"I took one of those fucking pills twenty fucking minutes ago," Ourcq snapped. He rearranged his leg on the pillow that he had swiped from the hotel, but it didn't seem to make any difference. Each time the Dodge went over a bump, he cried out in agony. "I am supposed to take one of them every four fucking hours, not every twenty fucking minutes."

"I was only trying to be helpful," Appleyard remarked, and he went back to imitating the sound of the windshield wipers.

For once, Ourcq didn't complain. The sound made him drowsy, and the drowsiness seemed to dull the pain in his foot. "How fucking far are we from—" He cried out as the front wheels of the car rippled over a washboard section of road.

"Maybe another hour," Appleyard called back over his shoulder. "Maybe forty-five minutes if I do not run into traffic when we get there."

Ourcq fumbled for another of the painkillers that the hotel doctor had given him. He had been fucking lucky in the end: fucking lucky that the bullet had passed cleanly through his foot, taking a toe along with it but not shattering any bones; fucking lucky, too, to have fallen on a doctor who, for a price, agreed not to report the shooting accident to the police. He had disinfected the wound, given him an injection against tetanus and another against pain, and pills to take when the injection wore off. He had even come up (again, for a price) with an old pair of wooden crutches, which Appleyard had imitated the sound of as soon as Ourcq hobbled across the floor on them.

"You want me maybe to pull over for a while?" Appleyard called from the driver's seat. He got a certain amount of satisfaction from being healthier than Ourcq, and he rubbed it in by being overly solicitous.

Ourcq, for his part, was touched by his colleague's concern. "You fucking want to do something for me?" he whined.

"You maybe name it," Appleyard shot back.

Groaning, Ourcq shifted his body to get more weight off his bad foot. "Imitate the sound of the fucking sun setting," he demanded. "You said you could fucking do it, but you never fucking did it."

Appleyard shook his head stubbornly. "I got to be in the mood," he explained. "I got to be inspired. Maybe later. Maybe."

33

Kaat was all for turning back when the Chrysler's high beams picked out the sign nailed to the stump of a dead tree at the end of the driveway. "Combes's Retreat, Whites Only," it read, and then in smaller print it specified: "No Animals, No Children Neither." But the Potter insisted on continuing. The rooming house at the bitter end of an unpaved road at the edge of the prairie, sixteen miles as the crow flies from the center of the city, was precisely what he was looking for. If the Prince of the Realm was really the target, if the Potter managed to figure out where the Sleeper would shoot from and find him, he would require an out-of-the-way place to take him to. They would need a breathing spell; time to put their heads together and come up with a permanent line of retreat. Between them they would have money, false papers, a clearer idea of what had happened; a clearer idea of where to go from here.

Assuming there was anywhere to go from here.

Assuming the Prince of the Realm was really the target.

Assuming the Potter managed to figure out where the Sleeper would shoot from.

"Mighty late to be sucking around for a place to spend the night," the owner of the rooming house said, squinting out suspiciously at the Potter and Kaat through the partially opened door. He was wearing a jacket without any shirt or undershirt beneath it. "Got half a mind to send you packing."

"We're whites," Kaat said with a straight face.

"There are whites, and there are whites," the owner muttered.

"Let's go," Kaat whispered, tugging on the Potter's arm. She regarded the house, large, Victorian, with bay windows and shingles and rusted drainpipes angling off in every direction, with apprehension.

"It is this way," the Potter told the rooming-house owner. "We are not married. What we need is a place to stay, if you please."

"It'll cost you," the owner, the Combes of Combes's Retreat, said. He scratched at a cheek that hadn't seen the cutting edge of a razor in days.

"Only name your price," the Potter said.

The rooming-house owner, a policeman who had been kicked off the city force several years before for shaking down illegal aliens, opened the door a bit more and studied his prospective clients closely. "Twenty a night," he finally announced.

"We will take it," the Potter said immediately.

"Plus five dollars a night for hot water."

"That will be fine," the Potter agreed.

"In advance," Combes insisted. He was annoyed with himself for not having asked for more.

The Potter counted out one hundred dollars in twenty-dollar bills and handed it to the owner through the open door. "This is for four nights, if you please," he explained.

"No refunds if you leave early," Combes warned.

"That is perfectly reasonable," the Potter said. "Can we come in now?"

The room they got was a large one with a bay window looking out over a copper-colored prairie that stretched off to where the horizon would have been if it wasn't too dark to see it. There was a tarnished brass bed with a mattress that sagged like a hammock in the middle, and threadbare carpets that smelled of cigarette ashes and mildew. Kaat went out to use the toilet at the end of the hallway, and came back with a look of sheer disgust on her face.

There was a washbasin in a corner of the room, but no hot water. Kaat wanted to complain; it was a matter of principle, she said. But the Potter told her not to bother. He would have paid three times as much for the room if the owner had had the sense to ask for it, he explained, and he sat her on the edge of the sagging bed and told her why.

"I never thought about what we would do after we found him," Kaat admitted. "That's very smart of you, actually."

"It is not a question of intelligence," the Potter said. "It is a question of experience. Generally speaking, people in my business live longer if they think about what to do *after*."

The Potter wedged a chair under the doorknob, placed his Beretta on a low table, loosened his tie and settled into the only seat in the room, an old easy chair that smelled as if it had once been in a fire. Biting nervously on a cuticle, Kaat asked why they didn't scout the downtown area immediately. The Potter said he preferred to wait for daylight because he would be able to see more, and because people strolling the streets would be less conspicuous. Kaat kicked off her shoes, propped the two old pillows up and leaned back against them. "You remember the other night?" she began. She left the rest of the thought hanging.

"The other night?"

"The other night, in the motel, when you wanted to make love to me," Kaat said. "You remember what I said about needing to share conspiracies?"

The Potter nodded tiredly. He wanted to sleep, not talk.

Kaat took a deep breath. "Here's the thing," she said. "I still think I need to share, but I'm not so sure about the conspiracies part. What I'm trying to say is, if you're still in the market to make love . . ." The sentence trailed off. Kaat smiled at the Potter across the room.

The Potter shifted in his chair, cleared a constricted throat. "You are an extremely nice human being," he told her. He spoke slowly, deliberately, anxious to express his own feelings without hurting hers. "Please understand, I did want to make love with you. I still do. But I am an old man, and I am getting older by the minute. I am tied up to the pier of old age. And the moment has passed. Which is not to say that it will not come again. Until it does, I thank you for bringing up the subject. I appreciate it. I appreciate you. Most affection between men and women these days is a matter of habit. But I am pleased to think that there is a real affection between us. Offered without being asked. Accepted without owing anything in return. Now go to sleep, my noiseless patient spider. In the morning we will find Piotr Borisovich, and then we will, all three of us together, contemplate the elusive thing called the future." The Potter reached over and switched off the table lamp. "Okay?" he asked into the darkness.

"Okay," Kaat replied in a puzzled voice.

34

⚜

The owner of the motel waited until he was sure the dwarf and his lady friend would be asleep. Then, taking his six-battery flashlight down from its hook, he went out to take a closer look at the Chrysler. Somewhere out on the prairie behind the house, a coyote howled. Combes flicked on the flashlight and played it over the car. Eventually he came to the license plates. They were from New York State, yet the sticker on the rear bumper advertised the advantages of vacationing in Ohio. Combes knelt and ran his fingers over the rear license plate. He could feel a crease in it where the screw held it to the body of the car, almost as if it had been pried loose and then replaced.

Combes straightened up. Maybe it had been the sight of the dwarflike man with a beautiful young girl trailing up the steps after him. Maybe it had been the way he spoke English with a foreign accent. Maybe it had been the ease with which he peeled off twenty-dollar bills from a wad as thick as a fist. Whatever it was, the dwarf had gotten on Combes's nerves. It would give him a certain amount of visceral pleasure to tag him.

The owner returned to the rooming house and dialed the number of his old precinct downtown. "It's me, Combes," he said when the patrolman on duty answered. "Who's minding the store? Pass him to me, will you? . . . Mac, it's me, Combes. Listen up. I got me a car out here with New York plates and an Ohio bumper sticker. I thought maybe you could see if anything was on the wire. . . . Sure I can." Combes described the Chrysler and gave the license-plate number. "Sure thing, Mac. I'll wait on your call." He hung up the phone and stared out of a window across the prairie. It would sure as hell tickle him to tag the foreigner. Yes, indeed. It would tickle the hell out of him.

35

❦

Studying the canyon formed by the buildings on either side of Main Street, the Potter sensed he had reached the end of the line. The sun was still out of sight behind the canyon, but shards of metallic light filtered through the narrow spaces between the buildings, sending alternating slats of shadow and light slanting across the gutter. Wielding canvas fire hoses that snaked back along the curb to a large mobile water wagon, two Chicanos in hip boots were hosing down the route the motorcade would take in a few hours. Up ahead, several men in impeccable three-piece suits looked on as sanitation workers pried up manhole covers and then lowered themselves through the openings to search for explosives.

"What about the hotel across the street?" Kaat asked.

The Potter sized it up with a professional eye. "Hotels," he said, "are the natural habitat of a very special breed called house detectives. The farther you stay from them, the better off you are. No, I don't see Piotr Borisovich marching up to the front desk, probably carrying some kind of package in which a rifle is hidden, and asking for a room with a view of the street through which the target will soon pass."

Around them scores of people, their heads angled against a nonexistent wind, were hurrying to work. Did they really think that getting there on time would change their lives? the Potter wondered. He made a mental note to tell Kaat how, in Moscow, people moved as if getting where they were going wouldn't change anything. Maybe he had put his finger on the real difference between the two countries, the two systems. Maybe hurrying to where you were going didn't have anything to do with an extra wet dream a week. He would have to talk to the Sleeper about it later, he decided.

The Potter strolled into the lobby of the mercantile bank building, and strolled out again two minutes later shaking his head. "Too much security," he muttered. "He would not pick this one." Making his way down Main Street, the Potter resembled nothing so much as a diviner searching for water, the only difference being he didn't have a forked stick. He examined several other buildings, always with the same result. One building he thought extremely promising until he discovered that it housed a factory on every floor.

Kaat asked him about the roofs. Even if he could get to them without attracting attention, the Potter explained, it was the last place a professional would shoot from, if only because every policeman was trained to scan rooftops for the silhouette of a sniper. Also, there was a good chance that the police would station snipers of their own on several of the highest roofs along Main Street to make sure the others were secure. If I were planning to pick off the target, the Potter reasoned, I would look for an open space. And if I would look for an open space, Piotr Borisovich would also look for an open space.

"What if you're wrong?" Kaat asked, biting on a hangnail.

The Potter looked down the canyon. The Sleeper was out there somewhere, he felt it in his bones. "I am not wrong," he told Kaat. "I cannot be wrong."

"What if?" Kaat persisted. But when she saw the expression on the Potter's face, she said, "I take back the 'what if.' "

Continuing down Main Street, the Potter investigated the construction site with several cranes lying on their sides, but saw the chain-link fence around the area and the uniformed guard checking work papers at the only door in the fence. The vest-pocket park sandwiched between two buildings on the right side of the street looked promising until the Potter discovered that it was in a slight depression, which meant that the people who would eventually line the route would mask the target from anyone in the park. At the far end of the downtown canyon there was an old sandstone courthouse, and a series of paved plazas around it, but for the life of him the Potter could not see where a rifleman could hide. Beyond the courthouse the motorcade would jog to the right and then left again, going directly toward and then passing under a rust-colored brick warehouse with a red-white-and-blue Hertz sign on the roof that told the time and the temperature.

"What's wrong with that building?" Kaat asked.

"Nothing," the Potter said, "which is what is wrong with it. It is probably the single best site for a rifleman along the entire route. The angle of fire, the distance to the target, are ideal. Unless the local police are fast asleep, they will post a man at every window."

"What are you staring at?" Kaat asked suddenly.

"I have found what I was looking for," the Potter announced in a low voice. "Look there, to the left of the warehouse building. Do you see it?"

"You mean the slope over there?" Kaat asked.

"Those bushes provide a perfect screen for a rifleman," the Potter said excitedly. "Come on, I want to get a closer look at it."

They crossed Main Street and skirted behind the warehouse, through the parking lot, to the top of the incline at the edge of the lot. The Potter studied the street below through the bushes. "This is it," he told Kaat. "The perfect place for a sniper. The only drawback is that the target will pass at almost right angles to the rifleman, but Piotr Borisovich is an excellent marksman and would not hesitate because of that. He would consider the parking lot at his back a great advantage for the escape, because he does not suspect that he is not meant to escape. He is meant to be caught."

Kaat looked at the Potter in awe. "How can you know all these things?"

"He will not come here until the last minute to avoid the possibility of running into anyone," the Potter continued in a low voice. He seemed to have forgotten that Kaat was next to him, and talked to himself. "In three hours and forty-five minutes, he will be standing where we are standing now. He will hear the cheers coming from Main Street, indicating the motorcade is approaching. The limousine will come into view, turn under the warehouse and pass directly under here. The guards accompanying the target will start to relax when they spot the freeway entrance ahead. Piotr Borisovich will aim for the jugular, as he did during the war." A distant look obscured the Potter's normally alert gaze. "Piotr Borisovich's father talked about myths just before he died. In one way or another, he said, all of us are acting out myths. Even Piotr Borisovich. Especially Piotr Borisovich," he said.

"What myths is Piotr Borisovich acting out?" Kaat wanted to know.

"What day are we today?" the Potter asked.

"Twenty-two November. Why?"

The Potter imagined he could hear the cheering of the crowds lining the canyon on Main Street, announcing the approach of the motorcade. "Have you ever noticed how autumn always makes people uneasy?" the Potter asked. "The days grow shorter and colder. Leaves fall from the trees and decay on the ground. The wind picks up and takes on a cutting edge. The clouds overhead appear to be lower and thicker and heavier than usual. The mountains on the horizon seem closer, more menacing. In ancient times the peasants began to worry that they had offended God. It was usually toward the end of autumn that they sacrificed their prince so that he could ascend to heaven and intercede with God, could make sure that spring would come again." The Potter took Kaat's elbow and drew her away from the line of bushes. "I remember something else Piotr Borisovich's father told me. He said he thought Piotr Borisovich was meant to be a prince, or kill a prince."

36

Looking out from the window of his room on the fourth floor, Francis observed with a feeling of infinite detachment—he had imagined the moment so many times, he felt as if he were watching an old film—the security precautions along the route the Prince of the Realm would soon take. He could make out a burly policeman armed with binoculars and a walkie-talkie on the roof across the way. Below, workmen in overalls were removing wooden police barriers from an open truck and stacking them next to the curb; at noon they would be used to close off the cross streets to traffic.

The phone next to the bed rang. Francis picked up the receiver. "Do you see what I see?" a voice asked.

Francis almost convinced himself that he could *hear* a facial muscle twitching in excitement. "You mean the cop with binoculars across the street?" Francis asked.

"They were pulling up manhole covers and looking for bombs earlier," Carroll said. He sounded as if he were feverish. Slurring his words, he hissed into the phone, "Poor saps." When Francis didn't respond, he asked, "What are you going to do now?" As if knowing how Francis planned to while away the morning would help him do the same.

"I am going to select an appropriate necktie to wear," Francis replied. And when Carroll finally hung up, he did exactly that. Picking the bow tie was, in fact, Francis' major preoccupation of the morning. He took one with mauve polka dots from his canvas tie case and held it up to his neck so he could see it in the mirror. It wasn't quite what he was looking for. He tried a solid-colored one next, a particularly generously cut bow tie in a washed-out orange silk. He eventually settled on one of his favorites, a pale green bow tie with rust-colored pinstripes running horizontally through it. Francis pulled up his collar, and with several deft hand-over-hand gestures knotted the tie, then adjusted the collar and studied the effect in the mirror. If he could save only one of his ties, this one would definitely be it. He detested the idea of abandoning the others, but he recognized the necessity and, as was his habit, bowed to it. If everything went according to plan, if the Sleeper were caught in or after the act, Francis would immediately dial the phone number he had been given before he left Washington. And wearing only the clothes on his back, the pale green bow tie with rust-colored pinstripes around his neck, the shoes on his feet and the Cheshire cat's pained smile that hinted at nothing more morally compromising than the death of an occasional rodent, he would disappear, within the hour, from the face of the earth.

37

Carrying a long, thin package wrapped in brown paper, Khanda turned up for work at the warehouse a few minutes early that morning.

"What you got yourself there, a fishing rod?" one of the older hands who passed Khanda in the stairwell asked.

"It's curtain rods," Khanda explained briefly, "for my room."

"Too bad it ain't a high-powered rifle to put a hole through that son of a bitch who's supposed to be passing by today," the other man said.

"I got nothing against him," Khanda said.

"Well, I reckon that makes you the only one in the whole entire state who don't," the other said, and muttering under his breath about how the punishment ought to fit the crime, and the crime was high treason, he went on about his business.

Using the stairway instead of the elevator to avoid other workers, Khanda made his way to the sixth floor. Near the window he had picked out, he shoved aside some cartons and slid the curtain rods in behind them. It occurred to him, as he went downstairs to report to work, that this was his last day on the job; that if things went well, he might never have to work another day in his entire life.

38

❦

A teenager outside the window of the motel room was walking across the gravel driveway in thick motorcycle boots. Watching from behind the half-drawn shades, Appleyard softly imitated the sound until he thought he had it right. Then he took a deep breath and did it at full volume. It sounded as if someone were walking across gravel *inside* the room.

Ourcq limped out of the bathroom on his wooden crutches. "Maybe you should fucking phone again," he said.

Appleyard stopped making the sound of a boot crunching on gravel. "He specifically said he would call us when he knew something," he reminded Ourcq.

"What I wouldn't give to get my fucking paws on him," Ourcq said. He leaned the crutches against the wall and sat down heavily on the bed, careful to keep his weight off his bad foot.

"What would you give?" Appleyard asked, his eyebrows dancing in curiosity.

"I would give a fucking year of my life," Ourcq replied with obvious sincerity. "I would give my fucking right arm. It is just not right to shoot somebody in the fucking foot. It causes too much fucking pain."

Appleyard came to the conclusion that the wound had had a humanizing effect on his partner; for the first time in memory, he seemed to hate the person he might have to kill. "If he had not shot you in the foot,"

Appleyard pointed out, "he might have shot you in the head." He cocked his forefinger as if it were a pistol and produced a perfect imitation of a gun going off. "At least," he added, "where there is pain there is life."

"Now you are imitating the sound of a fucking intellectual," Ourcq said in disgust. "Do me a fucking favor, go back to doing somebody walking on fucking gravel."

39

❦

It was twenty minutes to noon when the Potter went to pick up the Chrysler at the garage on Elm Street. One block to the south, crowds were already forming along the route. According to the newspaper clipping, the motorcade would jog past the red-brick warehouse—and the bushes on the rise just after it—at about twelve-thirty. The Sleeper, the Potter calculated, would wait until the last minute before taking up position. The Potter planned to pull the Chrysler into the parking lot next to the rise at twelve-twenty-five, and drive off with the Sleeper before the motorcade emerged from the Main Street canyon.

Kaat went into the garage to give the stub to the man on duty. Five minutes later she came hurrying out to the street with a strange look on her face; the last time the Potter remembered seeing it was when she had turned to stare at the lifeless body of her cat on the back seat of the car.

"What is happening, if you please?" the Potter asked in alarm.

"Here's the thing," Kaat said. "The attendant called on his intercom, and the man who moves the cars called back to say that the Chrysler had a flat tire. They said that for ten dollars they would fix it, so I told them to go ahead and do it."

The Potter stepped out into the street to see the time atop the brick warehouse at the end of Elm Street.

"Thirteen minutes to twelve," he said when he returned to the sidewalk. He made a quick calculation. "I am counting on the car to get the Sleeper to safety," he told Kaat. "Go back in and tell them you are in a hurry. Tell them you will give them twenty dollars if they will change the tire and get the Chrysler down quickly."

Kaat ducked back into the garage. The Potter paced up and down the sidewalk in front of it. Every once in a while he would step into the gutter and glance nervously at the time atop the brick warehouse. At one minute after twelve, Kaat appeared at the entrance of the garage. "They say they're bringing it down any minute," she called. She hunched her shoulders in frustration and returned to the garage.

On the side street that led to Main Street, the police were starting to drag wooden barriers over to block cross traffic. The Potter looked at the clock on the roof of the warehouse again. He had just made up his mind to go on foot and let Kaat follow him in the Chrysler when she dashed out of the garage. "It's on the elevator," she called, and raced back in.

It was twelve-seventeen when Kaat gunned the Chrysler out of the garage into Elm Street. The Potter jumped into the passenger seat. Before the door had slammed shut, Kaat had thrown the car into gear and started north so that they could come around behind the warehouse to the parking lot where, according to the Potter, the Sleeper would just be taking up position behind the hedges.

40

⚜

Khanda felt as if time were trickling away in a kind of suspended slow motion. When he held his wristwatch to his ear to check if it was still working, the spaces between the seconds seemed to be abnormally long, as if the moment were so exquisite it had to be drawn out. He glanced back at the cartons he had dragged over to form a wall so that anyone who happened to mount to the sixth floor wouldn't catch sight of him sitting in front of the partly open window, the homemade sling of his Italian military rifle wrapped around his left arm. The act of entwining himself in the sling had created the final intimacy between the shooter and the rifle; from that moment on, there had been no turning back.

He had decided to stay well away from the window when the motorcade appeared out of Main Street and headed directly for the warehouse, to reduce the possibility that any of the security people accompanying the Prince might spot him up ahead. Only when the limousine turned under the warehouse and started toward the overpass and the freeway, when the security people had their backs to the warehouse, would he move into firing position. He had placed three cartons on the floor next to the window, one on top of the other, and he planned to brace the rifle on the top box when he shot.

Outside, the canyons of Main Street formed a giant echo chamber. Somewhere up this echo chamber, peo-

ple were cheering. It sounded to Khanda like surf beating against a distant shore. He worked the bolt of the rifle, throwing the first round into the chamber. Then he brought his wristwatch to his ear again. The spaces between the ticks seemed even longer than before.

No matter. In a minute or two he would speed time up. He would accelerate it into chaos.

41

❦

Slipping through the open parking lot behind the line of hedges, his viola-da-gamba case tucked casually under one arm, the Sleeper sensed the wave of excitement approaching, like a groundswell, from Main Street. From his experiences in the war, he knew that he would soon reorder reality. When you looked at someone with the naked eye, you automatically put him into context; you related him to the world around. But when you observed someone through a scope fixed on top of a rifle, you *detached* him from the world around you; you isolated him; you created a very special relationship between the two of you, even if only one of you was aware of it.

The first vehicle in the motorcade emerged from the Main Street canyon. The Sleeper, alone at the edge of the parking lot, crouched and rested the viola-da-gamba case on the ground and undid the catches that held the lid. Cheers welled up from the crowd as the Prince's limousine came into view, then slowly jogged right toward the warehouse.

Moving with the deliberation of a sleepwalker, the Sleeper prepared the instrument that would detach the Prince from reality.

42

⚜

The Potter and Kaat had been delayed by the traffic backed up on Houston Street. It was twelve-twenty-nine by the time Kaat maneuvered the Chrysler into the parking lot behind the warehouse. "Wait here, if you please," the Potter instructed Kaat with unaccustomed sharpness, and he leapt from the car and darted between the parked automobiles toward the row of hedges at the far end of the lot.

On the street below, the Prince's limousine jogged left underneath the slightly open window on the sixth floor of the warehouse and headed toward the freeway. The Prince lifted a hand and waved at the people lining the route, and the crowd cheered back.

Crouched amid the hedges, the Sleeper worked the bolt, throwing a round into the chamber. Then he raised the sniper scope to his eye and sighted on the jugular of the target coming into view.

Breathing heavily, the Potter came around the front of a pickup truck and saw the familiar figure crouching in the hedges ahead, the right knee on the ground, the left elbow braced on the raised left knee, the rifle extended in the classical firing position used by the Red Army. "Piotr Borisovich," the Potter gasped, and then he filled his lungs with air and opened his mouth and cried out the name of the son he had always wanted with all the force he could find in his body. "*Piotr Borisovich!*" But even to his own ear his voice seemed lost in the roar of the crowd saluting the passage of the Prince.

At the mouth of the Main Street canyon, on the steps of the old sandstone courthouse, G. Sprowls was about to turn to the Sisters and make an ironic comment about the best-laid plans of mice and men when the sharp crack of a rifle, a dry twig snapping in a forest, echoed over the heads of the crowd. On the roof of the warehouse, several hundred pigeons nesting in the abandoned boiler swarmed into the sky in panic.

A second twig snapped.

And then a third.

And the world was accelerated into chaos.

"It came from the warehouse," Carroll blurted out excitedly. His cheek muscles went on a rampage. "I knew in my bones he would pick the warehouse."

On the street, the crowd spilled away in every direction. Several people fell to the ground screaming. A policeman pointed toward an upper floor of the warehouse.

"The first shot came from the grassy knoll," G. Sprowls said matter-of-factly. "I spotted the smoke from the cartridge." As if to prove his point, a motorcycle policeman skidded his machine onto the sidewalk below the hedges, and drawing his pistol, charged up the incline.

"My God," Francis said, "that means that there must have been *two* people shooting!"

For once, there was not the faintest trace of pained innocence on his face.

43

The moment was electrically charged. No one seemed quite sure what role to play. There was a father and a son, a teacher and a pupil, a betrayer and a betrayed; even a savior and a saved.

The Sleeper stared out of the window of Combes's Retreat at the prairie. "So you told them what they wanted to know," he was saying.

It had never occurred to the Potter that he would have to justify himself to the Sleeper when he caught up with him. "Please put yourself in my shoes," he pleaded. "I had no choice. They would have loaded us on the next plane to Moscow. Aside from everything else, there was the body at the airport to answer for." He fingered an empty coffee cup, unconsciously measuring the thickness of its walls between his thumb and third finger. "I had Svetochka to think of," he added plaintively.

"And yourself," the Sleeper answered harshly. "Let us not forget yourself."

"Since when is it a crime to think of yourself?" the Potter retorted.

The Sleeper turned on his teacher. "It is a crime for a teacher to betray his student."

"And what do you call it when the student betrays his teacher?" the Potter demanded. "You who are so offended by betrayals—tell me that if you can."

"So you found out about me and Svetochka," the

Sleeper said wearily. "Everyone was sleeping with her, Feliks."

"I knew that *everyone* was sleeping with her. I didn't know that *you* were."

The Sleeper drifted across the room, and then back to the bay window. "One thing has nothing to do with the other," he said finally. "Sleeping with Svetochka was an act without consequences—for me, for her, for you as long as you didn't know about it. But betraying me to an enemy service was pregnant with consequences." He turned his back on the Potter and breathed on the windowpane, fogging it. "If only I had known my father was dead . . ."

"I was trying to catch up with you to tell you," the Potter whispered. "He was dead, and you were free."

"Here's the thing," Kaat said. "It is frustrating enough to listen to the two of you argue. But to hear you argue in Russian is pure torture."

"Even if we spoke in English," the Potter told her, his eyes glued on the Sleeper, "there are things you wouldn't understand."

"He is not the hero he makes himself out to be," the Sleeper informed Kaat. "He betrayed me to get himself and his wife out of Russia."

"Then he crossed the Atlantic and trailed after you across America to try to save you," Kaat said. She looked from one to the other. "Don't you see, you're turning in circles." She stared the Sleeper in the eye. "Vicious circles! What's done is done. The important thing is to look ahead, not back."

The Potter shook his head sadly. "You have it wrong. Piotr Borisovich has it right," he told her. "In order to look ahead, we must first look back." And he quoted Akhmatova's line, " 'My future is in my past.' "

The Sleeper nodded grimly. "We must settle the business of the betrayal before we move on," he insisted. He turned to the Potter and switched into Russian. "You expect me to fall on my knees and thank you for saving me." The Potter started to interrupt, but the

Sleeper cut him off with a snap of his hand. "Don't deny it—it is written on your face. None of this would have happened if you hadn't betrayed me in the first place. That's what I can't swallow, Feliks. In my mind's eye, I try to put myself in your shoes. I really do try. But I don't see myself betraying you to get myself out. I would have killed myself first."

"You say that now," the Potter murmured. He held both hands to his stomach as if he had cramps. "But you can't be sure whose back you will climb on until you are at the foot of the wall."

"I had faith in you," the Sleeper said. "You let me down."

"I let myself down," the Potter observed acidly. He tried to muster a smile, but it only distorted his face more. "That's something else we have in common now," he added bitterly.

"I may not understand a word you say," Kaat told the Sleeper, "but you are hurting him very much. He doesn't deserve that."

The Sleeper eyed the Potter, then nodded. "I am willing to concede that you did try to undo the damage."

The Potter moaned. "I did try," he agreed, "but I failed."

"Maybe not entirely," the Sleeper said. "You are absolutely sure that it was the Americans you betrayed me to?"

"I was contacted by someone who called himself Oskar. He was probably German, and everyone knows the Americans have the Germans in their pocket," the Potter recounted. "In Vienna, I was debriefed by someone who spoke Russian with an American accent. In any case, the lengths they went to to get me out, to get access to a sleeper, only make sense if you assume the Americans are behind the whole thing."

"I might understand," Kaat announced in an exasperated voice. "If you spoke English, I might pick up a word now and then that seemed familiar."

"Your theory," the Sleeper told the Potter, "is that

the Americans awakened me and sent me on a mission so that I would be caught, and the Russians would be blamed."

"That is what I thought," the Potter agreed.

The Sleeper walked across the room and sat down at the small bridge table facing the Potter. "Do you still think it?" he asked.

"I am less sure than before."

"Because of the sweepers?"

The Potter looked up sharply. "So you spotted them?"

"I had a good teacher in such matters," the Sleeper said grudgingly. "The technique they used—lingering twenty-four hours—was straight out of the KGB sweeper manual."

"We ran into them several times also," the Potter said. "The first time they killed her cat. The last time I shot one of them in the foot. That was in the storage room of a hotel." The Potter frowned. "I recognized the man I shot. I had seen him once before. In Moscow."

The Sleeper's eyes narrowed thoughtfully. Tiny wrinkles fanned out from the corners of his eyes. Someone who didn't know him would have thought he was amused. "If the Americans were controlling me, as you say, how is it that the Russians were sweeping me? How did they know my route?"

"That," the Potter said, "is what the Americans call the sixty-four-dollar question."

"Go on speaking Russian if it gives you pleasure," Kaat snapped in annoyance. "To me it's all the same."

"There's another thing," the Sleeper said. "When you arrived in Vienna, you gave the American who spoke Russian with an American accent the line of poetry from Walter Whitman. But how could the Americans know where I was? How could they know where to deliver the line of Whitman poetry?"

"I told them," the Potter admitted morosely.

"How did you know?"

"From the picture postcard you sent me."

"What picture postcard?"

Now the Potter was staring at the Sleeper. "The one showing the Walter Whitman plaque on the door of a house in Brooklyn Heights."

The Sleeper said quietly, "I never sent you a picture postcard. It was against regulations to contact people in the homeland while on a mission. You know that."

"When you have finished with the past," Kaat muttered from the bed, "be sure to let me know."

"You never *finish* with the past," the Potter told her. "You take it with you, like baggage."

"Who did send me on this mission?" the Sleeper asked the Potter. "Who am I working for?"

"Do you think it is important to find out?" the Potter asked.

"If we don't find out," the Sleeper said, "we risk going on without baggage."

"If you don't talk English," Kaat said suddenly, "I'll scream!"

The Potter smiled faintly at his last, his best sleeper. "I think I know what we can do to find out," he said.

Kaat screamed.

44

❦

The building, lighted up like a Christmas tree, could have passed for an ocean liner in mid-Atlantic, a fact that several hands arriving late from various corners of the world would have commented on if they had had time. Which they didn't. The Prince of the Realm was dead. There was a suspect in the hands of the local police. There were rumors, fueled by vague reports of an entry wound in the throat, of a second shooter still at large, though cooler heads tended to discount this possibility. Sandwiches, beer, were ordered up, delivered by a downtown caterer with a security clearance. The bottoms of barrels were being scraped for leads, theories, coincidences, pieces out of place, people who had dropped from sight, others who were too conspicuously in sight. Anything and everything was being fed into the hopper.

Except telegrams that weren't addressed to anyone or signed by anyone.

"What you make of this?" the communications assistant, fresh from the Company's Farm and eager to be useful in a crisis, asked. The night watch, his head swimming from the message load, plucked it from the board. It had the look of a normal telegram; had in fact come in over the Western Union printer. " 'The hands of the sisters Death and Night incessantly wash again comma and ever again comma this soil'd repeat soil'd world stop,' " the night watch read out loud.

"Maybe it's a cipher," the communications assistant offered eagerly.

"Sounds more like the ravings of some crank," the night watch said. He was about to throw it into the burn basket when it occurred to him that the Company had in its employ two esoteric types known in the house as the sisters Death and Night. Could it be that the telegram was meant for them? "Listen up," the night watch instructed his communications assistant. "There are two guys up in Planning. Both have girls' first names. Carroll something, Francis something. The one who is named Francis always wears loud bow ties. Find out where they are and read this over the phone to them. Maybe they'll know what it's all about. Now, what else do you have on that message board of yours?"

45

❦

At first Francis assumed he was imagining things. Only when he lifted a tentative finger to his cheek did he realize what was actually happening. He had seen it often enough on Carroll's face to know what a twitching muscle looked like. Now he knew what it felt like.

What it felt like was exaltation rising, like a bubble in a still pond, to the surface of his imagination.

Thank goodness some idiot in Washington had had the good sense to try the telegram out on him. Francis had phoned Carroll immediately to share the good news, but Carroll was off God knew where with G. Sprowls. So as not to waste any time (who could say how long the birds would remain in the nest?), Francis had contacted Western Union and, citing urgent government business, had gotten from the supervisor the phone number from which the telegram originated. Flashing his laminated credentials in the general direction of a nearsighted telephone-company official, Francis had gotten the address that went with the telephone number. At which point he had put in a call from a pay phone to the special number in Washington reserved for extraordinary circumstances. "The Potter has caught up with the Sleeper," he told the person on the other end who lifted the receiver without a word of greeting and simply listened.

There was a long, awkward silence on the line. Then a voice, pronouncing each word meticulously in an effort to suppress an accent, said, "How can you know this?"

Francis explained about the telegram that had arrived in Washington containing, word for word, the line from Whitman that constituted the awakening signal for the Sleeper; explained the coincidence of him and Carroll being known, within the Company, as the sisters Death and Night; explained how because of this coincidence the telegram had been routed to him. "If the Potter and the Sleeper have put their heads together," Francis explained, "the Sleeper will know he was controlled by the Company and not his masters in Moscow. All we have to do now is arrange for them to be captured. The story they tell will eventually lead the authorities to Carroll and me. My disappearance, my written confession, the scribblings they will find hidden in my garbage pail will all confirm that the Sleeper was activated, and controlled, by the Company. Let the Director try to deny it when he is hooked up to a lie detector!" Once again exaltation manifested itself as a twitch of a cheek muscle.

The person on the other end of the line cleared his throat, almost as if he were embarrassed. "There is a complication," he said carefully.

It took a moment for the word to sink in, it was so unexpected. Francis repeated it to be sure he had heard correctly. "Complication?"

"The telegram that was sent to the Company was also sent to us at the embassy."

"To you?" Francis breathed into the phone. "Why would they send the awakening signal to *you*?"

"Several days ago, the Potter cornered one of our sweepers in a hotel," the voice on the phone recounted tonelessly. "Unfortunately for us, he recognized him."

"Recognized the sweeper?" Francis couldn't believe this was happening to him.

"He had seen him once before, in Moscow, some years ago, when the sweeper was given a medal," the voice said.

The phone started to buzz in Francis' ear. He force-fed his last handful of quarters down the slot. The line cleared. "Are you still there?" he shouted.

"So you see," the voice continued as if there had not been an interruption, "they will have posed the question: if the Sleeper was being controlled by the Americans, as the Potter said, why was he being swept by Russians who knew his itinerary?"

"How could you assign a sweeper whom the Potter could recognize?" Francis asked incredulously.

The person on the phone cleared his throat again. "Our resources in this hemisphere are limited," he said defensively. "When you told us you thought the Potter might be trying to catch up to the Sleeper and stop him from carrying out his assignment, we called in the Canadians, Ourcq and Appleyard. We have used their services for years. It did not occur to us to check to see if the Potter might know one of them. But then it did not occur to us that they would fail to eliminate him if, as you suspected, he was following the Sleeper."

Francis' mind was racing. "The telegram they sent to the Company, to you—it means they are not sure who is controlling the Sleeper. Of course, why didn't I see it! *They don't know!* So they fired off the awakening signal left and right, and are waiting to see which side *understands* it, which side responds to it. Then they will know who awakened the Sleeper. And knowing, they can try to save their skins. They can deal from strength."

"I can see," the voice on the phone said from what seemed an enormous distance, "that we have come to the same conclusion."

Francis transformed his face into a mask of pained innocence. "I will turn up at Combes's Retreat. Your telegram was routed to me, thank you very much for sending it, I will tell them. Yes indeed, I am your control. You want to know whom I work for? Surely you are joking! I work for the organization that arranged the Potter's defection, that awakened the Sleeper, that sent him across the country to terminate a Prince of the Realm we could no longer put up with. Why did we want a Russian sleeper? Because if you had been caught in the act, an eventuality that we had to plan for, the Russians would have been blamed. But you weren't caught in the act. You got away. The Prince of the Realm is no longer among the living, so we have accomplished what we set out to accomplish. You, in turn, seem to have figured out who was controlling you, else why would you have sent a telegram containing the awakening signal to the Company. We share a mutual interest now—you must both disappear. With the resources at my command, I can arrange this." Feeling his quarters were about to run out, knowing that he had used his last one, Francis began talking rapidly. "Only sit tight. Don't move. Give me twenty-four hours. I will organize everything—money, identities, travel plans. Of course they will agree. What choice will they have? After that it will only be a matter of an anonymous phone call to the local police. Detectives will capture a shooter who was controlled by the Company. I will disappear, leaving behind confirmation." Francis' cheek muscle twitched again. His voice soared half an octave. "It is still the perfect crime!"

"I quite agree with your analysis," the voice on the line said. "I authorize you to—"

The buzzing filled the receiver. Francis searched frantically to see if he had overlooked a quarter in one of his pockets. Reluctantly he placed the receiver back on its hook. I quite agree with your analysis, the voice on the line had said. I authorize you to . . . what? Fingering his pale green bow tie with rust-colored stripes running horizontally through it, Francis stepped out of the booth into the sunlight. He thought he knew what he was authorized to do.

He was authorized to put the finishing touch on the perfect crime.

46

Propped up amid the pillows at the end of the bed, nibbling nervously on an already mutilated fingernail, Kaat recognized it for what it was: an acronical (occurring at sunset) anagnorisis (denouement of a plot).

The Sleeper took his eyes off Francis for the first time since he entered the room. "She collects words that begin with the letter A," he informed the Potter, who was sitting at the bridge table, his eyes half-closed, his Beretta out in plain view on the torn green felt.

"He knows that," Kaat said from the bed. "He also knows what my first name is, which is more than you know."

"I see," said the Sleeper, and he did: the complicity between the Potter and Kaat was thick enough to cut with a knife.

Francis, leaning against a fireplace that had been bricked over, produced a particularly innocent smile. "To move on," he continued, looking from the Sleeper to the Potter and then back to the Sleeper again, "all I need is twenty-four hours to put together the package. There will be an appropriate amount of money. There will be passports, driving licenses, Social Security cards for everyone, including the girl. There will be plane tickets to the country of your choice. Do you prefer the southern or northern hemisphere? Sun or snow? Are you urban-oriented, or do you feel more at home in a rural atmosphere? I know you Russians put great store by your *dachas.*" Here Francis forced a dry laugh through his lips.

Kaat said, "That is an unusual bow tie you have on."

"Thank you," Francis said, taking Kaat's comment for a compliment. "I'm rather attached to it myself. If my apartment was on fire and I could save only one tie from my rather large collection, this is definitely the one I would pick."

The Potter said, "There is still the question of the sweepers to straighten out."

"If you were controlling me, as you say," the Sleeper asked Francis, "how is it that the Russians were sweeping my trail?"

With almost no effort Francis managed to project pained innocence. "You are referring to the Canadians who go by the names of Ourcq and Appleyard. It is true that they have been used on several occasions by our Russian friends; one of them, I don't remember which, was said to have been awarded a medal for services rendered. But they have nothing against accepting a free-lance contract now and then to augment their income. In this particular instance, we hired them to sweep your trail in order to keep the Potter from catching up with you. Obviously, if you had learned that he had betrayed you to the Americans, you would not have carried out the assignment we gave you. Using sweepers who employed Soviet techniques had an added advantage, from our point of view: if you spotted them, it would only reinforce your conviction that you had been awakened and sent on a mission by your legitimate control in Moscow. If you were caught in the act, we wanted the onus to fall on your masters in the Kremlin. You are both professionals. Surely you can understand our attitude even if you cannot sympathize with it."

"Personally," Kaat piped up from the bed, "I don't believe a word he says. He was a liar in his previous incarnations. He is a liar in his present incarnation. He will surely be a liar if he is lucky enough to have a future—"

Downstairs, the chimes that Combes's ex-wife had brought back from Memphis sounded.

The Potter reached for his Beretta. Francis fingered his bow tie. "Are we expecting anyone?" he asked into the silence.

The Sleeper shook his head.

"Maybe it is Combes," Kaat whispered, "returning from wherever he raced off to in such a hurry this morning."

"We would have heard his car," the Potter said.

"He wouldn't ring his own doorbell," the Sleeper said. He put his ear to the door of the room. "Someone's coming into the house."

"Francis?" a voice called from the entrance of Combes's Retreat.

"My God, it's Carroll!" exclaimed Francis. "Carroll, we are up here," he called back. To the others he explained, "Carroll is my partner. We are a team. I more or less specialize in forests, he in trees."

Carroll could be heard mounting the staircase. The Potter nodded at the Sleeper, who shrugged and pulled open the door of the room. Looking pale as death, Carroll appeared on the threshold. He was clutching a tiny pistol in his right fist and aiming it at Francis' stomach.

"If you come in and tell us who you are," Kaat said with a nervous laugh, "I'll tell you who you *were*."

Carroll stared at a point on the wall over Francis' right shoulder. "How could you have done it?" he asked in a voice that trembled with hate. He arched his neck and dispatched a finger to patrol the no-man's land between his neck and his starched collar. "We were colleagues, you and I. We were comrades in arms. We were *sisters*!"

Francis' mask of pained innocence started to melt. "What are you talking about?" he breathed in a barely audible voice.

Carroll stepped into the room. "You are not going to deny it, I hope. We are well past that stage. G. Sprowls saw you drop the empty matchbook under your seat after the film. He identified the woman who recovered it." He advanced on Francis, who shrank back into the wall. "I am going to end your life," he announced. "I am going to begin your death."

From across the room the Potter asked calmly, "How did you find us?"

Carroll never shifted his gaze from the wall over Francis' shoulder. "My colleague G. Sprowls has been looking for you. He had lines out. One of them paid off. The local police got a report of a stolen Chrysler turning up at Combes's Retreat. There were descriptions of you, of the girl, and after the death of the Prince of the Realm, of the Sleeper." Carroll must have noticed the Potter's finger curling around the trigger of the Beretta, because he said very quietly, "My colleague is nearby. He is not alone. I tell you this in case you are thinking of resorting to violence."

Kaat said, "I don't understand a thing he's saying, and he's speaking English."

The Potter stood up from the table, slipped his Beretta into his jacket pocket, walked over to the window and stared out at the sun dipping toward the edge of the prairie. It occurred to him that the Sleeper's father had been wrong—for him, there was to be no life before death. "I think I understand," he said, turning back to the room. "The Company of yours wanted to eliminate the Prince of the Realm, and put the blame for his assassination on the Russians in order to discredit those outside the intelligence and military communities who favor a détente with the Soviet Union. But one of the two principal planners was actually a Soviet agent working, in all probability, for Department 13, the assassination specialists of the Komitet Gosudarstvennoy Bezopasnosti. After the assassination, after the capture of the assassin, he would disappear. A confession would turn up in the mail of a senator known for his support of the Prince and his opposition to the intelligence community. If something happens to me, the confession would say, I have arranged for this letter to be mailed to you. Acting on precise verbal orders issued by my superiors, I and my partner organized the death of the Prince. We awakened a Soviet sleeper and used his services so that the blame would fall on Moscow. Something along these lines. There would probably be a cache of documents somewhere—transcripts of conversations, deciphered one-time pad messages, notes on my defection and debriefing—to support the story. There would be corroboration from the giggling idiot you sent to Vienna to debrief me; you probably sent him, as opposed to going yourself, just so there would be an outside witness to my defection."

Carroll raised his free hand to his cheek muscle. "You were supposed to shred the office notes, the messages, but you saved every scrap of paper," he told Francis. "G. Sprowls found them in the false bottom of your garbage pail."

Francis said weakly, "It was a perfect crime."

The Sleeper asked the Potter, "How did you figure it out?"

The Potter shrugged. "Once you told me you never sent the picture postcard with your address on it, everything became clear. The only people who knew *where* you were, who knew I had entered the Walter Whitman line that awakened you in your dossier in my own handwriting, were our Russian colleagues. So the plot originated with them. If an American had the good sense to get to you through me, he had to be working for the Russians too."

The Sleeper nodded thoughtfully. "You are still the *novator*," he noted.

The Potter turned to Francis. "Are the Cousins behind it? Is the blind man behind it?"

Francis managed to produce a sickly smile. "The blind man is my control," he said. "We met secretly in Mexico a year ago. He had heard people in high places rant against the Prince of the Realm after the humiliation they suffered at his hands during the missile crisis. He took this for an order. He and I devised a perfect crime. We would get rid of the Prince of the Realm in such a way that the blame would fall on the Company, on Carroll here. For this we needed the services of a Russian sleeper. To get the sleeper, we needed to force the defection of the man who trained him. Which is where you came in. We gave away the three sleepers you had inserted into the United States in order to ruin you professionally. Then we got you to defect and give us access to the agent you always referred to as your last and best sleeper."

The Sleeper looked across at the Potter. "Was I really your best?"

The Potter said, "My last and my best. Absolutely."

Francis' knees began to give way and he had to hang on to the bricked-over fireplace to keep from sagging to the floor. He felt drained of energy, of hope, of all possibility of exaltation. "For the blind man," he informed Carroll, "there was a bonus. Do you remember the German diplomat you brought in during the war? The one with the valise full of very useful papers?"

"What has that got to do with it?" Carroll demanded.

"There was a go-between in the affair, a Soviet agent working under deep cover in Germany," Francis told him. "You were already a rabid anti-Communist at the time. So you betrayed the Soviet agent to the Gestapo. One less Commie to deal with later, you probably said. They tortured him for weeks. At one point the Germans poured lye in his eyes. He was blinded for life."

The Potter said, "The blind man who runs Department 13 was the Soviet agent betrayed by your partner here?"

"The blind man worked nineteen years to get his revenge," Francis said. "He came within a hairsbreadth of having it."

Outside, the sun was knifing into the horizon. From

under the window of their room came the sound of someone walking on gravel—except there was no gravel under the window, there was just prairie. Everyone in the room stiffened.

"He may still get his revenge," Francis said. He stared vacantly at the tiny pistol in Carroll's hand. "Don't you see it, Carroll—to G. Sprowls we are all loose ends."

"You are *my* loose end," Carroll sneered. He lowered his gaze until he was looking directly into Francis' eyes. "I detest you as much as anyone can detest another human being."

Francis straightened with an effort and regarded his executioner. "I have loathed you from the moment I met you," he told Carroll. His lips seemed to curl insolently over the words he spoke. "If your life depended on it, you couldn't see the forest for the trees."

Carroll's tiny pistol jumped imperceptibly in his fist. Francis exhaled as if he had been punched in the chest. He looked down at the ragged hole that had suddenly appeared in the front of his tweed jacket. Blood oozed from it. He brought a hand up to cover the hole, almost as if it *embarrassed* him.

Carroll stepped up to Francis and pressed the pistol to a point over his heart and pulled the trigger again. When he removed the pistol, Francis sank to the ground.

Kaat, thoroughly frightened, leapt off the bed to join the Potter at the bay window. "Here's the thing," she whispered fiercely. "The Tibetans say that your last thoughts determine the quality of your reincarnation. Mine are of you. I hope to God we are reincarnated at the same time. I would like to spend an entire life with you sometime."

The Potter took the Beretta from his jacket pocket and pulled Kaat close to protect her from what was surely coming. He smiled at his last, best Sleeper as he spoke into Kaat's ear. "We will share conspiracies," he said. "It will be us against the world," he said. "For us, there will be life before death," he said. "If you please," he said.

47

⚜

"What did I do with the fucking lighter?" Ourcq muttered to himself.

Appleyard stopped imitating someone walking on gravel long enough to say, "Don't tell me you maybe can't find it."

Ourcq finally produced the lighter from a side pocket. "Stop imitating every fucking thing you hear and cover me," he ordered. Fitting a crutch under one armpit, gripping the homemade incendiary grenade filled with a flammable magnesium-like substance, he limped along the side of the house until he was directly under the bay window.

Appleyard fitted the silencer onto his pistol and bracing his arm with his other hand, aimed at the window. He caught a flicker of light—Ourcq would be igniting the fuse now, he knew. In a moment he would maybe arc the grenade up through the second-floor window. It would explode with a great whooshing sound, sucking up all the oxygen in a split second, suffocating every living thing in the room. The air would be sucked maybe out of their lungs even.

If ever there was an appropriate moment, this was maybe it. Filling his own lungs, drawing his lips back against his teeth, Appleyard began to imitate the sound of the sun setting.

In a car parked down the road, G. Sprowls heard a noise he couldn't identify, and then one he could—glass breaking, followed by a great sucking sound, as if all the air in the universe were being consumed. G. Sprowls frowned. He was not happy to be working with Russians, but it was unavoidable. The Director's instructions had been explicit. People in high places had communicated with each other; had decided that each side had too much on the other; that if they continued to play the game, there would only be losers. The only thing left to do was acknowledge the standoff and assign trusted people on both sides to tie up the loose ends. The suspect in police custody had been shot that morning by a local bar owner. All traces of a second shooter on a grassy knoll had been removed. The world would be invited to accept as fact that there had been one shooter, a demented loner acting on his own initiative. G. Sprowls had been given the phone number of the Canadians. Together they had just taken care of the other loose ends.

The idea flashed through G. Sprowls's head that someone might one day consider him a loose end. But he dismissed it as preposterous.

The Canadians were coming down the unpaved road toward the car now. The heavyset one was limping painfully along on two crutches, cursing with each step. The other one trailed after him, imitating the sound (so he claimed) of a noiseless patient spider spinning its web.

Ourcq thought he had finally tripped up Appleyard. "How come I can hear it if the fucking spider is fucking noiseless?"

"Concentration," Appleyard, unfazed, suggested, "is what it's a question of. You have got to listen with both ears so you can maybe hear what's there to be heard." And he repeated the sound that he said was produced by a noiseless patient spider.

About the Author

ROBERT LITTELL was born, raised, and educated in New York, and now makes his home in France. A former *Newsweek* editor, specializing in Soviet affairs, he left journalism in 1970 to write his first novel, and has been at it ever since. THE SISTERS is his seventh novel.